Mistress of Merrivale

SHELLEY MUNRO

Mistress of Merrivale

Copyright © 2023 by Shelley Munro

Print ISBN: 978-1-99-106311-3
Digital ISBN: 978-0-9951026-1-3

Editor: Evil Eye Editing

Cover: Frauke Spanuth of Octopi Covers

Munro Press, New Zealand.

First Munro Press electronic publication September 2017

First Munro Press print publication January 2023

For Paul.

Introduction

JOCELYN TOWNSEND'S LIFE AS a courtesan is nothing like the life she envisioned in her girlish dreams. But at least it allows her and her eccentric mother to live in relative security—until her protector announces his plans for marriage and no longer requires her services.

Desperate to find a new benefactor, one kind enough to accept her mother's increasingly mad flights of fancy, Jocelyn is uncertain when a lifeline comes from an unexpected source.

Leo Sherbourne's requirements for a wife are few. She must mother his young daughter, run his household, and warm his bed. All in a calm, dignified manner with a full measure of common sense. After his late wife's histrionics and infidelity, he craves a simpler, quieter life.

As they embark on their arrangement, Leo and Jocelyn discover an attraction that heats their bedroom and a mutual admiration that warms their days. But it isn't long before gossip regarding the fate of Leo's first wife, and his frequent, unexplained absences, make Jocelyn wonder if the secrets of Merrivale Manor are rooted in murder...

Warning: Contains mysterious incidents, a mad mother who screeches without provocation, scheming relatives, and a captivating husband who blows scorching hot and suspiciously cold. All is not as it seems...and isn't that delicious?

CHAPTER 1

London, 1758

"M-married?" Jocelyn Townsend clamped her hands in her lap and frantically sought the right words for the occasion. "Congratulations."

Tobias Sherbourne, the Earl of Melburn, beamed. Happiness lit his craggy face, taking it from ordinary to compelling. His eyes sparkled, the bright blue emphasized by his snowy white wig. "I've offered for the Neville girl."

"I wish you happy, Melburn." Jocelyn's spine pressed against the back of the damask sofa, the squeeze of her stays grounding her again. Gossip and rumors had circulated for months now. Yes, she'd known Melburn's declaration would come, but hearing it still hurled her into panic. She wanted to vent her frustration for everyone to witness, but of course, she didn't. Her mother was the only person who shrieked in this household.

She picked up the teapot. "Tea? Or would you prefer

something stronger?"

"Brandy, please." Melburn straightened from his casual lean against the mantle.

A raucous feminine screech pierced the air and tea sloshed from the spout. Jocelyn sighed inwardly, forcing her smile to remain intact while she set the china pot down. *Not again.* "Perhaps we would both benefit from something stronger."

She rose and maneuvered her skirts around her mahogany table and a square-backed chair to ring for a maid. The high-pitch scream repeated, louder and closer to the parlor. Jocelyn flinched, shooting a pained look at the closed door.

On her return, Melburn took possession of the seat opposite her, his large frame dwarfing the delicate furniture. "How is your mother?"

One would think the ear-piercing shrieks were nothing out of the ordinary, given his calm demeanor but, after two years as her protector, her mother's peculiarities no longer disturbed him.

A maid appeared, and Jocelyn relayed her request for a bottle of brandy and two glasses. It mightn't be the thing for a woman to drink strong spirits, yet if ever there was a time for her to imbibe, it was tonight. The maid's face blanked, although she curtseyed in acquiescence and hurried off to complete her errand.

"My mother is having a bad turn. She insists someone is watching the house and spying on us." It was a relief to share the latest drama with Melburn.

"Have you investigated to allay her concerns?"

Jocelyn resisted the urge to roll her eyes. "We have been more vigilant than usual. I haven't noticed anyone suspicious and neither has Woodley or Tilly, but Mother is steadfast in her charges."

Her butler and her mother's nurse were equally adamant no one lurked in the alley outside their Cork Street house. While it wasn't the best location in London, a night watchman patrolled the surrounding streets, and lamps chased away most of the gloomy shadows once evening fell.

The maid returned with a tray bearing the requested brandy.

"Would you like to adjourn to the bedroom, Melburn?"

"No, Jocelyn. I—"

Jocelyn leaned closer and covered his hand with hers, halting his refusal. "It's a love match. I understand." His bergamot and spice scent washed over her, familiar and comforting. He was a good man and a spurt of envy chased through her. Silently, she acknowledged her loss and the difficulties she'd experience in finding another protector of his caliber—someone she could trust not to abuse her.

"Ashleigh is a wonderful woman. I wouldn't see her hurt by spiteful gossip."

"I'd expect nothing less from you. It was a lucky day for me when you won me from Boynton." And even better he'd become a friend as well as her lover.

Melburn's eyes narrowed. "The man is a brute. The minute I saw the bruise on your cheek, my course of action was clear. Besides"—the tension in his upper body eased—"I like your red hair." He reached over to tug on an unfashionable red ringlet, grinning at her like an errant boy.

"Thank you." Her words acknowledged far more than the compliment. He'd rescued her from a bad situation and, for that, she'd always be grateful. She poured a measure of brandy and handed it to him before taking a smaller portion for herself. An abrupt ear-piercing shriek right outside the parlor made her wince. "Perhaps I should attend to my mother."

Melburn set his glass on the mahogany table. "Let me. I'll take a lantern and check outside in the alley. Help set her mind to rest."

Reality crashed over Jocelyn as she watched him stride from

the parlor and disappear into the hall, the door shutting behind him. This really was the end of their relationship. She'd miss his caring ways and passionate lovemaking. The Neville girl was lucky, and Jocelyn tamped down her envy. She fingered her gold locket and fought her growing agitation. A shiver crawled down her spine as she considered a search for a new protector.

No one could call her beautiful, and the last thing she wanted was to make another mistake, yet time would be of the essence because living in London was expensive. She was certain Melburn would give her a parting gift, yet even so, she'd have to tighten her purse strings until she found a suitable replacement.

The rise and fall of an emotional diatribe pierced the door. Jocelyn sipped her brandy and pulled a face at the harsh bite. At least the burn pierced the chill inhabiting her body. Her mother's crying ceased, and a reassuring masculine rumble filled the silence. She couldn't decipher the words but knew Melburn would offer comfort. It was his way. The respite allowed Jocelyn to ponder her predicament. Even if she located a protector, finding one who accepted her mother's presence would prove nigh on impossible.

She could approach her sisters... No, Georgina and Charlotte barely acknowledged her these days. They wanted to send their mother to Bedlam. Jocelyn hated to think of her one remaining parent incarcerated in the hospital, treated like an entertaining exhibit for those who possessed the price of admission. Her mind raced, attempting to fashion a workable solution. She drank more brandy, allowing the spirit to chase away her growing disquiet.

Ten minutes later, the door opened, and the earl entered the parlor. His cheeks were ruddy from the nippy spring evening.

"Did you discover anything unusual?" Jocelyn asked.

"Not apart from an old tomcat lurking in the alley. I informed your mother of my findings." He sent her a rueful grin. "She decided she'd scared the spy away with her warning cries."

"Thank you." Another burst of fancy on her mother's part.

Melburn sat again, a man with something on his mind, given the way he darted a searching look at her and toyed with his brandy. "What will you do now?"

"I don't know. I suppose I'll look for your replacement." She pulled a face, then let him know she bore no malice by adding a smile. After all, their involvement was basically a business proposition. She'd offered the use of her body in exchange for his financial support. The easy camaraderie between them had come as a bonus. "It won't be easy to find someone who suits my situation."

"I might have an answer to your problem." He hesitated as if he was unsure about his solution.

"Tell me. I'd like to think we're at least friends after all this time."

Melburn paused a fraction longer before appearing to come to a decision. "My cousin, Leo Sherbourne, requires a wife."

A shocked gasp escaped her. "But I'm a fallen woman. I—"

"You're not a mistress by choice."

"Well, no but—"

"Think about it. Marrying Leo would give you an opportunity to start afresh."

Most men wanted to distance themselves from their ex-mistresses. Jocelyn frowned at his quiet insistence, questions flying through her mind. "I see the benefits for me, but what about your cousin? What does he gain from such a match? Why would you suggest that I join your family? What if your betrothed learns of our shared history?"

"Leo lost his wife last year. He has a daughter, and he finds himself in want of a wife."

Jocelyn's brows rose. "Surely he could hire a nursemaid?"

"There are unusual circumstances that make a wife the better solution."

"What unusual circumstances?" Jocelyn wasn't sure she liked Melburn thrusting her into the middle of a mystery. "How can I make a decision if you don't give me the full facts?"

"Jocelyn, it's not my story to tell. I'm merely acting as Leo's agent in this matter, gauging a sense of your interest. What I can tell you is that my cousin is a good man. He's trustworthy. He won't beat or degrade you."

The chance of a new start wasn't something that occurred every day. "What about my mother? Where does your cousin live?"

"Leo knows of your situation."

"That wasn't what I meant. Is your cousin willing to give my mother his protection?"

"He'd like to meet with you tomorrow morning," Melburn said. "If you're agreeable, you can ask your questions then."

Jocelyn drank the last of her brandy and set her glass aside. She laughed lightly. "Very well, you wretched man. You've piqued my interest with your suggestion, and you know it. I'll meet with your cousin here at eleven tomorrow morning."

LEO SHERBOURNE HALTED HIS agitated pacing when he heard footsteps approaching the library. He ducked into the shadows, squeezed against the book shelves, and faced the door to wait. Melburn was the only person he wished to speak with this evening. If it was someone else, he'd prefer to remain alone.

The library door burst open. "Leo?"

Leo stepped into the light cast by the fire and the single candlestick sitting on the corner of a rosewood desk. "Did you see her? Did she agree?"

"I told you she'd have questions. She wants to see you tomorrow at eleven." Melburn tossed his cocked hat and cane aside and strode to an oak sideboard to pour two brandies. He handed one to Leo.

Leo cupped the crystal goblet in his hand and stared into golden liquid. "What sort of questions?"

"Foremost, she's worried about her mother, but she wants to know why you're willing to marry her when you know she's a courtesan. I think she's wondering why you'd want to marry your cousin's cast off, although she didn't put it into words."

Leo's answer was simple, though not one he intended to broadcast.

He wanted to send a clear message to Hannah. Despite her assumptions, he had no intention of chaining himself to his first wife's sister. He wished he could tell her bluntly, but given the circumstances...

Leo swirled his glass, watching eddies in the brandy with close attention. "You said she's trustworthy, and I know you said she's plain, but she doesn't need to be a beauty. I don't care about that. Her character is more important than her physical appearance."

After his debacle of a marriage, he wanted a woman he could easily control. Yes, this was the best way. He'd walk into a second marriage with a woman beholden to him—one who understood her place.

"Jocelyn is above all things sensible. I've known her for two years, and she's never done anything to draw attention to herself or our agreement. She's discreet, and I doubt many people know of our connection. The only time we ever met outside her house was at masquerade balls, and we always left before it was time to unmask. I believe she promised her two older sisters she'd keep a low profile, and she adheres to her pledge. From the little she's said, her sisters both married minor titles and don't wish to recall their merchant roots."

Leo dropped onto a chair in front of the fireplace and yanked off the cravat he'd disordered hours ago. "Most women in her position would use your alliance for their benefit."

"Jocelyn's not like that. From what I understand, her two older sisters refused to take in their mother when her behavior became erratic. Their father died leaving debts, and they lost their home. Jocelyn was desperate and fell into life as a courtesan. It was the only way she could keep her mother safe and a roof over their heads." Melburn took possession of the neighboring chair and stared into the flickering flames. "You won't find fault with her. I told you she's tall and possesses a pleasing shape. She has bright red hair and lots of freckles, while her eyes are an unusual light blue. If you're determined to go through with your plan, Jocelyn is the perfect candidate."

"You think I'm wrong to want to provide a mother for my daughter? A wife to bring peace to my household?"

"Of course not," Melburn said. "It's what we men want."

"The important thing is she has nothing in common with Ursula." A flicker of distaste swept Leo, the same one that struck whenever anyone mentioned his dead wife.

"You'll find Jocelyn is exactly what you search for." Silence fell, a companionable quiet. Melburn rose to refresh their drinks. "Jocelyn Townsend is a practical woman. As long as you word your proposition carefully, I think she'll agree to wed you."

Leo snorted. "Practical? I've yet to meet a woman who isn't ruled by her emotions."

"Not all women are like Ursula."

"The ones I've met to date are high-strung and anything but peaceful, although I'm sure your betrothed is the exception." Leo said all that was right to reassure his cousin, but he didn't believe Melburn. Ursula had been a traitorous bitch, and she'd cuckolded him whenever the opportunity presented itself. Hell, he was pretty sure Cassandra wasn't his daughter. His first wife had sucked him dry of emotion, and he wouldn't make the same mistake again. A mutual marriage of convenience with Melburn's mistress would give him leverage. He'd forever have the upper hand, and that was exactly what he needed to keep peace in his household.

AT PRECISELY THE STROKE of eleven, a sharp rap of the door knocker announced a visitor. Jocelyn set her needlework aside and rose. A flutter of nerves stirred as she smoothed her blue skirts and contrasting pale blue petticoats. It made her realize she'd already half-decided to agree to the proposition. She'd always thought she'd marry like her sisters, but fate and her father had set her on a different path. Under normal circumstances, her intuition would propel her to act with vigilance.

This wasn't a typical situation.

Her instincts were shouting "yes" because Mr. Sherbourne was Melburn's cousin. She trusted the earl, and marriage would solve several of her problems.

Out in the hall, Woodley's somber tones greeted her caller. Her hand crept up to smooth over her locket as she wondered for the hundredth time what Mr. Sherbourne would look like and how he'd react to her and her mother. A man who was willing to overlook her past and offer her the security of matrimony was unusual indeed. He'd most likely possess an appearance similar to Melburn. Yes, the resemblance would help Jocelyn to keep her composure and stifle the anxieties that had kept her from slumber last night.

Woodley tapped on the parlor door and entered. "Mr. Leo Sherbourne to see you."

"Show him in, Woodley." Amazed at her calm voice, she concentrated on presenting a serene front.

Woodley directed Mr. Sherbourne into the parlor, and she forced her lips to curve upward when she really wanted to gasp aloud.

Leo Sherbourne was stunningly handsome, his dark eyes piercing and direct. Taller than Melburn, he'd clubbed his midnight black hair in a tail, and this highlighted the stark planes of his face, his olive complexion. Impeccably dressed in a navy-blue suit with a pale blue waistcoat embroidered in a deeper blue, he appeared the wealthy gentleman. His choice of color matched her attire perfectly. A sign, perhaps.

"Good morning, Mr. Sherbourne." She finally rediscovered her manners.

"Miss Townsend." He regarded her steadily and not a measure of flirtation showed on his features. "Thank you for agreeing to meet with me." His deep voice caressed her senses, and she stared, mesmerized for an instant. He was...unexpected. Why would he want to take her as his wife? Young misses likely fluttered their eyelashes at him in flirtation, and she imagined older, more experienced women offered to jump into his bed on a regular basis. He didn't seem like a man who'd experience difficulty in attracting the fairer sex.

"Please take a seat," Jocelyn said, her mind twisting and prodding this new development. Her right hand rose to check her cap, and she forced herself to still the self-conscious action. Despite her fidgeting, her cap was likely still straight and hid a large portion of her red hair.

He waited until she seated herself before taking possession of the same chair his cousin had sat on the previous night.

"Why are you entertaining marriage with me, given my

history?" Jocelyn almost winced at her forthrightness. She caught the flash of surprise in him, the slight narrowing of his eyes then his slow smile. Her heart beat a little faster at his approval. It seemed devastating smiles were one trait borne by both cousins. She found it difficult to focus with his full attention directed at her, almost impossible not to gasp at her physical reaction to his potent masculinity.

"I have a young daughter and require help with her."

"Forgive me, but surely there is no shortage of women willing to accept you as husband." More candor. This was not the impression she wanted to present, yet she required answers. To her relief, he didn't take umbrage and merely scrutinized her closely in return.

"My first marriage wasn't an enjoyable experience. This time I seek a marriage where both parties know their duty from the beginning and are under no illusion as to how the liaison will proceed—the way I want."

Well, he was blunt too. Jocelyn wrenched her gaze from his face and concentrated on her lightly clasped hands. The romantic part of her faded under reality. This wasn't a love match. She had to remember that, yet the situation was strange. He hadn't told her everything. There was more. She lifted her head. "Did you beat your wife?"

His dark brows shot upward. "I'm not a brute." He half stood as if he intended to leave, and her hand shot out to grasp his forearm. Muscles flexed beneath her fingers, leading her thoughts directly to the marriage bed. Like a hot coal, his heat burned her palm, and she released her hold.

"Forgive me. Please, don't leave. This is an unusual situation and my nerves are ruling my manners. Stay. Tell me exactly what you expect from me."

Instead of sitting again, he prowled the parlor, putting her in mind of a caged beast. And, despite her growing alarm that she'd destroyed any chance of a marriage, she couldn't tear her gaze off him. He was a man in his prime, strong and sure of himself—an attractive quality in a husband. Her breasts prickled against her chemise, and her stays felt suddenly unbearably tight. Heat bloomed between her legs. The unusual reaction took her by surprise.

Mr. Sherbourne ceased his pacing and spun to face her. Determination etched his face, giving him the look of cool marble. "I want a wife who gives her loyalty to me, a woman to raise my child and warm my bed. Someone to instill order in my home and do things the way I direct."

Jocelyn nodded. That sounded reasonable. "And what would I receive in return?"

"In return, my wife will receive the security of my name and home. She'll want for nothing, and I hope she'll find happiness."

"What about my past relationship with Melburn? If I agree to wed you, there might be times when we socialize with Melburn and his new wife. Will that create difficulties?"

He laughed softly, a gleam entering his eyes. "Are you asking if I'll experience jealousy?"

"Yes." Nothing like a little honesty to get to the heart of a matter.

"Melburn and I have discussed this. He told me if you agreed to marry me, you'd also give your loyalty. He said you possess both honor and discretion. Integrity. I hadn't heard a single rumor of your relationship. This reassures me that we might suit. Will you miss your close...friendship with Melburn?"

"Melburn and I have always been friends. I hope our friendship will continue in the future—in a platonic way, of course. Your cousin is right in that I refuse to play games or pit gentlemen against each other to ensure a better offer or a richer lover. If I agree to become your wife, you'll receive everything you require in a spouse."

His brows rose again. "It's not often a woman surprises me."

"I'm not an ordinary woman."

"I'm coming to understand that."

"Thank you." Jocelyn found herself drawn to him. Along with his pleasing looks, he bore an air of confidence. But the stillness in him, the faint note of impatience hinted at hidden depths. Winning his friendship and perhaps his love would prove a challenge. Aware of the lengthening silence, she rushed into speech. "Did Melburn tell you about my mother? Her behavior is erratic at times, and she suffers episodes where she has mad fancies. Despite family pressure, I refuse to place her in The Hospital of St. Mary of Bethlehem. If we marry, I'll expect her to come to live with me."

He hesitated and acute disappointment gripped her. This point was nonnegotiable. If he didn't offer her mother protection, she couldn't accept his proposition.

"Is she violent?"

"No! Not at all. At worst, she shrieks loud enough to deafen everyone in the vicinity. I employ a nurse to oversee her and have found this is a satisfactory solution."

"Is she likely to harm my daughter?"

"I don't believe so," Jocelyn said. "You're welcome to meet her and judge for yourself. She does become agitated at times, but Tilly is good with her. Melburn will tell you."

The man stalked another tight circuit of her parlor, dodging an urn of flowers and the settee. "We could keep them apart if problems occurred," he said, almost talking to himself. "Yes, that should work." He focused on her then, his deep brown eyes searing through her.

A flutter of something—not fear—stirred in her belly.

"If you accept my proposal, your mother and any of your staff are welcome to accompany you."

"Thank you. My butler and my mother's nurse have been with me from the start and are husband and wife. I should like to offer them positions. The rest of the staff will continue to work for the next tenant who rents this house."

"As it happens, my current butler is past the age of retirement." One of his wondrous smiles flashed and her breath caught. "He worries about leaving me in the lurch, having been with our family since he was a young boy."

The glimpse of affection in his voice cheered her. "Melburn didn't say where you lived."

"Near the town of Tavistock in Devon."

"Dartmoor?"

"Yes, I'm a farmer and hold an interest in several mines. We live a simple life, although we socialize with our neighbors. You will find Merrivale much quieter than London."

A silent question hovered in his words, prompting her to rush into speech. "I have no problems with a country life." Devon was a long way from London and her two sisters. Their husbands both owned estates in Kent. The distance between Devon and Kent gave her the illusion of safety, especially from rumors about her past. "That sounds satisfactory. You'd better meet my mother." The poor man deserved to know exactly what he was letting himself in for, although the change of scenery might aid her parent. A thought occurred. "Do you have gardens and a stillroom?"

A bemused expression followed her question. "Yes. Merrivale Manor has extensive gardens. Is that important?"

"My mother enjoys working with herbs and flowers. A garden would help her settle and make her more amenable to a move."

"So you're seriously considering my proposition?"

"As long as you don't take a dislike of my mother when you meet her, I think we'll deal well together." A tremor went through Jocelyn. She'd share a bed with this man and perhaps

16

bear his children. "Do you want more children?"

A sensual gleam lit his dark eyes without warning. "Of course." His gaze traveled to her breasts and lingered before returning to her face. His avid attention left a raft of goose bumps creeping over her arms and legs. Sharing a bed with Mr. Sherbourne wasn't going to be a hardship.

"Is there anything else we need to discuss?"

"No, I think we've covered most things. I'll give you free rein in the manor, and you'll receive a quarterly allowance."

A thought occurred. "Do you travel to London often?"

"I don't enjoy the city. I visit Melburn at his estate in North Devon several times a year. Of course, you would come with me."

Jocelyn bore a fondness for Melburn, yet she frowned at the disclosure. "I wouldn't have thought Melburn would want me to meet his wife on a regular basis."

"Melburn and I discussed this at length. We decided to tell anyone who asks that we met in London. Melburn assures me you'll do nothing to blacken the Sherbourne name." Though spoken in a mild voice, his words carried an unpinning of coldness. His expression gave away nothing, yet Jocelyn sensed he'd be a bad man to cross.

"I agree to whatever story you've planned," she said. "I'll see if my mother has time to say good day." The entire journey to her mother's second floor chamber, she thought about Mr. Sherbourne. Jocelyn prayed her mother didn't take one of her instant aversions, for she'd instinctively liked the man. She wanted to embrace this chance to make a fresh start.

To her relief, Mr. Sherbourne charmed her mother and the pair chatted about gardening and plants for ten minutes before he needed to leave to visit his lawyer. By the time Jocelyn handed him his hat and cane and showed him out, they'd agreed a marriage between them would suit both parties.

THE CARRIAGE RATTLED OVER a rut, jolting the entire vehicle. Jocelyn braced her hand on the interior to hold her position. Once she'd committed to Mr. Sherbourne, affairs moved rapidly. With Melburn's help, she'd signed a betrothal contract and a few days later, she became Mrs. Leo Sherbourne. An urgent message came from Merrivale, summoning Leo home and he left London the same day, leaving Jocelyn to arrange the move to Devon.

Now that she was on her way to join her new husband, trepidation traveled with her. Anxiety jostled in the pit of her stomach each time the carriage struggled through a pothole.

"Are we there yet?" Elizabeth Townsend's querulous voice pierced her thoughts—an oft repeated question, that had grated Jocelyn's nerves raw.

They'd taken the journey in small stages over many days, but even so, by the time they reached the outskirts of Dartmoor, Jocelyn wanted to strangle her mother.

"We should reach Merrivale later this afternoon." Jocelyn pushed down the carriage window and tilted her face to the bright sunshine. Fresh air ruffled her hair, tugging the strands not covered by her cap.

The carriage labored up a slope, the wheels protesting and the coachman urging the horses on with a snap of his whip. When they reached the crest of the hill, Jocelyn's breath caught. The countryside stretched out before them—an endless carpet of greenery, studded with piles of rocks, stacked like a haphazard pile of oversize books. A cloudless blue sky completed the majestic panorama.

"Mother, look at the view. Isn't it glorious?" She'd heard the area could be inhospitable and eerie with dangerous mists and treacherous bogs, yet it wasn't today. For their arrival, Dartmoor was showing her finest.

"I can't see," her mother complained.

"Come and sit beside me," Jocelyn said.

They shuffled around the carriage interior until her mother could view the vista.

"Pretty," her mother said. "Are we there yet?"

"It won't take long now," Tilly said in a firm voice.

The hours passed and, after a brief stop for lunch and to change horses, they finally approached Merrivale Manor. Mature trees and extensive gardens surrounded a sprawling gray stone building, screening it from sight until the last minute. When the carriage came to a halt, several people hurried down the front steps of the manor.

"Are we there yet?"

"Yes." Jocelyn wiped clammy hands on her skirts, nerves striking her afresh now that they'd arrived. Today her marriage would start in truth, and tonight, she'd share a bed with her new husband.

The carriage door opened, and Leo appeared. He extended a hand to her. "Welcome to Merrivale Manor."

Jocelyn inclined her head, cautious and hesitant, unaccountably shy in front of her husband. She stepped from the carriage and waited for her mother and Tilly to alight. "Ah, Woodley," she said, spying her butler—posture erect and proper—amongst the somber servants. "How was your journey?"

He inclined his head respectfully. "Very good, Mrs. Sherbourne. We arrived three days ago."

"And you've settled in well?"

"Yes, Mrs. Sherbourne."

Jocelyn nodded, the small talk settling the worst of her

anxiety.

"Let me introduce you to the staff," Mr. Sherbourne said, placing her hand on the crook of his arm. His good looks dazzled her, stealing her breath as his dark gaze caressed her face. His focus dropped to her lips before his attention shifted to the waiting line of servants.

Men often scrutinized her thus, as if they wanted to strip her clothes from her body and take their ease, and that was despite her unattractive red hair and freckles. A burst of heat crawled across her skin and part of her wished it was time to retire now. She'd spent her waking hours since their marriage pondering Mr. Sherbourne's bedroom prowess. Would he hurry the act without regard to her pleasure? Or would he take his time, caressing and touching her until they both burned? Breathless, disturbed by her thoughts, Jocelyn swallowed rapidly, seeking distraction.

Ah, yes. The servants.

She scanned their faces and caught a glower from one of the maids, apparently aimed at Mr. Sherbourne. The rest of the faces were expressionless, absent of welcome, and that raised her curiosity. Did they not like their master? Fear him for some reason?

"This is Mrs. Green, the housekeeper." After a brief greeting to the stony-faced woman, Mr. Sherbourne led her down the line of staff, introducing her to the remaining maids and footmen without hesitation. He mentioned their families, his cool charm seeming to set the servants at ease.

Jocelyn inclined her head and murmured a small greeting to each servant, impressed with her husband's knowledge of his staff. The tension lifted from her shoulders. This wasn't a ruthless master. They were likely apprehensive about meeting a new mistress.

"Mrs. Green, will you show Mrs. Sherbourne's mother to her

room?"

"Of course." The housekeeper led her mother and Tilly away, and the servants dispersed, leaving Jocelyn alone with Mr. Sherbourne.

"I'm glad you're here," he said, his husky voice stirring her again. A tremor swept her, leaving a tingling awareness in its path. "Let me show you to your chamber."

She strolled up the steps into the entrance hall at his side. Flagstones covered the floor, her shoes tapping the surface as they progressed deeper into the manor. Mr. Sherbourne led her to a flight of stairs and together, they ascended to the next floor.

"When will I meet your daughter?"

"Cassandra has a nap at this time of the day," he said. "She isn't feeling well this week, and Arabella thought it would be best to keep Cassie in the nursery today. Perhaps tomorrow would be better. No doubt you're tired after your journey."

"Arabella?"

"She looks after Cassandra, and has done so since her birth."

Some of her enthusiasm faded. "Oh, I'm sorry to hear Cassandra isn't well." She'd looked forward to meeting her new daughter and had even purchased her a doll before leaving London. "Tell me about my new daughter. We didn't speak much of her before our marriage."

Mr. Sherbourne hesitated, as if considering his words. When they reached the top of the stairs, he guided her to the right, his hand a gentle pressure on the small of her back. Family portraits hung on the walls, most depicting serious gentlemen.

"Cassandra is four. People say she looks much like her mother."

Her husband's clipped tone suggested he didn't consider this a good thing. "I thought she'd be younger." Jocelyn hadn't realized Mr. Sherbourne had been married for that long. She didn't understand his strange reticence either but, no doubt, the coming weeks and months would aid her with insight into her husband. "I'm looking forward to meeting her."

Mr. Sherbourne guided her to the end of the gallery and around another corner. "The manor is easy to navigate. It's a U-shape. Our rooms are in the left wing while your mother's rooms and the nursery are in the right wing. The main reception rooms are in the center. My family has lived here since the late 1600s."

Interesting that he'd changed the subject. Jocelyn decided to let him. "I didn't realize your family had lived in the area for so long. Do you have any brothers or sisters?"

"I did have two older brothers. One died as a three-year-old during a plague and the other left home after an argument with my father. We haven't seen him since." The hard note in his voice repulsed further questions.

Jocelyn squeezed his arm. "Families can be difficult. I know from experience. I understand your parents passed away some time ago."

"Yes." The tenseness fell away from him at her words, and he smiled—a brief one that didn't reach his dark eyes. "Of course you do. I admire you for protecting your mother."

"Thank you." She hoped he'd continue to think this way because her mother had been at her charming best during their meetings to date. Heaven help them when she threw one of her screaming fits. At least her mother had ceased her avowals of spies lurking behind every corner. Something Jocelyn was thankful for, if only that lasted.

Mr. Sherbourne halted in front of a door and pushed it open. He stood back, pausing for her to enter.

Her husband.

A flicker of pleasure bloomed within her. The mantle didn't sit easily at present, but with time, she hoped her new status became comfortable. As she started to move past him, she caught his scent, a hit of bay rum and a pinch of spicy greenery. An urge to touch him struck her, yet she didn't act on the impulse. They needed time to build a friendship, intimacy.

She entered a large chamber. It was frilly and designed with a woman in mind. Jocelyn hated it on sight. "It's very..." Good grief. Words failed her, and she stared at her new husband.

His lips twisted. "Pink?"

"Ah, yes." That was the least offensive of descriptions for the overly fussy room and the multitude of cherubs. They covered every available surface and some even smirked at her from the wall. She looked up. And the ceiling.

"You're welcome to make changes."

Instinct told her he'd appreciate a transformation. She was certain of it when their gazes connected, because memories swirled in his eyes and etched into his facial muscles. This room held bad recollections of his first wife.

"I've always preferred simpler decoration." Jocelyn fought a shudder at the unrelenting pink frills everywhere. Her scan of the room drew her over to the windows. Ah, at least the view was beautiful. The garden spread out below, a blaze of summer color—red roses, yellow daisies and deep purple lavender. In contrast to the bright flowers, formal hedges grew in regimented green rows, all sharp angles to please the most exacting gardener. Gradually, the hedges gave way to mature trees, which sent dappled patterns of light and dark over their surroundings.

She crossed to a second window and gave a happy sigh at the greenery studded with rocks and trees, which stretched as far as she could see. "The views are lovely."

"Yes, they are."

She turned back to him and found her husband watching her. A pleased flush crept into her cheeks as she strolled toward him.

"This is my room through here." He opened another door.

She caught a glimpse of a four-poster bed and heavy oak

furniture. Deep green wallpaper adorned the walls, a white and gold trim bringing a touch more color. The room was masculine and far more to her taste. "Perhaps I could sleep in your room tonight." This cherub-festooned decoration was certain to give her nightmares.

"Mrs. Green will want to show you the rest of the house."

She'd thought he might take her suggestion as an excuse to at least offer a flirtatious comment in return. She was mistaken. Not a shred of carnal interest crept into his expression, and the lack of reaction brought a chill to her limbs.

"Yes, of course." She followed him from her bedroom and back down the stairs to the doorway of a parlor.

The housekeeper claimed his attention when she spied their arrival. "You have visitors, Mr. Sherbourne. Miss Hannah and Master Peregrine are here to see you."

Mr. Sherbourne cursed softly. "Where are they?"

"They're taking a turn about the garden."

"I'll go and meet them." He hesitated. "Jocelyn, why don't you come with me? Viscount Hartscombe is one of our neighbors. Peregrine and Hannah are his son and daughter. They live on the other side of the village."

Jocelyn turned to the housekeeper, hoping she hid her pleasure at his use of her name. "Mrs. Green, could you prepare refreshments for our guests please? It's such a lovely afternoon. Is there somewhere outside that's suitable to take refreshments?"

"Yes, of course. Mr. Sherbourne will show you to the terrace."

She took two steps and halted abruptly. Bother, her bonnet was no protection from the sun. Aware of her husband's impatience, she resigned herself to more freckles and hurried over to accept his escort. His mouth was firm, irritation making his face appear like stone. "I'm sorry to keep you waiting."

Mr. Sherbourne didn't reply, merely directed her from the

house and into a large garden. Roses perfumed the air and birds sang with gay abandon, as if celebrating a day full of sunshine.

"I do like the gardens." Jocelyn stole a glance at her husband, curiosity surging at the tension in him. Was it something she'd done or was it his unexpected visitors?

The murmur of voices ahead increased the rigidness of the muscles beneath her gloved hand. Not her, then. Her interest grew when a man and woman approached. They made an attractive pair, the brother tall and dashing in a black coat and breeches. The gold braiding decorating the coat caught the sun, sparkling like jewels. His sister was petite and very beautiful in a well-cut black riding habit. Both wore cocked hats, atop golden hair the color of ripe blades of wheat. It was the shade of hair she'd always admired, but not a single rinse came close to shifting the fiery glow from her locks.

Jocelyn smiled in greeting, looking forward to making friends in her new home.

Two sets of dark brown eyes stared at her in astonishment, the woman's gaze drifting to her arm linked with Mr. Sherbourne's. She scowled, her attention returning to Mr. Sherbourne. A brilliant smile bloomed, making her appear at one with the sunshine, despite her black garb.

"Leo! At last." The woman raced across the distance separating them with unladylike haste. "You've been in London for weeks. We heard you'd returned but Father and Mother have come home for a brief time. They brought visitors with them, which meant we couldn't ride over to see you until today. Aren't you going to greet us?"

Mr. Sherbourne released Jocelyn and caught the woman as she threw herself at him. His fingers banded her upper arms, holding her from his body and resisting her inclination to embrace. Shock flitted across the woman's face as he adroitly avoided her attempt at physical contact.

"Leo, you're hurting me."

Mr. Sherbourne set her away firmly, his countenance harsh. He moved closer to Jocelyn, curling his right arm around her waist. "Wish me happy," he said. "Jocelyn and I are married."

CHAPTER 2

"M-married?" The rosy color fled from the woman's cheeks and her posture went rigid. Her gaze flicked over Jocelyn, and she gave a disdainful sniff. "You're married? *To her?*"

"Jocelyn, these are my neighbors Hannah and Peregrine Richards."

Jocelyn dipped her head in greeting, her face stiff due to the open slight. "I'm pleased to meet you." She could do all that was polite, even if her new neighbor was lacking in manners.

"Your wife is scarcely cold in her grave," Hannah cried. "The period of mourning isn't over and you married *her*?"

"Ursula died a mere eight months ago." Peregrine hid his surprise better than his sister, but his words contained pain.

"I don't owe you explanations." Mr. Sherbourne's voice held a hint of cruelty, his arm a forceful band around Jocelyn's waist.

Jocelyn froze, neither understanding nor wanting to draw further attention.

"It's unconscionable." Hannah fisted her hands together, strain evident in her voice. "People are going to gossip and spread more rumors."

Rumors? What rumors? Jocelyn gnawed her bottom lip, unprepared for the seething undercurrents swirling around the trio.

"Let them," Mr. Sherbourne said with unconcern. "Mrs. Green is preparing refreshments."

"We're not staying." Peregrine grasped his sister's arm and propelled her from the garden without a farewell.

Jocelyn stared after brother and sister, watching until they passed a leafy bush covered with yellow flowers and disappeared from sight. "They seem a little upset," she said finally.

"Come, I'll show you the rest of the garden before we retire to the terrace." He led her down a gravel path, past several climbing rose bushes, resplendent with white flowers. Bees buzzed industriously, flitting from bloom to bloom. Some of the tension lifted from Jocelyn. It was only natural people were surprised at their marriage. But eight months? Oh, dear. What a pickle.

"The stables are down this path. It's a three-minute walk." He gestured in the direction her new neighbors had departed and strolled farther into the gardens. "We grow fruit and vegetables in the walled garden near the kitchen." Her husband pointed to the right. "See the hedging over there?"

"Yes."

"That's a maze my father designed when I was a child. My older brother and I used to enjoy scaring our friends whenever our parents held house parties. We'd don ghostly costumes and jump out at visitors."

"You didn't!"

Humor crinkled the corners of his eyes. "I assure you we did. Dartmoor abounds with tales of ghosts and witches, and we shamelessly used the legends to strike trepidation into our guests."

"Didn't your parents censure you? Your father?"

"Who do you think gave us the idea?" Pure wickedness curled across her husband's mouth as he unleashed one of his potent smiles. Her knees weakened under the impact, and she would have staggered if he hadn't held her arm. "Watch the path. It's a little uneven in places."

Heat crept into her cheeks. "Who tends the gardens?" she asked hurriedly, seeking distraction from the surge of awareness streaking through her veins. "My mother will enjoy them."

"I employ a head gardener and two under-gardeners to keep them in order." He directed her along another concealed path. The gravel crunched under their feet as they walked beneath an archway formed by trees.

Jocelyn cocked her head at a new sound. "Is that water I hear?"

"Yes, there's a stream that runs through the bottom of the garden. It flows into a river not far from here." His good humor faded, his mouth taking on a tight set.

Something else he didn't wish to discuss. Melburn hadn't mentioned his cousin was a moody man. "Do you fish?"

"On occasion," he said.

"Can we walk through the maze?"

"Mrs. Green is most likely waiting on us. We can explore the maze another time. It's a tricky one and most people get helplessly lost."

"But not you?"

"No."

Jocelyn noticed a hovering man who appeared to require a word with her husband. "Am I keeping you from your work?"

"I wanted to greet you, but I do need to help the men with the sheep."

Jocelyn understood obligations. "If you'll direct me to the terrace, I'll take refreshments with my mother and Tilly. You go and complete your chores, and we can talk later this evening."

"Are you sure?"

"Of course. I'll take the opportunity to speak with Mrs. Green."

"Thank you, Jocelyn." Mr. Sherbourne drew her closer, approval glinting in his brown eyes now. "You're very obliging. I appreciate your consideration."

"Think nothing of it."

"Follow this path. It will take you to the maze. Once there, turn to the left, and that will lead you to the terrace. I'll see you later." He lowered his head and brushed his lips over hers, his eyes dark when he lifted his head. "So sweet. Until tonight." With ground-eating steps, he strode away.

She watched him disappear from sight. Like the maze, he was a mystery, one she desperately wanted to solve. Her mind skipped ahead to the coming night and longing fueled a burst of pleasurable tingles and the urge to fan her face. Although nerves had come to the fore, a part of her was curious, and she looked forward to their marriage bed.

Her footsteps took her in the direction Mr. Sherbourne had indicated. Soon she came upon the maze, the tall hedges standing several inches higher than her head. *What fun!* With more time, she'd have ventured inside to challenge herself with the puzzle. The scents of more plants assailed her when she turned left—lavender and honeysuckle plus others she didn't recognize.

A whisper of sound behind her had her turning with an expectant welcome. "Good day."

There was no one there. Frowning, she scanned the vicinity. Nothing out of the ordinary struck her, yet the sense of an observer persisted. Finally, she shrugged and continued along the gravel path to the terrace. A maid and the housekeeper arrived at the same time. They placed a pristine white cloth over a round table and set out refreshments. A footman carried two chairs, arranging them around the table with two others.

"I've timed my arrival perfectly," she said to Mrs. Green. "I wonder if you could send a maid to ask my mother and Tilly if they'd like to join me."

"Of course, Mrs. Sherbourne."

"Mrs. Green, I'd like a meeting tomorrow morning, say around ten? I'd like to discuss a few household matters with you."

Mrs. Green pressed her lips together and drew herself up. "I hope you'll find everything to your satisfaction."

"Merrivale looks beautiful." The last thing Jocelyn wanted to do was tread on toes and create tension. "I'd like to discuss making changes to the furnishings in my chamber. I'm afraid the decoration is not to my taste."

"The first Mrs. Sherbourne had no concerns regarding the way I ran the household."

Jocelyn fought a grimace. She'd displeased the housekeeper, and on the first day too. "Perhaps Woodley could attend our meeting as well since I shall require some strong men to shift furniture."

"Yes, Mrs. Sherbourne. Will that be all?"

"Thank you, Mrs. Green." She watched the housekeeper march away, her back beneath her somber gown as rigid as a washing board. A pained sigh whispered from Jocelyn. Already, her presence at Merrivale had upset two of their neighbors and the housekeeper. Her husband was the only person who seemed genuinely happy with her arrival.

Melburn must have known the full details of Leo's first marriage, yet he hadn't mentioned a thing. Both men had led her to believe Leo's wife had died several years ago. How strange.

Her mother burst onto the terrace, followed by Tilly. Their appearance dragged Jocelyn from her marriage worries.

"Jocelyn, I love the gardens," her mother said, dancing

around the table and chairs like a child anticipating a treat. "I saw them from my window. And Woodley said there's a river with a waterhole suitable for swimming. Oh, I'm going to be so happy here."

"I'm sure we could have an excursion to the river," Jocelyn said, pleased with her mother's enthusiasm. "Do you like your room?"

"Oh, yes. I have my own parlor." Her mother plied her fan as she excitedly described the décor, the views of the garden from her rooms and the profusion of beautiful ivy clinging to the exterior brick walls. "I must explore the gardens immediately."

Jocelyn laughed at her exuberance. "We can walk after our repast. I find myself quite hungry after our journey." She busied herself with pouring. "Tilly, cease your hovering. Do sit and take tea with us."

Tilly sat on the edge of a chair and sent Jocelyn an unhappy glance. She started to speak, glanced at Elizabeth and closed her mouth. Jocelyn arched her brows, and Tilly nodded. She desired a private conversation.

"Mother, do you think you'll sleep well tonight?" Jocelyn asked.

"I'm sure I will," her mother said agreeably, swishing her fan. "Where is your hat, Jocelyn?"

Jocelyn pulled a face as she passed delicate porcelain cups to her mother and Tilly. "Mr. Sherbourne was in rather a hurry, and I didn't have time to collect one. Will you have a raspberry tart?"

The rest of the afternoon passed agreeably. The trio finished their refreshments and strolled through the gardens, her mother darting from one discovery to the next.

"Is something wrong, Tilly?"

"Your mother is exuberant since our arrival. I worry she'll have one of her episodes soon."

"She does seem rather euphoric this afternoon. Do you think we should administer a sleeping draft when she retires?"

"That's a good idea. You won't want interruptions tonight now that you're reunited with Mr. Sherbourne," Tilly said.

"No." They turned a corner and came across her mother speaking with an elderly gentleman—a gardener, Jocelyn presumed. Elizabeth's hands flashed as she indicated a plant in front of them. Her mother often displayed periods of clarity like this. In the past, Jocelyn had hoped it meant she was improving. Now she knew better. Soon her mother would return to her confused state where she screamed at imaginary creatures and spies who lurked in the night. Tears stung Jocelyn's eyes. She must treasure these moments whenever they arrived.

The gardener touched his hand to his cap and retreated when she and Tilly approached.

"Are the household staff welcoming?" Jocelyn asked.

Tilly wrinkled her nose. "From Woodley's experience, they are slow to warm to newcomers. They're a suspicious lot. It will take time for us to find our place here." She lowered her voice. "Then there's the business of the parlor maid from Hartscombe. She went missing over three months ago and yet they found her body displayed in the middle of the maze here at Merrivale."

"Body?" Jocelyn said sharply. "She was murdered?"

"Aye, I understand Mr. Sherbourne found her right in the middle of the labyrinth, not long after he arrived back from London."

"That's terrible." Jocelyn recalled the faces of the servants when they'd greeted her earlier, the unease she'd credited to her arrival. "Have they discovered the culprit?" It was odd Leo hadn't mentioned the murder. He'd said the maze was a challenging one—Jocelyn broke off, her skin prickling with apprehension. The culprit was familiar with the puzzle.

"No," Tilly said. "I intend to lock the doors and windows firmly against intruders each night. I shan't take any risks."

Suddenly the garden didn't seem welcoming or charming.

"I'm sure everyone is taking precautions already. The poor girl." Tearing her mind from the unfortunate maid and the disquiet that had seized her, Jocelyn said, "Please let me know if you have problems with the staff. Don't try to deal with them yourself."

"I will." Sincerity blazed on Tilly's wrinkled face. "But I'm sure things will fall into place as they're meant to."

Jocelyn smiled absently while her mind danced around the strange facts she'd uncovered since arriving at Merrivale. One detail wouldn't let go. How exactly had Leo's first wife died?

After spending a delightful hour exploring the extensive gardens, they made their way back inside. Tilly and Elizabeth decided to retire to her mother's suite, leaving Jocelyn to her own devices.

Cassandra. Despite Mr. Sherbourne promising she'd see her new daughter the following day, she was dying to get a glimpse of her. All these years she'd assumed she'd never have a child, and now excitement put a spring in her step.

Someone to love.

Recalling her husband's words about the nursery's location, Jocelyn headed in the same direction as her mother and Tilly. Tapestries lined the walls of the passage. She paused to study one showing the Trojan wooden horse, the colors vibrant and eye-catching, the stitching abrasive beneath her fingertips.

"Did you want something, Mrs. Sherbourne?"

Jocelyn whirled around, her heart banging against her ribs. She pressed her right hand to her breast. "Oh, you startled me."

A pretty dark-haired maid stood behind her, a polishing cloth and a feather duster in her hands. "I'm sorry. I wondered if you were lost."

34

Jocelyn shook her head. The maid's accent was broad, but not as thick as some of the other staff she'd met earlier. "Edna, isn't it? I'm looking for the nursery."

"It's Ella, Mrs. Sherbourne." Her manner was hesitant as if she feared Jocelyn might sprout a new personality complete with horns. Ella swallowed rapidly. "The nursery is at the end of the passage."

"Thank you, Ella."

Ella nodded, risking a glance at her. "Was there anything else, Mrs. Sherbourne?"

"No that's all." Jocelyn maintained her pleasant manner, despite the curiosity nudging her to ask questions. Gossiping with servants wasn't something a lady of the manor should do.

Ella scuttled away, leaving Jocelyn frowning after her thoughtfully. When the maid disappeared Jocelyn continued to the end of the passage. Aware of passing time, she opened the door and came to an abrupt halt.

The woman sitting by the window was stunning, the late afternoon sun falling on her face and highlighting her dark, exotic beauty. Her deep brown eyes were almond in shape and fringed with long lashes, and they widened fractionally at Jocelyn's arrival. A pale face with an olive cast held a wide, sensual mouth. Her faint smile lifted the corners of her lips in mockery and more. This was a smile of smugness.

She set aside her needlework and stood, revealing her crimson overskirt with matching red and white petticoats, spread wide with side hoops. A white tucker protected her modesty, yet did nothing to detract from her buxom curves. She was a woman who'd attract men, and her manner hinted she'd already made the comparisons between the two of them and found Jocelyn lacking. "Did you want something?"

Jocelyn roused from her stupor, a flash of heat storming her cheeks. "I came to see my stepdaughter."

"She isn't well. I'm afraid I can't permit you to wake her." Confidence filled the woman's voice, digging at Jocelyn's composure.

"Are you Cassandra's nursemaid?" For once, Jocelyn struggled with poise. She sucked in a deep breath and exhaled before stepping into the room. A taunting smirk drew her up short.

"Yes, I'm Arabella, Cassandra's nurse and a distant cousin of Leo's."

Nonplussed by the disclosure, Jocelyn reached for the polite society manners drummed into her by her mother from a young age. She ignored the sly insolence and quietly exerted her authority. "I'll peek in on Cassandra. Is she through here?"

The stack of wooden blocks and a discarded doll told Jocelyn this part of the nursery suite was where Cassandra played. A doll's house sat in a place of prominence, the design appearing much like Merrivale Manor. Jocelyn noted a doorway and noiselessly opened it. A small mound in the middle of the narrow bed drew her attention. She stepped nearer, ignoring the disapproving presence at her back.

Warm blankets swathed the child, and only the top of her blonde head showed above the covers. Each of her breaths whistled between parted lips, and every now and then, a cute snore erupted. Her cheeks appeared flushed, but when Jocelyn touched her fingers to the child's forehead, she found it warm rather than hot. Sleep would aid her recovery. She was a very pretty child, taking after her mother, or at least Jocelyn assumed her mother bore the same coloring as the siblings she'd met a few hours earlier. After smoothing the covers, Jocelyn retreated to the outer room.

Arabella confronted her, a scowl marring her dark beauty. "You have no right to barge in here. Leo has given me full authority."

The way the woman used Leo's name gave Jocelyn pause. Some of what she was thinking must have shown on her face because triumph glittered in the woman's brown eyes. Arabella let her gaze travel over Jocelyn. Jocelyn forced herself to remain at ease while inside every one of the hurtful remarks from the past emerged. It was true she couldn't lay claim to beauty but surely Mr. Sherbourne...no, he'd hardly install a mistress as a nurse for his daughter.

"I'll let you get back to your needlework," Jocelyn said in a stiff voice.

She left the nursery in a dignified retreat, unpalatable thoughts keeping her company while she walked down the passage. Hardly knowing how she got there, she entered her chamber and blinked.

The pinkness of the room didn't improve on second viewing. Furniture and knickknacks cluttered the space, making it appear small in comparison to Leo's chamber. The wallpaper coordinated with the furnishings, a deep blush pink that was almost red.

Jocelyn spun in a slow circle, barely suppressing her wince. Her gaze settled. Right, the first things to go would be those grinning cherubs. The plump statues bore salacious expressions, entirely too knowing for her liking.

Just like Arabella. She forced the notion away, determined to ignore the doubts the other woman had placed in her mind. She'd start clearing some of the clutter. When Mr. Sherbourne came to her room, and he would despite Arabella's silent insinuations, Jocelyn didn't want anyone or anything competing for his attention.

She plucked a plaster cherub off a table and placed it on the floor. Soon she had large pile of rejected items.

A brief tap announced the arrival of a maid. "Mrs. Sherbourne, my name is Susan. Mrs. Green said I'm to help you tonight, and if you like me, I'll become your maid on a permanent basis. I unpacked for you earlier." Breathless from her rushed words, Susan glanced at her feet.

She was on the plump side, wisps of frizzy dark hair escaping confinement beneath her white cap. However, her blue eyes shone with earnestness, making Jocelyn want to give her a chance.

"That sounds most satisfactory." Jocelyn approved of Mrs. Green's efficiency.

Susan burst into action, lighting several candles. The flicker of flames dispelled the gloom creeping into the corners now that the large trees around the manor hid the sun. The light brought a plaster angel into focus, one bearing a sly smirk. A vision of Arabella intruded, and Jocelyn scowled. Bother the woman.

"Which gown would you like to wear tonight?" A note of nervousness bled from Susan's voice, betraying her desperate desire to please.

"The green, I think." Jocelyn unbuttoned her gloves and peeled them off before starting to unfasten her current gown. Susan disappeared to retrieve the requested clothing. It was one of Jocelyn's favorites and never failed to boost her confidence. She and Mr. Sherbourne would dine in private tonight, and her stomach churned with both disquiet and hope. But now she clenched her jaw, determination heaping on top of nerves. She'd made a commitment and wanted to do a good job in *all* ways. She mightn't be a virgin, but tonight, the bedding part of marriage brought more trepidation than her first time.

Jocelyn freshened up with water Susan poured from an urn into a china bowl. A tremor slipped down her spine. The cold water had nothing to do with her burst of unease. It was the dread of losing her new husband to a beautiful mistress. *No!* She couldn't afford to let Arabella distract her from the important things—the chance of a new, reputable life.

Her mind in turmoil, Jocelyn reached for her scarlet stockings. She rolled them up her calves and secured them with garters just above her knees.

Once Jocelyn donned a clean chemise, Susan helped her with her stays, petticoats and gown. Her maid pulled the fabric up her arms and secured several buttons and tapes. She fussed with the skirts and twitched them into submission. With one final flick of her wrist, she nodded approval.

"How would you like your hair, Mrs. Sherbourne?"

"Something simple please. I think tidying my current style will suffice."

Susan bustled around the room, her initial tremors subsiding into quiet competence.

"Thank you, Susan. I won't need you again tonight, but tell Mrs. Green I'd like you to continue as my maid."

Susan's cheeks pinked with pleasure. "Will you require refreshments in the morning?"

"A dish of tea please."

"Thank you, Mrs. Sherbourne." Susan dropped a brief curtsey and left her alone.

A knock sounded on the connecting door of her chamber, and seconds later, Mr. Sherbourne stepped inside.

"Are you ready to go down?"

"I'm afraid I'm running a little late. My mother and I explored the gardens this afternoon, and when I came upstairs, I was pondering how to change this room to something more my taste. Time ran away with me." She stood and slipped her feet into shoes. Why hadn't she mentioned meeting Arabella?

"I have something for you—a wedding gift." Mr. Sherbourne pulled a sparkling necklace from his pocket. Emeralds and diamonds caught the flickering light from the candles.

"You didn't need to get me a gift, but thank you," Jocelyn said with pleasure. "I adore emeralds. Could you fasten it for me? I'll wear it tonight."

"This necklace belonged to my mother." Her husband closed the distance between them and placed the necklace around her neck. "She brought it with her from Spain."

"Your mother came from Spain?"

"Yes, my father met her during his travels on the continent and brought her home as his bride."

"Oh. I met Arabella earlier. Is she from Spain too?"

Mr. Sherbourne shrugged. "A distant cousin."

How distant? The stones chilled her skin. Had his first wife worn this necklace? And did Arabella have designs on the jewels and her husband too? A frisson of alarm set her mind awhirl, but the warmth of his callused hands at her neck countered some of her trepidation. A tremor of an entirely different kind swept her, heating every inch of her skin. Her eyes fluttered closed, and she breathed in his bay rum scent, her pulse racing with anticipation. The urge to reach for him, to slide her palms over his cheeks and draw his face down for a kiss teased at her. Aware she needed to act like a wife instead of reminding Mr. Sherbourne of her seductive mistress days, she curled her fingers into her palms until the inclination faded.

"There you go." He stepped away from her, seemingly unaffected by their proximity.

"Thank you." Jocelyn surveyed the necklace in her looking glass. "It's beautiful."

"I thought the necklace would suit you." Satisfaction glowed in his stern features, telling her she'd pleased him. "There are earrings to match. I'll give them to you later. Shall we?" He offered his arm to escort her to dinner.

The cook excelled herself with a delicious meal of oyster soup, roast venison, lamb stuffed with flour and raisins, and salmon. Jocelyn tried a little of everything, including the vegetables of chopped spinach and asparagus. Over their food and several glasses of red wine, they talked about the manor and Mr. Sherbourne's normal routine. They ended their meal with a fruit pie served with custard.

"Tell me about the village," Jocelyn said.

"It's small, but adequate for our needs. There's a baker, a blacksmith, a draper, a chandler and a coaching inn."

"And a parish church?"

His grin dazzled her. "Yes, we have one of those. We go to Tavistock on market day for some of our supplies, but I try to support those in the village."

"I look forward to a visit. I hear Tavistock is a decent size town." Her needs were few, but her mother would enjoy purchasing fabrics and sewing supplies. "What about neighbors?"

"You've met Hannah and Peregrine," Mr. Sherbourne said. "I grew up with them. Viscount Hartscombe, their father, operates several copper mines and owns much of the land around here, although he and the viscountess are often traveling due to their interest in ancient civilizations. You'll probably meet Vicar Allenby and his wife, Mrs. Allenby, very soon. There's a retired army man called Captain Cartwright. He's the elected parish constable. Then there's Duxton, the home of Sir James Harvey. When I was a child, my parents used to attend social gatherings in Tavistock. I haven't participated as much as my parents did when they were alive."

Something in his clipped tone suggested he was thinking about more, but Jocelyn bit her tongue to still her questions. *Patience.* The last thing she wanted was to start off their marriage with a disagreement.

"I can't wait to explore your estate and the village."

"Always tell someone where you're going." A clipped demand to obey. "Take one of the footmen with you. They will make sure you don't get lost or wander off the path should a mist drift onto the moor."

Jocelyn's brows rose at his abrupt order. "Yes, of course." Some of her surprise must have shown.

"The moor is a hazardous place and the weather can change on a whim."

"Dangerous?"

"There are hidden bogs. It's easy to wander off the path if a fog descends without warning. People have disappeared and never been seen again. A child wandered off only three months ago. Despite our search, no one has seen him since."

"I'll keep that in mind." Jocelyn suppressed a shiver with difficulty. Why wasn't he mentioning the murder? Perhaps the servants had exaggerated. "I'll make sure Mother and Tilly take an escort if they go in search of wild herbs."

"They can take the carriage to the village if they wish to make a visit."

"I'll let them know." She glanced up from her fruit pie to find Mr. Sherbourne studying her mouth. His eyes rose, darkening with desire when their gazes met, and she fought an impulse to lick her lips.

"Would you like to take a turn around the garden? We could wander along the banks of the stream. The path is smooth, and the moon is almost full. We won't require a lantern."

"I'd like that very much." Jocelyn pushed aside her plate, indicating readiness even though disappointment followed his suggestion. She'd thought he might whisk her off to his chamber. Masking her emotions with the ease of long practice, she smiled at her husband. It was odd interacting with him. She was acutely aware of him physically, yet he was essentially a stranger.

He stood and helped her rise, attentive and gentlemanly. He was like his cousin in that respect, although she'd never experienced this level of longing with Melburn. Mr. Sherbourne led her from the dining room. They exited the manor via the double doors that opened out onto a terrace.

Full darkness had fallen while they dined and, despite the moonlight, shadows loomed in parts of the garden. To their right, a loud rustling commenced, and Jocelyn jumped, moving closer to her husband in a silent request for reassurance.

"It's only a night creature—a hedgehog or similar."

"Whatever it is, I hope the creature doesn't decide to scuttle over my feet. The outdoors appears very different at night." Tree branches stretched out like naked limbs, leaves rustled and other mysterious sounds, scratches and creaks, made Jocelyn doubt she'd want to wander alone after dusk.

"This way," Mr. Sherbourne said, leading her confidently down the steps into the night.

Away from the house, it was easier to see the stars studding the black sky and the moon hanging overhead, huge and bright. The scent of roses and a hint of lavender filled the air, mixing with her husband's bay rum. Somewhere in front of them, a night bird called a sharp warning. She started and Mr. Sherbourne laughed.

"Just a bird," he said.

"There aren't any ghosts hanging around the manor?" Despite the lovely evening and his presence, a preternatural nippiness kept her glancing over her shoulder.

"None that I know of," he said. "But the servants will tell you of ghosts and spirits wandering the moors. Witches and goblins and even the odd dragon."

"Now you're trying to scare me."

A rusty chuckle came from him. "I was aiming for romantic. Don't most women enjoy a romantic tryst with their husbands?"

"Yes." Jocelyn sensed he was trying to put her at ease. He wanted her happy in their marriage. The knowledge soothed her dread, and she pressed closer, her reservations about Arabella fading under his attentions. "I've heard it said a kiss adds to the romance."

He stopped abruptly and turned to face her. Shadows screened his face, making her guess at his expression. Her pulse beat a little faster. He cupped her face, and lowered his head until his breath warmed her lips.

"Mr. Sherbourne." She laced her hands behind his neck and rose on tiptoe to reduce the inches separating them. Their lips met, tentatively, then with decadent warmth. Heat and sensation darted along her veins, and she pressed against his chest, straining to move as close as possible. Her breasts brushed his vest, shooting awareness, yearning through her body. *Proof.* This area of their marriage wouldn't present problems, despite the contrasting unease fluttering through her body.

"Leo," he said and trailed a finger down her cheek. Then he tugged lightly on a red curl that lay against her collarbone—a tender gesture that rocked her to her toes. "Come, let us walk off our dinner."

By common consent, they ambled along the path hand-in-hand, the silence companionable, thoughts of ghosts fading far from her mind.

"I peeked in on Cassandra earlier. She's beautiful."

"She can be a bit of a handful, at least when she is feeling well."

"We'll get along fine," Jocelyn said. "You don't need to worry about your daughter. I will care for her as if she's my own."

"Thank you." Leo wanted to place his faith in her words but intended to reserve judgment. Time would tell. At least Jocelyn's presence would stop Hannah's constant attention. His new wife brought hope to Merrivale Manor, something he hadn't felt for a long time. He shot her a quick glance. Lust too.

The instant he'd stepped into her chamber tonight, he'd wanted to strip off her green gown and explore her luscious body. He'd badly wanted to discover if freckles, like the ones on her face, covered other parts of her torso. Even now, he fought the urge to drag her to a private spot, to ravish her until her beautiful blue eyes darkened with passion.

The waiting since their nuptials had been difficult, yet he didn't regret the lost opportunity. She deserved time to become used to him. Her light floral scent teased him, and he sent her a grin. "I'm having trouble keeping my hands off you."

"Oh." She paused, the subdued lighting not hiding her expressive face. Her lips curved upward. "Good."

A bark of laughter escaped him, and he hugged her, enjoying the way she relaxed in his embrace. "Not many women would react that way."

"Which is why men seek out mistresses, I presume. I'd much rather you wanted me than another woman."

"I don't have a mistress." Melburn had mentioned her no-nonsense nature. Leo found her practicality intriguing, and when he compared her with Ursula—

He broke off the thought abruptly, angry at himself for letting his first wife soil what should be a special evening. "I've no intention of taking another woman to my bed."

"Other men do it."

"My first wife took many lovers during the course of our marriage. I disliked it and won't accept disloyalty of that nature in you or myself." Leo resumed their walk, requiring motion to rid himself of painful memories and betrayal.

"I'm sorry."

"I want you to feel free to make changes in the manor. I believe there is more furniture in the attic. Mrs. Green will know." The shift of subject wasn't exactly adroit, but recollections of Ursula brought fury and regret for allowing his heart—lust—to rule his mind. One mistake and he was still paying. He wouldn't make the same errors with this marriage.

Jocelyn nodded with enthusiasm, dragging his focus back to the present. "I thought I'd give the rooms themes. What do you think of cherubs for the main reception room? Maybe rename it the Greek room."

"Cherubs?" Leo barely restrained his shudder of horror. The ones Ursula had placed in her chamber gave him nightmares. "Ah, if that's what you'd like."

Her throaty chuckle brought him to a halt. "I wish I could see your face more clearly. Your voice..." She trailed off, laughing without restraint.

Leo's brows rose, and he found himself smiling at the joyful sound. "I can see I'll have to watch you."

"Yes, Leo."

With a lighter heart, he guided her past the maze.

She glanced at the opening between the hedges. "I heard there was a murder."

"Yes." Damn, he should've guessed the staff would gossip.

"I thought the maze was difficult to navigate?"

"It is. I'd rather not talk about murder. Not tonight." The challenge of the labyrinth pointed the finger squarely at him. The local authorities had already mentioned this fact. He'd have to be careful or he'd find himself implicated again.

She heeded his strong suggestion, and they strolled in silence, the bubble of the stream and the croak of a frog providing background music. Leo guided her along the loop path and soon they found themselves back on the terrace. "I find myself longing for privacy."

"Oh?"

"I've half a mind to spank you, just to draw a line, you understand. I can't have you teasing me about cherubs."

"No, Leo."

"No, you're agreeing or no to spanking?" Damn, he found he liked the coquette in her manner. A spear of lust struck his loins. He wanted her naked, under him, over him. He cast her a considering glance while wondering if she'd take his cock in her mouth.

"I've heard rumors of men and women who enjoy giving and receiving a spanking." Moonlight highlighted the mischief dancing in her eyes.

"And what conclusions have you drawn regarding the reports?"

"I think I'd like you touching my bottom." A tiny smile played on her lips, impish in nature and one he found intriguing.

The more he came to know this woman the better he liked her. It meant he could let his guard down and simply enjoy the evening instead of feeling as if he'd wandered into a Dartmoor quagmire. His strides lengthened, his pace quickening until she was trotting at his side.

"Leo! Could you slow down?" Her breath came in rushed pants, her chest rising and falling rapidly, drawing attention to the plump curves of her breasts and a cinnamon freckle that sat a scant distance above the fabric of her bodice. "You don't want to fatigue me this early in the night."

Leo ripped his gaze off the freckle, and with a chuckle, slowed to scoop her into his arms. Jocelyn let out a squeak of surprise and clutched his shoulders. "This way is faster."

"Why did you suggest a walk if you were eager for privacy?"

"I didn't wish to appear uncouth." Honesty from him, once again. Hell might freeze over.

"I'm a good judge of character. It's a skill I had to learn to survive." She stroked his cheek, a gesture of tenderness. "Besides, I wouldn't travel all the way to Dartmoor if I feared you."

"I'm glad you're here." Another truth. Already Jocelyn's presence had lightened the tension wrapped around the manor. Cassie would love her, as long as Hannah didn't try to interfere. Leo set Jocelyn down to close the terrace doors before sweeping her off her feet again and hurrying up the stairs to his chamber. He shouldered the door open and shoved it shut once he'd entered.

A maid had already turned down the bed and lit several candles. He glanced down at Jocelyn and couldn't hold back his amusement at her impish grin and pink cheeks. The candlelight illuminated her hair, making it glow like fire.

"I like it when you smile." She traced his lips with her fingertips. "You should do it more often."

"There hasn't been much happiness about recently." Damn, that wasn't what he wanted to say. Her honesty was having a bad effect on him.

But instead of pursuing the opening he'd given her, she nodded. "Are you going to put me down?"

"I suppose I must." Her enticing scent made him think of sunshine and lazy summer days. And that single freckle—it was sending him toward madness. He let her slide down his body, his cock reacting in a predictable manner given the friction of clothes and supple limbs. God, he wanted her. He'd desired her from the moment he'd seen her in London. She wasn't beautiful but her glorious red hair and sparkling blue eyes were mesmerizing. She'd charmed Melburn and hearing his cousin talk about her had raised both his curiosity and a sense of longing. A woman who garnered his cousin's loyalty was someone he'd wanted to meet. "Do you know what I'd like?"

She tilted her head to one side and bestowed him with a mysterious feminine smile. For once the sight didn't send alarm shivering through him. "Should I disrobe?"

"You read my mind." Leo kicked off his black shoes and

shrugged out of his jacket. With deft fingers, he unbuttoned his vest and set that aside too. He tugged his shirt from his breeches, dispensed with it and settled on his bed. His gaze fastened on his new wife, who'd watched him the entire time. "I'm ready now."

"You'll need to help me with my buttons."

Hell, in his hurry he'd forgotten the difficulty of women's attire. "Come closer."

Obvious humor lit her face, and she glided toward him, all feminine elegance and subtle flirtation. A confident woman. And so far, she seemed to have integrity. His former wife had never understood there were times when honesty achieved more than falsehoods.

Irritation seared him then, and he forced his mind to Jocelyn. She flirted with her eyes, the sinuous sway of her body. Slowly, she lifted her hands, the graceful rise snaring his attention. She plucked a jeweled comb from her hair and started on the concealed pins. Mesmerized, he watched their removal. Then his gaze met hers and held, the heavy pulsation of sensual awareness humming between them. Jocelyn removed the final one and down the heavy mass toppled.

His breath caught at the sight. Long fiery locks danced around her shoulders and halfway down her back when she moved closer to his four-poster bed. His hands clenched as he imagined winding the curls around his fingers. They'd feel silky to his touch, and if she knelt in front of him, took his shaft into her mouth...

A shudder racked his frame, his mind shaping the scenario, his hands gripping her hair, controlling her movement while she sucked his cock. Suddenly his breeches were far too tight. He cleared his throat without taking his attention off her. She sashayed up to him and angled her back for him to unfasten her gown. To his chagrin, tremors shook his hand when he reached to deal with her buttons. He tightened it to a fist and, this time, it held steady when he unclenched his fingers.

Soon the silk gaped away from her body. Her eyes danced with a provocative note as she glanced over her shoulder.

He drew a sharp breath. His new wife was a bloody witch, captivating him with a glance. "Do you intend to tease me all night?"

"No, it would be difficult not to taunt myself at the same time."

"A double-edged sword."

"Exactly." She beamed at him, making him puff up like an innocent receiving praise, except tonight, he sure as hell didn't feel childlike. To his relief, she stepped away and let the fabric slide over her hips to puddle at her feet. She plucked the green silk from the floor and draped the gown over the back of a chair.

Leo couldn't take his eyes off her. Beautiful. Graceful. Honest. Melburn hadn't mentioned her teasing nature, but Leo liked her harmless impudence.

Jocelyn removed frothy petticoats, stepping closer when she required assistance with the lacing of her stays. In a trice, the task was complete and all she wore was her filmy chemise, the emerald necklace and her footwear.

"Jocelyn, you're stunning."

"Thank you." Her throaty tone told him her flirtation had taken a toll of her too.

She planted her pert backside on a chair and bent to take off her shoes. With a playful glance at him, she untied her garters and made a production of rolling her scarlet stockings down her legs. She started to remove her chemise.

"No, leave that on for the moment."

"Will you kiss me now?"

"And more," he promised.

Jocelyn joined him on his bed, and they stared at each other, potential shimmering between them.

"What do you mean to do with me, my husband?"

Pure pleasure struck him at her words. "I intend to touch and learn your shape. Kiss you." Leo cupped her shoulder, savoring the warmth of her smooth flesh. "I want to kiss your lips again, your breasts. By tomorrow morning there won't be an inch of your body I haven't kissed or tasted."

She licked her lips. "And then what?"

"I intend to fuck you until this hunger inside me is sated."

"Do I get a turn?"

Interesting, his bluntness and vulgar language didn't scare her into blushing silence. "Later," he said, drawing her against him. He intended to start his seduction. He crushed his lips to hers, loving the way she responded immediately. Her hands curled around his neck, and every idea he'd entertained of taking his time flew out the window. Hell, he needed her, and if he didn't get these breeches off soon they'd strangle his cock and cut off his circulation.

"Chemise off," he demanded, springing off his bed to deal with the fall of his breeches and remaining clothes. When he glanced back at Jocelyn he found her exactly where he'd left her, her eyes big and wide as she watched him disrobe. His hands settled at his sides, and he stood before her naked and aroused.

CHAPTER 3

JOCELYN ACHED FOR HIS touch and, when he stalked toward her and finally drew their naked bodies together, a hard shudder seized her. She gripped his shoulders and strained to get even closer, her quim weeping and ready for his possession. This man—her husband—she scarcely knew him, yet he touched places inside her, made her hunger for his hands on her skin, his smile. Especially his smile.

Their lips met, communicating urgency on his part. Jocelyn didn't mind. Their thoughts ran parallel. She didn't want cautious and easy. Tonight she needed to know she belonged to Leo. She wanted to experience every gut-wrenching emotion she'd missed in the past because she'd chosen—been forced on a different life path.

This time was for both of them, for pure pleasure and pleasing each other. For once, she experienced no pressure to perform or boost egos. It made a big difference.

His kisses fueled her need for more until she went dizzy with desire. Finally, desperate for air, she pulled away, her chest heaving. Before he could speak or ask questions, she pressed a quick kiss to his throat. That peck became another kiss, this one long and lingering while she discovered his flavor and drank in his heady scent of bay rum and masculinity. Her new favorite bouquet.

He gripped her upper arms, gently pushing her away. His eyes glittered with both laughter and triumph as he rolled and covered her trembling body.

"I can't wait any longer," he said. "Let me pleasure you."

Amusement simmered and prompted a burst of humor. "You want a clear conscience when you finally pounce on me and lose control."

"Of course." His grin held a hint of rogue, and her heart beat a little faster at his playful manner. "You've discovered my evil plan."

Jocelyn couldn't contain her mirth. "Your plan doesn't sound wicked to me."

"I'm pleased to hear I don't scare you." One hand smoothed over her collarbone, his callused fingers creating a sensual drag across her skin. Awareness pulsed in her, his touch shooting sparks through her veins, his blatant regard making her feel feminine and seductive despite her ordinary appearance.

"I'm not frightened of you." She'd known fear, and it bore little relation to the feelings coursing through her now. The murder...no, she mustn't think the worst. "A bit nervous maybe, but I think that is to be expected with a new marriage." Her smile felt as if it were ragged at the edges.

"Understandable. You have freckles all over." His fingers moved in a seductive stroke from one golden spot to the next.

"The bane of my life." She clutched his shoulders, her fingernails biting into his flesh, yet he didn't protest. Instead, he licked a lazy path across the curve of one breast, making it difficult for her to concentrate. "Freckles are not fashionable," she added.

"I like them." His warm breath washed across her skin as he spoke.

Her nipples beaded to hard points, a silent plea for him to touch her with greater intimacy. Her head dropped back. "Leo, *please*."

Luckily, he didn't attempt to tease her or draw out the waiting. One big hand covered her breast, his fingers circling then tugging on her nipple and sending desire sizzling across her skin. She gulped in air and gasped when his mouth closed over her other nipple. Oh, this was exactly what she needed. She turned liquid deep inside, moistening for his possession, yearning for him to hasten his pace.

"Leo." This time her voice held approval as he palmed her left breast and stimulated her nipple with deft fingers. His mouth worked harder, spreading a prickling trail of pleasure. She stirred restlessly, desperately craving more, yet contrarily wanting to draw out his attentions and commit them to memory so she could recall every perfect detail once she was alone again.

"I like the way you smell," he said when he lifted her head. "But you taste even better. All sugary and sweet with a hint of spice."

"My mother makes lotions and special rinses in the still room. I use them to wash my hair and to keep my skin smooth."

"I must commend her."

She'd ask her mother to make something for Leo. She'd enjoy working on a special project. Then thoughts of her mother faded because Leo moved down her body. He parted her legs and placed a kiss directly on the heart of her quim. She gasped at the skill and purpose in his touch. Soon her entire body hummed under his seductive plundering. A lap of his tongue. A faint nibble and an open-mouthed kiss. Her hips moved restlessly as she sought deeper contact.

"You like that."

"Yes. More please, Leo." Her hips canted in silent encouragement. She felt...empty. She craved his touch, his cock filling her. A soft moan escaped when he teased her nub, his stroke a tug deep in her core. Her stomach hollowed, and she trembled, unraveling with each of his caresses.

Laughing softly, he licked downward to her entrance, the stubble on his jaw abrading the tender skin of her inner thighs. This man...her husband. He knew how to pleasure a woman. Part of her wondered at his experience, about the other women in his life. They both came to this marriage with history. *No!* She needed to concentrate on their future.

"Leo." Her pelvis rocked. She pressed her needy flesh against his mouth in silent demand.

"I know what you want." This time he answered her plea. He pushed a finger inside her and her breathing went shallow. She squirmed when he closed his mouth over her and applied steady suction. A sharp breath filled her lungs, and she released it in a low moan. His touch was too much. It wasn't enough. Flames swarmed over her entire body. Her pulse spiked sharply, then the molten force inside her exploded. The fire banked high and gradually reduced to languorous waves that seemed to go on forever. Finally, she sighed, a heartfelt sound of satisfaction.

Leo removed his finger and slid up her body. His lips settled over hers, urgent and inflammatory. He tasted wild and sweet, his eyes feral with passion as he gripped fistfuls of her hair and surged into her, filling her with one powerful thrust.

Fully embedded, he paused and lifted his head, his fingers toying with a springy red curl. "This surpasses my imagination."

"I'm sure we can do even better yet." This flirtatious nature was new to her, but she found she enjoyed the way her words teased humor from him, a bright smile.

Leo nuzzled her neck, and she gripped him in a possessive

hold, running one hand down his back and coming to a rest on his rump. He began to move in decisive strokes that fueled a renewed surge of desire.

"Hell," he muttered.

His hoarsely voiced curse brought a rush of amusement, an awareness of her feminine power. Determined to propel him into pleasure, she caressed his neck with a trail of kisses. At the place where his shoulder and neck met, she deepened her attention with hot suction and used her teeth to introduce a hint of pain. He groaned and, if anything, his cock grew harder, filling her to capacity. With a convulsive heave of muscles, he quickened his strokes, shoving her into the feather mattress.

Jocelyn gasped, a shimmer of sensation overtaking her. Her channel pulsed around his cock and another harsh cry escaped him. He invaded her body and stilled, throwing his head back and letting out a harsh cry of enjoyment. Jocelyn watched his stark visage, eyes screwed tight while he rode out the carnal stimulation. Gradually, he relaxed, his eyes popping open.

"Thank you," she whispered, emotion welling in her, clogging her throat and preventing further discourse.

He might have thought she was thanking him for the satisfaction that came with their bed-sport, but it was for so much more. He'd shown her tonight how their marriage could be—the promise of a happy future. They suited each other. Instinctively she'd known that, but his behavior and care proved her instincts correct. They were a good match.

"Don't thank me yet," he said. "I've barely started."

He parted their bodies and started kissing her anew. Her muscles pulled tight with each tormenting stroke of his hands and mouth. Their breaths mingled and she clung to him, reveling in every tempestuous sensation.

"Good," she said when their lips parted. "I haven't finished either."

His rich chuckle thrilled her, the echo of his amusement filling her mind as they loved each other into the small hours of the morning.

THE TUNEFUL SINGING OF a maid roused Jocelyn. Her eyes opened to register the bright sunshine attempting to burst through a crack in the curtains. She stretched, the stiffness in her muscles bringing to mind the previous night. A faint smile played around her lips. She and Leo were compatible in the bedroom, and she looked forward to the coming evening.

Jocelyn slid from the tangled sheets and slipped on the shirt Leo had worn last night. She opened the connecting door to their chambers and stepped into her pink room.

"Good morning." Susan helped Jocelyn don a robe. "Mr. Sherbourne said to let you sleep. I'll go to fetch your tea now."

Before her maid disappeared, Jocelyn asked, "Is there water to wash?"

"Of course," the maid said. "I'll arrange hot water while you drink your tea."

Once Jocelyn was alone, she padded over to a window and surveyed the garden. She caught a glimpse of white from the corner of her eye. When she focused where she'd seen the flicker, she saw nothing. She shook her head and stepped away. Spending so much time with her mother was propelling her into flights of fancy. She'd most likely caught sight of one of the gardeners.

Susan arrived bearing a tray. The scent of the raspberry jam and the sight of two slices of bread brought pangs of hunger. Her stomach gave an unladylike rumble.

"Pardon me."

Susan cast a knowing glance. "Your mother is asking after you, Mrs. Sherbourne."

"Is she agitated?" Immediate tension tightened Jocelyn's shoulders as she waited for more information.

"Oh, no. She was singing with Cassandra. They seemed very happy."

"I'll go and find them once I'm dressed," Jocelyn said, then remembered the housekeeper. "After my meeting with Mrs. Green."

Jocelyn hurried through her wash and changed into a serviceable brown gown to meet with the housekeeper.

Mrs. Green greeted her with a frosty grimace. Her black dress and cap were immaculate, spotless and crisp with starch. A simple bun confined her dark brown hair and not a wisp strayed out of place. Jocelyn fought an urge to check her own rebellious hair.

"I've brought the meal plans for the next week," Mrs. Green said. "Mr. Woodley asked if he might meet with you later."

"That will be fine. Please have a seat."

They went through the menus, which were satisfactory. Mrs. Green appeared efficient, and Jocelyn didn't want to upset her by changing everything. Not yet anyway. Thankfully, by the end of their meeting, Mrs. Green managed a wider, albeit tight, smile that told Jocelyn the housekeeper still bore reservations about the new mistress of Merrivale.

"Does Cassandra eat with the adults?" Jocelyn asked.

"She takes her meals in the nursery."

Jocelyn nodded, deciding to speak with Leo regarding her stepdaughter. In her experience, it was best to start training a young girl for polite company as soon as possible. Cassandra would become used to conversation and able to hold her own if she joined the adults more regularly. Of course that meant Arabella would dine with them too. Dismay grew at the realization. Jocelyn straightened her posture as if preparing for battle. It would be best if she acted decisively and demonstrated that Leo was her husband in all ways. Jocelyn was here to stay.

"I'd like two footmen to help me move the furniture in my chamber, and if you could spare a maid to remove the curtains, I'd be most appreciative."

"The color is bright to the eye," Mrs. Green conceded.

"Do you know if there are suitable furnishings to replace those that are there?"

"The furniture Mr. Sherbourne's mother used is in one of the attics. I can get the footmen to bring it down and the maids to polish it before you choose the items you'd like to use."

"Excellent, thank you, Mrs. Green. I have a feeling you'll know exactly what I have in mind." At least Jocelyn hoped she did. "I have several things that require my attention today. Why don't you decide on the replacement furniture for me?"

The faint approval that crept into the housekeeper's cheeks told Jocelyn she'd read the women correctly.

"Do you require everything done today?"

"There is no hurry." Jocelyn preferred to sleep in Leo's chamber. She suspected they would share a bed again this evening anyway. "Thank you for your help, Mrs. Green."

Jocelyn stood and went in search of Woodley. A quick conversation with her butler told her he was enjoying the change and wasn't experiencing any difficulties, other than a little frostiness from the rest of the staff. He assured Jocelyn it wasn't a problem.

"Do you know where I'll find my mother and Tilly?"

"I believe they are taking a turn around the gardens," Woodley said. "They have Miss Cassandra and her nurse with them."

Jocelyn strove for an impassive expression. "Thank you. I think I'll join them."

Voices and childish giggles guided Jocelyn in her search. She spied the group by a lavender hedge. Arabella strolled ahead, a lacy parasol shading her face while her mother carried a basket and was busy gathering flowers and herbs. Tilly and Cassandra followed in the rear, her stepdaughter chasing a blue butterfly.

"Good morning. Mother, did you sleep well?" Jocelyn shot a quick glance at Tilly, her raised brows asking her mother's nurse silent questions.

Tilly dipped her head in a quick nod while her mother burst into excited conversation, much of it about her room and the gardens. Jocelyn listened with half an ear while studying the child.

"You must be Cassandra," Jocelyn said when her mother stopped talking.

"No, I'm Cassie." Her stepdaughter wore a daffodil yellow dress covered with frills, and someone had arranged her golden hair in tight ringlets. Jocelyn saw none of Leo in the young girl.

"I'm pleased to meet you, Cassie. I hope you're feeling better today."

"Belle gave me medicine." Cassie crept behind a leafy bush and peered at Jocelyn uncertainly.

"I'm glad you get to spend time with us then. Mother, let me carry the basket for you," Jocelyn said.

"No, I wish to carry it to keep my cuttings safe."

They walked through the garden picking rosemary, yarrow, angelica, more lavender and handfuls of rose petals.

"Could you make a special rinse for Leo to use in his bath?" Jocelyn asked, glad that Arabella had vanished around the bend in the path. No mocking eyes to offer Jocelyn discomfort. "I thought he might like one."

Her mother started thinking out loud, muttering about herbs and spices and craning her neck as she searched for the various plants in the garden. She darted away to pluck leaves and blooms from a geranium and exclaimed loudly when she sighted a patch of marigolds. Her mother disappeared with Cassie skipping after her.

Tilly sighed. "I'd better follow them before they get up to mischief."

"I'll keep an eye on them," Jocelyn said. "You find Woodley. Spend half an hour with your husband. I'll send for you once we're indoors again."

"You're an angel," Tilly said.

Jocelyn shook her head since they'd repeated this conversation many times. Tilly was the saint for dealing with her mother during her bad spells. "Go before I change my mind."

Tilly left, and Jocelyn trailed her mother and Cassie. The childish chatter and her mother's soft replies reassured Jocelyn that neither of her charges required aid. She turned a corner and came across a young man trimming a hedge. He nodded in greeting before continuing his task.

A harsh scream cut the air without warning.

Jocelyn started running, lifting her skirts to navigate the twisting path. The young gardener raced behind her, his boots sending gravel flying.

A second scream came from Jocelyn's right, followed by a high-pitch childish shriek of alarm. Jocelyn changed direction. She sprinted around a corner, her breath emerging in harsh pants and came to an abrupt stop. Her mother was cringing in a corner, a hedge at her back with Cassie squashed behind her rigid frame.

"Mother?" Jocelyn approached slowly, aware of the wildness in her mother's eyes. "It's all right. Everything is going to be fine."

The contents of her mother's basket littered the path, sprigs of herbs and delicate rose petals crushed beneath her feet. Her fierce eyes scanned a copse of oak trees, and she trembled violently.

"Mother?"

Hurried footsteps behind Jocelyn announced Arabella's arrival. "What have you done to Cassie?" she demanded.

"Nothing," Jocelyn said tersely. "Mother?"

Cassie started crying and the tears exacerbated her mother's panic. Elizabeth's facial muscles twitched. Another violent quake shook her thin shoulders and she shrieked, long and loud. The harsh, grating cry made the small hairs at the back of Jocelyn's neck lift in foreboding.

"Mother, what is it?"

"The spy. He followed us. He's here."

"What spy?" Arabella demanded.

Not again. Jocelyn ignored Arabella to scan their surroundings. She could discern nothing in the garden or amongst the shadows in the trees. "There's no one there, Mother."

"There is. There is! He's hiding." Her mother's voice grated with shrillness and she shook uncontrollably.

Jocelyn frowned, concerned about Cassie, who was wailing in earnest. "Mother, you're scaring Cassie. Can we go inside and talk about it?"

"But the spy will come closer when we're not looking," her mother shrieked. "We can't let him."

A frustrated sigh escaped Jocelyn. Her mother wouldn't budge until she proved there was no spy in the vicinity. Meanwhile Cassie continued to cry, her small body almost hidden by her mother's skirts. Jocelyn turned to the gardener. "Could you check the copse for strangers please?"

"Yes, Mrs. Sherbourne."

"Thank you. Look for footprints or anything out of the ordinary." Jocelyn wrinkled her forehead, realized it could cause creases and smoothed her expression. "I don't suppose you saw any strangers loitering in the area?"

"No, Mrs. Sherbourne. The only people I've seen are the ladies and Miss Cassie."

"Arabella, did you see anyone?"

"Of course not." Arabella sniffed, the twirl of her parasol highlighting her disdain.

Jocelyn suspected her mother was seeing ghosts again where there were none. She issued more instructions to the gardener. "Search the garden and the edge of the trees. Let Woodley know when you've finished and if you discover anything."

The young man touched his cap in a respectful manner and trotted away.

"Search amongst the oaks first," her mother screeched. "Look for a white ghost."

A ghost? First she'd seen a man and now she was changing her story. Jocelyn fought for patience. Losing her temper wouldn't help—she knew from past experience. "Mother, the gardener will search for an intruder. Please, stop screaming. You're frightening Cassie." She approached her mother cautiously, knowing a sudden move could set her off again. "Let's get you both inside. I'm sure Mrs. Green will make us a cup of tea. She might even have a special treat."

Cassie peered out at Jocelyn, her face tearstained. "Jam tarts?"

Jocelyn bit back her relief and held out her hand. "Let's go." She recalled the flash of white she'd seen earlier and discounted as nothing out of the ordinary. Could her mother have seen a bird? A dove perhaps?

"We should get Cassie inside," her mother said. "It's not safe out here." She glanced around them, her gaze darting wildly as if she expected someone to pop from behind the bushes. Then abruptly, she fell to her knees and pawed through the sprigs of plants and flowers she'd picked. "My herbs and flowers are ruined."

"I'll pick more for you." Jocelyn seized her mother's arm and helped her to her feet while maintaining her grip on Cassie's small hand. She started walking, silently praying her mother wouldn't become even more difficult. To her relief both Cassie and her mother fell into step.

"I'll take charge of Cassie," Arabella snapped.

"Of course." Now wasn't the time to make a scene. Jocelyn let Arabella take Cassie's hand and focused on leading her mother to the house, only releasing her breath after ushering Elizabeth inside.

Tilly came running, her lined face edged with concern.

"Tilly, the herbs I picked are ruined."

Jocelyn shot a sharp look at Tilly. Her mother was building up to another one of her screaming episodes.

"I intend to collect more for you," Jocelyn promised. She rang for a maid and ordered refreshments, then she crouched in front of Cassie. "Are you all right, sweetheart?"

"Of course she isn't." Arabella let out a scoff that was almost a hiss, her dark eyes flashing with a hint of triumph.

Jocelyn ignored Arabella's dramatics to concentrate on her stepdaughter. "Cassie?"

"The bad man scared me."

Jocelyn's mouth dropped open. "Did you see the man?"

"N-no."

Jocelyn barely stopped her shoulders from sagging in disappointment. Cassie hadn't seen anyone but was taking her cue from Elizabeth. Jocelyn stretched out her hand to Cassie. "Let's dry your eyes. I'm sure Cook will send some of her special cakes for us."

"Jam tarts," Cassie said, her bottom lip sticking out in a pout.

Relieved at her stepdaughter's resilient nature, Jocelyn hid her amusement as she ushered everyone to the parlor. "I'll ask if Cook has tarts today."

While they waited, she settled Cassie on a chair and wiped the last of her tears away. Tilly encouraged Elizabeth to retire to her rooms.

A loud commotion outside drew everyone's attention.

Halfway to the door, Elizabeth whirled to face the window, her eyes wide with alarm. "I told you there were spies. They followed us from London. I told you!" She clapped her hand to her heart, her words growing progressively louder and strident.

"Your mother belongs in an institution," Arabella said.

"I suggest you return to the nursery," Jocelyn said in an icy tone. "I will personally deliver Cassie to you this afternoon."

"You can't—"

"I can," Jocelyn snapped. "Go now before I decide to hire a new nurse for Cassie." A cold stare met hers. The two women dueled in silence before Arabella broke the connection and flounced away. Jocelyn watched through a narrowed gaze, her body tense to the point of pain. When Arabella disappeared from sight, Jocelyn dragged in a noisy breath and turned to face her next trial.

"Mother, cease your cries." Her mother was upsetting Cassie again. "Please."

"He's over there." Elizabeth pointed a dramatic finger, and Jocelyn caught herself glancing over her shoulder, peering out the window for a glimpse of a skulking man before commonsense reasserted itself. This was yet again one of her mother's imaginary phantoms.

"Is there something wrong, Mrs. Sherbourne?" Woodley burst into the parlor, his calm demeanor taking in everything at a glance.

"Elizabeth is upset," Tilly said. "I think it's best if we take her to her room."

"I saw someone outside," her mother insisted.

"I'll send someone to scare them off," Woodley said, his voice pitched to soothe.

"They won't search properly," Elizabeth said. "You go, Woodley."

Woodley inclined his head. "Very well, Mrs. Townsend. I'll do a search the minute we've escorted you safely to your chamber."

Tilly took Elizabeth's arm and Woodley the other. Together, they directed her mother toward her quarters and peace settled in the parlor. Jocelyn relaxed and smoothed her skirts. With relief beating a tattoo through her veins, she pinned a reassuring smile to her lips, ready to settle Cassie. "Cassie, we'll—Cassie?" A shocked gasp escaped.

The child had vanished.

CHAPTER 4

"Cassie?" Jocelyn rapidly searched behind the chairs and the larger pieces of furniture, alarm tightening her throat. She peered under a sturdy table but didn't see her stepdaughter.

"Good morning." Amusement colored the voice of the feminine speaker.

Jocelyn's head jerked upward, colliding with the edge of the table. "Ow!" She backed out from underneath the desk, rubbing her temple. Face flushed with heat, she climbed to her feet and turned to face the mystery woman.

Oh, the neighbors—Hannah and Peregrine. *Just perfect.* Jocelyn pasted on a smile and pretended her new neighbors hadn't seen her on the floor with her backside poking from beneath a table. She brushed her face with the corner of her apron, aware of her messy appearance. No doubt, her cherry-red cheeks clashed with her hair and freckles. Her callers, of course, wore smart clothes suitable for visiting.

"Good day to you. I didn't see you there. I was looking for Cassie." She restrained herself when instinct told her to fuss with her hair. She couldn't begin to compete with Hannah's beautiful cream riding habit and pale golden perfection. There was no black garb in evidence today.

"We heard screaming. Is something wrong?" Masculine approval glinted in Peregrine's eyes as he focused on the upper curves of Jocelyn's breasts.

"My mother received a fright." Jocelyn ignored Peregrine's rude ogling to visually search the parlor for a glimpse of her stepdaughter.

"Aunt Hannah!" Cassie appeared from the far corner of the room and threw herself at the woman, burying her face in the skirts of her aunt's riding habit.

Jocelyn wanted to sag onto the nearest chair. *Thank goodness!* The last thing she wanted was to explain to Leo how she'd lost his daughter.

"Poppet, what's wrong? You're not usually shy." Hannah took a step back and stooped to kiss her niece's face. "Why have you been crying?" She shot a reproving look at Jocelyn, and Jocelyn felt the full weight of the woman's censure. "Where is your nurse?"

To Jocelyn's relief, a maid arrived with refreshments, the rattle of the tray providing a welcome interruption. Providing explanations of the last hour to her new neighbors, even if they bore close ties to Cassie, wasn't something she wanted to do either.

"Please take a seat," Jocelyn said, gesturing at the Egyptian-style settee and the ornate matching chairs. She accepted Peregrine's escort to a spot near the tea tray and immediately wished she hadn't when his touch lingered overlong. Experience had taught her how to deal with unwelcome advances, but she held herself in check, reminding herself these were her neighbors. She arranged her skirts and waited expectantly for Hannah to follow suit.

"Where is the fair Arabella?" Peregrine asked in a lazy drawl.

"I volunteered to look after Cassie for a few hours," Jocelyn said in a tight voice.

Hannah led Cassie over to a chair—one with elaborately carved feet—and lifted her up. "Would you like some fresh milk and one of Cook's raspberry tarts?"

Irritation tightened Jocelyn's chest, and she aimed an incredulous glower at Hannah. The woman had no business usurping her rightful place as hostess. The hint of malice in the other woman's eyes stiffened Jocelyn's spine. She curled her right hand around the arm of her chair, counseling herself to patience. Her marriage to Leo was a shock and she needed to make allowances.

Hannah placed a tart on a plate for Cassie, and Peregrine caught Jocelyn's frown.

"How do you like Dartmoor?" he asked, directing the conversation with a flirtatious grin, probably in the hope of avoiding an unpleasant disagreement between the two women. "It must be a change from London."

How did he know she came from London? She hadn't told anyone simply because she didn't want to cause Leo embarrassment or open herself to nosy questions. "I haven't been here long, but so far I love the countryside." An evasive answer, but it seemed to satisfy him.

"Dartmoor is a dangerous place." Peregrine leaned over and placed a too familiar hand on her forearm. His blue eyes twinkled and, to her discomfort, Jocelyn detected a hint of lust.

"In what way?" Jocelyn shifted and his hand dropped away. Personally she thought both Hannah and Peregrine needed a lesson in manners.

"Did you hear about the murder of our maid? Her body was found in the maze here at Merrivale." His blond brows rose, his eyes strangely intent. His lazy manner faded as he leaned closer to speak in an undertone. "Then of course, there was my sister's murder. If I were you, I'd be watching my back."

A chill rippled through Jocelyn, stirring the hairs at the back of her neck. "Whatever do you mean?"

Peregrine's brows drew together. "I'd listen to the rumors because there is more than a little truth in them."

"Stop being so secretive." Jocelyn drew in a rapid breath, attempting to claw back the anxiety his words set loose. There was something about his tone, the way his teasing nature had receded to expose a hint of his inner self. "Tell me what you mean."

Peregrine shrugged and insouciance settled on him again like a cozy woolen cloak. "I'm warning you to take care. All is not as it seems at Merrivale."

Confused about his meaning, she stood abruptly. "Can I get you a dish of tea or would you like something stronger?"

"Do you have claret?"

"Of course." Having learned a thing or two while dealing with her sisters, she calmly reclaimed the reins from Hannah, bustling about to pour claret and prepare a plate of cakes for Peregrine. "Hannah, would you care for a slice of butter cake or perhaps a raspberry tart?"

"Thank you." Hannah smiled graciously, although her fingers tightened around the handle of the milk jug before replacing it on the table.

An awkward silence fell. Jocelyn wanted to check on her mother and make certain Cassie was all right after her fright. But, aware of her responsibilities, she sat beside Peregrine again and introduced a neutral topic. "Tell me about the village. Is there a good dressmaker?"

"We came to invite you to a party." Hannah's gaze swept Jocelyn's serviceable brown and her top lip curled. "I doubt you'll have time to order a new gown beforehand. The village dressmaker might aspire to London designs, but the results are hopelessly provincial."

"Hannah!" Even Peregrine blinked at her rudeness.

"A party sounds lovely," Jocelyn said, ignoring both comments. "I look forward to meeting Leo's friends and neighbors. Will there be dancing?"

Hannah shrugged. "Of course. Peregrine has the invitation." She turned her back on Jocelyn and Peregrine to chat with Cassie. Another show of ill manners.

A distant shriek severed the taut calm.

Cassie dropped her milk and started wailing. Jocelyn jumped to her feet, but Hannah took over, soothing her niece while ordering Peregrine to summon a maid. In the end, Jocelyn rang for a servant, moving away to let Hannah deal with Cassie. There was no need to complicate the situation by arguing with the woman, but Jocelyn's lips pursed in irritation. If Hannah attempted to behave like this during her next visit, she'd learn Jocelyn wasn't afraid of claiming her rightful place.

"Aren't you going to investigate the commotion?" Peregrine asked, leaning closer than necessary. His focus was on her breasts again, and a scandalous smirk lit his eyes. It wasn't difficult to imagine the direction of his thoughts.

"No." Jocelyn straightened, irked by the man's flirtation. There was nothing she could do that Tilly wouldn't already be doing. "My mother's nurse will take care of her."

"Your mother is making that racket? She sounds as if she belongs in Bedlam," Hannah snapped. "No wonder Cassie is upset with a lunatic living in the manor."

"Hannah," Peregrine rebuked. "That was unpardonably rude."

"I'm speaking nothing less than the truth. I don't know why Leo would marry *her*."

Peregrine grimaced, but his attention wandered to Jocelyn's bodice. "I must apologize for my sister. I'm sorry, Jocelyn. Can I call you Jocelyn since Leo's family and ours are such old friends and none of us stand on formalities?"

Why couldn't he address her face instead of her breasts? "Yes, of course." She wanted to refuse, yet it seemed silly to insist when they'd see each other on a regular basis.

"We'd better leave you to calm your mother." Peregrine stood and bent over her hand. A perfectly polite gesture yet he made it into a lurid one. His fingers traced the tender skin of her inner wrist, lingering over the scatter of freckles in an overly familiar way. A reckless grin lit his face when she jerked from his touch. "Remember what I said. Merrivale is a dangerous place." Raising his voice, he said, "Come, Hannah. We have callers arriving this afternoon. I told you we couldn't visit for long."

"I don't want you to go," Cassie cried, clutching her aunt's cream skirts with her jam-covered fingers.

"Look what you've done," Hannah said in a sharp voice. She yanked from Cassie's grasp and backed away with a scowl.

Cassie started wailing, her sobs breaking Jocelyn's heart. *Poor mite.* She'd had a trying morning. Jocelyn scooped up the child and hugged her tightly, but Cassie's crying didn't diminish.

"We will visit again later in the week," Hannah promised, shooting a triumphant look at Jocelyn.

"I want to go home with you," Cassie cried.

"That will be enough, Cassie." Leo stood in the doorway. He grimaced as a volley of shrieks echoed from her mother's wing. "Hannah. Peregrine. I didn't think to see you so soon." He ignored Jocelyn to concentrate on their visitors.

"We came to invite you to a party," Peregrine said, smiling warmly at Jocelyn.

"Cassie," Leo remonstrated.

Cassie's noisy sobs abated somewhat at her father's stern tone, and Leo glowered at Hannah and Peregrine before leveling his dark expression on her. Jocelyn stiffened, annoyance striking her like an abrupt bump against the shins. She drew a sharp breath and attempted to tamp down her exasperation. Surely he didn't suspect she returned Peregrine's obvious interest? That she wanted his flirtatious attentions? Compared to Leo, Peregrine was a rambunctious puppy, acceptable in small doses but not fit for polite company.

Cassie started to struggle, and Jocelyn set her down. The child immediately ran to Hannah and hid her face in her aunt's skirts. This time there were no rebukes, merely sweet smiles that made Jocelyn long to lash out with sharp words of reprimand.

Hannah sparkling with the good cheer she hadn't demonstrated before Leo's arrival. "Do say you'll come to the party." She placed one gloved hand on Leo's arm, all charm as she batted her lashes at him. "It won't be the same without you."

"Please excuse me," Jocelyn said in a stiff voice. "I must attend my mother." With a nod at Peregrine and a strained smile at Hannah, she hurried to the doorway. When she passed Leo, her lips warmed into a genuine beam. "I won't be long."

Leo glanced in the direction of the hoarse screams. "We'll talk once our visitors leave."

"Of course." Jocelyn tried not to read too much into his glower. She had nothing to worry about, because she hadn't encouraged Peregrine. Still, anxiety stalked her all the way to her mother's rooms. She wanted Leo to trust her. Her thoughts slid to Peregrine and uneasiness joined her concern. His warning words implied something was amiss at Merrivale. Was he implying Leo was the source of the danger?

The screams grew progressively louder until they drowned out Jocelyn's doubts.

Grimacing, she tapped on the door before entering. "Mother, is this shrieking necessary? You're upsetting Cassie and making her cry."

The caterwauling ceased abruptly.

"Have you collected herbs for me? I need them to make my rinse for your husband."

Jocelyn fought an urge to bang her head against the nearest wall. In a quicksilver change of direction her mother appeared to have forgotten the spy she'd spotted lurking in the garden. "No, Mother. I had unexpected visitors. Leo is with them now, but as soon as they leave, I'll collect the herbs and flowers you require." She wanted to speak with the gardener anyway. Hopefully, he'd reported his findings to Woodley already.

Leaving Tilly to organize her mother, she returned to the parlor. To her relief, only Leo and Cassie remained. Arabella arrived at the same time and, after a glare in Jocelyn's direction, took charge of Cassie and marched the child from the room.

"I'm sorry my mother upset Cassie."

"I suspect Cassie is still unwell," Leo said, his words clipped and precise.

Jocelyn winced, wary of his mood. She didn't know him well enough to predict his temper. "Did you hear about the party?"

"Yes, Hannah informed me of the invitation."

Jocelyn bit her lip. *Stupid.* She'd heard Hannah repeat the invitation herself. "I'm looking forward to meeting our other neighbors."

Leo prowled to the nearest window. He stared out over the garden, his back stiff. Yesterday he'd reminded her of a graceful beast. Today his prowling seemed faintly menacing, especially in light of Peregrine's strange warnings. Leo whirled to face her, the sudden move making her jump. "Are you bored with living in the country? Jaded with my company already?"

Jocelyn gaped at him. "Of course not."

"You appeared to enjoy Peregrine's company." Leo's harsh tone surprised her too. Had last night meant nothing to him?

"They weren't here for long before you arrived. Mother had

one of her episodes out in the garden."

"I heard." Leo's tone was short.

Someone tapped on the door, halting the tart reply trembling at her lips.

"Enter," Leo said without taking his gaze off her.

Woodley stopped just inside the door. "Mrs. Sherbourne, the gardener is here to see you. He said you'd told him to talk to me, but I felt you should hear what he has to say in person."

Leo's eyes narrowed, but Jocelyn's gaze didn't waver. There was something in Leo's past—something relating to his first marriage—that made him distrustful. Part of her understood his testy attitude because he didn't know her well. Not yet. It'd take time for him to believe she'd never betray him. Taming Leo would require patience and resilience, which thankfully she possessed in abundance after dealing with her sisters and mother and the hellish mess her father had landed her in on his death.

"Of course. Tell him I'll be out in a few minutes. I promised to collect some herbs and flowers for my mother anyway."

"Yes, Mrs. Sherbourne." Woodley backed from the parlor and closed the door.

Leo stared at her until she wanted to squirm.

"Ah, I'd better go and speak with the gardener." The words burst from her, a reaction to his frosty demeanor.

"Why do you need to speak to the gardener?" Once again, suspicion colored his expression.

She was innocent of wrongdoing, and his attitude stirred even more uneasiness. Jocelyn reminded herself she'd made the decision to marry him, and she had to make the best of her new situation. "Why don't you come with me?"

Her suggestion obviously startled him. Good. Perhaps keeping him off balance might mellow his mood. She bustled to the doorway and spoke over her shoulder. "I'll explain on the way. I need to collect a basket and scissors to pick more flowers and herbs for my mother. The ones we picked were destroyed—trampled underfoot during the earlier tempest."

Leo nodded, strangely reticent now.

Satisfied with her strategy, Jocelyn led the way outside, pausing to collect her supplies from the still room. "I asked the under-gardener to check for signs of a stranger loitering in the garden. Mother was insistent she saw someone spying on us while we were picking flowers."

"And you think your mother was imagining things?"

"Yes. No." Jocelyn frowned. "I'm not sure. I sensed someone watching us while we were in the garden, but thought it was my imagination. I also saw a flash of white."

"Most likely it was a bird or a sheep."

"That's what I decided, but that was also before Mother started screaming about spies." Another thought occurred—one she didn't voice. The riding habit Hannah had worn today was pale in color. She and Peregrine had arrived at roughly the same time. No, Hannah mightn't like her, but her affection for her niece appeared genuine. She wouldn't want to upset Cassie.

The jam episode...

No, Jocelyn was positive of Hannah's innocence in this case. They'd arrived on horseback and left their horses at the stables, which were in the opposite direction. "Have you experienced problems with intruders before?"

"Strangers tend to stand out in the village." Leo's mouth twisted, but she wouldn't call it a smile. "We live in a beautiful area and do have visitors, but I'd have heard of new arrivals, where they'd come from, along with their intentions and length of stay. Gossip spreads rapidly around here."

"I suppose that must be how Peregrine knew I was from London. There he is," Jocelyn said, changing her direction abruptly. "Good afternoon, did you discover anything out of the ordinary?"

The young gardener bobbed his head in a show of respect. "I didn't see anyone or come across footprints." His words were slow and thick with a Devonshire accent. "The ground's dry after the fine weather."

"Oh. Well, thank you for looking for me." Jocelyn had expected this report. Her mother wasn't the most reliable witness. She started to turn away when the gardener spoke again.

"There was something strange," he said. "Someone had trampled the undergrowth at the edge of the oak forest. No footprints, see, but broken branches and crushed grasses near the trees."

Jocelyn considered the information. "Perhaps it was an animal. Maybe sheep?"

"How old were the signs?" Leo took over the questioning, his gaze probing.

"Recent," the gardener said without hesitation. "Sap still oozed from the broken branches."

"Could one of the other gardeners have caused the damage?" Leo asked.

"None of us have worked in the area today," the gardener said.

Jocelyn nodded. "Thank you."

The gardener went back to his work, leaving her alone with Leo. He was frowning again, but this time his displeasure wasn't aimed at her.

"What do you think?"

"I don't know," Leo said. "I'll speak to the rest of the outdoor staff and ask them to watch for strangers."

"We're assuming it's a stranger, but it could be anyone," Jocelyn pointed out. "It could be a local or one of the staff."

"At least you're not trying to tell me your mother saw a

ghost."

"You don't believe in ghosts?"

An indelicate sound escaped Leo. "Of course not. I'm sure there's a perfectly logical explanation." He studied his wife's impish expression, and his bad mood disappeared as quickly as it had arrived. Seeing Peregrine touching her in the overly familiar manner had reminded him of Ursula's flirtations. At the start of his first marriage, he'd been so smitten he hadn't noticed Ursula's shortcomings. Besides, she'd hidden her lovers carefully until he'd discovered her in bed with an actor from a touring troop. After that episode, she hadn't bothered to hide her indiscretions, her behavior outrageous and designed to rouse his jealousy.

"I'd hoped Mother would settle easily. She was so happy out in the garden picking flowers." Jocelyn grimaced. "I'm sorry about the drama. I'd better pick these flowers and herbs before Mother makes her displeasure known again."

"Jocelyn?"

"Yes?"

"Take care with Peregrine." He'd confront his worries—his jealousy—instead of ignoring the situation as he'd done with Ursula.

She cocked her head, the sun glinting on her red hair and turning it to flame. "I hate to say this, but your neighbors lack manners. Peregrine is a child, although he probably wouldn't thank me for saying so."

"What happened?" The fire in her eyes darted a frisson of heat to his groin, and memories of the previous night added to the warmth. She was incredible, and he'd been looking forward to the coming evening.

"Hannah attempted to usurp my place as hostess, and

Peregrine kept speaking to my breasts," she snapped.

Her distaste went a long way to soothing his distrust. "I hope you managed to put her in her place." Melburn had told him she was loyal, but while he'd nodded at the information and professed himself glad, he was finding it difficult to deal with reality. Jocelyn mightn't have beauty, but men responded to her easy, friendly manner and her shapely form. They looked at her hair and translated it to a sensual nature.

"I didn't resort to rudeness," Jocelyn said. "It's a tricky situation because they're Cassie's aunt and uncle."

"There was a time when Hannah and I discussed marriage." Leo winced, surprised he'd admitted this.

"What happened?"

"Her younger sister happened," he said drily. "I hadn't met Ursula since we were children. I'd been away at school and spent time with Melburn in London. Ursula and I met at a Christmas ball and ended up getting married mere weeks later." Leo watched Jocelyn the entire time, but her expression didn't so much as flicker.

"I see."

Leo doubted Jocelyn's understanding. Ursula had fooled him with the skill of an expert loo player. "I'd better get back to work. I ran across the vicar, and he invited us to dinner. I thought I'd better give you notice."

"Thank you. I look forward to dinner."

"You'll like the vicar and his wife. I always enjoy their company."

Jocelyn gripped his arm suddenly. "Is that a sheep?" she asked in a whisper.

Leo turned slowly to face the direction she indicated but saw nothing.

"Bother. It's gone," Jocelyn said. "I don't think it was a sheep, but I can't swear it was a person either. I caught a glimpse from the corner of my eye. It was near the oak tree with the stump in front. Do you see it?"

"Go back to your flower picking," Leo said. "I'll check before returning to help the farm hands." He leaned close to steal a kiss then turned on his heel and strode away. The weight of a stare at his back brought a grin, and he put an extra swagger in his step. When he didn't let his jealousy get to him, his wife made him happy. A good start to their marriage.

THE DINNER WITH THE vicar and his wife turned out to be a pleasant experience, and Jocelyn found herself liking Vicar Allenby and his wife. The vicar enjoyed his food, being rotund in shape. A yellowed wig covered his head and sat off-center. By contrast, Mrs. Allenby was tall and angular, her pale blue eyes bright with intelligence. Her artfully arranged dark hair held streaks of gray. Although they were older, conversation passed easily between the couples.

The vicar and Leo spoke of farming, the mines and village matters while Mrs. Allenby nattered to Jocelyn about the village and the sewing circle, which was currently making children's clothes for an orphanage in Tavistock.

"Would you like to join?" Mrs. Allenby asked. "And perhaps your mother too?"

"My mother isn't well," Jocelyn said, fighting to keep regret at bay because socializing with other women was something her mother had always enjoyed in the past. "But perhaps she could stitch some articles at the manor?"

"Splendid," Mrs. Allenby said.

The two men stood. "I'm off to show Leo the new books I purchased in Tavistock," the vicar said. With the advance of the night and numerous drinks, the vicar's wig had drifted askew, and he now had a lopsided appearance.

Mrs. Allenby's eyes twinkled. "I know you're off to taste the brandy that appeared at the doorstep three nights ago. Don't be too long."

"You can use the time to gossip," the vicar shot back. "You don't require our presence for that."

Laughing, Mrs. Allenby made shooing motions with her hands and the men departed.

"Have you met Viscount Hartscombe's son and daughter?" Mrs. Allenby asked.

"Yes." Jocelyn abhorred gossip, a remnant of the horrid days after her father died. "They seem pleasant." She managed to get the words out without choking.

"Hartscombe and his viscountess are lovely, although they don't spend much time in Dartmoor. Hartscombe prefers the pleasures of the Continent these days. He's very interested in ancient civilizations and the viscountess travels with him. It will be lovely to see them at the party. I presume you're attending?"

Tension eased from Jocelyn. "Yes, I'm looking forward to meeting everyone. Tell me about the village," she prompted, eager to learn more of her new home.

Mrs. Allenby's brow crinkled, and a heavy sigh escaped. "Normally I'd say the village is a lovely place to live, but since the murders..." She trailed off, worry making her appear much older. "I suspect you've heard about them."

"A little, but I wasn't sure if the gossip was exaggerated."

"I'm afraid not. First poor Ursula was discovered strangled down by the river, and a few weeks ago a maid who disappeared from Hartscombe was found in the maze at Merrivale."

"Do they have any suspects?"

Mrs. Allenby grimaced. "A lot of people are saying your husband is the murderer."

"That's ridiculous," Jocelyn burst out, aghast that anyone would think Leo capable of the crime. Thoughts careened through her mind, so rapid they tripped over one another. She shook her head. "No, not Leo. I can't believe it of him."

Mrs. Allenby reached over to pat Jocelyn's hand. "Of course not, but I'm afraid the facts point in his direction."

"What is the evidence?" Jocelyn demanded, anger replacing her initial shock.

Sympathy chased across Mrs. Allenby's face as she hesitated.

"Tell me. I'd rather hear it from you. Please, don't let me enter a social situation unprepared."

Mrs. Allenby gave an unhappy sigh but acquiesced with Jocelyn's plea. "Witnesses saw Leo and Ursula fighting the evening before they discovered her body."

"But—"

Mrs. Allenby held up her hand, and Jocelyn cut off her objection. "Captain Cartwright, the parish constable, questioned Leo. Of course, Leo denied everything. One of the shepherds saw Ursula early the following morning with two men. They never identified the men. Ursula was discovered a few hours later, and the authorities released Leo."

Jocelyn found herself shaking her head. No, she couldn't believe Leo was a murderer. "And the other murder?"

"I'm afraid the disappearance of the maid who worked at Castle Hartscombe is a mystery. No one knows what happened to her, but there is no doubt she was found at Merrivale. The village is awash with speculation."

Not good. No wonder Leo was so insistent on her taking a footman with her during every outing. "Everyone suspects Leo."

Mrs. Allenby patted her hand again. "I'm afraid so. Those of us who know Leo understand the accusations are nonsense, but unfortunately this doesn't stop gossip. The best thing you can do is stand at his side, your head held high and smile."

"I can do that." After all, she'd had lots of practice at pretending everything was right in her world.

ONCE HOME, LEO AND Jocelyn hurried inside to escape the chill of the evening air. Leo's hand sat warmly on her hip, his arm curved around her waist as he escorted her up the stairs. At her chamber doorway, he paused, his arm slipping away. She missed his touch immediately.

"Why don't you join me once you're ready for bed?" His eyes glowed with banked lust, firing an answering call in her. Her breasts developed a sensual heaviness and desire tugged low in her quim.

Her tongue flicked out to moisten her lower lip as she stared up at him. "I'll do that."

"Good." His fingers stroked across her cheek for an instant before he turned away. "I'll see you soon."

The firm click of a door closing broke the spell he'd cast with a few words and a mere touch. She blinked then reached for the door of her room with a flash of anticipation. How could anyone suspect this man was a murderer? She knew his cousin and trusted him implicitly. Leo had shown such kindness to her mother. No, she'd never believe the vicious gossip circulating the village.

She found Susan asleep in a chair, waiting for her return, and chagrin filled her. She hadn't thought to tell her maid not to wait up for her.

"Susan." She shook the girl gently, not wanting to scare her.

Two candles flickered on the dresser, highlighting the lack of cherubs. Although the room wasn't yet to her taste, the removal of knickknacks and the pink curtains was a vast improvement. Mrs. Green had ordered the airing of some of the stored bed linens and promised they'd be ready the next day. Jocelyn nodded with approval, enjoying putting her stamp on the manor.

The girl was in a deep sleep, and she hated to wake her. "Susan." Jocelyn spoke louder this time.

The maid's eyes flew open. A sharp squeak escaped her before she came fully to her senses. "Mrs. Sherbourne? I'm so sorry. I must have fallen asleep."

"Susan, you shouldn't have waited up for me."

"It's my job, Mrs. Sherbourne." Susan's broad accent wrapped around her stiff, affronted words as she stood. "Would you like me to remove your gown and brush out your hair?"

"Yes, please," Jocelyn said. Her maid acted as if she'd insulted her when all she'd wanted was to save her work. She stood still while Susan unfastened her garments and removed layers of silk. Jocelyn presented her back and Susan worked on her stays. Finally, Jocelyn stood in only her stockings and chemise.

"Take a seat, Mrs. Sherbourne."

Meekly, Jocelyn sat and half an hour later, Susan finished with her hair.

"Would you like me to help you with your stockings?"

"No, thank you, Susan. That will be all for tonight. Good night."

"Goodnight, Mrs. Sherbourne."

When the door closed behind her maid, Jocelyn allowed herself a wry smile. Susan took her position seriously and was determined to do a good job. Jocelyn would need to quell her independent ways and become used to letting her maid do everything for her.

"Jocelyn?" Leo appeared at the connecting door to their chambers.

"I'm almost ready. I need to take off my stockings."

"I'll do it for you."

Jocelyn beamed. "Let me blow out the candles."

"Go and wait for me. I'll take care of the candles."

Jocelyn padded through the connecting door and sat on Leo's bed. Leo followed her, mere seconds later, closing the door behind him. He prowled nearer in the way of a beast, yet she didn't experience alarm. He blew out one of the two candles lighting his chamber, enclosing them in a bubble of intimacy.

"Why don't you have a valet?"

"I did, but he ran away with one of the parlor maids. Stay right there," he instructed, parting her legs a fraction so he could kneel comfortably in front of her.

Her breath caught, a warm glow suffusing her limbs. When she started to get dizzy, she gasped in air to combat her breathlessness.

Leo chuckled, his amusement bringing a wash of heat to her cheeks. "After he disappeared, I decided to do without a valet."

"Oh." It was difficult to concentrate with Leo's fingers trailing over the delicate skin of her inner thigh.

"You like red stockings?"

"I like red, yet it's difficult to find a shade of red that suits me."

Amusement glowed in his dark eyes, the corners of his lips twitching a fraction as he reached for a lock of her hair and gently tugged. "Red is my new favorite color."

"You are in a minority, I fear."

"Their loss." He released her hair to yank at her garter. Soon he was sliding woolen fabric down her calf. After a pause to place a kiss on the skin he revealed, he removed and tossed her stocking aside. Every inch of skin he touched turned tingly. His contact might be innocent, yet they both knew where this would lead. The other stocking followed the first. Leo stood and held out his hand to her. "Time to remove your chemise."

Once she was naked, he swooped her off her feet and set her in the middle of the mattress. He dropped his robe on the floor, allowing her a glimpse of his muscular body and rampant erection before he blew out the last candle, plunging the room into darkness.

CLOUDS SKITTERED ACROSS THE night sky, obscuring the moon for long minutes before racing off again and allowing dull light to pierce the darkness. The faint sound of chanting carried on the breeze, low and harmonious and out of place in the moor.

The man stood on the hill, surveying the scene below, watching for oddities. Deep shadows, cast from the ruined abbey, made it difficult for him to survey the scene, but nothing odd captured his attention. When clouds drifted across the moon again, he made his way down the hill, leading his horse behind him. His cape swirled in the puffs of wind, and his footfalls remained cautious in the darkness.

A woman's scream rang out. High and ear-piercing, it made the hair at the back of his neck rise. His mount danced a few steps, and he reached out to soothe the beast. "Steady, boy," he said in a low voice.

He paused to listen and could discern only normal sounds of the night. As he neared, it was easier to see the outline of the ruins, left when Henry the Eighth had ordered many of the country's monasteries destroyed.

The woman screamed again, and he frowned. They should have waited until they'd entered the secret crypt to start the ceremony. Anyone could hear her, and that was all they needed. One nosy person, a farmer tending his flock, and their sweet setup here at the abbey would cease.

Hastening his pace, he led his horse to the shelter of a lean-to. Disguised from public scrutiny, it already contained four horses. One nickered in welcome, and he covered his own horse's muzzle with his hand in a sign for his mount to remain silent. He didn't think anyone had followed him, but he had to take care to minimize the risk. After one final scan of his surroundings, he retrieved a candle from within the temporary stable. He lit the wick while his mind wandered over the last two months—the good and the bad.

Placing the body in the maze had been a mistake.

It cast suspicion, distrust he could do without at present. No, it wasn't time. Not yet.

He picked his way through the ruins, stepping more confidently now that he carried illumination to light his path. He wove past pillars and crumbling walls, striding deeper into the old abbey.

They'd left the secret chamber open for him, which made his progress rapid. Once through the door, he took care to seal the doorway, shutting him away in gloom, only pierced by his flickering candle. He stalked down a long passage. The downward slope took him deeper into the earth, the rush of the nearby river becoming louder.

The monks had left a convenient legacy, perfect for their needs.

A scream, much weaker this time, rang through the dark. It was a pity he'd had other prior business. His loins tightened at the promise of the evening to come. He looked forward to the entertainment and relieving the tensions of his day.

AN ABRUPT NOISE JERKED Jocelyn from sleep. For an instant she froze, her heart pounding as she attempted to make sense of whatever had awakened her. *Mother?* She strained to hear, tension seeping from her muscles when she couldn't discern the frantic screeches that signaled a mad fit from her parent. Not her mother then. Feeling more alert, she rolled over to find an empty space where she'd expected Leo.

Puzzled, she slipped from bed and strode to the window. She jerked the curtain aside to stare down at the gardens. A flash of movement caught her attention.

Leo? Squinting didn't aid with identification. She watched until the figure disappeared from sight, before the cold morning sent her fleeing to her bed.

Something amiss in the stables perhaps. Jocelyn tossed and turned, trying to get comfortable, fatigue weighing down her limbs. She must have dozed off at some stage because she woke to daylight streaming through the window.

Susan arrived with her tea. "Here you go, Mrs. Sherbourne." Instead of her normal competence, her lips quivered and her hands trembled so much splatters of liquid sloshed over the rim of the porcelain cup.

"Whatever is wrong?"

Tears welled at her maid's eyes. One trickled down her cheek, rapidly followed by another. Her shoulders slumped inward, and an audible sob broke free.

"Susan?"

"It's my sister, Ella," Susan said. "She went for a walk with Gavin, one of the footmen, last night after we finished our duties. They argued, and now Ella is missing. She didn't return last night."

Alarm shot through Jocelyn. "Has someone talked to Gavin?" Surely this was a misunderstanding. "Have the grounds been searched?"

Susan gave a miserable nod and another tear rolled down her cheek. "Some of the servants are saying Ella has run away, but she wouldn't. She wouldn't do anything without telling me she was leaving."

"Help me get dressed," Jocelyn said. "Has Leo been informed?"

"No one can find him."

A chill skipped down Jocelyn's torso, but she lifted her chin and grasped for confidence. There was a logical explanation for Leo leaving his bed in the small hours of the morning, a good reason for his absence now.

Jocelyn hurriedly dressed. "Leave the tidying," she said, when Susan started to right the bed. "You'll feel much better if you're helping to search. We'll consult with Woodley."

Their search produced nothing except hoarse voices and sore throats. Jocelyn grew increasingly concerned, her gaze flitting from person to person. Where was Leo?

A new arrival spiked a spark of relief until she realized it was the vicar and his wife. Jocelyn forced a gracious welcome and ushered Vicar and Mrs. Allenby toward the steps leading inside the manor. When she noticed Susan wringing her hands, her stomach flipped in sympathy.

"Susan, please go and order refreshments from the kitchen, then I'd like you to continue your duties in my chamber. I'm afraid I ripped the hem of my brown gown yesterday." When a mulish frown appeared on Susan's face, Jocelyn spoke rapidly, forcing herself to issue the order when she wanted to embrace her maid and offer comfort. "I'll send word as soon as we hear something."

Susan's face crumpled, but she gave a crisp nod and left.

"Why whatever is wrong?" Mrs. Allenby asked. "Have we arrived at a bad time?"

"One of our maids has vanished. She's normally very reliable, and her disappearance is quite out of character."

"Oh, dear," the vicar said.

"This doesn't sound right, especially since the other maid turned up dead," Mrs. Allenby said in a troubled voice.

"Is Leo out searching for her?" Vicar Allenby asked.

"Yes," Jocelyn said, guiding her guests into the parlor. She bit her lip, wondering why she'd lied.

Mrs. Allenby sat on one of the damask chairs and Jocelyn dropped onto the settee.

"Have you summoned the parish constable?" the vicar asked, selecting a sturdier chair more suitable for his robust frame.

"No, we're still searching the grounds and the riverbank in case of an accident."

"But you don't think an accident has befallen the girl," Mrs. Allenby said.

Jocelyn grasped her hands together, tightly in her lap. "No."

Silence filled the parlor.

"I think it would be a good idea to summon Arthur Cartwright, given the similar circumstances to the other maid's disappearance. Do you have paper? I'll pen a note for Arthur," the vicar said.

A maid appeared with a tray of refreshments, and Jocelyn bade her escort Vicar Allenby to Leo's study to procure paper and ink, all the while hoping she wasn't making a mistake. She hated to implicate Leo.

With the note dispatched, the vicar returned. Jocelyn sat on the edge of the settee, ignoring her tea, while she strained to hear any new arrivals outside.

"Mrs. Sherbourne?"

Jocelyn shook to alertness. "I'm sorry. I'm worried about Ella's disappearance." A vexed screech sounded in the distance. It repeated again, this time much closer.

Mrs. Allenby's brows rose. Vicar Allenby leaped to his feet.

"My mother," Jocelyn said wryly. "I'd know that sound anywhere." Heat suffused her cheeks. Heaven knows what her visitors thought. Sometimes she wished... No, this arrangement was working well. Her mother was enjoying the move to Merrivale. Besides, Leo had agreed to house her mother. He wouldn't go back on his word. A third squeal right outside the door had Jocelyn moving. She wrenched open the parlor door. "Mother. We have guests. Come and meet the vicar and his wife."

"Jocelyn, Tilly won't let me go outside. I want to walk in the garden."

"Mrs. Allenby, Vicar, this is my mother, Mrs. Townsend."

"I'm so pleased to meet you." Mrs. Allenby walked forward with an outstretched hand. "I understand you're a very talented seamstress."

Jocelyn held her breath until the tension seeped from her mother's shoulders. A broad smile broke out on her face, showing a hint of the beauty both of Jocelyn's older sisters had inherited. Ah, it seemed the period of relative calm would continue. Jocelyn hid a grimace. At least as long as they let Elizabeth go for a walk later.

After several minutes of animated chatter between Mrs. Allenby and Elizabeth about stitching and fabrics, Vicar Allenby said it was time for them to leave. Trying not to display anything apart from a polite social facade, Jocelyn escorted her visitors outside.

"Let us know how the search progresses for your maid," Vicar Allenby said in a gruff voice. "We'll keep our eyes and ears open."

A horse and rider approached down the driveway.

"That will be Captain Cartwright," Mrs. Allenby said. "He's a good man."

Jocelyn nodded, trying to ignore the trepidation churning the few sips of tea she'd managed to swallow. Leo hadn't returned yet.

CHAPTER 5

LEO CUT THROUGH THE moors, fatigue like a heavy sack of wool bearing down on his back. The scratches on his cheek throbbed, but at least the wound had stopped bleeding, and he'd helped the woman to escape her captives. Loud shouts drifted on the breeze, jerking him from introspection. His eyes narrowed against the glare of the sun as he noted the even spread of the men. They were searching for someone or something.

Leo hastened his pace. As he took the turn in the path, he came face-to-face with one of the Merrivale footmen. "What's happened?"

"Ella disappeared last night."

"Susan's sister?"

"Aye."

Leo's left hand curled against his thigh, and he ignored the footman's curiosity to hurry in the direction of the manor. At the edge of the copse of trees that bordered the gardens, he slowed to a brisk walk. This might prove difficult. He'd have to play cool and limit the information he gave or else he'd become a suspect. If he didn't say anything he'd appear guilty because of the bloody scratch on his face.

Damn.

The first person he saw was the parish constable standing on the front steps with Woodley and Jocelyn. Captain Cartwright was a scrawny man with fair skin. At present his nose was pink, burned by the hot summer sun. A knife scar dissected one cheek, courtesy of a brigand he met while soldiering in France. Now retired from the army, he wore a cocked hat on top of his pristine white wig. The man was honest and known to refuse bribes. He was also intelligent and determined when it came to seeing wrongdoers receive punishment.

Leo changed course, deciding to clean up first. Minimize the damage. He slipped around the back of the manor and entered via the library window, left conveniently open by one of the servants—a man creeping about his own home.

A startled gasp made him stiffen. He whirled around to face the source.

"Leo, what are you doing?" Jocelyn slapped a hand to her breast on seeing his cheek. "What happened to your face?"

How the hell had she got here so quickly? He struggled for a plausible excuse. "I stopped by the inn and thought a man was going to injure his wife. I got into the middle trying to stop him."

Her gaze flickered to the scratches again, and he witnessed the exact moment she jumped to her own conclusion.

"Where have you been?"

"My sheep have been disappearing. I think someone is stealing them, and I decided to watch the flock to see if I could catch the culprit." He maintained eye contact, despite the brazen lie, despite wanting to stare at the shelves of books instead. The ease with which he managed his deceit made his gut swirl with an edge of nausea.

"I see." She paused without taking her attention off him. "Ella is missing."

He didn't have to force his concern. "Is it possible she has run off with a man? The footman she was walking out with?"

"You knew? I didn't think you'd approve of servants courting after your valet ran off."

Some of his tension slipped away. He even managed a laugh. "My staff—our staff deserve the same happiness as us. As long as their trysts don't interfere with work I see no reason to stop them."

Jocelyn nodded, her hands gripped in a bunch of fingers, constantly moving, clasping and unclasping. "She hasn't run away. She and Gavin argued last night. Gavin stomped off and left her alone, and she hasn't been seen since." Jocelyn's gaze searched his features, lingered on the scratches again. "Captain Cartwright is interviewing everyone. He'll want to speak with you."

Damn. Cartwright would take one look at his face and start asking the same questions that were rattling around Jocelyn's mind. "I'll clean up and meet the constable in the parlor. Offer him refreshments and tell him I'll be down shortly."

"Of course." Jocelyn's modulated tone held no inflection, and the turmoil in him started afresh.

A screech of feminine rage roared down the passage and into the room where they stood. Leo had never been so happy of an interruption from Elizabeth. "Perhaps you should attend your mother."

"Of course." Jocelyn walked away without a backward look, yet her disapproval swirled around him like eddies of Dartmoor fog. She didn't believe him.

Leo strode from the library and up the stairs to his chamber. He needed to prepare himself for Arthur's interrogation, and he couldn't afford a slip.

Dressed in fresh clothes and with the scratches on his face

treated, Leo walked down the stairs to meet his fate. He encountered Woodley at the base of the stairs.

"Woodley, have they found Ella?"

"Not yet, Mr. Sherbourne. We're widening the search out onto the moor."

Leo gave a curt nod. He'd search for her in the abbey ruins this afternoon, not that he thought he'd have any more luck than those already searching.

"Sherbourne." Captain Cartwright stretched out a hand in greeting, a frown forming when he noted the scratches on Leo's face. His gaze grew intent. "Meet up with a she-devil?"

Leo barked out a laugh. Trust Cartwright to get straight to the point. "I committed the cardinal sin of getting between a woman and her man. They were fighting, I thought she was in danger, and when I tried to rescue her, she turned on me."

"Where was this?"

"The Running Footman in Tavistock." Leo wanted to rush into speech, to add more details but knew it would be a mistake. Too much information would raise Cartwright's suspicions even more. "I understand one of our maids has disappeared. Which areas have been searched? Does it look as if she's run off?"

"My gut tells me there is more to this situation than a maid running away after a tiff with her suitor. Everyone I've questioned confirms she's a good girl, one unlikely to run away. Time and again this morning I've heard she's a hard worker, a responsible woman. I fear someone has taken her unwillingly." Cartwright's voice grew harsh, his need to find the girl resonating in his voice. "You didn't see her on your way back from Tavistock?"

"No, the road was quiet today."

Cartwright's eyes narrowed. "So no one can vouch for your whereabouts?"

"No," Leo said. "Apart from the man and woman in the pub,

and I don't know their names."

"That makes things tricky." Arthur rubbed his chin in an absent manner.

Leo wasn't fooled and worried Arthur saw too much. A problem. He remained impassive, his practice with Ursula bearing him in good stead. "Was there anything else? I'd like to join one of the search parties."

"If I think of anything I'll ask you later."

Leo gave a curt nod and strode from the parlor, glad to have the interview finished. For now. Gut instinct told him Arthur would seek him out again to probe more about his visit to Tavistock.

This wasn't over.

Tavistock market, one week later

Jocelyn strolled through Bedford Square and studied the St. Eustachius church. The fine stone building dominated the square, but today farmers, merchants and shoppers brushed past her without a second glance, impatient to complete their tasks. Hawkers hollered over the shouts of their competitors, tempting customers to purchase their wares.

The scent of food, fresh flowers and perfume warred with the less appealing aroma of animal entrails, droppings and unwashed bodies.

"Get yaw 'ot pies here!"

"Oranges. Oranges!" A young girl jostled Jocelyn, trying to get her attention. She held up a glossy orange, waggling her wrist to better display the fruit.

"No, thank you." Intent on catching Leo and her mother, Jocelyn forged through the crush of bodies, taking care to watch for pickpockets. She was glad of the footman at her back. The hubbub of market day vexed her after the peace of the moors. Even so, she was happy to be away from the tension of Merrivale for a few hours. Since Ella's unexplained disappearance, everyone was on edge, glancing over their shoulders with suspicion.

Her nose wrinkled at the acrid cooking smoke coming from the nearby stall. The stallholders were doing a brisk trade in bowls of meat and turnip stew. The vendors next door were roasting chunks of venison over a fire.

"Jocelyn, do hurry," her mother called.

"I'm right behind you." Trailing Leo and her mother, she held her breath until they reached the sweeter smelling cloth stalls. Leo had promised her mother they'd purchase several lengths of fabric. The dressmaker would be the next stop, and her mother danced with her excitement.

Leo... Jocelyn's mind kept returning to his absence the night of Ella's disappearance, the scratches on his cheek he said had occurred in a fight. Her gaze lit on Leo's solid back, and a heavy sigh gusted from her. She didn't know what to think. Her heart kept telling her he was a good man, but her head refused to let go of the facts. Two murders and one disappearance. They all pointed at her husband.

She bumped into someone, and their bread toppled to the ground.

"Watch where ya goin'." The owner of the bread shot her a black glare before snatching up her loaf and brushing off the dirt.

"I'm sorry." Jocelyn stopped abruptly to avoid a further collision. Now was not the time to think about Leo's duplicity. She darted around the bread seller and hastened to catch up.

Jocelyn saw Leo maintained a firm grip on her mother's arm to stop her darting from stall to stall. An excellent strategy. The last thing they needed was a frantic search through the crowded marketplace. Still, it was good to see the bright color in her mother's cheeks and the way she chatted with Leo with nary a sign of madness.

"Look at that blue damask," her mother screeched. "See the color. The fineness of the fabric."

Jocelyn chuckled as her long-suffering husband allowed her mother to drag him over to inspect the bolt of cloth. She glanced along the line of stall holders, studying the rest of the fabric with a practiced eye. Was there a stall selling lace and trimmings? She turned to scan the offerings in the other direction. A gap appeared in the crowd and a familiar face loosed a startled gasp from deep in her throat.

Boynton? Here?

Shock held her rooted to the spot before self-preservation asserted itself and propelled her to scurry behind a large woman carrying a basket laden with vegetables. God, had he seen her? Apprehension twisted through her veins and nausea shot upward to clump in her throat. She swallowed rapidly, her breathing hoarse with panic.

He must've seen her.

Boynton hadn't been a gracious loser when Melburn won her off him in the poker game. He'd threatened to blacken her name, but Melburn had whisked her away and used his influence to protect her from harm. But now...now Boynton—he was here.

She peeked from behind the woman and glimpsed Boynton again. Her ex-protector hadn't changed. His dress was immaculate, his coat well-tailored and elegant. He wore a wig and his ruddy features told of his love of port and roast beef. His bulldog face bore a long, narrow nose while his lips curled upward in a cruel twist.

He was scanning the crowd, as if searching for someone. Oh dear. She'd have to tell Leo, would have to involve him in the nastiness of her previous life. Dread lent her speed. She elbowed her way through the crowd with scarcely an apology for her rudeness. She scuttled behind the nearest stall, her breath coming in harsh pants. From her hiding place, she watched Boynton. He cut through the crowd, using his size to bully anyone who dared bar his way. His pugnacious face was set with determination. She crouched against the side of the stall, a tremor weakening her knees.

Questions ran through her mind with breakneck speed. How had he discovered her location? Was it a coincidence or had he followed her from London? And even worse, had he known her address in London all along and simply bade his time?

"Lady, you all right?"

Jocelyn's head jerked in the direction of the young woman, towing a grubby child. "I'm fine. I felt ill for a moment." She had to move. Soon. Her mother would require Jocelyn's opinion on the bolts of cloth available for sale. Where was the footman? He'd be frantic, wondering what had happened to her. "I believe the feeling has passed now."

The young woman trudged on her way, juggling control of the child and her basket of shopping.

"'ere, you! Wot you doin' loitering behind my stall?" an irate woman demanded.

"I'm sorry." Jocelyn repeated her excuses and stepped furtively from hiding, craning her neck in her search for Boynton. If she remained lurking here, Leo would start asking the same questions. Besides, he wouldn't leave her mother on her own in the market. He'd want to turn her mother over to her before he left to view livestock. She glanced left and right. Boynton had gone—at least for the moment.

"Mrs. Sherbourne." The footman's voice held relief.

Jocelyn offered him a wan smile. She spied Leo and her mother in the row of fabric stalls and made her way over to them, maintaining a wary eye for Boynton.

"Leo purchased three lengths of cloth for me," her mother said, almost girlish in her enthusiasm.

"And I thought you'd need my advice on your purchases," Jocelyn teased, fighting her impulse to scan the faces in their vicinity.

Leo grinned, the curve of his lips doing strange things to her pulse rate. Despite her worry, Leo only had to turn his charm on her and her anxieties lessened. It was his Sherbourne smile. He flashed it in her direction and every sane thought fled. She squeezed her thighs together as her mind drifted to the joy she found with him in private.

"If only the other women in my life were so easily satisfied. Cassie wants a new doll and was very specific with her requirements." His good humor faded. "Hannah put her up to it."

"Why don't you purchase some extra cloth, and ask Mother if she'll stitch new clothes for Cassie's existing doll? That might keep her happy." She gave into her need and glanced around her, tension bleeding from tight muscles when she didn't glimpse Boynton's gloating, cruel visage.

"Is something wrong?" Leo asked.

"No. No, I'm fine." Now wasn't the time to discuss the matter with Leo, and besides, she was possibly worrying about nothing. After another surreptitious glance over her shoulder, she allowed Leo to direct her and her mother to another stall.

She caught Leo watching her and offered a bright smile. He didn't return the sentiment, and her breath caught, uneasiness filling her now. She didn't know him well enough to decipher what his changeable moods meant.

"I need to go," he said. "The footman will escort you to the dressmaker and then to the public house."

"Of course," Jocelyn murmured. "You must attend to your

livestock. We'll see you later."

Leo tugged on a lock of Jocelyn's hair. "Make sure you keep Gavin with you at all times."

"We will," she promised.

Once Leo left, they walked directly to Madam Marie, the dressmaker, with the footman trailing them.

"Ah," Madam Marie said. "The new Mrs. Sherbourne." She shifted her gaze. "And your mother. I can see the likeness in the eyes."

"Good day," Jocelyn said.

"How can I help you today?" the dressmaker asked.

"My mother requires new gowns, and I'd like to purchase two dresses for my stepdaughter."

"But of course." Madam Marie clapped her hands briskly, and one of her seamstresses appeared to help with the measuring. "Did you have any specific styles in mind? Is the dress for a special occasion?" As she spoke, she started to take Elizabeth's measurements, her competence telling Jocelyn that despite Hannah's assertions, Madam Marie was a capable seamstress. The measuring took no time at all.

"Is it possible to get dresses stitched for my stepdaughter's doll? I thought it would be a good idea to match the fabric with Cassie's new gowns," Jocelyn said. "Mother is going to sew several, but I thought garments from the dressmaker would make her very happy."

"Mrs. Sherbourne, but of course." Madam Marie pursed her lips. "I heard another girl has disappeared from Merrivale."

"Gossip travels fast."

"Two girls have gone missing from Tavistock," Madam Marie said. "The butcher's daughter vanished last month, and no one has seen her since."

Jocelyn stiffened and glanced at her mother. She seemed content to look at pattern books plus the additional fabrics and trim the assistant brought to show her. "Two?" Why hadn't anyone mentioned this? "Did they disappear without warning?"

The assistant unwound a length of apricot silk and held it against Elizabeth's face.

"Neither of the girls had bad reputations. They were hardworking and well-liked." Madam Marie leaned over and flicked the fabric to make it drape better, a faint frown marring her brow. She *tsked* under her breath. "No, I don't think this color will do. Try the dark gray silk."

Not the kind of women who would run off with a man, then. No, something more sinister was at work here. Surely Leo—*no!* The knowledge she had of him refused to let her suspicions gain root and grow. There had to be another reason why young women were disappearing from the towns on and around the moors. "Have there been disappearances from other villages?"

Madam Marie cocked her head, intelligence glinting in her sharp gaze. "It's possible, although, I haven't heard of others."

Jocelyn nodded, not inclined to discuss the matter further, and wandered over to look at the selection of hats and shawls. A green hat with a large brim caught her attention—the perfect thing to cover her distinctive hair. And if she added a shawl in a different color—yes, a change in her appearance might help her avoid Boynton until she spoke with Leo.

"Do you have your stepdaughter's measurements, Mrs. Sherbourne? The measurements for the doll?"

"Yes, certainly." Jocelyn rattled off the relevant information, having committed it to memory before they left home.

"And which fabrics would you like?"

"Mother, would you like to help me choose fabric for Cassie?"

"I think you should take the pale blue and the red floral," Elizabeth said decisively. Her cheeks glowed with exhilaration, an emotion that echoed in her eyes. No one looking at her, clad in her smartest yellow gown and a lacy cap, would suspect her of madness. She'd dressed carefully for her trip to Tavistock, driving Tilly to distraction with her demands, yet Jocelyn couldn't help but smile. This challenging woman was the mother of her childhood—the ambitious one who pulled off splendid matches for her merchant class daughters. A pity the family situation had changed before it was Jocelyn's turn.

After Jocelyn extracted a promise from the dressmaker to complete the gowns and deliver them to Merrivale Manor within the week, they left the shop. Gavin pushed away from the wall and took up the rear, a silent sentinel.

"I told you they'd manage to complete a gown in time for the party," her mother said, practically skipping down the street. She skirted a smelly pile of refuse in the middle of her path. "You should have ordered a new gown too."

"Yes you did say that," Jocelyn said, scanning the busy street in her peripheral vision. "I have plenty of gowns. I don't require a new one."

"Your husband might decide to never purchase a dress for you again if you tell him that," her mother said sharply, once again reminding Jocelyn of the past, and the shrewd woman who'd snared titles for Georgina and Charlotte.

"He was very generous with you and Cassie."

"Yes, I was surprised. You were lucky with your choice of husband. Most men wouldn't have married *you*."

"Mother," Jocelyn hissed, her gaze darting to check for Boynton and eavesdroppers.

While she was pleased her mother was showing signs of her old self, she could do without the criticism. She bit back the sharp words on the tip of her tongue—the fierce resentment because if it wasn't for Jocelyn embracing the life of a courtesan, they would've ended up out on the street, penniless and desperate.

"The Bull and Bear. This is our destination." Thank goodness. Hopefully her mother would focus on something else now that they'd arrived at the pub.

Leo had booked a private room, and Jocelyn gratefully followed the innkeeper who directed them to his best parlor. Although small, the room was clean and comfortable with several upright chairs and a sturdy wooden table.

Jocelyn wandered to the window and massaged her right temple, pressing carefully with her fingertips in an effort to shift the dull throb that had settled since leaving the dressmakers. A respite from the flurry of the marketplace would prove welcome, give her time to think. She let out a muffled snort, directed more at herself than anyone else—a chance to sulk because her mother wasn't appreciative of her sacrifices.

A heavy sigh followed, the burden heaped on her as she considered the choices she'd taken since meeting Leo. Foremost came the worry that she'd made a huge mistake in accepting his offer. What if she'd placed her mother directly in danger?

"What do you think of Tavistock, Mother?" Jocelyn caught a glimpse of a tall man who looked a bit like Boynton, and she drew back from the window in two jerky steps.

She was a married woman. Boynton no longer held power over her, but he could cause trouble for Leo if he decided to inform every one of her past. Jocelyn's hands trembled, and she clenched them in an effort to calm her escalating dread. There was no reason for Boynton to visit Dartmoor. His family held estates in Yorkshire. And Leo...what would he think when she told him? She and her mother had brought a stack of problems to Merrivale Manor.

Leo arrived after seeing to his business, and her mother immediately regaled him with their activities since they'd parted. Her husband listened closely, and Jocelyn felt her heart turn over. Gratitude filled her at the way Leo treated her mother—like an adult instead of an imbecile.

"And what about you?" Leo asked. "Did you also attempt to spend all my money?" His eyes glowed, and Jocelyn basked in the warmth of his regard. When his charm focused on her like this, her concerns and doubts about their marriage seemed trivial.

"I managed to spend a little," she said. "I didn't expect the market to be quite as crowded. Are the weekly markets always this large?"

"The locals use the market to sell their wares and exchange news and gossip."

"So the market is mainly for locals?"

Leo shot her a dissecting glance. "Why?"

Jocelyn checked on her mother and saw she'd moved to another window to watch the antics of a juggler down on the street. She leaned nearer to Leo and lowered her voice. "I saw Boynton in the crowd. I know he saw me."

"Boynton? The man Melburn mentioned from your past?"

"Yes."

"You're safe at Merrivale."

She groped for Leo's left hand as she recalled Boynton's frequent rages. "What if he spreads gossip about my past? Surely you don't want rumors spread throughout the parish?"

"To my knowledge, the man hasn't been near Merrivale. His presence is a coincidence, and he's merely traveling through the area."

Jocelyn doubted that very much and feared nothing good could come from her sighting. Boynton had seen her, and the man wasn't a good loser. "His estates are in Yorkshire."

Leo smoothed his fingertips across one cheek. "Sweetheart, you're worrying unnecessarily. He can't hurt you, but if it sets your mind at rest I'll make discreet inquiries."

"Thank you." She shivered when she registered his hot intent. If it wasn't for her mother's presence, she was positive he'd haul her into his arms. Warmth suffused her cheeks.

He smiled down at her. "I'm sure there's no need for concern."

Despite her qualms, Jocelyn nodded and released her desperate grip on her husband. "I'll give you a description. He's about your height but stockier in build. He usually wears a wig, and keeps his blond hair clipped short. He enjoys his food and drink, and it shows in his body."

A tap on the door announced the arrival of their meal. The innkeeper's wife and a maid entered the parlor bearing trays. The moment they lifted the covers on the food, the delicious scent of beef and oyster pie drifted through the air. Lunch was a gay affair, full of laughter and good spirits, and Jocelyn allowed the delicious food and jolly atmosphere to lull her trepidation.

JOCELYN WOKE IN AN empty bed again, despite the early hour. When she'd first arrived at Merrivale, Leo had risen early, but not before kissing her awake. Slowly, things had changed. He visited her bed and sometimes left after they'd made love. Last night he'd stayed, or at least he'd remained until she fell asleep. She stared at the ceiling, trying to quell the doubt demons popping to life.

There was a good reason for Leo's absence. Yes, he was likely in his chamber now. She found herself out of bed and halfway to her dressing room before the thought properly formed. The Oriental rug was soft beneath her bare feet, her footfalls silent as she approached the connecting door. She opened the door and peered into Leo's chamber.

He wasn't there.

His bed hadn't been slept in, the covers smooth and unruffled.

Deep in thought, she retraced her footsteps, but instead of returning to her bed, she drew back the curtains. A wash of light lit the horizon, backlighting the contrasting dark silhouettes of the trees and piles of stone. On impulse, she let the curtains fall back and dressed rapidly in one of her simpler gowns. A peaceful walk in the garden would be a lovely way to start the day.

Outside, the cool breeze tugged at her hair, and she wished she'd taken the time to confine her locks. She grasped her hair with one hand and tucked the long ends haphazardly beneath her shawl. The sky was lighter now, and the cheerful chorus from a nearby thrush was almost deafening. Her skirts brushed the dew-covered plants, absorbing the moisture and dragging under the weight.

Choosing to take a path she hadn't explored before, she strolled without purpose, merely enjoying the slice of morning quiet. She rounded a corner and came to an abrupt halt, her hand rising to cover her gaping mouth. Hurriedly, she drew back out of sight but not before the image of her husband embracing Arabella seared to her mind.

Anguish gripped her chest, making it difficult to draw breath. She stumbled in the opposite direction, only wanting to escape. Leaves and branches grabbed at her clothes and clung. She burst into a clearing she hadn't seen before and sank onto a seat in a folly overlooking the moors. She couldn't stop trembling.

The betrayal...she should have expected it. Most men had mistresses. She'd been a mistress, seen the way men behaved and heard the way they spoke about their wives with contempt and sniggers.

She wrapped her arms around herself, suddenly aware of the tears pouring down her cheeks. She wiped them away with an abrupt rub of her hand. Their marriage—despite the odd way they'd come together—she'd expected they'd deal well together because they'd started with honesty. A snort erupted. At least there had been openness on her part.

No wonder Arabella treated her so shabbily. She resented Jocelyn's presence at Merrivale. Perhaps she'd expected Leo to offer her marriage.

Gradually her tears stopped. A chill from her damp clothes sped through her, yet she was hesitant about returning to the manor. The last thing she wanted when she felt so raw was to confront Leo and Arabella. She took a deep breath, striving for composure. After smoothing her hair, she stood and retraced her footsteps.

Jocelyn nodded to the footman as she entered the Great Hall. Low feminine laughter came from the morning room, and when she heard the rumble of a masculine voice, she turned in that direction. Lifting her chin, she sailed through the doorway, scanning the dark-paneled room to ascertain the occupants.

Leo and Arabella.

"Good morning," Leo said in a warm voice as he walked toward her, his obvious intention to embrace her written on his handsome face.

She dodged behind the table and slipped into one of the vacant chairs. "Summon a maid please, Leo. I require hot chocolate."

"Of course." Leo's smile of greeting faded into a frown, and she could feel his disapproval. Too bad. She wasn't the one in the wrong here.

"Good morning, Arabella." Jocelyn couldn't keep the bite from her voice.

Arabella quirked an eyebrow, a hint of mischief twinkling in her brown eyes. "Whatever is your maid thinking? Surely she didn't send you out this morning looking like that? Your hair..."

She trailed off, her gesture toward Jocelyn leaving little to the imagination.

"I went for a walk in the garden." Jocelyn's pulse raced a little faster. "There is a heavy dew on the ground this morning, and the wind was blowing up on the hill." She swallowed and knew she couldn't pretend. "I saw you this morning, out in the garden."

CHAPTER 6

ARABELLA STARTED LAUGHING, THE sultry tones irking Leo. No wonder Jocelyn had seemed standoffish on her arrival in the breakfast room.

"Leo and I—"

"Stop." The malicious expression on his cousin's face thrust Leo into action. He wouldn't allow Arabella to taunt Jocelyn. "You've made your views clear, cousin, and I choose to ignore your advice."

"You shouldn't have married her."

"But he did," Jocelyn snapped. "Leo is my husband, and I wish you'd accept the fact instead of sniping at me."

Leo was pleased to see his wife wasn't allowing Arabella to bully her. "That's enough from both of you."

"Why were you embracing Arabella in the garden where anyone could see?" Jocelyn asked.

Honest and to the point. Leo almost smiled. The more time he spent with Jocelyn, the more he liked her, and he didn't regret his marriage in the slightest.

Arabella smirked, her brows arching. Without saying a word

she was throwing out insinuations, implying their relationship was less than proper. "Why do you think we were embracing?"

"Enough, Arabella." He went to his wife and squeezed one hand before releasing it. "Arabella is homesick for Spain and her family, and I was comforting her. She's decided to return, but she worries about Cassie."

"Of course you must go home." Jocelyn helped herself to several slices of bread and took a seat at the table. She spread a lavish spoon of raspberry jam over one of the slices. "I am sure one of the maids would be willing to look after Cassie."

Leo admired her calmness, given Arabella's provocative behavior and the scene confronting her in the garden.

"If it weren't for my sister's illness I'd remain here at Merrivale." Arabella became defensive, as if worried she was disappointing him and she needed to make excuses.

Leo knew better. He could see the steam building. It was time to step in before Arabella had one of her tantrums.

"Arabella, I've told you how much I appreciate the way you've helped with Cassie, but you must do what is best for you now. Your sister needs you," Leo said, ringing a bell to summon a maid. With the order for hot chocolate and more tea for him dispatched, his attention returned to Jocelyn. "What do you intend to do today?"

"Mother wishes to visit the village, so I thought I'd take her on an outing this morning. I believe we're to have visitors this afternoon."

Leo nodded, taking a mental note to stay away from the manor until the callers departed. "Don't forget to take a footman with you."

"Of course," Jocelyn said. "Arabella, would you like to come to the village with us?"

"Thank you, but I have to pack." Arabella smiled sweetly, yet it didn't reach her eyes. It was a smile he'd learned to dread in a woman. Perhaps it was best his cousin was leaving. The last thing he needed was her causing more trouble.

"What are you doing today?" Jocelyn nibbled on a piece of bread, averting her gaze from him when Leo glanced in her direction.

Something in her expression gave him pause. When her attention wavered to Arabella and her face clouded, his mouth compressed. Jocelyn wasn't convinced of his innocence.

"I'm helping the men muster the cattle. We're going to sell some at the next Tavistock market."

"I see," Jocelyn said. "Will you be home late?"

"Your wife doesn't trust you," Arabella said with a touch of glee.

"That's enough, Arabella." But Leo saw she was right. Jocelyn was wary of him. No, maybe not of him. She'd been distant since their trip to Tavistock. He opened his mouth to question her then came to a halt. This could wait until tonight. While Arabella was family and wouldn't gossip, he didn't want to broadcast Jocelyn's past to her. His cousin didn't require more ammunition to wound Jocelyn.

JOCELYN USHERED HER MOTHER outside, the footman following at their heels. Elizabeth came to an abrupt halt, almost causing an undignified pile of bodies.

"Mother."

"We should take the child to the village."

"There isn't room in the carriage for all of us," Jocelyn said. Not quite the truth, but Cassie's presence would require another invitation to Arabella plus a delay in their departure. "Perhaps we can go for a walk together in the gardens later this afternoon. Did I tell you I discovered a folly this morning?"

Diverted, Elizabeth clapped her hands together. "How exciting. We'll take the child with us when we explore the folly."

"Of course we can," Jocelyn said, forcing a smile. She waited until her mother and Tilly were seated before accepting help from the footmen to ascend into the carriage.

The drive to the village didn't take long. Her mother prattled about everything and anything that caught her attention. Jocelyn tuned her out, only replying absently in the conversational gaps. Instead she visualized the scene she'd witnessed this morning, trying to see the clinch in light of Leo's explanation.

The seclusion of the garden.

The intimacy of a handsome man and a beautiful woman alone.

An embrace.

Jocelyn flinched, the recollection hurling her into unease. No matter what Leo said, she'd feel better once Arabella departed Merrivale. Arabella's smug laughter echoed through her mind, bringing a rush of anxiety.

"Arabella is intending to return to Spain. Her sister is ill." Maybe if she confronted the dragon, she could slay it and emerge unscathed.

"When is she leaving?" Tilly asked.

"I'm not sure. Soon, I think. She mentioned doing some packing this morning." Jocelyn continued to stew, another thought occurring. The other morning when she'd woken to find Leo absent, had he been with Arabella? Of course that didn't explain the wound on his cheek. To her they'd looked like the claw of fingernails. She worried her bottom lip, recalling the suspicion on Captain Cartwright's face. Still, he hadn't returned to question Leo again.

She didn't want to believe the facts she kept stumbling over, but Leo held secrets close to his chest, and it was difficult not to feel concern over their nature.

The carriage swayed over the uneven ruts made by bullock carts. Jocelyn flew against the side of the carriage, an unladylike grunt emerging at the slash of pain at her ribs.

"Jocelyn," Elizabeth said. "It's not polite to make noises like that in public places."

Jocelyn steeled herself as the carriage shuddered on hitting another pothole, a throb radiating down her side.

Tilly sent her a worried glance. "Are you all right?"

"Just a bump," Jocelyn said.

"Are we there yet?" Elizabeth asked.

"Another five minutes," Jocelyn said, hoping it was true. The ache in her torso traveled to her head. Surreptitiously, she lifted one gloved hand to rub her temple.

"Whoa there!" the driver called to the horses. The carriage slowed to a creaky halt outside the draper's shop.

"Oh, look!" Elizabeth cried, off at a trot before Jocelyn or Tilly could react.

With a sigh, Jocelyn scrambled from the carriage, faltering a fraction when pain streaked through her. She watched her mother disappear into the draper's store. "It's all right, Tilly. Something in the window has caught her attention."

"Between her and Miss Cassie, I'm forever running," Tilly said.

Jocelyn drew a sharp breath. "I know she's not easy."

"I don't mean to complain. When Arabella leaves who is going to look after Cassie? She can be a bit of a handful."

"I know. I talked to Susan before we left. She suggested I stop by the baker's shop and talk to the baker's wife. Evidently her eldest daughter is good with children. Perhaps she'll be willing to help with Cassie."

Tilly nodded. "That seems like a sensible solution."

"I thought I'd go and see her now." Jocelyn shot a glance at the window of the draper's store. From where they stood, they could see Elizabeth's enthusiastic hand gestures and the lengths of scarlet ribbon a woman was showing her.

"Off you go." Tilly made a shooing motion with her hands. "I'll supervise Elizabeth's ribbon purchases."

Jocelyn continued down the dusty road to the bakery. She smiled at two young children teasing a kitten with a piece of rag and string. A plump woman swathed in shawls offered a curt nod but didn't stop to speak to her. A scuff on the dirt behind her made her jump. She twisted, let out a pained cry.

"Mrs. Sherbourne?" The footman stood there, surveying her strangely.

Heat flooded her face, and her gaze slid away. Good grief, everything was making her jumpy today. People would start to speculate on her mental condition and whisper she was taking after her mother. "Please stay with my mother and Tilly. I'm going to visit the baker and will return to the drapers. I doubt you'll shift my mother for at least an hour."

The footman nodded. "Yes, Mrs. Sherbourne."

Jocelyn stepped over a pile of horse dung, aware of the local women staring at her. She forced her smile a little wider and inclined her head, acknowledging everyone she passed before arriving at the bakery. The scent of loaves, hot from the oven, floated through the open door.

A young woman set an uncooked pie on the counter and waited patiently for service. A toddler clutched her skirts, his big blue eyes fixed on Jocelyn.

"Good morning," Jocelyn said softly and glanced up at the mother. "What a beautiful little boy."

"Thank you," the woman said.

The woman behind the counter took the pie and set it on a shelf. "'Twill be ready this evening."

The young woman nodded and left.

"Are you Mrs. Samson?" Jocelyn asked.

"Aye, Mrs. Sherbourne," the woman replied with a grim smile.

Jocelyn's own smile faltered. "Susan, my maid, suggested I speak to you. I wish to employ someone to look after Cassie. I understand your eldest daughter is very good with children."

"Aye, she is." Her eyes flashed and resentment twisted her lined face into a grimace.

Jocelyn took an automatic half-step back when the woman continued to glare. "Is something wrong?"

"I won't let my Agnes work at Merrivale Manor."

"Why?" Jocelyn asked faintly. Surely this wasn't anything to do with her mother. She was only a danger to herself, not to other people.

"It's not safe," Mrs. Samson said. "I'm not letting my Agnes anywhere near your husband."

"Leo?"

"Aye, Sherbourne. I know what's going on at Merrivale. First his wife, then a maid is dead. Other girls missing. He's selling them into slavery and murdering those what don't agree."

Jocelyn drew herself up. "The parish constable hasn't arrested him."

"It's not what you know. It's who," Mrs. Samson snapped. "My Agnes is not going anywhere near the manor and that's final."

Jocelyn gave a civil nod and kept her tongue still. How could she protest when Mrs. Samson's words dovetailed so neatly with her own doubts?

CHAPTER 7

Hannah and Peregrine's party, three days later.

"I'M SORRY ABOUT MOTHER making us late," Jocelyn said. "She's been so good recently. I didn't expect her to have one of her episodes. Normally we have more warning."

But that was changing, and it was an alarming trend. The silence inside the carriage was rubbing her nerves raw. If Leo decided to cease his support, Jocelyn didn't know what she'd do. She forced herself not to fidget but couldn't prevent the curling of her gloved fingers while she anxiously awaited her husband's reply.

Leo reached out, his hand landing unerringly on her knee. He squeezed lightly. "It's not as if I wanted to attend to this party," he said gruffly. "With any luck we'll miss the receiving line."

Some of the tension leached from her. "I'm looking forward to meeting more of our neighbors."

Leo caressed her lower thigh through her skirt, the warmth of his hand shifting her anxiety to other sensual avenues. "Some of Hannah's friends are...difficult. There will be gossip. Snide comments. I don't want you to get upset by the things you might hear."

"Don't worry. I can handle anything they throw at me." The past had taught her confidence went a long way in social occasions. It didn't matter if she was falling apart inside, she could still portray a lady, a woman calm and above the vulgarities of others.

"You might find them unwelcoming. Everyone loved Ursula, and my remarriage has caused talk." The tone of his voice suggested he was grimacing. "Gossip."

"What sort of comments?" He must have realized a second marriage so swiftly after Ursula died would initiate gossip. Her mind tugged and pulled at the reasons he'd given her. He required a mother for Cassie. Not true—not when he had Arabella in residence. "Leo?" she prompted a reply.

The pause lengthened until she wondered if he intended to answer at all.

Finally, he sighed. "Most people expected me to marry Hannah once the period of mourning ended, and they're likely to make that clear during the course of the evening. They can be petty, and I find their cruelty untenable."

"I understand what you mean. People judge my mother and laugh behind her back. She can't help her behavior."

The carriage coasted to a stop. A footman opened the door and the faint tinkle of music carried to them. Leo stepped from the carriage and turned to assist her to alight.

"I didn't realize they lived in a castle." Jocelyn stared up at the tower that loomed in the darkness. A face stared down at her, partially obscured by shadows. "There's a face—oh! It's a gargoyle. How interesting."

"Hartscombe is full of such things," Leo said. "It's not a place for children." He placed her gloved hand on the crook of his arm and turned toward a flight of steps. "This way. Watch your footing. The steps are crumbling in a few places."

Jocelyn strolled at Leo's side, glad of his warning and the smoky torches lighting the uneven steps. At the top, Leo guided her through a doorway. A maid took possession of her pelisse and Leo's hat, then Leo directed her right toward the music. They entered a large salon, brightly lit by candles and full of strangers.

"Leo!" Hannah pushed her way through the crush, her welcoming smile only for him. Her black gown with white accents was stunning in its simplicity, yet it clung to her curves and grabbed every male eye in the vicinity. "You're here at last."

"I'm sorry we're late, Hannah. We had a small problem at home." Jocelyn smiled brightly at the woman everyone had expected her husband to marry. She turned her attention back to Leo and caught him eyeing Hannah's charms. Some of her anticipation and pleasure in the evening faded.

"Jocelyn." Hannah turned her gaze on her, and Jocelyn couldn't help but notice the malicious glint as the other woman took in her green gown, the splendid emerald necklace and earrings and Jocelyn's bright red hair in its intricate twist. "Is your mother not well? I hope she isn't scaring Cassie again."

"Hannah." Leo's voice held a touch of warning.

Hannah's smile faltered before burning bright again. She approached Leo and took his arm in a familiar manner. "Leo, darling, come and meet my friends from London."

Jocelyn sucked in a swift breath, humiliated by the way Hannah was ignoring her. The slight hadn't gone unnoticed by others, and two young women clad in the latest London fashions openly tittered. Her cheeks started to burn.

Leo removed Hannah's hand from his arm. "Let me introduce Jocelyn to our neighbors first, Hannah." A rebuke shaded his words, and Hannah shot Jocelyn a scowl before flouncing away.

"Is she always like that or does she save her rude behavior for me?" Jocelyn asked in an undertone.

"She tends to worry about her needs more than others." Leo looked as if he wanted to say more but politeness forbade him. "Ignore her bad manners. It's best that you do."

Leo led Jocelyn over to a group of men and women in the far corner of the salon and started his introductions. She felt the waves of the curiosity from Leo's friends, and her stomach churned despite the confident tilt of her chin. She observed the whispers, partially hidden by flickering fans, and the way the confidences increased when they noticed the healing scratches on Leo's face.

"Jocelyn, this is Sir James Harvey from Duxton."

"Mrs. Sherbourne, charmed." Sir James took her hand and bowed over it, his lips brushing the back of her glove. Tall and slim, he wore the latest London fashions from the top of his powdered wig to the jeweled buckles on his shoes. His red suit and matching ruby jewels made him stand out from the more somberly clad locals.

"It's lovely to meet you. Is Duxton very far from Merrivale?"

"About ten miles if you have the skills to fly like a crow," Sir James said, straightening from his bow. "A bit farther if you choose to travel by carriage or horseback. You must ask Leo to bring you to Duxton to visit, my dear. We have many things from exotic places. The ladies love the sparkling treasures."

Jocelyn had met men like Sir James before—a wealthy rake. Unconscionable, they seduced every woman crossing their path and if they were virginal or unobtainable, so much bigger the challenge. When they weren't whoring, the scoundrels gambled with weaker men who should know better. She tugged her hand from his grasp and gave him a chilly smile. "Thank you for the invitation."

The music started again, and one of Leo's friends solicited her hand in a dance. Once again, people stared, but she went through the measured steps with grace and her head held high. Let them stare.

With Jocelyn safely dancing, Leo made the rounds of his friends and acquaintances, keeping a close ear to pick up any useful gossip. Unfortunately, it appeared most of the rumors circulating were about him—his marriage to Jocelyn and the murders.

"Leo," a crisp voice said from behind him.

Damn, he'd hoped the parish constable wouldn't attend tonight. Composing his features, Leo turned to face Captain Cartwright.

"Have you made any progress in the search for our maid?" He might as well raise the subject first.

"How did you get the scratches on your face?"

Leo sighed. Straight for the throat. "I told you. I fell when I got between a man and his wife during an argument."

Another new arrival caught his attention. Leo felt a vein start throbbing at his temple and the blood pounded in his ears. The bastard. Leo clenched his fists, fighting the urge to march over to Jaego Woodburn and issue a challenge.

Their gazes connected across the crowded ballroom, and Leo grit his teeth as he stared at the man who'd once been his best friend.

"Leo. Leo!" Cartwright attempted to retrieve his attention.

"What?" Leo barked.

"I'll be at Merrivale early tomorrow morning. I have more questions for you."

Leo shrugged. "I have sheep to dip."

"The questions won't take long. I thought you'd prefer privacy." The veiled threat came through clearly. Cartwright intended to get his answers one way or another. If he refused to entertain an interview, Cartwright would voice his queries in a public venue.

Aware of interested bystanders, Leo gave a curt nod. "I'll see you tomorrow. If I'm not at the manor, I'll be at the sheep yards."

"Thank you." Cartwright moved away to mingle.

Leo scanned several familiar faces and noticed some acquaintances looked away in firm snubs.

"Leo, how are you?" Hannah's mother, Viscountess Hartscombe, approached him.

Leo offered a stiff smile and relaxed when she behaved in her normal, friendly fashion. "I'm fine. How long are you home for this time?"

"Only for a few weeks while we prepare for another journey to Egypt. I hear you've remarried," she said abruptly.

"Yes. I'll introduce you to Jocelyn." Leo scanned the dance floor and couldn't see his wife. "When I find her."

Jocelyn couldn't help but be aware of the pointed stares and speculation. She scanned the crowded room, searching for Leo. On locating him, she witnessed his ease with everyone, his apparent unconcern about their opinions. She took her cue from her husband. No doubt there were rumors flying around about her mother's behavior along with the ones about their abrupt marriage.

The murders.

Hopefully, the gossip would die. All she needed to do was grit her teeth and smile. And hope that Leo wasn't involved with the murders...

There! She'd actually admitted her concerns. Leo might share her bed, but he was still an enigma—an unknown quantity.

"Would you like to dance?" A man Leo had introduced her to earlier stood in front of her.

"Thank you. That would be lovely."

One dance moved into another. Jocelyn suspected everyone wanted to gather information to add to the gossip vine, but she was politeness itself, exchanging pleasantries with each of the men who secured her hand for a dance. Finally, Jocelyn excused herself to visit the ladies' retiring room. On the way back, she dawdled and, on seeing a set of open doors, sought brief respite from the constant surveillance of strangers.

Lit by torches, the gardens were wild and untamed compared to those at Merrivale, yet they bore a certain charm. She breathed in the scent of roses, the sweet perfume relaxing her and bringing a spurt of pleasure. Her mother would love to use these petals in her potions. Perhaps she could ask Hannah—no, maybe not.

"Don't you think he has a nerve appearing in public, especially at a party at Hartscombe?" A woman's tart voice carried on the night air. "Sherbourne is a murderer."

Jocelyn came to an abrupt halt, her heart jumping in a noisy *thump-thump*.

"I daresay Hannah and Peregrine thought they had to invite him. I mean, they used to be related by marriage," a man drawled, amusement clear in his lazy tone.

"But he murdered her," the woman snapped. "If I were his new wife, I'd worry about my safety."

Jocelyn caught back a gasp, her hand fluttering at her breast.

"The officials cleared his name," the man said.

A tinkle of laughter came from the woman. "He paid them off."

"Maybe," the man mused. "He certainly had reason to rid

himself of Ursula. No man wants a wife who cuckolds him."

The voices sounded closer and, afraid of discovery, Jocelyn ducked off the path and pressed into a corner. Luckily, she blended into the shadows. A rose branch dug into her arm, the jab of thorns piercing her long gloves. Wincing, she froze and prayed the couple wouldn't linger.

"Do you think the child is his?" the woman asked.

"It's difficult to say since she takes after her mother. Only Leo would know the truth."

"What do you think of his new wife?"

Jocelyn's breath hitched when they paused mere feet away. *Please don't let them catch me eavesdropping.*

"She's plain," the man said. "But with good lines. Leo has a discerning eye."

"Discerning...she has bright red hair and is covered in freckles!"

"You have no imagination, my dear." His voice lowered to a seductive croon. "All that fire combined with a pleasing figure. I'd wager she'll breed well."

Jocelyn bit back her instinctive cry of protest. The man was talking about her as if she were a prized broodmare.

"Do you know anything about her? How did he meet her? Do you think she is with child?"

"All I know is that Leo went to London to visit his cousin and returned with a wife. Hannah is beside herself," the man said with a touch of malice. "She might cease her snobbish manner and accept one of the local men now that Leo is out of circulation."

"Perhaps," the woman said.

To Jocelyn's relief, they recommenced their ramble through the garden and, after a few minutes, she could no longer hear them. Cautiously she detached herself from the rose bush and crept from hiding. She reached the house without meeting anyone else.

In the salon, she searched for Leo and finally located him on the dance floor with Hannah. The other woman appeared happy and free of her normal spiteful air. Leo, on the other hand, didn't appear quite as pleased. His mouth was pinched as he went through the steps.

"You'll have to watch that one," an elderly woman said.

Jocelyn turned to face a tiny woman dressed in the fashions of twenty years prior.

The woman let out a rusty cackle on searching Jocelyn's expression. "Come, escort me to a chair. My legs aren't what they used to be."

Hiding her amusement, Jocelyn allowed the elderly woman to lean on her arm. She led her over to a grouping of chairs overlooking the dance floor.

"Sit, sit," the woman said, once Jocelyn had seated her. She clicked her fingers at a footman. "Bring us two glasses of punch."

Jocelyn joined the woman and arranged her green skirts so they wouldn't crease.

"Did you know Hannah fancied herself as the next mistress of Merrivale?"

"So I understand," Jocelyn said cautiously, accepting a glass of punch from the footman on his return. "Thank you."

"I knew Leo was smart, but I didn't see another marriage coming so quickly. Are you breeding?"

Jocelyn blinked and sipped her punch to give herself time to reformulate her instinctive retort about manners.

"Don't be reticent, girl. Can't stand young misses who don't have opinions of their own."

Jocelyn met the nosy woman's gaze with a direct one of her own. "No, I'm not with child."

"Was it a love match?"

"Yes," Jocelyn lied, realizing anything she said could make the rounds of the village. "Leo is a wonderful man. I'm sorry, but I don't recall your name. I've met so many people tonight."

The elderly woman reminded her of an alert bird, her bark of laughter like a warning squawk, attracting the attention of several women standing in the vicinity. "I'm Lady March, Hannah and Peregrine's godmother."

"Oh."

"Don't worry. I don't spread dubious rumors, girl. I've always liked Leo—a handsome rogue, that one." She made a humming sound. "Yes, I think you'll do well together. You have a head on your shoulders. Not flighty."

"Thank you."

The dance ended, and Leo joined them.

"Lady March, you're looking well." He bent to kiss her wrinkled cheek, and Jocelyn saw he was genuinely pleased to see the elderly woman. Some of her tension dispersed when he pulled up a chair to join them.

"Aren't you going to ask your wife to dance?" Lady March asked.

"After we've spent time chatting with you," Leo said.

Lady March clapped her hands together in girlish delight. "Do you have any good gossip? I do so like to know what is happening in the district."

"As long as it isn't about me," Leo said drily, eliciting a cackle from Lady March.

"Pooh, where is the fun in that? I wanted to ask about your wife's mother." Her lips pursed. "I've heard rumors from Hannah and Peregrine."

Leo grunted. "I can imagine."

"My mother has times where she becomes confused," Jocelyn said stiffly. "She requires rest."

"Hannah told me she shrieks like a banshee," Lady March

said.

"Hannah is rude." Leo's reply was curt.

Lady March cackled again. "Age gives me advantages, my boy. I can say what I think, and no one takes me to task." She tilted her head to the side. "Do you think your mother would welcome a visit from me?"

"Thank you for the suggestion, but my mother is going through a bad patch at present." A pang cut Jocelyn at the admission. It was for the best. The last thing they needed was for her mother to confide about Jocelyn's past.

"I think she'd enjoy a visit because you have a lot in common," Leo said. "Send word before you come to make sure she is up to receiving guests."

Lady March nodded. "I'll do that."

A footman materialized in front of Leo and handed him a message. Leo scanned the contents. "Have the carriage brought around." He turned to Jocelyn. "We'll leave immediately."

"Is something wrong?" Lady March asked.

"We have a problem to attend to at home."

Worry bubbled up in Jocelyn as Leo helped her rise from her chair. "Is it Mother?"

"I'll explain everything in the carriage."

Jocelyn swallowed her alarm. It was difficult acceding control to Leo when in the past the responsibility had fallen to her. "It was lovely to meet you, Lady March."

"I like your wife, Leo. You've chosen well."

Leo studied Jocelyn for an instant, his gaze warm. "I think so."

When Leo exerted charm in this manner, it was easy to forget her concerns.

"Surely you're not leaving?" Hannah asked, appearing behind them without warning. "Father was saying he hasn't had a chance to speak with you yet."

"I'm afraid I'm not feeling well," Jocelyn said before Leo could answer.

"Leo could send you home in the carriage," Hannah said.

"I don't think so," Leo said. "I want to make sure Jocelyn reaches home safely." He didn't give Hannah a chance to argue. "Thanks for inviting us, Hannah. We'll say goodbye to your parents on the way out."

Jocelyn caught the ripple of interest, imagined the guests' thoughts. In truth she was glad they were leaving because she had much to consider. It seemed everyone was convinced Leo was a murderer, and she couldn't help the shiver of foreboding that slipped down her spine. Someone was murdering poor, unfortunate women and spiriting away others. All the signs still pointed to her husband.

CHAPTER 8

AFTER THEY SAID THEIR goodbyes, Leo hustled her to the carriage.

Jocelyn's mind danced over the possibilities, each one worse than the next. Terror made her shake, the punch she'd drunk earlier sloshing uneasily inside her. When Leo settled beside her in the carriage, she clutched his arm. "Is it Mother?"

"She's missing," Leo said. "Woodley has organized a search party, but they thought we should know."

Fear tightened her chest, and she had to force herself to breathe. "It's unlike Mother to leave the house at night. She doesn't like the dark." Another thought occurred. "Do you think someone has kidnapped her? Like Ella?"

"I'm afraid the note didn't say much." Leo threaded his fingers through hers and placed her hand in his lap. "They'll find your mother before we reach the manor."

"I hope so." She didn't have a good feeling about this.

"You disappeared for a while," Leo said.

"Ah, yes." A frisson swept her as she recalled the woman's words. *She feared for Jocelyn's safety.* Oh dear. What should she tell Leo? Her eavesdropping didn't show her in a good light. "I went for a walk in the garden," she said finally.

"Alone?" His question fired at her like a pistol, and her anxiety ramped up another notch. Surely he didn't suspect her of meeting with another man? Her shoulders slumped. Of course he did. He was judging her by his first wife's standards. He probably didn't even realize, but this early in their marriage she'd make allowances and give him time to understand she'd never betray him—as long as he was innocent of murder.

"I needed a break from the intense scrutiny. Everyone kept staring at me." Now she was starting to babble when she needed to remain matter-of-fact. She needed to placate him. Reassure him she was nothing like his first wife.

"And?" There was a clear edge to his voice.

"I heard a couple talking out in the garden."

"You eavesdropped?" Now he sounded disbelieving, definitely disapproving.

"Um...yes." Not her finest moment. She wished she could scrub her mind clean, but now that she'd overheard accusations of murder...

"Yes, what?" His tone hovered close to snappish, and she tugged her hand free.

"Yes, I'm guilty of eavesdropping on a private conversation." Her words echoed in the silence of the carriage, crisp and tinged with anger. She took another breath, willing herself to relax. She was acting exactly like him, jumping to conclusions. The parish constable hadn't arrested Leo for murder, and trust needed to go both ways.

"You might as well tell me, Jocelyn."

She hesitated, wishing she could see his expression. "The couple intimated that you murdered your first wife."

Silence fell—an uneasy one.

"Do you think they'll have found my mother by the time

we arrive at the manor?" She repeated her earlier question, desperate to change the subject. She didn't need to give him ideas about murder.

"Do you believe them?" Leo asked finally, his voice devoid of nuance.

"I didn't mean to snoop. It happened by accident because I was too embarrassed to show myself. It wasn't well done." And she hadn't answered his question. Disquiet rippled through her as she waited for more questions. Relief when they didn't come allowed the tension to ease from her muscles.

"What else did they say?"

He'd noticed the way she'd prevaricated. It was clear from his clipped words. "They...implied you murdered your wife and paid off officials to avoid imprisonment."

"Is that all?"

Again Jocelyn wished she could see Leo's expression. "They talked about Hannah and how she thought she'd marry you once the mourning period ended."

"I see."

Jocelyn wished she could *see*. She didn't understand a thing. While she didn't know Leo well, the things she'd learned showed a good man. He was generous with her mother and a kind and lusty lover to her. While he was distant with Cassie, he didn't neglect his daughter. He might have remarried a short time after the death of his first wife, but that didn't make him a bad man. He'd wanted a mother for his daughter.

But some people were adept at covering their true characters, and that was the confusing part.

The springs creaked as he shifted his weight, and her pulse suddenly raced. As the silence grew, more questions formed in Jocelyn's mind. She kept returning to the same one. What had really happened to Ursula?

For peace of mind, she needed to learn more about her

without providing fodder for gossip or upsetting Leo. Whether the answers she found would help—

What if she discovered Leo was responsible? No, she shouldn't pursue this matter. "Do you think they'll have found Mother by now?"

"I hope so," Leo said.

She swallowed at his harshness and wanted to say something to placate him, yet her uncertainties wouldn't let her offer the support.

Finally, the carriage pulled up in front of the manor. Leo pushed the door open and leaped out before turning to aid her descent.

The manor was ablaze with light, and Jocelyn's heart sank. Obviously, they hadn't located her mother. Shouts rang out, some close and others more distant. Lights bobbed in the garden, indicating the progress of searchers.

"You're back," Tilly said in clear relief. "I'm sorry, Jocelyn. Your mother retired with a headache. I gave her a powder and looked in on her several times. She was asleep when I made a final check before I retired for the evening. The maids, Mrs. Green and I have searched the manor from top to bottom." She wrung her hands in clear agitation.

"When did you become aware she was missing?" Leo asked. "What made you check on her?"

"Mrs. Green heard a noise and thought it was a footman sneaking around with one of her maids. When she went downstairs, she discovered the front door wide open. She notified Woodley. When we discovered Elizabeth missing, we commenced a search."

"When was that?" Leo asked.

"Almost three hours ago."

"Three hours!" Jocelyn exclaimed.

Tilly shot her a look of apology. "We thought we'd find her

without difficulty. You know how she wanders off. We've always found her in short order." Tilly clutched a handful of her skirts, twisting and tugging the fabric. "No one has seen Elizabeth. It's as if someone has spirited her away." Unspoken was the fear that this was a repeat of Ella's disappearance.

"Where is Susan? Is she all right?" Jocelyn asked.

"She's in your chamber, awaiting your arrival," Tilly said.

Jocelyn nodded. "I'll get Mrs. Green to check on her."

"Jocelyn, I want you to search the house again," Leo said, after returning from speaking to several of the servants. "I'll help the men outdoors."

"But I can help—"

"Please, Jocelyn. I don't want to worry about you too. I'll send word as soon as we find her."

Jocelyn watched Leo stride away and told herself her mother had wandered off. She'd keep telling herself that because the alternative was unspeakable. Yes, if her mother had strolled out of the gardens to the moor she'd be frightened. Cold. The thought galvanized her to action. "Blankets. Warm bricks. Come, Tilly. We'll prepare for my mother's return and do another search of the house."

Leo grabbed a lamp and located Woodley. Wisely, Woodley had sent footmen in various directions and stayed near the stables to coordinate.

"Any luck?" Leo asked.

"No. We've combed the house, the stable area, and most of the gardens. One of the footmen found a scrap of white cloth snared on a branch. We're not sure if it belongs to Mrs. Townsend or not."

"Where was it found?"

"Near the walled garden."

Frighteningly close to the gate leading into the moor. "It's time to hunt farther afield."

Woodley nodded. "Which areas should I send the footmen to search? Some of the locals have arrived to help too."

Foreboding swept Leo, memories of Ursula swamping him, the sense of helplessness, the knowledge everyone suspected him. "I'll scan along the riverbank to the west. Tell the next group of men who report back to you to check the shore from the east. If we don't find her near the river we'll spread out and start to scour the moor."

Leo held his lamp high, his gaze sweeping the area as he strode through the garden to the river. "Elizabeth!"

God, he hoped they located her soon. If she'd wandered onto the moors they might never find her. As it was, they'd need to wait for first light to search the open ground. There were dangerous bogs nearby that were nigh impossible to navigate during the day. They'd likely lose men if they attempted to comb the area now.

He thought of the missing maid and rolled his shoulders to loosen the tension flooding his mind and body. Although Elizabeth's moods were unpredictable he couldn't think why she'd leave the manor in the middle of the night.

Hollers drifted on the air, voices increasingly urgent. Once the path ended, Leo examined the riverbank as best he could. Gravel and stones crunched beneath his shoes. Nothing appeared out of the ordinary. Leaving the small open area, he pushed through the undergrowth, grimacing when mud squelched into his evening shoes and seeped through his stockings. He should've taken time to change, but the idea of finding Jocelyn's mother in similar circumstances to Ursula had urged him to haste.

"Elizabeth! Elizabeth!" He paused and heard nothing but the scolding of a night bird. It burst off the branch of a nearby tree, the frantic flap of its wings giving him a start.

He checked the ground for footprints to no avail. It looked as if the sheep had escaped the care of their shepherd during the afternoon since animal prints studded the ground. His progress was slow, the limbs of a willow impeding his advance.

"Elizabeth!"

Leo scrutinized his surroundings, holding his lamp aloft to gain maximum illumination. He ducked his head to avoid an overhanging branch and tripped on something in his path. Cursing, he flailed his arms, but he went sprawling headfirst anyway. The lamp flew from his grasp, struck a tree trunk and flickered out.

"God's blood." Leo pushed to his feet. His evening clothes would never be the same.

A soft noise caught his attention. Foreign, it took him a few seconds to place the sound.

"Elizabeth?"

A pained cry. A whimper.

Cautiously, Leo moved through the dark, using his hands to feel for protruding branches while waiting for his eyes to grow used to the inky black beneath the tree.

The third time the cry sounded, he recognized it as human. "Elizabeth?" His fingers came into contact with a muddy hand and relief filled him. He didn't need to tell Jocelyn the search had failed. "Elizabeth, I'm here. You're safe now."

When she didn't reply, alarm rose within him. He felt her wrist for a pulse and found a weak one. Thank God, she was still alive.

Leo crawled from beneath the tree and let out a holler. "I've found her. Over here by the river!"

"She's found," someone shouted from over to his left. The cry was picked up, the message passed on to Woodley.

Leo returned to Elizabeth, worried when she didn't stir. He

rapidly checked her limbs for sign of injury and didn't find anything amiss until he ran his hands over her head. Wetness met his touch. Blood? Damn, he needed a light. Blankets. Her skin felt like ice against his palms.

He glanced up, relieved to see lights heading in his direction. "Over here," he shouted. Aware of the cold wind, he removed his jacket and covered her. "We're here," he said, giving the search party a direction.

"Is she all right?" Woodley asked.

"She's not responsive—nothing apart from the odd whimper. I think she's hit her head."

Woodley squatted beside him, the glow from Woodley's lamp showing blood on Elizabeth's face and hair.

"We need to get her back to the house. I'll carry her," Leo said. "You light the way."

Several other searchers arrived, the extra illumination from their lanterns making Leo's progress easier. They arrived at the house after a brisk fifteen-minute walk.

"Mother? Is she all right?" Jocelyn reached out to touch her mother's arm, anxiety shading her breathless queries.

His wife's pale face made his heart twist. He wanted to hold her, comfort her, but instead he kept walking. "She's hit her head, probably on a branch because I found her underneath a tree with low-lying branches. Where do you want her? In her room?"

"Should I summon the doctor?"

Leo frowned. "I doubt he'd get here for a couple of days. There was a mine accident in the south. He's been called to treat the injured."

"Never mind. We'll manage. Her room is fine," Jocelyn said with a hint of steel. "Tilly and I will take care of her."

In the chamber, Leo set Elizabeth on her bed and, once he was sure the women didn't require his assistance, he left to join the men who'd helped with the search. "A bottle of rum is in order, I think, Woodley."

"Yes, Mr. Sherbourne."

Leo ushered the men into the servants' dining room because he knew they'd feel more comfortable there. He busied himself with stoking the fire while Woodley passed around tots of rum.

"Thank you for your help," Leo said, lifting his glass.

"We're glad to be of service," one of the men said.

"'Tis a pity we didn't find the young maid wot went missing," another of the men said.

"Aye," someone agreed. "'Tis a bad business."

"Someone said she ran away with a lover."

"No, not Ella. She be a good girl," the first man said.

"I don't believe that of 'er," one of the men agreed. "I've known Ella and Susan since they were nippers. Good girls, both of 'em."

Leo frowned, remaining silent. This wasn't a topic he wished to become embroiled in tonight.

Woodley arrived with a platter of cheese, pickles and bread and passed this around. Conversation shifted to farming and the mining accident down south.

Leo remained near the fire, intermittently joining the conversation. His thoughts went to Jocelyn and her distress when he'd strode in with her mother. He stalked over to the table to set down his glass.

"I'm going to check on Elizabeth," he said to Woodley. "Thank you," he said to the men who'd left their beds to aid in the search.

He hurried down the passage and took the servants' staircase to the second floor at a run. He knocked, pausing until he heard Jocelyn bid him to enter. "How is she?"

"Apart from the wound on her head and a few scratches, she appears unharmed," Jocelyn said. "I'd feel happier if she regained consciousness."

"Can I do anything?" Leo asked gruffly.

"No," Jocelyn said, her gaze remaining on her mother. "I'm going to sit with her for the rest of the night."

"No, Jocelyn," Tilly objected. "You go to bed."

"Tilly, you can watch her tomorrow morning. She'll likely wake soon, and you'll have your hands full. You know what a difficult invalid she is. She'll run us both ragged."

Leo wanted to object. He hadn't handled things well during the conversation in the carriage. He'd known Jocelyn would hear gossip, but it still hurt to imagine the questions she must have after the conversation she'd overheard. In hindsight, the carriage had been a bloody stupid place to force the conversation. "I'll see you in the morning. Summon me if you need help in any way."

Jocelyn nodded, but her manner remained distant. He didn't know her well enough to tell if it was merely worry for her mother or if she felt disdain for him after their exchange.

"Good night." With a stiff bow, he withdrew. Damn, her words had struck like a rejection, even if she hadn't meant them that way. He stomped down the passage, part of him aware he was behaving like Cassie, sulking because Jocelyn's attention was on her mother. As it should be, he reminded himself.

He and Jocelyn had time. He'd have to woo her and make her understand he viewed their marriage as a good thing. Hell, he was already half in love with his new wife. How could he not admire her sunny disposition and loving manner to her mother and Cassie? The servants liked her too. Even Mrs. Green had thawed quickly under Jocelyn's deft management.

Leo entered his room and prepared for bed. He yawned and dropped onto the corner of the bed, exhaustion arriving now that the excitement had ended. Cold made him fumble in removing his filthy shoes. Maybe one of the footmen could do something with them. He struggled with the buttons of his vest and shirt, fingers clumsy. When he stood, he noticed splotches of mud clinging to the bedcovers. Guilt struck, and he grimaced at the mess he'd made.

After a quick wash with cold water, he doused the candles and crawled between the sheets. Despite his fatigue, his mind chased in circles, refusing him the rest he sought. He missed Jocelyn, the warmth of her curvy body and the tiny sighs she made in her sleep, the spill of fiery hair across his pillows.

But she didn't trust him, and there was nothing he could do about it.

Then there was Hannah. He'd known she'd expected him to offer for her once the period of mourning ended. He hadn't heard much gossip though—perhaps because the locals didn't like to air rumors to his face. He wished the treatment had extended to Jocelyn.

Eavesdropping.

His lips tightened in distaste, although he could hardly blame her for remaining concealed. Some of Hannah and Peregrine's friends bore wicked tongues.

A loud scream rippled into his musings. He jerked upright, startled for an instant. The terrified scream repeated, and his tension eased. This sound was a familiar one and good news. Elizabeth was awake and in full voice.

CHAPTER 9

.

"I SAW SOMEONE OUT in the garden," Elizabeth said.

"Who did you see?" Jocelyn raised a weary hand to her face and tucked a stray curl behind her ear. When her mother remained silent, irritation seared Jocelyn. The hour of sleep she'd managed earlier hadn't countered her fatigue, and her head pounded. "Why didn't you summon Tilly or one of the maids? Why did you go outside in the middle of the night? Everyone was worried about you."

"There is no need for you to take that tone with me, Jocelyn Anne."

Jocelyn barely caught back a snort. Her mother's mind hadn't suffered from the knock to her noggin. Her mouth twisted at the irony because if anything, the jolt appeared to have improved her memory. She seemed her old self, avoiding answering Jocelyn's questions while treating her daughter like an unruly child.

"Mother, why did you go outside?"

"The ghost summoned me. How could I not go? It was an order."

"An order?" Jocelyn spluttered. Of all the ridiculous things. *A ghost*. She shook her head and mutely stared at her mother.

"Well, if you want the truth, I thought it was your father."

"Father." Jocelyn was starting to feel like the parrot one of their neighbors had owned when she was a child, repeating everything said. She counted to three under her breath. Her father had been an idiot, gambling away his estate and his daughter. She shoved away the memories and continued. "You couldn't have waited until the morning to commune with him?"

"The ghost was most urgent with his summons. I couldn't miss the opportunity to speak with him."

"But Leo said the moors are dangerous, especially at night. Remember what Leo told us? You could have fallen into a bog and disappeared. As it was you hit your head. You could have died if Leo hadn't found you."

"Your husband scared off the ghost."

"I don't think so," Jocelyn snapped. "Ghosts are fictitious beings."

Elizabeth took on a mulish expression. "The maids say the ghosts of lost travelers wander the moors during the night. Apart from your father, I didn't see any."

Jocelyn could feel a lecture coming on and spoke rapidly to forestall it. "If Leo hadn't found you in time you'd be joining the ghostly wanderers. Promise me you won't leave the house at night again. It's dangerous, not only for you, but for all the servants and the kindly locals who left their beds to search for you."

Her mother's forehead scrunched into lines. "But what if your father summons me again?"

"He's certainly not here at Merrivale. Father is dead." Saint Bridget, give her strength. "If anyone summons you again in the middle of the night, come and get me or Leo. We'll invite them

142

in for a drink, and you can have a chat in cozy warmth."

Elizabeth frowned. "I didn't like to wake you."

Yet her mother didn't seem to worry about disturbing them with her shrieks at random times during the night and day. Jocelyn sent a silent prayer skyward since Saint Bridget wasn't granting her appropriate strength. "Promise me, Mother. Please. I don't want to see you hurt or worse."

"You're a good girl," her mother said, reaching out to pat her hand. "I'll let you know the instant the ghost appears to me again. Maybe you could talk to your father to learn where he stashed his money. I'm sure that's what he wishes to discuss."

"Thank you, Mother." Jocelyn exchanged a glance with Tilly, who had returned from a short break.

Anything Jocelyn said to her father would *not* be polite. His selfishness during his life had caused lasting repercussions. Yes, all the money he'd possessed was long gone, spent on wine, gambling and loose women. It was a pity he had hadn't taken after his father—her grandfather.

Jocelyn stood abruptly. "Would you like me to retrieve your needlework basket? I believe I saw it in the Blue parlor."

"I have a headache," her mother said. "I believe I'd like to rest."

"As you wish. I'll check in on you later." Jocelyn smiled at Tilly and left the room. Downstairs, she consulted with Mrs. Green. They'd decided to refresh several of the rooms and remove the accumulated clutter. While Jocelyn could have left the task to the household staff, she liked to keep busy and involved with the running of the house.

"We can start on the room at the far end of the passage," Jocelyn suggested.

"That's the Chinese room," Mrs. Green said. "Mr. Sherbourne used the room when the first Mrs. Sherbourne was alive. For privacy, he said." Mrs. Green paused, a faint trace of red appearing in her cheeks. "I beg your pardon. I didn't mean to gossip."

Aware of a chance to learn more about Ursula Sherbourne, Jocelyn waved her hand to dismiss Mrs. Green's concerns. "You're not gossiping, Mrs. Green. There is a difference between knowledge and the passing of hearsay."

Mrs. Green thawed enough to give her a stiff smile.

Jocelyn sought the right questions to retrieve information without upsetting the woman—any details to help her discern the truth of the relationship between Leo and Ursula. "For what purpose did he use the room?"

"I believe Mr. Sherbourne read and did his correspondence there. He uses the study near the salon now. The maids dust once a week, but no one has used the Chinese room for months."

Jocelyn pressed her right hand to her temple, gingerly rubbing in an effort to dispel the dull ache. That was strange. Why would Leo bypass his perfectly good study to use another room at the far end of the manor? Yet another puzzle to add to her list.

"If you have a headache, we could do this another day," Mrs. Green said.

Her shrewd observance confirmed Jocelyn's summation of the woman. Mrs. Green didn't miss much in her domain. Jocelyn checked the pins holding her cap in place and fiddled with them until she was satisfied it would remain on her head. "Today is fine, Mrs. Green. I require a task to occupy my mind."

Mrs. Green gave a brisk nod. "I'll summon two footmen to shift the furniture and a maid to help with the dusting and cleaning."

"Thank you." Jocelyn made her way to the Chinese room. She drew back the heavy curtains to flood the room with light. While no dust covered the surfaces, it was obvious the room hadn't been used for some time. For one, no one would manage to move with the amount of clutter filling the space. Stacks of books sat on top of the two side tables near the window. There were more books sitting on the upright chair near an open fireplace and several piles on the floor.

Jocelyn started to collect the books into one area, ready to return to the library. She dislodged an embroidered cushion when she leaned over to pick up a leather-bound book from the back of a chair. A scrap of parchment caught her attention. Tucked down the back, it must have escaped notice. Curious, she tugged it free and discovered it was part of a letter. Most of the salutation was missing.

ula,

I will wait for you in the copse by the river at midnight. I can't wait to hold you in my arms. Until then, my darling.

J.W.

Ursula perhaps? This note was proof of an affair, but how had it come to be tucked down the back of the chair? Leo had used this room. Her breath caught, thoughts whirring through her head faster than the turn of a mill wheel. Had Leo intercepted this note? She knew his first wife had been unfaithful, knew of Leo's displeasure regarding the fact. But many husbands and wives had discreet affairs once an heir plus a spare had been produced. She studied the contents of the note again. If Leo had felt cuckolded would this propel him to take action?

Would it drive him to murder?

A crinkling sound made her realize she was crushing the note. She smoothed the paper out and stared at the words.

Had Leo murdered Ursula and attempted to pass it off as an accident?

Approaching footsteps galvanized her to action, and she tucked the note inside her bodice.

Mrs. Green appeared in the doorway with two footmen in tow. "Too much furniture," she said in her decisive tone.

"I agree. Some of the chairs and at least one of the tables could go," Jocelyn said. "I rather like the Chinese furniture. Perhaps we could leave that and stay with a Chinese theme to match the paintings on the wall?" She gestured at the stylized bird and bamboo paintings.

"Perfect," Mrs. Green said.

"Do we have a basket or a box we could use to pack up these books? They should all be returned to the library."

"Yes, I have just the thing. I'll retrieve it after I've given the footmen directions."

Jocelyn continued to gather the books to a central point, and Mrs. Green gave orders to the two footmen. While the housekeeper remained a little frosty, they worked well together, their tastes much in line. It made for a harmonious working relationship and hopefully reduced Mrs. Green's anxiety about having her position usurped.

During her task, she kept her eye out for more notes, but didn't find anything else to help her come to an understanding about Ursula. The rest of the morning passed and, by the time they'd completed the task, Jocelyn was ready for a rest. One—no—two things plagued her the entire time. Who was J.W. and had Leo taken action to make sure his wife never strayed again?

In her chamber, she removed her cap and tidied her hair, smoothing frizzy red strands until she appeared respectable. It was time to check on her mother. When she turned into the corridor leading to her mother's suite, the screams started.

Jocelyn sighed and hastened her steps. She burst through the doorway, took one look at her mother and relaxed a fraction when nothing major appeared amiss. Completely random things set her off, and Jocelyn had given up trying to discern the reasons behind her mother's erratic behavior.

Jocelyn placed her hands on her hips, taking time to catch her breath. "Is there a problem?"

"Elizabeth wishes to walk in the gardens. I think she should wait until the morrow." Tilly glowered at her charge.

Jocelyn studied the stubborn jut of her mother's jaw. The heightened color in her cheeks indicated more to come. Another raucous screech started Jocelyn's ears ringing, almost before she'd completed her thought. "Mother, really! What sort of example is this for Cassie? Do you want her to learn bad habits from you?"

"But I want to go for a walk."

Jocelyn strolled over to the window and peered down at the garden. "That's impossible right now." She turned back to her mother. "Come and look out the window at the mist rolling in. You won't see your hand in front of your face shortly. I hear it's easy to become disorientated."

Elizabeth stamped her foot and drew a sharp breath.

"Do not scream. Please, Mother. I have a pounding head."

Elizabeth's breath whooshed out. "I am feeling a trifle tired. Perhaps I will stitch more clothes for Cassie's doll," her mother said in one of her lightning-quick mood changes.

"That's a good idea. Perhaps Cassie can spend time with us this afternoon." Crisis averted. Jocelyn beckoned for Tilly to join her outside. "Why don't you have a rest? I'll supervise Mother."

Tilly smothered a yawn, the dark circles beneath her eyes telling of her fatigue. "The bang on the head hasn't slowed her down. I have a horrid feeling this is just the start."

"Please don't say that." Jocelyn tried to tamp down her concern because she understood exactly what Tilly meant. The periods of rationality were less frequent, and Jocelyn couldn't help but worry about the future.

STRATEGICALLY PLACED LANTERNS LIT the way, a twinkling path through the darkness of the abbey. Leo watched from the hillside, taking in as much as possible in the gloomy ruins. Finally, he slipped his mask into place and half slid, half walked down the hillside to join the line of drunken men and women traipsing deeper into the abbey. He merged with the laughing stragglers, so drunk they teetered and swayed.

Like him, each of the men and women wore a mask to conceal their identities, their long capes obscuring their clothing and personal items that might hint at their names.

Leo drifted with the group and ended up in a part of the abbey that was still intact with walls and a ceiling. Separate cells divided the spacious room, formerly used by monks before the dissolution of the monasteries. Lanterns lit some of the cells. A low chanting drifted from the far right corner while moans of passion came from in front of him.

He stepped nearer, the flash of a pasty bum almost blinding him with its whiteness. The rhythmic grunts and thrusts brought an answering feminine cry.

In the next cell, a masked woman knelt before two men, tonguing and sucking on their cocks while the men carried on a low conversation. The woman, obviously tired of being ignored, lifted her head. The men paused and one of them placed his hand on the woman's head, guiding her mouth back to his rod.

Leo wandered on, nodding at the masked people he passed but not stopping to speak to anyone. He entered another room, this one larger and crowded with masked people. Sconces held flickering torches and a strangely sweet scent carried on the air. Palpable excitement filled the abbey, fueled by sexual tension and the copious amounts of wine served by women wearing transparent gowns. Their masks were more substantial than their clothing.

One of them sauntered up to him. "Like a drink, love?"

Leo gave a curt nod and accepted one of the glasses from her silver tray. She pranced away with a twitch of her scantily clad arse.

"Want some company?" A woman hooked her arm through his, tugging him to a stop. "You're a fine figure of a man. I could show you a good time."

"I'm searching for someone special," Leo said.

She cuddled her breast against his arm. "I could change your mind."

Leo didn't recognize her voice. "Not tonight. I have particular needs in mind." He removed her arm from his and stepped away. His scan of the room showed several people wearing maroon cloaks and masks. Edging closer, he propped himself against a cold stone wall, taking intermittent sips from his glass.

A shrill whistle cut the din and the excited chattering faded. The men and women standing around Leo turned to face a man standing on a dais. A maroon cloak disguised his form. Eagerness pulsated through the abbey, most mouths curved in leering grins. The women to Leo's right appeared plain bored. Leo turned his attention back to the man, noting a large square item beside the man's makeshift platform. A thick maroon cover hid concealed the contents.

"Fellow monks," the man hollered. "We have a very special event for you tonight." He paused, the final notes of his husky voice still echoing through the central room. Leo couldn't place him. The pause lengthened as the man skillfully played his audience, stoking expectation. No one shuffled or quaffed their drinks. No one spoke to break the silence. Instead they focused on the man, the pending announcement.

"Let me present, Marguerite!"

On uttering the words, he gestured at two monks on his right. They whisked the maroon cover off to reveal a gilt cage. Inside a woman perched on a tall chair. Practically naked, she wore a transparent chemise, her rouged nipples showing clearly through the thin fabric. Her dark hair rippled down her back, a contrast to her creamy skin.

Along with everyone else, Leo stared at Marguerite, mesmerized by the image presented. She looked vaguely familiar. Who—? The answer sprang into his mind.

This was Ella.

He studied her afresh and wondered why she was sitting so calmly, then recalled the unidentified sweet scent. They'd drugged her into submission.

"This morsel of feminine loveliness is available to the highest bidder. I'm sure you've noticed her beauty."

"Is she a virgin?" someone asked.

"Of course. Why would you suggest anything else?" His toothy smile encompassed the audience. "Her virgin status brings added value."

A low buzz of chatter filled the room before the man lifted his hand. "Let the bidding begin."

Leo tensed, as the bidding raced to a rapid start. He lifted his hand to indicate a bid of his own.

CHAPTER 10

LEO LOST THE BIDDING to another man. The victorious bidder swished his maroon cloak aside and pushed his way to the dais to receive his prize. The man conducting the bidding produced a key from his pocket and, with great ceremony, unlocked the cage.

He reached inside and took Ella's hand. She stumbled as she exited, only her contact with the man helping her to maintain her footing. The man handed her off to the winning bidder, sending her on her way with a familiar pat on the arse.

Leo plunged through the crowd, shoving his way past the masked men and women. Instead of stopping at one of the cells, the man towed Ella from the ruins and lifted her into a waiting carriage.

"Damn." He'd tethered his horse over the hill out of sight. Leo raced to catch up. For a while he managed to keep up with the carriage but once the road leveled, the horses increased their speed from a trot to a canter.

In desperation, Leo cut across the moor. He plunged through a copse of trees and ran around piles of stones. The contour of the land changed radically, but the steep slope barely gave him pause. He raced down, desperate to cut off the carriage before he lost sight of it. Mud splattered his evening clothes. His cloak flared out behind him, his pistol thumping against his hip in painful digs.

Gasping for breath, he screeched to a halt with the carriage almost on him. Glad of the mask, he pulled out his pistol and stood square in the middle of the road.

Now that Leo was closer he recognized the matching chestnut horses—Sir James Harvey. Leo knew him as a man who treasured his reputation. That might work to Leo's advantage.

The driver glimpsed him, noted his raised pistol and visibly hesitated. The team shied and slowed.

"Stand and deliver."

The driver hauled on the reins, slowing his team further.

Keeping a wary eye on him, Leo opened the carriage door and brandished his weapon. "Out."

"We have nothing to steal." The masculine voice contained a thread of fear. Not such a rake now.

"Get out of the carriage." Sir James obeyed, albeit unwillingly. "I'll take your money pouch," Leo said, taking care to lower the timbre of his voice. "Who is inside the carriage with you?"

"No one important."

"Out." Leo gestured with his pistol. When Ella didn't stir, Leo pointed his weapon at the baronet. Stealing the carriage wouldn't work. Everyone would know it was Harvey's carriage. He'd have to get Ella away on foot. "Both of you—out of the carriage."

The man cursed under his breath. "You won't get away with this."

"Do it. Now." Leo tensed, watchful and ready for Sir James to make his move.

Sir James took a step toward the carriage and spun around, springing at Leo without warning. Leo blocked a punch and backhanded the man. Shorter and slimmer than Leo, he was no physical match. Leo's second punch knocked him cold. The man fell to the side of the road and didn't stir when Leo kicked him with the toe of his boot. He wrenched the maroon cloak off the man and rapidly amended his plan. He reached inside the carriage and covered Ella with Harvey's cloak. She didn't react.

Scowling, Leo closed the carriage door and climbed up beside the driver. "Drive us down the road."

The driver clicked his tongue, urging his horses into motion. In tense silence, the horses trotted down the narrow lane. They slowed at a hill and at the top Leo ordered the driver to halt.

"Wait while I get the passenger. Once we're gone you can return to collect your master."

The driver gave a curt nod, and some of the tension released from Leo's shoulders. He swung down and wrenched open the door. Ella lay sprawled along the seat, the drug or whatever they'd given her still in her system.

"Easy there, I'm not going to hurt you." Leo moved cautiously, not wanting to traumatize her any more than she was already. To his relief, she scarcely blinked as he scooped her into his arms and backed from the carriage.

With rapid steps he carried her into the cover of trees, out of sight of the driver. He paused and set her on her feet, while waiting for the man to drive off. After several long moments, he heard the driver's guttural click to the horses and the creak of the carriage. Still not safe, but at least he'd managed to grab Ella.

She lay passive in his arms, her face a deathly white. Each of her breaths came in a shallow pant. Leo hastened his steps. The walk to Merrivale was a long one, and treacherous, since he'd need to keep to the back paths and cut across the moor. They'd traveled a fair way from the abbey already. Better to collect his horse in the morning.

"Can you walk?"

Ella stared at him, not appearing to comprehend. She hadn't recognized him, and he was thankful for the mask screening most of his face.

Leo grasped her arm and took two steps. She staggered and would have fallen if he hadn't caught her. He cursed under his breath and swept her into his arms. With a purposeful stride, he followed the narrow sheep track through the trees and deeper onto the moor.

Dartmoor was a silent place in the small hours of the morning—inhospitable and unforgiving to the naïve.

"At least there's a little moonlight," he said.

Ella didn't reply, but she was awake, her eyes wide and staring. Leo frowned and cautiously moved down a sheep track. He set one boot down after another, testing his footing before distributing his full weight.

Time passed and clouds skittered across the moon, plunging the moors into darkness. Leo spat out an oath, took two steps and stumbled. He staggered, thankfully regaining his balance. Part of him wanted to take shelter and wait out the rest of the night. It wasn't safe. Sir James would have raised the alarm now. He mightn't feel he could make a report to the parish constable, but he could seek help from his fellow monks.

Doggedly, Leo trudged along the track, aided only by his night vision. As they crested a hill, the wind struck them, biting cold despite the summer month. The trail ended abruptly, and he hesitated, unfamiliar with the terrain in this area. He took two steps and sank to his knees in bog. Ella's extra weight threw him off, sending him lurching forward. She screamed when he sprawled on top of her. She struggled weakly, wriggling beneath him, sobs of terror filling his ears. Each frantic move sucked her deeper into the bog.

Water and mud soaked into their clothes, splashed their faces. And the entire time Ella thrashed. Leo attempted to soothe her, but like a terrified horse she fought wildly, placing them both in danger.

No time for him to panic. He battled mud, backing cautiously away from Ella. His pulse raced, urgency thrumming through him. Damn. He didn't intend to die in the night, sucked under by a Dartmoor bog. He kept edging away, an inch at a time.

It took him a moment to realize he'd hit firm ground. Thank God. Trembling, he turned his attention to retrieving Ella.

He groped in the mud for her hand, gave up and grabbed one of her legs despite the impropriety.

"Help." Her cry was weak, ineffectual.

"Cease your wriggling." He'd had his fill of screeching females. After making sure he had solid purchase, he put some muscle into his yank. She freed her leg and kicked him square in the chest. He grunted and maintained his grip.

"Damn, woman. Stop fighting. I'm trying to help you." He heaved again, and she came free, sending him tumbling onto his arse.

They landed in an ungainly heap, Leo cursing again when her foot made contact with his balls. He grasped her arms and pushed her forcibly away before the ungrateful woman made a eunuch of him.

Her screech cut off abruptly, and she curled up like a hedgehog under attack. Understandable after what she'd suffered.

The moon peeked from behind a cloud, allowing him to see more of their surroundings. The nearby pile of rocks would offer shelter from the wind until daylight broke.

Gripping Ella's arm, he dragged her toward the tor, relief

SHELLEY MUNRO

striking him once they reached protection.

"Let me go." Ella wrenched her arm from his touch, eyes fearful and still showing no recognition of him. "Please let me go."

Leo gave her the illusion of freedom but watched her closely in case she decided to bolt. Her slight body tensed, and she tried to stand. Her legs failed, toppling her back to the ground. He winced at the loud clunk and her groan of pain. But at least she ceased her fidgeting.

Exhausted, Leo scanned their surroundings, searching the gloom for danger.

The hours passed, and gradually faint rays of sunshine lightened the horizon. In the growing daylight, he studied Ella. Pale and thin, her eyes were closed and purple shadows highlighted her exhaustion. A trail of dried blood decorated her right temple and ear.

Now able to discern the borders of the bog, he nudged Ella awake. Her eyes opened, and she climbed sluggishly to her feet, teetering the whole time. Her gaze remained unfocused, confused. What the hell had they done to her?

Taking her arm, he skirted the marsh, relieved when they reached safe ground. This time she didn't struggle, merely let him lead her. Leo picked his way through the landscape, using both vision and gut instinct to guide them to safety.

A holler drifted to him. Leo froze and scanned their surroundings, finally making out two figures in the distance. Damn, this was going to complicate matters. The shout sounded again, and he ripped off his mask, shoving it into the waistband of his breeches.

Leo started walking again, half dragging the girl when she stumbled. She fell, and he wrenched her arm, trying to help her regain her footing.

She whimpered, her eyes wide in an ashen face. "Don't hurt

156

me. Please let me go!"

Leo released her arm, and she dropped to the ground. The air whooshed out of her, and when he offered a hand to help her up, she cringed and let out another whimper.

"Oy, you there! Leave her alone."

Leo recognized the voice and backed away.

"Turn around. Put your hands above your head where I can see them."

Leo complied, angling his body to face Captain Cartwright, the parish constable.

"What are you doing with this girl?" Cartwright asked, his face devoid of expression.

"It's not the baker's daughter," the village blacksmith said, his eyes narrowing, large body poised to attack. "But seems the rumors are true." He lunged at Leo, ham fists swinging.

Pain struck Leo's shoulder, the force of the blacksmith's blow sending him off balance. He tripped on a stone and staggered. The blacksmith darted forward to repeat the punch, but Cartwright gripped his arm and wrenched him to a stop.

"Wait," he said harshly.

"He's a murderer."

"Wait," Cartwright repeated.

Leo fingered his jaw while meeting Cartwright's gaze. "This is Ella, the maid missing from Merrivale." He climbed gingerly to his feet, keeping a wary eye on the blacksmith.

"Murderer," the blacksmith snarled, and he turned his back on Leo and Cartwright to help Ella. She flinched when Leo moved, shaking her head back and forth, distressed moans issuing from her. Her cries made the hair at the back of Leo's neck prickle.

"She's terrified of you," the blacksmith said.

"I didn't spirit her away." Leo stretched out a pleading hand to Ella. "Tell them."

But instead of clearing his name, Ella started screaming, and she didn't stop for a long, long time.

"Tell me again," Captain Cartwright said.

They'd arrived back at Merrivale and given the care of Ella over to Jocelyn and Susan before adjourning to Leo's study. Now Leo paced from one side of his study to the other, his fists clenched at his sides. When he spun about to face Cartwright, he noticed the watchful air of the constable and forced himself to relax. "Would you like a drink?"

"No, thank you. Tell me about finding Ella."

"You think I murdered those two women."

Cartwright's bushy brows rose. "Did you?"

"No! I did not." Leo sank onto a chair, trying to maintain a calm air. Everyone thought the worst of him. Even his wife refused to meet his gaze. He took a deep breath and recounted his experience for the second time.

Cartwright nodded slowly when Leo finished. "I'd prefer you to keep this close to your chest until I have time to investigate."

"So you believe me?"

"I didn't say that." Cartwright's bushy mustache twitched, and Leo straightened abruptly, aiming a glower at the man. "I've seen the worst of men in my duties as constable. I like to gather the facts before I pass a judgment, especially one that would sentence a man to the gallows."

"I did not murder Ursula or the woman I discovered in the maze. You know I didn't murder Ursula."

"But you had the opportunity, which is why I'm going to take you into custody."

Leo leaped to his feet, no longer able to contain himself.

"Everyone will think I'm guilty."

"Exactly," Cartwright said. "We're going to flush out the guilty party."

Leo gaped at Cartwright. "We?"

"I've known you for a long time, Sherbourne. I'd understand if you'd murdered your wife because she was a bitch." He made the sign of a cross. "But you have a creditable alibi for the time after you argued. You didn't, as far as I can fathom, have any reason to kill the first maid. And I doubt you'd be stupid enough to wander the moors in the middle of the night with Ella if you had nefarious intentions. You're an intelligent man. If you were the guilty party you'd have a plan for every contingency. And that's why you're going to help me catch the murderer and put a stop to the orgies going on in the abbey."

"How is Anna?"

"My stepsister has caught the eye of Lord Lawtin." Clear relief sounded in Cartwright's voice. "I'm hopeful of an offer. Let another man have the reins," he said gruffly.

"What a pity," Leo said, unable to resist a sly dig at the parish constable. "We had a rather delightful time—"

"That's enough." Cartwright slashed his hand through the air. "Don't think I'm happy my stepsister is your alibi for the night of Ursula's murder. Push me hard enough, and I might conveniently forget the truth."

Leo sighed, his shoulders slumping. "Fine. What do you want me to do?"

LATE EVENING, FOUR DAYS later, jail cell, Captain Cartwright's house.

Leo picked up his glass of whisky and gulped some down.

What a bloody week. Everyone thought he was a murderer and Jocelyn...

He set his glass down and rubbed his chest, but the empty ache remained. Jocelyn had looked at him with her big blue eyes, a combination of disappointment and dread shining in them, then she'd turned her back and walked away. The slight had cut, made him shrivel inside. It bloody hurt—the knowledge she thought him capable of killing for pleasure.

Arabella believed him innocent. She'd visited him, ready to protest and do whatever it took to get him released, even put off her return to Spain. He'd had to tell her the truth, swearing her to secrecy, before she'd consent to leave Merrivale as planned. His cousin was an attractive woman, and he'd hate to have her in harm's way. No, it was best for her to leave for Spain. It was distressing enough worrying about Jocelyn and the rest of the female servants.

A key turned in the lock and Cartwright entered the cell adjoining his house where Leo was kept incarcerated for appearance's sake. "Are you ready to leave?"

"We'll probably find nothing." Each night since his arrest, they'd kept watch on the abbey. So far they'd discovered nothing suspicious. Meantime, the locals were baying for his blood, and Cartwright had hired more men to keep watch in case the villagers decided to take things into their own hands. "Did my wife send a message?"

Cartwright's hesitation was all the reply Leo required. Jocelyn believed the stories and his imprisonment served as confirmation of his guilt. The only person, aside from Arabella, who seemed to believe in him was Hannah. She visited him each day, filling him in on the gossip and public opinion.

Leo swallowed the last of his whisky. "Where are we going tonight?"

"I thought we'd stake out Sir Harvey's property. I want to see if he has visitors."

Interest stirred in Leo. "You think he might entertain them at the abbey?"

"It occurred to me."

"He wasn't the man in charge on the night. It was someone else. I didn't recognize his voice."

"He could have disguised his voice."

Leo shrugged. "What about other locals?"

"Peregrine Richards?"

"I don't know. There were women present. Some were prostitutes, and they didn't wear masks, but there were other women who wore masks to obscure their identities. That says to me they have a reason to hide their faces."

"Were you invited to join in with the...festivities?"

"Yes," Leo said instantly. "I declined. The only reason I became suspicious was because I came across a large number of footprints, hoof marks and carriage tracks while I was helping the shepherds muster sheep. It roused my curiosity, and I decided to investigate. I came across sheep entrails." Leo frowned. "Is it possible they're doing some sort of ritual? Could that explain the missing women? Some are sold and others are used in the ritual?"

"A sacrifice?" Cartwright rubbed his chin. "We both saw the blood on the ground. The woman dumped in your maze bore stab wounds to the chest area. It's possible, I suppose."

"Unless someone is rustling, butchering the sheep to sell at the local markets. I don't know," Leo said. "We've discussed the topic to death."

"We're close. My gut tells me this."

"I'd feel better if the locals weren't baying for my blood." And if he could see Jocelyn, to explain. Cartwright didn't want him to confide in anyone, and while part of him understood, he wished he could speak with his wife.

"Put this on," Cartwright said, tossing a black cloak and mask at him. "We'll go prepared again."

Leo donned the cloak and stuffed the mask in the top of his breeches, ready to grab in case of need. "Are we walking again?"

"We'll take the horses part way and leave them on the boundary of Harvey's property. Walk the rest of the way."

Leo nodded and followed the parish constable from the cell.

"Wait in the study while I distract the watchmen."

Leo did as he was bidden, all the while praying they'd find proof to clear his name. He wanted to sleep in his own bed with his wife curled in his arms.

Glimmers of sunshine crept through a sliver between the curtains, waking Jocelyn from a light slumber. She kicked off the remaining covers and sat, rubbing the sleep from her eyes.

A brief tap on the door announced her maid's arrival. At Jocelyn's invitation, Susan entered. She set down her tray and poured a dish of tea. "Miss Hannah and Master Peregrine sent word they intend to call this morning."

Jocelyn grimaced. Their departure always left Cassie unsettled and rebellious. Since the parish constable arrested Leo for murder, Merrivale Manor had received many callers. Everyone wanted to poke and pry before they dashed off to whisper about the wife of the murderer. "The vicar and his wife intend to visit this morning too."

"I had best get you dressed then, Mrs. Sherbourne. Which gown would you like to wear?"

"The pale blue with stripes, I think. How is Ella?"

Tears filled Susan's eyes. "She lies in bed all day and refuses to talk. She won't even speak to me, and we were always close."

Jocelyn reached for Susan's hands and gave them a gentle squeeze. "I'm so sorry. I..." What could she say when her husband was the responsible party? It galled that she'd misread his character so badly. "Please let me know if I can do anything to help. Anything at all." Somehow she managed the words, when her throat ached and her chest felt so tight she wondered if she might snap under the strain. She hadn't contacted Melburn yet, putting off the task of writing the missive. Soon Leo would appear before a Justice of the Peace and then—

She abruptly cut off the thought. "Yes, the blue gown today please, Susan."

Half an hour later Jocelyn left her chamber. She checked with Tilly and found her mother stitching another gown for Cassie's doll. Her mother seemed happy, showing no evidence of her earlier screaming fit. "Did you have a good night, Mother?"

"I only heard the ghost once," she said. "He tapped on my window."

"Oh?" Jocelyn glanced at Tilly and received a shrug.

"I told him to go away, and he did."

"That's good," Jocelyn said. "You should tell him the same thing next time too." Inwardly, she sighed. Her mother's room was on the second floor. It would take an acrobat to knock on her window.

"Yes, it worked well. I'll definitely do that if I see the ghost again." Elizabeth held up a tiny green dress. "What do you think?"

"It's beautiful. I wish I had your talent with a needle and thread," Jocelyn said.

A maid tapped on the door. "The vicar is here."

"I'll be there shortly. Please let Mrs. Green know we'll need refreshments."

The maid bustled away to undertake the chore.

"They'll be coming to ask you about the Harvest festival," Tilly said.

"What festival?"

"The Sherbournes have always hosted a summer festival. I understand they stopped after Mr. Sherbourne married his first wife."

"Go on," Jocelyn prompted, glad of a distraction. "Mrs. Allenby hasn't mentioned the topic. Tell me everything you know."

Tilly hesitated, looking unhappy. "According to gossip, the festival went ahead the first year Mr. Sherbourne married. Mrs. Sherbourne created a scene—the first Mrs. Sherbourne, that is. Some of her friends came down from London. They were rude and one of them tried to force their attentions on a local girl. That's all I know."

"I suppose I'd better go and find out what they want," Jocelyn said. "A gathering might be fun. Mother, I'll see you later. If the weather stays fine, we can go for a walk in the garden this afternoon."

Elizabeth clapped her hands. "Oh, yes. I'd like that."

Jocelyn pasted a welcoming smile on her face and sailed into the parlor where Vicar and Mrs. Allenby were waiting for her. "How are you? I'm so pleased you dropped by to visit. Do have a seat. Will you take refreshments?"

"That would be most pleasant," Mrs. Allenby said. "Thank you."

"We were lucky with the weather," the vicar said. "I thought the mist might settle and keep us confined indoors for the day."

Mrs. Allenby nodded, the trim on her blue hat bobbing erratically with every jolt of her head. "We have been lucky recently. During the winter, the fog comes down and doesn't lift for days."

"Something for me to look forward to," Jocelyn said, taking a seat. They passed pleasantries and danced around the subject of Leo until Jocelyn's mouth ached with smiling. The maid's arrival with a tray of refreshments provided a respite, and Jocelyn busied herself pouring glasses of the cook's sweet lemon drink. She passed a glass to Mrs. Allenby, glancing up as she did so. A face wavered in the window.

One from her nightmares.

She gasped, fumbling the glass. It slipped from her grasp, and the contents splattered the Oriental rug.

Mrs. Allenby lurched to her feet as splashes struck her skirts.

Jocelyn shot off her chair. "I'm so sorry. I'm not usually this clumsy." She rang for a maid and risked a frantic glance at the window.

Boynton.

He'd found her.

A maid appeared, and Jocelyn issued instructions. He *had* seen her at Tavistock and followed her home. He'd always been sly. The hair at the back of her neck rose, and she fought to still the tremor of her hand as she helped Mrs. Allenby sponge the stain from her gown. Boynton was likely enjoying his furtive game, stalking her as if she were a helpless mouse.

"I'm so embarrassed," Jocelyn said, taking another peek at the window. "I don't know what happened." It hadn't been her imagination. Had Boynton been the one terrorizing her mother? Perhaps he was the ghost.

"No apologies necessary." The vicar patted her hand. "You've been under a lot of strain recently."

"Of course you don't need to apologize," Mrs. Allenby agreed. "Have you seen Leo?"

"No." Jocelyn straightened in her chair, determined to hold her composure.

The maid exited and everyone settled again. Jocelyn kept glancing out the window. She wanted to confront the wretched man and demand he leave her alone. Surely she had enough to deal with at present?

The clearing of a throat jerked her attention back to her guests. She forced a smile and focused on them.

"There," the vicar said. "I knew she'd approve of the idea."

Oh, dear. That was what happened when a person didn't pay attention. "I'm sorry," Jocelyn said. "I haven't been sleeping well, and I'm a bit scattered today. What were you saying?"

"The Harvest Festival is a Sherbourne tradition," the vicar said. "It would be good to have it back at Merrivale Manor."

"We thought the gathering would help things return to normal," Mrs. Allenby said, sympathy filling her eyes. "I understand this situation is difficult for you, and that many of the villagers are treating you as guilty too, but the festival might be the thing to cement your presence here. Once Leo..." She trailed off, her gaze darting away while a red tide surged into her wrinkled face. Mrs. Allenby inhaled deeply. "This is your home. We are your friends, my dear. If you act normally, the villagers might get past their distrust of you."

Everything Mrs. Allenby said was true. When...when Leo was gone, Merrivale would belong to her. Melburn was Leo's nearest kin, and she was confident he'd allow her to remain in the house. Yes, they were right. Maybe she'd redeem herself a little instead of appearing a total lackwit. "Did the festival take place last year?"

The vicar's nose twitched in clear distaste. "At Castle Hartscombe."

Oh dear. "I can't give you a definitive answer today. Let me consider it overnight, and I'll send a footman with my decision."

"If you won't host the festival, we won't have one," Mrs. Allenby said.

Jocelyn's brows rose. It was what Mrs. Allenby *didn't* say that prompted intrigue. "Oh?"

"The goings on at Castle Hartscombe during the last festival were scandalous. Hannah and Peregrine invited guests from London." Mrs. Allenby pressed her lips together then made a faint *tsk* of disapproval.

"The visitors behaved badly. Very badly." The vicar's wig

slipped a fraction to the side during his vigorous nodding. "It was a disgrace."

"I'll send word of my decision tomorrow," Jocelyn repeated.

"Thank you. That's all we ask," Mrs. Allenby said.

A brief tap on the door sounded seconds before it burst open.

"We're here," Hannah trilled. "It's such a beautiful day we thought we'd take Cassie riding. Oh." Her hand flew up to cover her mouth. "We're interrupting your visit."

Peregrine stepped into the parlor behind his sister. A languid figure in white and maroon trimming today, he smiled broadly, and the flash of his teeth competed with the sparkling silver embroidery on his vest. "Vicar. Mrs. Allenby. It must be time to discuss this year's Harvest Festival. We're looking forward to hosting it at the castle again."

Mrs. Allenby drew herself up, the steely glint in her eyes failing to hide her dislike. "We have asked Mrs. Sherbourne to host the festival at Merrivale Manor."

Hannah's brows rose in surprise. "Do you think that's appropriate with Leo in jail for murder? Surely it would be better to remain in seclusion." The consummate actress, she gave a delicate shudder. "I know I wouldn't risk further gossip. Isn't your reputation stained enough already?"

Peregrine glanced from his sister to Jocelyn and back with avid interest, treating their conversation like a bear baiting.

"Leo said he never wanted to hold the gathering again," Peregrine said.

"He was most definite on that point," Hannah agreed.

Jocelyn shot a reproving glance at the vicar who had the grace to flush. They'd left out vital facts during their request.

Mrs. Allenby shot back. "He said that because—"

"Mrs. Allenby," the vicar said in an unusually sharp voice. He pushed to his feet. "It is time for us to leave. I have several parishioners to visit this morning." He turned to Jocelyn.

"You'll let us know?"

Jocelyn inclined her head, unwilling to inflame Hannah and Peregrine further. Thankfully Cassie arrived, diverting attention. Hannah cooed over her niece's brand new red dress while Jocelyn escorted the vicar and his wife out and bid them farewell.

Before reentering the parlor, she glanced through a window overlooking the garden and saw nothing out of place. Had she imagined the face at the window? Boynton had seemed so real, even down to his carefully tied cravat and elaborately embroidered black waistcoat, his immaculate wig atop a ruddy face. Deep in unhappy thoughts, she joined Hannah and Peregrine.

"You don't want to go to the trouble of organizing the festival," Hannah said. "Especially not at present. It wouldn't seem right to have a celebration at Merrivale when you're... Let's face it. You're married to a murderer. Do you want to face the public?"

"Are you taking Cassie riding?" Jocelyn asked.

"Leo said it's all right to take out Cassie," Hannah said, a trifle defensively.

"Hannah will lead Cassie around on the pony," Peregrine said. "Don't worry. She'll be perfectly safe. Besides, Cassie has natural talent. She takes after Ursula with her love of horseflesh."

"It's me you need to ask," Jocelyn said, keeping her voice mild when she wanted to scream with vexation. "Until it is decided otherwise, I am responsible for Cassie's wellbeing."

"I—"

"Hannah." Peregrine squeezed his sister's shoulder in warning.

"We'll see about that!" With a backward glare, Hannah ushered Cassie outside, and Jocelyn and Peregrine trailed after them.

Irked by Hannah's attitude, Jocelyn wished Hannah would quit trying to get one up on her all the time. Now that Leo... She broke off the thought and forced herself to concentrate on Peregrine. "Everyone says Cassie looks like her mother."

Peregrine laughed. "You're lucky she doesn't have the same temper tantrums."

"Ursula had tantrums?"

"Oh, yes." Peregrine shook his head ruefully. "If everything was going her way, she was all smiles and charm. The minute someone didn't do as Ursula wanted, watch out!"

Jocelyn sucked in a quick breath. "What happened to Ursula?"

Peregrine came to an abrupt halt. "What do you mean?"

"How did Ursula die?"

His ever-present smile faded, and he scanned their vicinity before turning back to her.

This was a time for bluntness. "Why do the locals think Leo killed her?"

"She'd been strangled." The lack of emotion in his voice told of pain. "People heard them arguing only two hours earlier."

"But no one saw Leo do it. What did Leo say?"

Peregrine's mouth twisted. "He denied doing it, but of course he's now in jail awaiting trial."

Something she couldn't stop thinking about, her feelings conflicted on the matter. The fact her judgment had failed her so badly. "Do you think he killed Ursula?"

Peregrine avoided her gaze, staring off into the distance instead. Jocelyn's heart thumped hard against her rib cage. He did. He blamed Leo for Ursula's death. "Yes," he said finally.

"What about Hannah? Does she think Leo killed Ursula?"

Once again Peregrine's silence was telling. Jocelyn puffed out a frustrated breath, angry on her own behalf. She'd never have come to Dartmoor or exposed her mother to this situation if she'd known of Leo's first wife and her traumatic death. While he might have still tricked her into marriage by professing his innocence, she would have thought twice if she'd had possession of all the facts. Since their marriage, she'd witnessed his icy anger. Added to the facts now she could see why Captain Cartwright had locked him up.

"I'd better join Hannah and Cassie," Peregrine said.

"Why did you keep visiting Merrivale Manor and seeing Leo if you both thought he was responsible for your sister's murder?"

Peregrine looked at her then, for the first time since she'd introduced the topic. His eyes blazed with emotions. Fear, definitely. The rest flickered through his eyes too quickly for her to decipher. "We can't leave Cassie alone with him. What happens if he hurts her? I'm sure he's just biding his time, waiting for suspicions to lull. Leo is dangerous."

"I won't let anything happen to Cassie," Jocelyn said. "Arabella protected your niece while she was here."

"Arabella was good with Cassie. That's the only thing that's keeping us from taking her," Peregrine said. "And of course, your presence helps keep Cassie safe."

Why, then, had Hannah wished to marry Leo? Jocelyn stared, conflicting emotions stilling her tongue. This wasn't a nightmare she could wake up from to escape. All his words rang with truth. He truly believed Leo had killed his sister.

CHAPTER 11

JOCELYN DAWDLED OVER HER preparations for bed.

Susan finished deftly braiding her hair. "Will that be all, Mrs. Sherbourne?"

"Yes, thank you, Susan. I'll see you in the morning." She reached out to still her maid for an instant. "I'm very sorry about Ella. Please, if there is anything I can do to help you have only to ask."

Pain flickered over Susan's face. Her mouth worked before she dipped her head in curt acceptance and withdrew, leaving Jocelyn alone with her nightmare. Leo—a murderer. The evidence was conclusive. After her mistake with Boynton, she'd listened to her instincts and trusted Leo. It was only after her arrival at Merrivale and witnessing his strange behavior that she'd become confused and wondered about his innocence.

The facts remained. Someone had murdered Ursula and the maid. Someone had kidnapped Ella and left her traumatized, her mind addled. If Leo wasn't the murderer, then who'd committed the crime?

Despite the late hour, restless energy filled her. Perhaps she'd find a book in the library. Jocelyn tightened the belt on her wrapper and left her chamber. Several candles still burned in the wall sconces, and she found her way without difficulty. She scanned the library shelves, searching for a book to pique her interest.

A loud creak made her pause. She cocked her head and heard the distinct scuffle of feet. Her breath caught, her thoughts skipping ahead to murder. She listened for a few seconds longer, trepidation making her indecisive.

Finally Jocelyn gathered her wits and slinked to the door, glad she hadn't pulled it fully shut. The front door creaked as it opened. Familiar muttering propelled Jocelyn to action.

"Mother, what are you doing out of bed? Where is Tilly?"

"I saw lights outside. Someone is beckoning me. I have to go." Before Jocelyn could remonstrate, her mother ran outside.

"Mother!"

"W-who goes there?" Somewhere to Jocelyn's right, a servant called a high-pitched query. The nervous stutter sounded like the youngest footman.

"It's Mrs. Sherbourne. Summon Woodley and tell him my mother is outside." Jocelyn dallied no longer. She grabbed the closest pair of boots and thrust her bare feet into them. They were wet inside and too big. Ignoring the damp ooze, she clenched her toes and clomped down the steps into the night. After pausing for precious seconds to listen, she hurried along a gravel path, almost tripping over her feet in her haste. *St. Bridget's nose!* She should have taken the time to grab her own footwear.

"Mother!"

A cloud slid across the partial moon. Jocelyn slowed, her progress more tentative now that her vision was obscured. Dew covered the grass and plants, weighting down the hem of her wrapper. A chill nibbled her bare ankles with every step.

"Mother!" She bit off a second call, recalling the face she'd seen at the window. She proceeded cautiously, approaching a fork in the path with vigilance. The crisp crunch of a branch underfoot stopped her in her tracks. "Mother?"

A familiar mumble came from the right *Ah!* "Mother," Jocelyn said. "You have to come back inside. It's not safe wandering around in the dark."

She raced around a corner and plowed into someone. "*Oomph!*" The air whooshed from her lungs. Hands wrapped around her upper arms like containment cuffs. Squeezing. One hand fastened around her throat. Fingers pressed deep. The scent of horse and a whiff of soap wrapped around her. She fought, lashed out with her feet. One boot fell off.

"Stop fighting," a muffled voice snarled.

"Help!" Jocelyn screamed. She wriggled frantically and lashed out with her feet. Her bare foot connected with her captive's legs and pain radiated up her shin. "Help!"

A loud screech rent the air. Jocelyn turned her head to see something white hurtling toward them. Ghostlike and terrifying, the creature waved its arms and wailed. Abruptly, she was freed, a hand shoving her in the middle of her back. Jocelyn lurched forward, her arms flapping for balance. Her knees collided painfully with the gravel path, her palms striking seconds later. Agony shot through her limbs.

"*Ow.*" She groaned and slowly pushed herself off her hands and knees.

"Ghost!" A familiar shriek sounded near her ear.

"Mother?" Jocelyn flinched at yet another screech right next to her ear. She grasped her mother's shoulders and shook her. "Mother, it's me. For pity's sake, please stop that infernal racket. You're deafening me."

The high-pitched screams halted abruptly. "You're not a ghost?" Hands patted Jocelyn—her face, her torso. "You're not a ghost. Georgina, what are you doing outside?"

"It's Jocelyn, Mother. Georgina is in London."

"I don't know any Jocelyn. Where's Georgina? Or Charlotte? Get Charlotte. She'll know what to do."

"Mother, Charlotte and Georgina are both in London with their families."

A violent tremor swept her mother. "It's cold out here. I'm cold, Georgina. Cassie said there would be fairies. I wanted to see the fairies dancing."

"Mother, someone is playing tricks on you. Let me help you back inside. You'll catch a chill out here."

"Jocelyn!" a familiar voice yelled.

"Over here," she shouted.

Seconds later, Woodley appeared on the path. "Are you all right?"

Jocelyn shivered. "Woodley, someone was out here. I don't know who it was, but Mother frightened him off."

"Where is Georgina? I want Georgina." His mother's querulous voice cut through Jocelyn's explanations.

"Oh, dear," Woodley murmured.

"Indeed," Jocelyn said, sadness engulfing her at the confusion in her mother.

"Come, let me escort you both inside." Woodley grasped her mother's arm and assisted her down the path, leaving Jocelyn to fend for herself. Her shoulders slumped as she clomped along in one too-large boot and a bare foot. She longed for a warm bed, and a good night's rest. Unfortunately, she didn't think tonight would contain much sleep.

LEO SLIPPED FROM THE shadows under the trees. He didn't

know what to think. Someone was skulking around the manor, and since it was in the middle of the night, their presence didn't bode well.

After a slow, careful search of the grounds with no sightings, Leo suspected the person had departed. At least Jocelyn was safe. Leo prowled another circuit of the gardens, and once satisfied the intruder no longer lurked in the vicinity, he searched for access to the manor. The only door open was the one to the servants' entrance. With noiseless steps, he slipped inside.

A deep snort drew him up abruptly. A junior footman sat on a chair, his eyes closed and mouth agape. Leo's arm snaked out to shake him awake, ready to demand an explanation before he thought better of the action. He'd face all sorts of questions if anyone other than Jocelyn saw him. Leo grimaced. He was taking a risk as it was. Cartwright didn't realize he'd flitted away from his post early, and Leo hoped to return to Cartwright's residence without the constable realizing he'd gone back on his vow.

Leo crept past, increasing his speed once the slumbering footman was behind him. With the ease of familiarity, he moved up the dimly lit stairs, skipping over the stair second from bottom to avoid a nasty creak. He entered his chamber and closed the door before making his way to the connecting entrance to Jocelyn's room.

Her flowery scent drifted to him as soon as he stepped inside. His lips curved into a smile as memories drifted through his mind. She wore a dab between her breasts and another behind her ears. He'd discovered that while exploring her body with his mouth. He couldn't wait to rain kisses on her neck but first...first he had to make sure she didn't scream bloody murder.

"Jocelyn." He sat on the edge of her bed and gently shook her shoulder, poised to slap his hand over her mouth if she attempted to shriek. "Jocelyn."

"What is it? Is it Mother again?" Her voice slurred with fatigue. Her eyes opened, focused, and a thin scream escaped.

Grabbing her, he cut off most of the sharp cry. "It's Leo. Jocelyn, it's Leo. Your husband. Don't scream again. Please." God, she had to believe in his innocence. "I'm going to take my hand away, but if you scream again, I'll gag you. *Please don't scream, sweetheart.* "Nod, if you're willing to talk."

She nodded slowly, her eyes big and wide.

Watching her warily, he released her.

"Leo, what are you doing here?" She bolted upright, her voice carrying an edge of dread.

Her terror made his chest tighten, his breath catch in regret. How had it come to this? Him, a suspected murderer and his wife afraid of him. "Let me light a candle." He made short work of the task, relaxing when she didn't raise the alarm. "I didn't murder those women, and I had nothing to do with Ella's disappearance."

"Then why has Captain Cartwright charged you with the crime?" Her blue eyes accused him, her body tense as if she was poised to flee. "Does Captain Cartwright know you've escaped?"

Disappointment coursed through him, and he scarcely contained his wince. She didn't believe him. "He knows I'm not guilty."

"If that's the case, why have you been taken into custody?"

Leo sighed. "I can't tell you."

"That's convenient," Jocelyn said.

Despite his frustration, Leo fought a flash of humor. Jocelyn's straightforward approach was refreshing, and it was part of the reason he liked her so much. The rationale for offering her marriage, despite her past. "I can't stay past dawn," he said instead of expressing his delight in her.

"Why are you here?"

"I came to see my wife." Leo caught her gaze with his. "I came to make love with her."

"I—you're meant to be in jail."

Her clipped response wasn't reassuring, but tonight would not go the same way as the previous evenings. Jocelyn was his wife, and they could have a good marriage. She enjoyed their bed sport and could hardly refute it. Still watching her, he stood and started to disrobe. Her eyes widened a fraction, but she didn't call out or speak. Instead her blue gaze followed his progress, skimming his chest then lowering to stare at his engorged cock.

"This isn't right." She glowered at him, her mouth in a mulish set that reminded him of Elizabeth. "I don't want this."

"Because you believe I am guilty of murder."

"Yes."

"On the night of Ursula's death she and I argued. I was so angry I returned to the party at Hartscombe. I spent the rest of the evening with a woman."

"Who?"

"I can't give you her name. I don't want to harm her reputation."

"Huh! A plausible excuse, I'm sure." Her tongue darted out to moisten her lips, leaving them glistening in the candlelight.

Naked, he closed the distance between them. At the edge of the bed, he halted, meeting her glower with one of his own. "You can shriek for help, or you can spend a few hours with me."

"Trust you?"

"Yes." He sat on the edge of the bed and, unable to resist, tugged lightly on her fiery red braid. "Is that so difficult?"

She nibbled her bottom lip, a frown creasing her forehead. "I don't know what to believe," she said. "Captain Cartwright must have had a good reason not to arrest you for Ursula's murder. He doesn't strike me as one who'd accept a bribe."

"And what else?" He could tell something else bothered her.

"Captain Cartwright is an intelligent man. From what I've seen of him, he's both honest and efficient. I doubt you'd escape his custody, which means he released you for some reason." Her gaze felt as if it drilled through him, and he wasn't sure what she'd decide. Yet even with his freedom hanging in balance, pride swelled within him. Jocelyn didn't miss much, which made her skepticism galling.

Leo caught her gaze darting to his chest. Maybe he had an edge after all. "Are you going to let me into your bed or not?"

Her gaze slid down his naked body and a sultry smile bloomed on her lips. It didn't reach her eyes, which told him she held serious reservations. "Haven't you made the decision for both of us already?" She wriggled across the mattress, leaving a space for him. For reasons known to her, she was letting him have his way, but uncertainties roiled in his gut. Would she betray him?

They stared at each other for a long moment, and the residual worry left his shoulders. He'd trust her—for now. Satisfaction replaced his earlier disappointment. As always, Jocelyn's presence calmed him. Never had the contrast between Jocelyn and Ursula yawned so wide. Grateful and desperate to touch his wife, he slid beneath the covers and pulled her rigid body against him. Unable to resist, he nuzzled her neck and placed a kiss on the curve of her cheek. A pity she'd bound her hair in a tight braid. He rather liked the heavy mass loose and glinting like flames flickering in the night.

"Leo?"

"Yes."

"You scared me half to death, popping into my chamber like a magical creature. You're lucky I didn't wake everyone. Does Captain Cartwright know you're here?"

"Who did you expect it to be?"

"You haven't answered my question." She scowled before a

chuckle burst from her, another sultry sound that grabbed him by the balls. "A strange man intending to seduce me?"

"Your husband is interested in seduction. And no, Cartwright doesn't know, but he did release me for the night."

"Why?" She wriggled, until her breasts flattened against the wall of his chest.

"We're investigating together." Leo hugged her tight, his relief palpable. She might harbor doubts, but for now she was accommodating.

"Tell me about Ursula."

The words pricked him like a sharp needle. "What?"

"Tell me about your first wife."

"I don't wish to discuss her."

Jocelyn drew back, and he forced his expression to impassive. He couldn't allow her to witness the fury coursing through him, couldn't risk what she might see on his face.

"If you want me to trust you, I need something in return."

"No." Leo pulled away. Hell, he was making a mess of this, but thoughts of Ursula, the way she'd played him always shoved him into anger. "We can talk about anything you like, anyone except Ursula." He tried to soften his tone but didn't pull it off. When the determined waves coming from her continued, he struck with a low blow. "I've never asked you why you didn't marry like your sisters or how you came to the situation Melburn found you in."

She flinched, and his insides felt as if someone had knifed him with a rusty blade. *Guilt.* Damn it, he refused to soil their marriage with memories of that traitorous bitch.

"You're asking a lot from me." She didn't attempt to keep the tartness from her tone.

He hated to see her disillusion. And it didn't help that she was right. He was asking for trust without reciprocating. With a hand that trembled, he reached for her again. "I'm sorry,

Jocelyn. I—it's a part of my life I don't wish to dwell on any longer. We both have pasts we'd prefer to forget. I want to concentrate on our future, on Cassandra and any children we might have together." He stared down at her, taking in every minute shift of her expression, the flicker of her rapid thoughts.

Please, let her accept his direction in this matter.

His fists clenched. Hell, he'd wanted Ursula to die. No, he hadn't killed her, yet he couldn't help feeling glad he was free of her viperous tongue and her mischief. *Fool!* Even now his first wife cast tall shadows.

"If that's what you wish," she said finally.

"It is." Relief swept him, despite her grudging capitulation. Full of gratitude, he drew her close and kissed her, putting everything he couldn't say into his caress. His touch spoke of his approval, his growing friendship and physical lust for her. He demonstrated their future, his hopes, his dreams, and by the time he lifted his head they were both breathing rapidly.

Unable to resist, he traced the plump curve of her bottom lip with his thumb, approval joining the growing raft of emotions thrumming inside him. Her tongue flickered out to lick his thumb. His breath hitched, his gaze shooting to hers. Desire filled her eyes, and something stirred in him. Not lust exactly, but something else. Something precious.

She opened her mouth and closed her lips around his thumb. He started, heat streaking straight to his cock. A groan escaped him, and humor danced in her eyes. She sucked hard and his cock lengthened. The minx knew exactly what she was doing, exactly how to thrust him into stark need. He cupped her cheek with his free hand, savoring the warmth of her silky skin. Every breath he took contained the scent of flowers. Whenever he saw flowers now, he thought of Jocelyn.

"I want to run my fingers through your hair." The hoarse words burst from him, scarcely louder than a whisper.

Her mouth opened and his thumb popped free. "Are you volunteering to brush the knots out in the morning?"

"Anything. I like your hair, the feel of it against my skin. It always looks so alive." And the visual of seeing the liquid fire spread across the pillow appealed to him on so many levels.

She tugged the end of her braid free, her eyes now full of seduction. The vague sense of being played flitted through his mind, but he let it slip away, too entranced by her sultry attractions.

"Please, let me." Performing mundane services for her enchanted him. Hell, it made him crave her body all the more. The simple act of unfastening a button or tying a lace forged a connection, an intimacy between man and woman that he'd come to enjoy.

She turned her head to give him better access. He made short work of the ribbon and used his fingers to separate the silken strands. Once he'd completed the self-imposed task, he tugged on the thin chemise she wore. "This should go too."

Minutes later, he'd divested her of clothing and she lay facing him. Her hair cascaded over her shoulders, hiding one of her breasts. She blinked at him, the action seductive and snaring him tighter.

"What now, husband?"

A curl of emotion wrapped around his heart. *Husband*. Swallowing to dispel the tightness in his throat, he rolled to lie flat on the mattress. "Ride me. I have a yearning to see your pretty breasts bounce while you take your pleasure."

Dimpling, she straddled his hips. Her hands smoothed across bulging pectoral muscles, glided across his shoulders, leaving a trail of prickling enjoyment. His mouth dried, his gaze seeking the damp flesh between her thighs. Her fingers followed the trail of hair leading to his groin, her hands small and capable, fingertips silky against his skin.

SHELLEY MUNRO

"Yes," he whispered.

Every muscle pulled taut, the need to hurry a frantic beat of his heart. He wanted to hasten but fought the inclination, part of him curious about what she'd do next. Fleetingly, he thought of the men in her past. A flash of jealousy, which he shoved away. Nothing should interfere with their marriage.

"Are you ticklish?"

"No."

"I might check to see if you're fibbing."

He was no liar. He opened his mouth to remonstrate then flinched when she plucked his nipple between two fingers. Predictably, her touch echoed in his cock. She skimmed her fingers along his rib cage, seemingly satisfied when he didn't squirm. She took her time, learning his body and his reactions in a way she hadn't done to date. Leo discovered freedom in allowing her to take the lead. Joy. She nuzzled his neck, kissing and alternatively nipping his flesh, torturing him with sensual bites until he trembled like a green lad.

"God's teeth, Jocelyn. Please take me inside you."

Solemnly, she studied him. "I want to learn you."

"We have plenty of time. Years to study each other." The unspoken words—if he didn't hang for murder—rang between them.

Her smile faltered before she rallied. "You haven't given me leave to explore you before."

"All you needed to do was ask."

She squirmed down his body until he could feel her damp heat against the base of his shaft. Each time she moved, he bit his lip and steeled himself against taking the reins.

At last, she lifted her hips, and he sighed in relief. Finally. But once again, she surprised him, moving lower so she straddled his upper thighs. She gripped his cock firmly, sent him an impish grin and lowered her head. The air whooshed out of

182

him as her mouth enclosed the tip. The wet heat seared him. Unable to hold completely still, he reached for her hair, gripping handfuls like an anchor. God, her mouth felt good—the lash of her tongue even better. With minimum effort, a few practiced moves, she hurled him toward ecstasy. His balls drew tight, aching in a bite of pleasure. Holding back took effort, and he trembled.

"Jocelyn, I'm going to spill in your mouth if you keep that up."

She lifted her head, her mouth making a faint popping sound when she released his shaft. "I don't think that would be a problem, Leo. I've already learned you care about pleasing your lovers and give in return."

"Lover," he corrected, his voice stiff.

"Did you not say you took a lover once you knew your wife was unfaithful?" As she spoke, she maneuvered her body and guided him to her entrance. She pushed down, slowly impaling herself. Her brows rose, silently demanding an answer.

"One," he said finally.

She nodded. "Understandable. And what happened to your lover?" She pressed down, taking him to the hilt, questioning him while he was at his weakest.

"I'd prefer not to discuss the matter." He owed Anna his silence. She'd faced her brother's wrath for him.

Jocelyn narrowed her gaze. "I applaud you on your discretion." She lifted and settled again with a sigh, her breasts swaying, her delight in the sexual act evident. "Are you going to tell me more?"

"No. Cup your breasts. Pinch your nipples. I might reconsider if you tell me about your past."

"Touché." Her head tilted to the side, the shift of her weight repositioning her hair to screen one breast. "Do you like watching?"

"I like watching you." A parade of faceless men marched through his mind before a focused blink scattered them to the winds. *Stupid.* He'd thought about jealousy and accepted her past. "You're a beautiful woman."

"I'm not beautiful."

He caught her pained expression, the way she closed down and her hands dropped away from her breasts. She stopped moving. "Hannah is beautiful. Arabella is beautiful."

His mind fixed on a truth. While he was experiencing jealousy, she was in an equally challenging position. One of uncertainty, and now wondering if she'd married a murderer. As a man, he had the power to set her aside and withdraw his support. If anything, her risk was greater than his. Because of her responsibility for her mother, she had more to lose.

"You're beautiful to me." He tugged on a lock of her red hair and smiled. Her internal muscles flexed, caressing his shaft and shooting a burst of pleasure to the depths of his body. "Your red hair reminds me of sunsets. I like to kiss and lick the scatters of freckles on your face and chest because they remind me of tart spices. And I like you, Jocelyn. Always."

Doubt still marked her solemn face, so he hooked his hand around her neck, dragged her down and kissed her, using all the experience he'd acquired through the years. After seconds of resistance, she melted. She made a soft *woof* of sound, kissing him hard in return, her hands clenching his shoulders. When she finally lifted her head, passion darkened her eyes. Her delight sparkled in her blue eyes, lighting her features with mischief. She started to move again, rising and falling above him. His gaze drifted down to her breasts. They bounced in a delightful manner, grabbing his appreciative attention.

"Touch yourself."

Her measured rise and fall faltered.

"Do it," he insisted.

"It's not ladylike."

"I don't want a lady in my bed."

"Are you sure about that?" Her grin suffered under restraint, dimming the joy in her eyes, and he wanted it back.

"Jocelyn, I want you."

To his relief, her tension receded as she appeared to come to a decision. She caressed his hip and increased her pace. Leo had trouble biting back a groan at the incredible friction massaging his rod. Heat rampaged through him. His balls ached so much he had to grit his teeth against the throb of pain.

"Jocelyn." A plea full of emotion.

She sucked in a breath. Her fingers trailed down her thighs and slipped between her nether lips. She stroked firmly, and on the down strokes, he felt the pressure of her finger on the base of his cock. It was too much. Not enough. He caught his breath, releasing it on a moan as pleasure flooded his body. He was vaguely aware of breathy sounds emerging from Jocelyn. The flush on her cheeks intensified. Her eyes squeezed tight, and he felt the rhythmic pulse of her, clutching his shaft. Finally, she stilled and her eyes opened.

"Come here," he said softly.

She fell against him, and he wrapped his arms around her, peace rippling through him. His instinct to join her had been a good one. While they still didn't know each other well, the bedroom was a place where they were well-matched. At the very least it would bring the possibility of a child closer. A baby would tie them together because he knew, without a doubt, no matter what she might think of him, Jocelyn would never walk away from a child.

CHAPTER 12

He was gone when Jocelyn woke, and it left her wondering if she'd imagined the entire encounter. Only the faint bruise on her left breast and her naked state gave her proof of his visit. She slid off the bed, ignored the twinge of sore muscles, and started to wash briskly with a cloth and cold water. She frowned, still uncertain if he'd told her the truth. Even so, it'd be best if no one suspected Leo's visit.

Susan knocked on the door and entered. Two steps into the room, she came to an abrupt halt, her right hand clasping her breast. Her mouth formed into an O of surprise when she spied Jocelyn's unbound hair.

"I'll wear my blue floral gown today, Susan." Jocelyn glanced at her looking glass and barely suppressed a wince. Her hair resembled a stork's nest.

"Yes, Mrs. Sherbourne."

If Leo was in jail this morning, she'd know he spoke the truth about Captain Cartwright believing him innocent. But if she discovered Leo had lied, she'd inform on him herself. Jocelyn took the opportunity to finish washing, new resolve pouring through her now that she had a purpose. She picked up her brush, but Susan returned with her gown and undergarments before she could restore her hair to tidiness.

"Did you have a restless night, Mrs. Sherbourne?"

"Yes," Jocelyn said, hating that Leo was turning her to subterfuge. Leo...drat the man. She didn't know what to think. Last night he'd soothed some of her concerns. It was once she was alone or when other people spoke of him that her doubts returned.

She noticed Susan eyeing the faint bruise on her breast. "I think I'll dress first. I'm feeling chilly today." She gave a theatrical shiver and stood to allow Susan to help her don her chemise.

Susan dressed her with her normal efficiency, and Jocelyn chattered aimlessly, but the tightening of her maid's lips and her increasingly short replies told of Susan's suspicions. She thought Jocelyn was conducting an affair. If only she knew.

After breaking her fast, Jocelyn began her plans for the festival, glad of the task to keep her mind busy. She requested a meeting with Mrs. Green. They retreated to the parlor to go through the notes Leo's mother had made regarding previous festivals.

"Mrs. Sherbourne liked to have games and contests." Mrs. Green actually smiled. "She disliked drunken revels and kept everyone occupied before serving the feast."

The parlor door burst open, striking the wall with a noisy thump.

"You can't do this!" Hannah stormed into the room. "You can't hold the festival at Merrivale."

Mrs. Green started, sending papers flying. She shot to her feet, a dull tide of color flooding her cheeks. A snap of annoyance showed in her dark eyes as she retrieved the papers and reclaimed her seat.

"There is nothing to stop you from holding a festival." Jocelyn didn't understand why Hannah was so determined. Maybe she wanted to take credit for the organization.

"Thank you for being so understanding. I'll let the vicar know." Hannah beamed, becoming gracious with her perceived victory.

Jocelyn rose, not wanting to feel at a disadvantage with Hannah looming over her. Standing, she had several inches over the other woman. "No, you misunderstand. I intend to revert to tradition and host the villagers and neighbors here at Merrivale. Your course of action is up to you."

"You can't. I—"

"This is pointless." Jocelyn drew herself up, unwilling to let Hannah push her into emotional turmoil. "I will not change my mind. Our people work hard, and I wish to show my gratitude for their service and loyalty." Jocelyn strode over to the door and waited. When Hannah stood rooted to the ground, Jocelyn tapped an impatient foot, stirring the hem of her gown with a sharp rustle. "Hannah?"

"You haven't heard the last of this," Hannah spat, and she flounced from the parlor, muttering obscenities under her breath.

Mrs. Green *tut-tutted* at the etiquette breach.

"What happened last year?"

"I didn't attend since my sister was sick and I was busy nursing her back to health. From what I understand there were many strangers present—friends of the Richards'. They arrived two days before the festival and, from all accounts, behaved like drunken louts. I can't say if the local women were willing or not. Many of them ended up with child. The visitors picked fights with the locals. The evening ended in a nasty brawl."

"And that's why the vicar wishes us to host the festival."

"That is my supposition, Mrs. Sherbourne."

"Although with the gossip about Mr. Sherbourne, I wonder how many locals will attend."

"Curiosity will bring them," Mrs. Green said, speaking plainly.

Jocelyn settled back in her chair with a sigh. "I think you're right. Perhaps we should get back to our plans. Is there any mention of games for children?"

An hour later, Jocelyn and Mrs. Green concluded their meeting, their strategy for the festival underway.

Jocelyn went to check on her mother.

"Tilly, how is Mother this morning?"

Her mother bolted upright in her bed. "I'm not an invalid. Georgina, tell Tilly I can get out of bed."

Every time her mother called her Georgina, Jocelyn's heart fractured a little more. She forced a smile to cover the hurt. "It's another lovely day. Would you like to go for a walk in the garden this afternoon?"

Her mother beamed and let out a cry of delight. "I want to make a special lemon wash for Charlotte's hair. She has such pretty hair. Unfortunately, there is nothing I can do with your hair. That red is beyond my help."

"Of course, Mother." A rush of tears stung Jocelyn's eyes, and she blinked rapidly. Her mother was confused and didn't mean to wound. She withdrew and hurried to the opposite wing and the haven of her chamber. By the time she closed her door and leaned against the hard wood, tears poured down her cheeks. She covered her face with her hands and sobbed for the mother she used to know, the one who scolded her when she played in the mud with the village children. The one who held her after she fell and scraped her knee. The one who disapproved of her life as a courtesan even as she ignored the fact Jocelyn's father had gambled away his daughter's virginity. She cried for her mother of old.

THE DAYS PASSED, TURNING into weeks. Leo grew increasingly worried as the end of the month neared. Despite staking out the abbey, not a soul ventured near the ruins in the dead of the night. From his hilltop position, he glared down at the silent pillars, the piles of glowing gray stones revealed whenever the moon peeked from behind a cloud.

"The next quarter session takes place soon. The justice of the peace will be here in less than three weeks."

Cartwright's disclosure shot ice through his veins. "You could always let me escape," Leo said.

"That would make me look inefficient." Cartwright shot him a sideways glance, one that Leo had no difficulty reading despite the black of the night. "I give you free rein as it is. I know you sneak off to visit your wife."

"But you believe my innocence?" If he went to trial, he wouldn't have a chance with the evidence pointing at him. The locals were scared. Angry. And so they should be, but they were looking for someone to blame, to punish.

He was an innocent man.

"I wouldn't roam the moors at all hours if I didn't place credence in your story."

"Each time I've seen groups of people at the abbey it's been after the abduction of a woman," Leo said thoughtfully.

"We can't exactly place a trap for them. Your rescue of Ella scared them, made them extra cautious, and the local women aren't going out at night or walking alone. That must make it more difficult for them to grab someone else. We'll have to wait until the culprits relax enough to resume their activities. Hell, they're probably looking sideways at each other, wondering who released Ella, since you're sticking to your story about finding her wandering the moor."

"Depends on the tale Sir James spun about that night. And there's the fact Ella says I kidnapped her." Leo hated this. From the little Jocelyn said it appeared Ella's mind was damaged from her experience, and he wouldn't wish that hell on anyone. "Have the abductions coincided with house parties?"

"Within a few days," Cartwright replied.

"So someone decides on a target and makes off with them. A secret society along the lines of the Hellfire Club?"

"That's what I think," Cartwright said.

"What do we do next?" Discouragement dogged his heels, weighing down his spirit tonight. He wanted to live openly with Jocelyn, instead of paying clandestine visits. Damn it, he needed to walk tall with his name cleared of suspicion.

"I'll keep an ear open while I do my rounds. Keep track of the comings and goings at Castle Hartscombe and Duxton." He paused, his face contorting into deep set lines. "Might have a quiet word with the constables in the neighboring parishes to discover if they have unexplained disappearances."

"And at night?"

"We'll continue to stake out this place. If any visitors arrive, we'll track their movements."

Leo gave a stiff nod.

"Go and visit your wife, lad. Make sure you're back in time for me to lock you up."

"Thank you." Cartwright was doing him a favor, even if the restrictions governing his liberty chafed him. Intending to melt into the darkness, he came to an abrupt halt when a foreign sound cut through the air. He slinked back to Cartwright's side and peered down at the abbey ruins.

"Two men on horseback," Cartwright murmured. "Do you recognize them?"

Leo stiffened on seeing the gray stallion one of the men was riding. His gaze darted to the man's face, but it was shadowed and impossible to identify from this distance.

"What?" Cartwright prompted.

"I know the horse. I sold it to Jaego Woodburn about three years ago. The other horse looks like one from the castle stables. Maybe that's Peregrine."

Cartwright drew in a sharp breath. "Jaego hasn't been around for a while."

"Not since the party at Hartscombe," Leo said in a tight voice.

"You didn't know Jaego was sneaking around with your wife?"

Leo tracked the movements of the two men as they swung off their mounts. "No," he said. "I knew she was seeing other men, but I didn't realize my best friend numbered among them."

Silence fell between the pair as they watched from their hilltop. The two men led their horses out of sight.

"Do we follow them?"

"No," Cartwright said. "There are just the two of them. I'll watch them and see what eventuates. Tomorrow, I'll ask a few questions and discover where he's staying."

"Probably with Peregrine at the castle."

"Something always puzzled me," Cartwright said. "Everyone suspected you murdered Ursula, yet Hannah and Peregrine and their parents stood by you."

"I think they knew what she was like, that she was meeting other men. Not that they discussed it with me. Ursula spent a lot of nights at the castle. A lot of people knew our marriage was a failure. I told the viscount I didn't murder their daughter, and he seemed to believe me."

Down below, the two men reappeared, still leading their horses. Both mounted and rode off.

"I wonder what that was about," Leo said.

"Hopefully I'll learn more tomorrow," Cartwright said. "Go. Visit your wife. I'll keep an eye on these two."

"Thanks." Leo slipped away to where they'd left their horses, his mind full of the past. The smirk on Ursula's face, the bruises on her body from where she'd said Jaego had spanked her. And Jaego, his friend of many years—the man he'd called brother. He hadn't denied his perfidy when Leo confronted him.

Even now, the memories held the power to hurt, to sling him into fury. A red haze formed in his mind, and he had to fight the urge to grab his horse and gallop after Jaego. What the fuck was he doing back in Merrivale?

Leo reached his mount and swung into the saddle. Despite his urge for vengeance, he steered his horse to the manor and Jocelyn.

JOCELYN LINGERED IN HER bed, exhausted, despite a good night of sleep. The indentation on the pillow beside her indicated Leo had joined her at some stage, but she hadn't heard him arrive or depart.

Susan bustled into her chamber bearing a tray of her normal tea and bread and jam. The scent raised Jocelyn's gorge. *Oh, St Bridget.* She was going to be sick. She flung back her covers and leaped off her bed, barely making the chamber pot in time.

"Mrs. Sherbourne?" Susan set the tray aside and hovered like a mother hen. "Mrs. Sherbourne."

Jocelyn caught another whiff of the fresh bread and vomited again. She hovered near the chamber pot and, once she was certain her belly wouldn't revolt, she lifted her head. "Please take the tray away. I'm not feeling well."

Susan's sharp glance dissected her appearance. She gave a curt nod and hurried to carry out Jocelyn's order. "I'll be back in a thrice."

Wearily, Jocelyn straightened and trudged to her bed. She sank onto the edge of the mattress. Something she'd eaten last night hadn't agreed with her system.

Five minutes later, Susan returned. She handed Jocelyn a piece of dry bread. "Try nibbling on this. It should settle your stomach. My mother swore by it."

Jocelyn stared at the bread dubiously. "Are you sure?"

"Quite sure, Mrs. Sherbourne. I suspect you're with child."

Jocelyn's head jerked up, and she stared at her maid in bemusement. "A baby?" She hadn't considered the possibility with all that was going on at the manor.

"Yes, Mrs. Sherbourne." Susan didn't smile. Instead she glanced over at the indentation on the spare pillow, before shifting her attention back to Jocelyn. Although she didn't comment, her disapproval was clear. "You're showing all the signs."

"But I haven't noticed—" Frowning, she thought over the past weeks. She'd felt tired, but this was the first time she'd felt physically ill. Her courses hadn't arrived. She'd put it down to her change in circumstances, worry about her mother, the apprehension and ever-present confusion when she thought of Leo. Hope surged through her now. Excitement. *A baby. Her own child to love and nurture.* "Do you really think I'm with child?"

"You're displaying the same symptoms my older sister experienced earlier this year. Would you like to go back to bed?"

"No." Jocelyn nibbled absently on the piece of bread. "I have too much to do for the festival."

"Do you feel a little better?"

"Yes." Surprisingly she did.

"My sister swore by the dry bread. She'd nibble on a crust

194

every morning before she started her day."

"Thank you." How would Leo take the news? Some of the shine went off her happiness when she thought of her incarcerated husband. Surely he couldn't sneak around for much longer, not when he'd face the court soon and stand trial. She scowled. She hadn't managed to wriggle any details from him, despite her questions. It was most vexing.

She stood cautiously, a hand going to her still flat stomach. She felt almost normal, apart from the suspicion of a child dancing through her mind. She was going to have a baby. A warm glow expanded throughout her body, and she couldn't seem to keep still.

Despite her fidgety twitching, Susan managed to get her dressed, and Jocelyn left her chamber clothed in a lilac gown with matching petticoats in a darker hue. She made her way down the corridor, past an alcove bearing a tall marble urn, the jet-black patina reflecting her face back to her when she paused. Smiling, she continued on her way, her hand cradling her belly.

A loud shriek echoed from the room they used to break their fast. Oh, joy. What had upset her mother now? When a second higher-pitched scream joined the first, she hurried toward the screeches.

She found her mother hovering over Cassie, her face contorted into a horrendous expression. Cassie crouched in a corner, her small mouth open in preparation to release another terrified squeal.

"What is going on?" Jocelyn's stern voice cut the tension, and her mother backed up, the extra distance between them giving Cassie the façade of security.

"Who is this child?" Elizabeth spun around to face Jocelyn. "Who are you?" Her frown intensified. "Where is my daughter? Charlotte? Charlotte! This isn't Charlotte's child. Who is she?"

Cassie let out a squeak, pressing her tiny body deeper into the corner, her eyes large and fearful.

"Mother, take a seat. You're scaring Cassie." Jocelyn glanced at Tilly, before attempting to steer her mother to one of the vacant seats. Elizabeth resisted, wrenching her arm free and whirled around to glower at Cassie. With her dark gown and the untidy wisps of hair escaping her cap, she appeared crazed, and she was certainly acting in the same way. "Perhaps Mother's medicine would calm her," Jocelyn said.

"I don't require medicine." Elizabeth's gaze darted frantically around the room, searching faces. Unhealthy red splotches grew on her cheeks. "If Charlotte isn't available, then where is Georgina? I want Georgina."

But Georgina doesn't want you, Mother. Jocelyn strove for patience. "Georgina is in London. Please, let me get you something to eat."

Finally, her mother moved away from Cassie, and Jocelyn scooped up the small girl, giving her a cuddle. "I'm sorry my mother scared you, sweetheart." Now that Arabella had left, she needed to find someone to take her place. This current arrangement wasn't working, especially with Elizabeth taking exception to Cassie's presence. Maybe Mrs. Green would have a suggestion as to someone suitable.

Cassie's small hands curled around Jocelyn's neck. For once the child accepted comfort from her instead of rejecting Jocelyn. Her mouth wobbled and tears filled her big blue eyes. "She doesn't know my name."

"Yes," Jocelyn said with a trace of sadness. "She forgets mine too."

"Hannah says she's mad. Why is she mad?"

Hannah needed to stop her unguarded speech. "My mother isn't feeling well. It makes her unable to recall some things." Jocelyn made her explanation simple enough for Cassie to understand while attempting to keep her irritation contained.

Although she preferred not to confront Hannah and cause further ill-will, she didn't like the way the woman manipulated her niece. It was time to have a word and request her to desist.

LEO SNEAKED INTO THE manor, dirty and exhausted, after skulking around Hartscombe Castle for most of the evening. He'd like nothing more than a bath but resigned himself to a cold wash. At least he'd confirmed Jaego was staying at the castle. Hannah and Peregrine were playing host to several other friends as well, which made Leo's hopes surge. Maybe an end was in sight. He was tired of spending his days locked in a cell and sneaking around the moors in the middle of the night. He hated having to creep into his own home to visit his wife.

Inside his chamber, some of the tension left him. He pressed his ear to the door and heard the faint murmur of feminine voices. Damn. How long was the maid going to stay? He'd promised Cartwright he wouldn't reveal himself to anyone except Jocelyn.

At least his farm employees were carrying out the instructions he'd given them before Cartwright had arrested him. Most landowners expected their workers to attend to the day-to-day toil on the land. Leo liked to participate. It was a point of pride to know what was happening with each part of the farming process even if he arrived home looking like a laborer. Days of sitting in his cell, unable to do more than pace, put him in a bad temper. He missed the physical labor. He missed freedom.

He listened at the door again and heard nothing. After waiting for another three minutes, he carefully opened the door. A hipbath sat near the doorway, steam still rising from the scented water.

Cautiously he peeked into Jocelyn's chamber. To his relief, he found her alone.

"Jocelyn." He waited until he was sure she'd seen him, not wanting to scare her. Sometimes he thought she was frightened of him, although she hid it well.

"Leo," she said, taking in his disreputable appearance. Her blue eyes rounded. She held her nose with her thumb and finger. "Something smells."

Leo chuckled. "Am I that bad?"

"Worse." She backed up a few steps.

"Is your maid returning?"

"No, I told her to retire for the evening. She spends her half day off looking after her sister and doesn't get much rest. The poor girl was almost asleep on her feet."

Leo started to disrobe, dropping his soiled clothes at his feet. "It would be silly of me to wash with cold water when there is a warm bath available."

Jocelyn inclined her head. "That is why I told Susan not to bother with removing the bath until the morning."

"A wife beyond compare," Leo said.

Naked, Leo could feel the weight of her stare and put a swagger in his step, twitching his arse. On reaching the bath, he glanced back. She wasn't watching him. Some of his good mood shriveled. Shaking his head, he sighed. He was charged with murder. Doubts on her part were understandable.

The bath was a small one and the lukewarm water smelled of flowers, but after days of cold water he sank into the water without complaint. He scrubbed the dirt from his chest and legs, relishing feeling clean and human again instead of like a caged monkey.

"Would you like me to scrub your back?"

"I can't think of anything I'd enjoy more." Her open smile went a long way to ease his concerns and exhaustion. "How was your day?"

"Interesting."

Something in her tone drew his attention. Excitement blazed in her, her lips curved in a secret smile.

"What sort of interesting?"

"Wait until we eat. I ordered a late supper."

"Now I'm curious."

She tapped her nose, before she stepped behind him. She grabbed a cloth, lathered it with soap and started to wash his back, her earlier reticence no longer in evidence.

A groan of pleasure whispered from him. "I should get dirty more often."

"Would you like me to wash your hair? I have a special cleanser my mother makes."

Leo caught the way the good humor drained from her. Ah, her mother had experienced another episode. He sought a topic to take her mind off her mother's declining health. "No one has offered to wash my hair before."

"I hope you enjoy the experience. Tell me about your day," she said. Color stained her cheeks when she realized what she'd asked. "I'm sorry."

"As it happens my day was entertaining. Cartwright locked away Bill Jakeson, the blacksmith until he sobered up. I had to listen to his bad singing and slurs against my character for two hours. Once he fell asleep it was peaceful for ten minutes, then the man started snoring. I hold great sympathy for his wife."

While he talked, she poured water over his head and massaged his head.

"You have magic hands." The firm press of her fingers made him want to groan. His breath caught as her scent surrounded him. The minutes passed, and his eyes closed to better savor her attentions. Finally, she ceased her rubbing and poured more water over his skull, rinsing away the soap.

"All done."

"Thank you." He grasped her hand and pressed a kiss to the delicate skin of her inner wrist, wishing things were different, that shadows didn't slide over her face when she was with him.

"You're welcome."

If Ursula had ever offered to assist him in this manner, he'd have wondered what she wanted in return. Jocelyn aided him because she enjoyed his company. Most of the time. His thoughts led to more sexual ones, the relaxation in his muscles giving way to lust. "How hungry are you, or have you already eaten?"

"I did eat a little, but I find myself hungry again."

He stood abruptly, the water pouring off his body as he stepped from the bath. Time spent with Jocelyn always made his mind turn to other appetites, ones that had nothing to do with food.

She handed him a towel, which he accepted, giving his body a cursory rub to dry the worst of the moisture clinging to his skin.

"Let me dry your back."

"Not necessary," he said, stalking her.

"What are you doing?" Alarm flickered across her face before most of it smoothed away. A small crease remained between her brows.

He checked himself, coming to a halt on seeing the fear she tried to hide. He forced a rueful smile. "I'm not doing a very good job of seducing you."

"I...sorry. I don't know what I was thinking."

"Would you like me to leave?"

"No! No, of course not."

"Come, let us go and eat." He took care to move slowly, so as not to alarm her, and offered her his arm. He escorted her to her bed, a smile tugging at his lips because he was naked and she wore a thin chemise. "I'm sure we appear very dignified."

She grinned, and he relaxed a fraction.

He seated her on the edge of the bed and stepped away, casting a rueful glance at his erection. Likely, she had no doubts regarding the direction of his thoughts. He picked up a plate bearing a large slice of meat pie. "This will do nicely."

Leo took the plate back to the bed and fed her morsels of food. Under his attentions, she unwound. "Tell me about your day," he said.

"Mother scared Cassie half to death," Jocelyn said. "I need to find someone to look after Cassie. The baker's daughter was recommended to me, but her mother flatly refused to allow her to work at the manor."

"Because of me?"

She avoided his gaze, the action answer enough.

"I'm sorry."

"You said you didn't murder those women, and I believe you."

"Thank you." Leo set the plate aside. "I'm going to kiss you now. I'm telling you so I don't frighten you again."

"Why don't I kiss you? That way you can be sure it's what I want."

Leo couldn't resist pressing a kiss to the tip of her freckled nose. "That sounds like a good idea to me."

The brush of her lips against his was almost innocent, yet it propelled hunger through him. His hands tightened on her shoulders, and he gently pushed her down on the mattress. This time he kissed her, taking tiny bites from her mouth, her neck and the creamy curves of her upper breasts. Moving down her body, he kissed the fragrant skin of one inner thigh, tracing his tongue over a small cluster of freckles. "What is that scent?" He breathed deeply, catching the note of lavender and something else. Citrus, maybe?

"Lavender, orange and a hint of cloves."

"I like it, especially on you." His lips moved closer to her feminine flesh. Her hips jerked. He smiled against her skin, breathing in her scent. Already her folds glistened, beckoning him to taste. As always, he was torn between haste and a leisurely loving. This time speed won out. He buried his tongue in her hot center, feathered his thumb over her nub, delicately teasing while he consumed her. Each moan and twitch he drew from her pushed him harder. He coaxed out another groan and licked her swollen flesh.

"Leo," she whispered, her hands tugging his wet hair in a silent urge to make her come. "Please."

Carefully, he closed his mouth around her and sucked. She let out a low moan, her body arching upward and into him. He felt the tiny pulses against his tongue, and before she'd fully relaxed into the mattress, Leo moved and guided his cock into her. He pushed deep and savored her flesh caressing his length. Damn, he liked this part of their marriage. He plunged into her time and again while she held him, murmuring encouragement. A shudder passed through her, and her silken sheath tightened around him. Pleasure grew to a hot, almost painful ache. He kissed her roughly and powered into her with a decisive shove. His muscles locked and he spilled his seed, groaning at the soft, yielding whispers against his ear. For a time, he lost himself in the sensual haze, floating on a cloud of satisfaction.

Finally, he shifted his weight, separating their bodies. He grinned at her. "That was much better than sleeping in my cell."

"How long is Captain Cartwright intending to keep you locked up?"

"Not for much longer, I hope."

"I see." She sat up. "Would you like something else to eat?"

"You don't usually eat in your room." Frowning, he pondered her reply as he stood to grab some bread and meat. What did she see? He had a feeling it wasn't his innocence.

"It's a special occasion."

Something in her voice grabbed his attention, warmed him through. "Why?"

"It's not every day a woman learns she's going to have a child."

Leo stared, her words not registering at first. He replayed them in his head. "What did you say?"

"I'm expecting our child." She grinned at him, clearly delighted. "Are you pleased?"

Joy burst through his chest, broadened his smile. "God, yes!" Leo crossed to her side with three giant steps. He plucked her off the bed to hug her tight. "Are you happy?"

"Oh, yes. I couldn't be happier. I never thought...I'm very happy, Leo."

CHAPTER 13

LEO COULDN'T STOP SMILING the next morning. Not even another day spent with the blacksmith who'd gone on another drunken binge when he'd learned his wife had run off with a travelling salesman could dim his mood. A child. Now if only he and Cartwright could catch the murderer.

"Leo!"

He turned at the hail, his good humor faltering when Hannah entered, Cartwright locking the door after her.

She gave a delicate sniff, her nostrils flaring. He didn't blame her—the drunken blacksmith smelled of vomit and stale alcohol. The stench clawed the back of his throat every time he returned to the cell.

"How are you?" She set down the basket she carried and looked both left and right. Neither of the battered chairs passed her scrutiny. Her nose wrinkled and she remained standing.

The blacksmith plunged into another chorus of his song about a limber barmaid named Nelly.

Hannah scowled. "How can you stand this?"

"I have no choice. It's good of you to visit."

"I notice your wife doesn't."

Leo didn't bother to reply. In truth he was glad Jocelyn kept her distance. He didn't want his wife to see him here.

"You're up early." He didn't want to deal with Hannah. Her flirtations were uncomfortable, and she was much like her sister, thinking only of herself, which made her regular visits out of character.

She shrugged. "We have visitors down from London. With their drunken revels I can scarcely hear myself think. I needed a ride to clear my head."

"Ah, something to distract me. Tell me about your visitors. Anything to take my mind from my present situation." Leo spoke loudly so Hannah could hear him above the blacksmith.

The man halted his singing mid-verse, his head dipping toward his homespun linen shirt. His eyes closed and he snorted, a string of drool dribbling from the corner of his mouth.

Leo's voice rang out above the partial snores. "It's better when he's asleep."

"Disgusting! It's no wonder that man's wife ran off."

"Is it certain she left with a man?"

"Vicar Allenby saw her leave on a cart packed with possessions. The gossips say the vicar tried to talk her out of leaving. Think positively, Leo. At least no one can blame you should they find her body on the moor."

Leo snorted, aiming a careful smile in her direction. "Divert me."

Hannah dimpled at him. "I could do this task better if we were alone in a romantic setting."

"I'm married," Leo snapped, cursing inwardly at her grimace. Damn, farming sheep was easier than questioning people about possible crimes.

Hannah rallied. "Pooh, she's a poor wife to you. I hear she's going mad like her mother."

Anger gripped Leo. His fists tightened at his sides, but he ruthlessly suppressed his natural inclination to snap at her again. "Who told you that?"

"I heard she's seeing faces in windows and wandering from the house in the middle of the night. Everyone knows it's dangerous to navigate the moor. Only an imbecile would attempt Dartmoor at night."

"I'm sure these are merely rumors." Leo wanted to say more. Jocelyn was no more mad than he was a murderer.

She shrugged. "Rumors always bear an element of truth."

Her smug laughter poked his temper. He fought it, not wanting to upset Hannah when he needed her to speak of their visitors. "That is true. Come, I don't wish to discuss my wife." He thought of the way Jocelyn had curled in his arms the previous night. She didn't exhibit any of her mother's symptoms, and he refused to listen to Hannah's viperous tongue.

"Several of the usual crowd have come down from London. Peregrine's friends mostly." A malicious gleam sparkled in her eyes, and Leo tensed as he wondered the cause. "A few people I hadn't met before. Peregrine is taking them grouse shooting later today. Sir James is coming for dinner tonight and bringing his house guests with him. I believe we shall be quite a party. I'm sorry you can't attend." She glanced over her shoulder and leaned closer. "We could break you out of jail."

The blacksmith snored on, undisturbed by their conversation.

"If I escape it will look as if I'm guilty."

"My sister was no angel. I could understand someone murdering her," Hannah said lightly.

"Be that as it may, I didn't kill your sister."

Hannah waved a gloved hand in dismissal. "Of course you

didn't, Leo. Peregrine and I still talk to you. My parents don't speak badly of you. We know Ursula was difficult."

An understatement in Leo's opinion. "You and your family are in the minority."

Despite Hannah's many annoying qualities, she'd never snubbed him, even though the death of her sister must have come as a shock.

Cartwright entered the jail, his keys rattling with each step. He unlocked the door and nudged the blacksmith in the ribs with his mud-splattered boot. "Oy, time for you to go home."

"Can I leave too?" Leo asked.

Cartwright chuckled. "You could try."

"I'd better get back to our guests," Hannah said. "I asked Cook to pack some treats for you."

"I'll search the contents first," Cartwright said in a stiff voice, playing the part of jailer to the hilt. He guided the blacksmith to the unlocked door. "You first, Miss Richards."

Leo listened to the murmur of voices, the loud protests of the blacksmith and the jangle of a horse's harness. A cart rolled away with a squeak of wheels. Seconds later the gallop of hooves indicated Hannah's usual reckless departure.

Cartwright returned five minutes later.

"Did you learn anything?"

Cartwright shook his grizzled head. "Nothing of import. They have visitors, but I couldn't get close enough to identify them."

"Hannah said they're friends from London. They're going grouse shooting later this afternoon, so you might get luckier if you follow them. Sir James is going to the castle with his guests this evening."

A bark of rusty laughter emerged from Cartwright. "You've learned more than me, despite being locked up."

"Do you think they'll visit the abbey tonight?"

"We saw two men there last night, after seeing no one for weeks."

Leo nodded. "Will we watch again tonight?"

"Yes."

"Are you sure the blacksmith's wife left the town of her own free will?"

"Aye, as sure as I can be."

Leo paced to the small, barred window and stood on tiptoe to peer outside. "I find it hard to believe Jaego is part of this. I don't like the man, but he's not capable of murder."

"People change. Some are masters at concealment. In this job I see the worst of people. Nothing surprises me anymore."

THE WEEK PASSED IN a pleasant fashion. Jocelyn enjoyed Leo's attentions, although he appeared distracted at times. Understandable since the next quarter session took place soon. A tremor darted down her spine. What would she do if Leo was charged with murder? While there was no proof, everyone believed he'd committed the crime. Even she wasn't sure some days and wondered if she lacked sound judgment.

While Leo hadn't told her he loved her, it was obvious he enjoyed her company. The babe clearly pleased him. Her hand crept down to cradle the swell of her abdomen. The mornings of sickness were nothing. Soon she would have a child of her own—another child. Cassie was with Cook, learning the intricacies of making gingerbread. For some reason Hannah and Peregrine hadn't visited this week, and Cassie's improved behavior meant a more harmonious home.

Jocelyn wandered past the rose gardens, enjoying the sunshine after an unexpected day of rain. The sweet perfume of the roses fought with the musty scent rising from the branches the gardeners had collected in preparation for a bonfire.

On a whim, she turned toward the maze. After swearing her to secrecy, Leo had told her the trick of the maze, and now she was eager to test her skill.

The jumble of twists and turns and dead ends became easy to navigate if one knew the secret pattern. She stepped forward with confidence, passing through the opening. She strolled along the gravel path, counting the turns. When she paused, the towering green hedges, straight as soldiers on parade, filled her vision. From the middle of the maze, the *clip-clip* of shears and the low murmur of the under-gardeners carried as they trimmed the hedges into submission.

Jocelyn continued until she'd almost reached the center. Not wishing to disturb the gardeners, she retraced her steps and exited the maze without difficulty.

The gardens burst with color and precise plantings, a real credit to the gardeners. Every single bush and hedge were trimmed to perfection for the festivities in two weeks. Mrs. Allenby was fussing, her frowns indicating panic, but Jocelyn felt confident with their plans. The games for the children were organized, the games to entertain the adults were almost finalized, and the menu for the Harvest feast was complete. They'd planned for every contingency. As long as the weather cooperated, everyone should enjoy the event. Mrs. Allenby had little reason to worry.

A ladybird landed on her hand, and Jocelyn watched the spotted insect before gently relocating it onto a leafy plant. She wandered past a lavender bush, running her hand over the flowers to release their pungent scent. Slowly, she made her way back to the house.

"Jocelyn, there you are. I've been searching for you everywhere." Hannah aimed her displeasure at Jocelyn, the whip she was holding *tap-tap-tapping* against her black skirts.

"Hannah, you should have called for me. I told the servants I intended to walk in the garden. Did you want to visit with Cassie? She's in the kitchen with Cook. If you want to take her riding, you'll have to tear her away. Gingerbread is her favorite."

"No, I don't wish to see Cassie. She's an ungrateful brat."

Jocelyn blinked at Hannah's sharp tone. Cassie became sulky at times, but her behavior had improved recently, and she'd finally accepted Jocelyn's presence. "If Cassie is acting badly, please let me know."

"All she wants to do is play with her dolls and dress and redress them countless times," Hannah muttered.

Jocelyn laughed. "No doubt she'll be back to ponies next week."

"I don't know if I want to look after her."

"Do you mean you don't wish to visit her any longer?"

Hannah lifted her shoulder in an irritable shrug. "I mean that Peregrine and I don't know if we want her living with us when you have your baby. She's disruptive."

Jocelyn stared at Hannah in shock. How did she know about the baby? "Why would you—nothing will change. Cassie is our daughter. Of course she'll live with us." As if they'd ever consider letting Hannah have sole charge of Cassie.

"But you are having a baby?"

"Yes, but...how did you know?"

"Servants talk. There are rumors going around the village."

Alarm surfaced in Jocelyn. Surely they didn't know about Leo's frequent absences from jail. He took such care to return before anyone noted his absence. "What rumors?" Jocelyn asked faintly.

"Why, it's very obvious to anyone who can count that this baby is not Leo's. You're having an affair."

"That's not true!" A sick sensation forced its way up her

throat. *St. Bridget's nose*. She couldn't deny the rumors without placing Leo in danger. She swallowed, frantically searching for a way out of the moor-like bog that was her life.

"Say what you like. It's difficult to ignore the truth when it stares one in the face. How are the plans for the festival?" Hannah changed the subject abruptly.

"Ah, very well, thank you." The shift left her feeling like a passenger on a runaway carriage. Jocelyn groped to order her thoughts. "Um, the vicar and his wife are pleased with the progress."

"Interfering old busybody." Hannah plucked haphazardly at lavender heads and tossed them on the ground. "She spoils anything remotely connected with fun. I wanted to invite a friend."

According to the vicar, the troublemakers were the strangers who'd attended the last festival, but there was no reason why Hannah and Peregrine couldn't invite a couple of friends. "Is there someone special you'd like to invite?"

Jocelyn walked farther down the path, intending to head back to the house. At the rate Hannah was going the plants would end up bare, stripped of flowers and foliage.

The crunch of rapid footsteps on the gravel path indicated Hannah was following her. Once they reached the end of the path, Jocelyn slowed for Hannah to catch up.

"There is someone I would like to invite," Hannah said. "Someone special."

"You're welcome to bring him with you. Is there someone Peregrine would like to escort to the fair?"

Hannah smiled suddenly, lighting up her entire face. She looked so angelic that Jocelyn blinked under her radiance. "Yes, I believe there is."

"That's settled then," Jocelyn said. "I'll add two more people to my list."

"Thank you. I might visit Cassie after all, if that is all right with you."

Despite Hannah charging her with an adulterous affair, Jocelyn's lips twitched before she regained control of herself. Hannah and Cassie were clearly related with their quick changes of mood. "You're her aunt, and you're welcome to visit at any time."

An agitated screech filled the air as they neared the manor.

Jocelyn turned to Hannah. "I assume you know the way to the kitchen?"

"Of course."

"I'll say goodbye then." What had upset her mother this time? Some days Jocelyn wanted to scream herself. She ran up the steps and turned toward the parlor. Another furious shriek told her she was heading in the right direction. Her chest ached at the sudden exertion, and she slowed to regain her breath. When she rounded the corner, she came to an appalled halt in the doorway.

"Mother!"

Elizabeth paid no attention as she held Tilly at bay with a pair of shears. Her mother wielded them with expertise, intent to wound written on her distraught face.

"What is going on here? Explain yourself instantly." Jocelyn forced the words out, acting the stern disciplinarian because that was the only method to which her mother responded. "Why are you threatening Tilly?"

"She stole my sewing basket," her mother cried, not lowering the shears. "She wouldn't give it back."

Another of her mother's strange fancies. Tilly would cut off her hand rather than steal. Her father had hanged for stealing, and Tilly had sworn she'd never follow in his footsteps.

"Elizabeth dropped her basket. The contents spilled over the floor. I merely picked them up and replaced them," Tilly said, her voice as stiff as her posture.

"Mother, put the shears down. You'll take out someone's eye waving them around like that."

After a fraught few seconds, her mother lowered them, and the tension drained from her thin shoulders. Her thin brows arched as she stared down her nose at Jocelyn. "I don't know who you are, but I'm not your mother. Where's Georgina?"

"She's in London," Jocelyn said for about the fifth time that day. She pushed away the ache in her chest and focused on Tilly. "Are you hurt?"

"Elizabeth gave me a bad fright, that's all."

"You look exhausted. Why don't you have a rest? I'll watch her for a couple of hours."

"No, I'll cope. You need to take care of yourself with a babe on the way."

Her mother blinked. She glanced down blankly, frowning at the shears in her hand. "I need to finish my sewing. The little girl asked me to make a dress for her doll." She bustled over to a chair and calmly picked up her task as if nothing had happened.

"She's deteriorating," Jocelyn said. "I hate the idea of keeping her confined, but I can't have her attacking people."

"You mustn't blame yourself. None of this is your fault," Tilly said, reaching out to pat Jocelyn's hand.

Jocelyn knew that, but what would happen if Leo refused to protect her mother any longer? She could hardly blame him wanting her mother gone from Merrivale, given her recent behavior.

Footsteps approached, and Hannah appeared in the doorway.

"Cassie is finished her baking. Can I take her to the castle for a ride? I'll bring her back later this afternoon."

Despite Hannah's moodiness and periods of rudeness, she appeared to care for Cassie. There was no reason to deny the request. "Of course."

"You!" Elizabeth tossed her sewing aside and sprang to

her feet. Moving with uncharacteristic speed, she rushed at Hannah, her fingers outstretched like talons, face contorted in a mask of hatred.

Shocked at the ferociousness of the attack, Jocelyn froze, taking precious seconds to gather her wits. "Mother!"

"Elizabeth!" Tilly shouted.

"You. It was you. Get out. Get out!" Elizabeth gouged Hannah's cheek before Hannah could strike in self-defense.

"Mother!"

Elizabeth struggled, batting away restraining hands. She shrieked—an eerie cry that raised the hairs at the back of Jocelyn's neck—and lashed out at Hannah again. "Quick, Tilly. Seize her arm. I'll grab her other."

"Summon help first," Tilly ordered.

Of course. Tilly was right. Jocelyn hurried to the bell and rang it stridently. Thankfully, Woodley arrived seconds later. Between him and Tilly, they dragged her mother away from Hannah.

"Let me kill her!" Elizabeth screamed, wriggling and kicking at Woodley and Tilly. Thankfully, they kept her restrained.

"You'd better lock her in her room," Jocelyn said in a worried voice. "I'll take care of Hannah."

"She belongs in Bedlam," Hannah spat, probing the wound on her cheek with her fingers. "I didn't even look sideways at her. She attacked without provocation."

Hannah had every right to her fury. Jocelyn winced on seeing the blood oozing from the scratches her mother had inflicted. She swallowed, stunned by the suddenness of the attack and concerned for Hannah and her mother.

"Let me treat your face." Jocelyn crossed the room to summon a servant. On her return to Hannah's side, she urged her to a seat and inspected the wound. Jocelyn pressed a clean handkerchief against the scratch in an attempt to halt the bleeding. Scratches were nasty and often became infected. *St. Bridget's nose!* What had come over her mother? Hannah had done nothing to inflame the situation. She hadn't acted rude and didn't deserve the treatment her mother had meted out.

After holding the handkerchief to Hannah's face, Jocelyn lifted it to inspect the damage. She grimaced.

"Is it that bad?"

"I'm afraid so," Jocelyn admitted, heartsick. "I'm sorry. I don't understand why my mother attacked you."

"She should be locked up."

At this point Jocelyn couldn't dispute the fact.

A maid arrived, and Jocelyn issued instructions. Soon the maid returned with the requisite supplies and a bowl of warm water. Jocelyn set about cleaning the wound, her mind replaying the moment of the attack. No, she didn't understand. Her mother had been entirely at fault, her behavior like an unpredictable beast. And if she could attack both Tilly and Hannah, what would happen if her mother took a sudden dislike to Cassie?

With the bleeding slowing, it was easy to see the tracks of gouged flesh. It would take time to heal. Jocelyn hoped it wouldn't leave a scar. She'd never forgive herself.

"I have ointment I've used with great success. It keeps infection at bay and speeds healing." As she spoke, Jocelyn carefully rubbed the herbal scented salve into the wound.

"Will it scar?" Hannah asked.

Jocelyn bit her lip. "I don't know. I'm so sorry."

"What if she'd attacked Cassie?" Hannah demanded.

"I'm sorry," Jocelyn repeated. "I'll make sure it doesn't happen again."

"How?"

"I..." Jocelyn trailed off because saying more would mean admitting the truth. Her mother was out of control, and she needed to be locked away for everyone's safety.

"JOCELYN, I UNDERSTAND YOU'RE reluctant to secure Elizabeth, but what if she hurts someone else? One of the servants or Cassie?" Leo's arms tightened around her in the darkness of her chamber. The warmth emanating from him went some way to pierce the chill filling her body. "What if she hurts you?"

Jocelyn scowled against his shoulder. Knowing he spoke the truth didn't make it any more palatable. "She doesn't recognize me any longer."

"That must hurt after the sacrifices you've made for her."

Her eyes stung, and she blinked to clear them. "I wouldn't do anything different."

Leo pressed a kiss to the top of her head, his understanding and the lack of accusation helping her to think more clearly. He was right.

"I want one of the footmen present when you spend time with your mother."

"But strangers seem to set her off. She becomes even more disorientated."

"I won't compromise on your safety." His tone told her he meant every word. "The footman won't need to enter the room. He can wait outside. Frank would be a good choice. He's a sensible lad and is big for his age. Speak to him tomorrow."

"Very well." Jocelyn didn't think her mother would hurt her, but she'd blame herself if Elizabeth injured Tilly or Cassie.

True to her word, she spoke with Frank the next morning, warned him of her mother's behavior and took him to meet Elizabeth. She'd decided to spin her mother a tale, but the falsehoods weren't required in the end. Her mother took a liking to Frank, which meant he could sit inside the room and keep a close eye on proceedings.

Preparations for the festival continued. Jocelyn and Cassie walked in the garden and watched the gardeners haul huge logs to fuel a bonfire. One of the under-gardeners clipped the grass on a flat field near the river in readiness for running races.

"What sort of games will we play?" Cassie skipped beside Jocelyn, her inquisitive gaze darting this way and that while she took in the different activities.

"We'll have races. There will be a treasure hunt and people can explore the maze."

"I like the maze. Father took me inside. It's dark in there." She shivered theatrically. "Hannah says there are ghosts."

"I suspect it can be scary if you get lost and take a wrong turning," Jocelyn said. "But I don't think Hannah is right about the ghosts."

"Is the festival tomorrow?"

"No, not tomorrow. Ten more days. One day for each of your fingers and thumbs." Jocelyn held up her hands to demonstrate.

"Hannah is bringing a friend. She told me."

"Yes, she is." Jocelyn couldn't contain her flinch. Hannah's face looked terrible, the scratches swollen and angry. Jocelyn and Cassie had visited the castle earlier in the day to deliver more salve. She bit her lip as she recalled the wound marring Hannah's smooth cheek. She hoped Hannah's friend wasn't put off by the disfigurement.

A yawn struck Jocelyn without warning. "Oh, dear. I think I need a nap."

"I'm too old for naps," Cassie said.

"A person is never too old for naps," a masculine voice said.

Jocelyn let out an *eep* of shock, grabbed Cassie, and placed the child behind her as she whirled to face the newcomer.

"Peregrine," she said weakly when she recognized the man standing on the path.

"Sorry to startle you. I wanted to see how your mother is today."

He hoisted Cassie on his shoulders, laughing at his niece's cry of delight.

"I can see the whole sky," Cassie said. "And the trees."

"Can you see the maze? And the fruit trees in the orchard?" Peregrine asked.

Jocelyn forced a smile and listened to their chatter. Gut instinct said Peregrine hadn't just come for a visit.

"Will you go back to London? After Leo..." He trailed off uncomfortably, but Jocelyn had no difficulty understanding him.

"Leo says he's innocent."

"Then why is he locked up?" Peregrine demanded. "Maybe it's because he's guilty."

CHAPTER 14

JOCELYN TURNED OVER ON her other side, attempting to find a more comfortable position. She'd waited for hours, expecting Leo to arrive. He hadn't come, leaving her alone with her worries, her confusion. Fatigue weighted her eyelids. She had to try to sleep—for the sake of the babe.

At some stage she must have dozed off. Loud hammering on her chamber door woke her. She had no idea of the hour since the room still lay in darkness, the heavy curtains pulled to shut out the night.

"What is it?" she called, pushing to an upright position.

Tilly burst into her chamber. She gasped for breath before blurting. "She's dead. I found her in her bed, her body as cold as ice."

"Who is dead?"

"Elizabeth."

"Mother? But how?" Jocelyn flung back the covers and grabbed her robe. A surge of nausea struck, and she held a hand to her stomach, gulping several times. Once she was certain she wouldn't vomit, she hurried into the passage still fastening her robe.

Tilly trotted a few steps behind her, talking the entire time. "Elizabeth was fine when I left her last night. Happy even. She showed no sign of illness."

The door was ajar when they entered, the room chilly with a stiff breeze pouring through an open window.

"Was the window open when you left Mother last night?"

"Why, I never noticed the open window. I was that shocked at seeing Elizabeth. I came to get you straightaway. I closed the window myself before I left her for the night. I locked the door as usual."

"And the key?" Jocelyn slowed as she approached the bed. Her mother looked as if she were in one of her rages, face contorted, her mouth twisted into a grimace. With a trembling hand, Jocelyn checked her mother's pulse.

"She doesn't look peaceful," Tilly said.

"No, she didn't die easily." This raised all sorts of questions. Jocelyn tugged her mother's night gown away where it bunched around her neck.

At her side, Tilly gasped. They stared at each other wordlessly before turning back to view the livid marks around her mother's throat.

"We'd better summon the constable," Jocelyn said finally.

"Aye, 'tis murder right enough," Tilly said in a grim voice. "And the sleeping draft I gave her last night would've made the murderer's job easy."

Jocelyn focused on her mother's hand, part of her ashamed because her initial reaction had been relief. No one deserved this sort of death.

"I'd better speak to Woodley and question the staff. Maybe one of them heard or noticed something," she said.

"Woodley and I didn't hear a thing and our quarters are nearby."

Jocelyn nodded but didn't speak her mind. The truth was Tilly would have slept through a violent thunderstorm without stirring. Her mother had interrupted several nights recently with her ceaseless screaming. The constant disturbances had made Jocelyn consider murder herself. It was the reason they'd upped the dose of sleeping draft—so all everyone received a good night of rest.

Captain Cartwright arrived, and the morning passed in a whirlwind of questions and investigation of the scene. He spoke to everyone from the scullery maid to Woodley and Mrs. Green, allowing Jocelyn to sit in on the interviews. Not one of them had seen or heard anything out of the ordinary.

"At least Leo can't be blamed," Jocelyn said.

When the constable hesitated, she shot him a sharp look.

"Leo was at the manor last night," the man said.

"No."

"We were together for part of the night until I told him he could visit you."

They stared at each other, Jocelyn frightened to ask questions. Finally, she croaked, "I didn't see him last night." A chill marched down her spine, and she wrapped her arms around herself in an effort to get warm. "Do you think Leo…" She closed her eyes, the lump in her throat preventing further speech.

"I don't know what to think," Cartwright said. "I haven't discussed the matter with Leo yet."

Jocelyn shivered, still cold. "He doesn't know?"

"I thought it was best if I discovered the lay of the land here. I told him I needed to attend to parish business."

"No one heard anything unusual. The door was locked. My mother didn't have a chance." Tears prickled at her eyes again. Why would someone kill a defenseless woman?

"Tell me again," Cartwright said, his manner intense,

reminding her of a hound dog scenting a fox. "Who had keys to Elizabeth's room?"

"Tilly has a key and I have one. Tilly said she unlocked the door this morning, which leaves the window as the only possible point of entry. It was wide open."

"Could someone have taken one of the keys?"

Jocelyn shook her head. "I don't see how."

"I'll go through the room again. But first, you'd better show me which window was open. Maybe we can discern something that way."

"Of course."

"Mrs. Sherbourne?"

Jocelyn halted and turned to face the constable. "Yes?"

"Are you sure you're up to this? I understand you're with child."

"It's better for me to keep busy. I...I don't like to think about how my mother died." A tear trickled down her cheek, and she had to concentrate on her shoes because she couldn't hide her distress. "Do you know what my first reaction was on seeing my mother? It was relief. I was glad because all I did recently was worry about how I was going to look after her. She didn't recognize me any longer. I...I worried about the future and about Leo sending us both away."

"I've come to know your husband well, Mrs. Sherbourne. Despite what everyone thinks, he's a good man." Captain Cartwright patted her awkwardly on the shoulder. "I don't believe he'd send you away."

After two deep breaths, she gathered her composure. With a choppy gesture of her hand, she indicated he should follow her. "This way. I'll show you the window." She escorted the constable to the wing her mother and Tilly used. Her mother's room was empty now, the vacant bed stoking her guilt higher. She was a heartless daughter. *By St. Bridget!* Who was grateful for the death of a parent? "It was the window overlooking the gardens. Tilly is positive she shut the window before she retired for the evening. My mother often complained of the cold, so I doubt she opened the window."

"Her companion indicated she'd given her a sleeping draft." Captain Cartwright opened the window and leaned out, surveying the surroundings. "I wonder," he mused out loud. "The creeper is strong enough to support the weight of a person." He drew his head back inside the room. "Can you direct me to the garden? I wish to inspect the window from below."

Captain Cartwright escorted her down the stairs and out the front door. They walked around the house, the loose gravel crunching beneath their footwear. The scent of flowers hit her the instant they turned the corner and entered the garden. Her stomach clenched, a hint of queasiness creeping into her consciousness. She swallowed rapidly and started breathing through her mouth.

Her footsteps hastened, and she was thankful once they'd passed the strongly perfumed carnations.

"This is the window. Hmm, no footprints, but it hasn't rained for some time."

"There's a broken branch up there." Jocelyn pointed out the withering branch of the creeper. The wiry creeper clung to the brick of the manor like a living green ladder. "Do you think it would bear the weight of an adult?"

"Only one way to find out."

Before she could protest, Captain Cartwright shrugged out of his jacket and tossed it on the ground. He turned to the vine and grasped a section, testing it for strength. It made a cracking sound but held when he exerted his might.

"As I suspected," the constable said. "It's holding."

"Be careful." Jocelyn tried not to sound too anxious. He'd fall heavily if the vine tore from the brickwork.

Cautiously the constable made his way up the wall toward the window. Halfway up, he halted. "I'm going to come back down. I think I've proved it would be easy enough for a determined individual to climb up and enter the manor via this method."

Jocelyn nodded mutely.

Minutes later, he stood at her side. "I'm certain this was the method of entry, Mrs. Sherbourne."

"You've proved it's possible to climb up, yes. But how did they obtain access? Tilly is adamant she closed each window before she left Mother."

"Perhaps one of the locks is faulty." The constable cocked his head, as if considering the mystery. "It's even possible your mother opened the window for some reason."

Jocelyn nodded, even though she held doubts. Her mother's body was cold, which meant the death happened hours ago. She would've remained drowsy from the sleeping draught for some time. Jocelyn puzzled at the known information, twisting it this way and that, trying to make it fit before giving up. Her mother's behavior had grown so unpredictable. Until this week she'd never suspected her mother would physically attack anyone.

"Do you require me for anything else? I need to write to my sisters. They'll want to learn of the news." Her sisters would likely dance on her mother's grave in celebration—if ever they deigned to make an appearance.

Cartwright didn't like to leave her alone. A crusty bachelor, he didn't know how to help her. Mrs. Sherbourne's face was snow-white, her freckles standing out in stark relief, and she wavered on her feet. His arm snapped out. He hesitated then curled it around her waist to keep her upright.

"Send word to your sisters later. A few hours won't make much difference."

"I suppose you're right. I...I am tired."

Cartwright escorted her to the parlor and gently guided her into the paneled room. "Have you eaten today?" He helped her sit on a Queen Anne chair near the window.

"No."

"You should eat, Mrs. Sherbourne." Glad of a course of action, Cartwright rang for a maid and issued concise instructions once she arrived. The maid scurried away to carry out his orders. "I need to leave to take care of other matters."

"You'll let me know if you learn anything further."

"Of course." Cartwright backed from the parlor, his heart heavy. Leo hadn't been with him the entire night. Jocelyn said she hadn't seen her husband since the previous day, so where the hell had Leo gone last night after they'd parted ways at the abbey?

"There's a problem," Cartwright said the minute he sighted Leo. During the ride back to his residence, his thoughts had run wild. No matter which way he looked at the situation, the bodies were piling up. His own stepsister had given Leo an alibi for the time of his wife's murder, but the others...

Leo walked over to the door, staring at Cartwright. Something in him shriveled on seeing the expression of the constable's face. "What is it? What's happened?"

"Elizabeth Townsend is dead. Someone strangled her last night."

"How? What happened? Jocelyn?" Leo asked hoarsely.

"It appears someone climbed up the side of the building and gained access via a window."

"Hell. Jocelyn?"

"Your wife is distressed but safe. Where were you last night?"

Leo's mouth twisted. "Ah, you've discovered I wasn't with

Jocelyn."

"Tell me where you were."

"I went to Duxton and skulked around Sir James's gardens. His visitors are still in residence."

Cartwright's shoulders lost their tense set. "Who did you see?"

"Sir James was at home. He has three male guests. He also had a carriage load of women arrive for entertainment."

"They didn't go to the abbey. I wonder why. Sir James told me the men were there for hunting and fishing. He told me their names without me prompting him." Cartwright pulled out a notebook and flicked through the dog-eared pages. "Harry Weatherall, Adam Beacham and Jack Boynton." He looked up. "Do you know any of them?"

"Boynton? Which one was he?"

"Tall. He wears a wig. Red face. A bit on the portly side."

Leo frowned. "There's a Boynton in Jocelyn's past. She thought she saw him in Tavistock. She's frightened of him."

"Why? You think it's the same one?" A scowl creased Cartwright's brow, and Leo could see his brain ticking through the relevant information. A woman of good birth would never come into contact with a brute like Boynton—not unless she married him. After a while Cartwright asked, "Did any of the men leave Duxton?"

"No one left while I was there. I need to talk to Jocelyn. Make sure she's all right."

"Tonight," Cartwright said. "All the players are in position, and we need to keep an eye on everyone. I need your help. Besides, I want to know where you are at all times. It's starting to look as if someone is trying to frame you, although no one should blame you for Mrs. Townsend's death."

"I should be with Jocelyn. I can't protect her if I'm in custody." An unwelcome thought popped into his mind. Was

Elizabeth's murder something to do with him? Someone might have known he'd rescued Ella when he'd told everyone he'd found her wandering his land. He'd been careful, but there was always a chance someone other than Cartwright knew the truth. "I need to be with Jocelyn."

"I'm sorry. We can't even risk a note in case the wrong person intercepts it."

Leo gave a curt nod. "If anything happens to Jocelyn I—"

"Nothing will happen to Jocelyn as long as she doesn't wander off on her own."

On edge for the rest of the day, Leo couldn't relax until he saw his wife. After spending long hours reconnoitering with Cartwright, he finally headed to the manor and sneaked inside. Relief assailed him once he spied her tucked up in bed. He padded farther into her chamber.

"Jocelyn," he whispered, not wanting to take her by surprise.

She stirred immediately, sitting up in bed. "Leo?" Her voice trembled.

"I heard about Elizabeth. Are you all right?"

"It's my fault." Her voice broke, and he heard a tiny whimper of pain.

He was at her side in an instant. He tugged her into his arms, and she started crying in earnest while he ran his hand up and down her back. Her floral scent surrounded him, and he luxuriated in her sweet smell after the musty, rough cell. He recalled Cartwright's words about someone trying to frame him. That, he could understand, if he was still free, but Elizabeth's murder didn't make sense.

He kept stroking her back, mind busy, seeking answers to the puzzle.

When she stopped crying, he started to talk. "This isn't your fault. You've done everything in your power to protect your mother. You've sacrificed much to secure her wellbeing, so please, don't blame yourself or think you could have done more. I know it's not true."

"But I left her helpless, drugged in a locked room."

"Jocelyn." He spoke sternly this time, his tone indicating he wouldn't stand for her blaming herself. Someone had wanted Elizabeth dead, and they'd successfully committed the crime. "What was Boynton's Christian name?"

"Jack." She stirred in his arms. "Why?"

"He's staying at Duxton with Sir James."

The air hissed through her teeth—a sign of alarm. "You think he murdered Mother?"

"No, he was at Duxton at the time. Is he capable of murder?"

"He's more of a bully. He preys on those weaker who have no means of retaliation. He knows I'm here," she said. "He'll cause trouble and spread rumors about my past, if he hasn't already."

"Jocelyn. Listen to me." Leo grasped her upper arms, forcing her to focus on him. "He can gossip as much as he likes. You're my wife, and nothing he says will make me turn you away. Nothing," he said in a fierce voice.

A shudder rippled through her. "You probably know my father gambled. He lost everything my grandfather built through clever trade, and when Father had nothing left to stake, he tossed me into the pot. My virginity. He lost, of course, and after informing me of my fate, he attended a cock fight. There was a carriage accident, and my father broke his neck."

Weak fool. Leo wished *he* could break the man's neck, but he merely waited for Jocelyn to continue.

"My older sisters distanced themselves. They didn't wish to get caught in the gossip. Father lost our house and land. The man who won them wanted his property and gave us days to leave. We had nowhere to go, so when the man who won me arrived, I did the only thing I could. I negotiated a roof over our heads and a small stipend in return for my services."

A tremor racked her body, and Leo tightened his hold as he acknowledged the courage his wife had shown in a situation that would've broken most. She gave an audible swallow. "He soon lost interest, and I found someone else. Then there was Boynton. He...he forced me to commit acts with other men."

"That is your past," Leo said, running his hand down her back in a soothing motion. "I will *not* turn you away. I know you were utterly loyal to Melburn, and you've stood by me when other women might have faltered. I can hardly offer less in return."

A COLD SQUALL BLEW across Merrivale Manor on the day of the funeral. The clouds sank down to meet the moors, reducing visibility to three or four feet, while rain lashed the landscape into a sodden mess.

Jocelyn stared out the window and prayed the rain would subside long enough to see her mother off. She hadn't heard from her sisters, not that she'd expected them to change their stance, but it would have been decent of them to acknowledge her communication.

Leo strode into the parlor, his boots tapping loudly until he reached the square of Persian carpeting. "It's time."

Captain Cartwright followed him, a silent sentinel, his presence the condition for allowing Leo to attend her mother's funeral.

"I'm ready." She reached for a heavy shawl and wrapped it around her shoulders, covering her simple black gown. Leo took her arm, and she leaned into his warmth while she battled her queasy stomach. Merrivale seemed quiet now that her mother's screams no longer echoed down the halls. Too quiet.

When they exited the manor, a closed carriage pulled up outside.

"I thought we were walking to the plot," Jocelyn said.

"We are since it's not far."

A footman ran out into the rain and opened the door. Hannah and Peregrine exited, both dressed in elegant black.

"We came to offer our support," Hannah said. "Leo, what are—oh. You have a guard."

"Cartwright has given me leave to attend Elizabeth's funeral."

"Well done," Peregrine said.

Touched by their support—a very nice gesture—quick tears formed in Jocelyn's eyes. She sniffed. "Thank you for coming."

The vicar and Mrs. Allenby arrived in the carriage Leo had sent for them, alighting and offering sober greetings. Woodley and Tilly joined the solemn party. The rain continued, and Jocelyn was glad of the umbrellas a second footman handed them. It was a small procession that walked to Leo's family plot.

Jocelyn half listened to the vicar's words. They vied with the guilt still stalking her. Despite her mother's murder, the days since had been peaceful. Without drama. Her sense of relief warred with the feeling it was wrong to think this way. She kept telling herself this was for the best—not the murder, of course, but her mother's passing. Yet her heart cried out for the vibrant person her mother had been before debt and her father's death had changed everything.

A cough startled Jocelyn, her head jerking.

"Jocelyn," Leo murmured, curling his arm around her waist. "Do you want to say something?"

She lifted her head to stare at the expectant vicar. "No. I-I can't."

Leo's grip tightened momentarily before relaxing. "It's all right," he whispered against her hair, his warm breath a startling contrast to the chill in the air. "She knew how much you cared

230

for her."

Jocelyn sighed. If only that were true. Her mother—*no!* She couldn't think these disloyal thoughts now. Her mother had loved her, despite her rejection toward the end.

The ceremony continued, and by the time the vicar finished, ice seeped deep into her bones. She shivered, despite her woolen shawl and Leo's body heat. Finally, they walked away with the sound of clods of earth striking the coffin ringing in her ears. Jocelyn didn't blame the gravediggers for their haste. No one with any sense would wish to linger on a day such as this.

Back at the manor, they peeled off their wet outerwear and entered the parlor to partake of tots of brandy for the men and hot, sweet tea for the ladies.

Jocelyn murmured a few words of thanks to the vicar before crossing the room to join Hannah. "Thank you for coming today." It meant a lot to her when her own sisters hadn't made an effort to attend. She had delayed the funeral for as long as possible, so they couldn't make the length of the journey an excuse. Even Melburn had sent his regards and words of sympathy, but her two sisters remained silent.

Hannah shrugged, as if their presence was nothing, yet her cheek still bore the remnants of her mother's attack. "We're neighbors. This is what neighbors do in Dartmoor. I thought you had family in London. Could none of them attend today?"

"My sisters are both unable to travel at present," Jocelyn said. "One is with child and the other has children who are unwell. They decided it was best not to attend the funeral." More lies to hide her past. At least with her mother gone she could settle into something resembling a normal life—as long as her husband didn't hang for murder.

"I'm sorry to hear that." Hannah frowned. "I understand the constable hasn't discovered the person responsible for her death."

"No." Jocelyn still couldn't understand how someone had gained entry without anyone hearing. "The constable has questioned everyone who was present that night."

Peregrine joined them, wrinkling his nose when he caught the tail-end of the conversation. "Rumors are doing the rounds of the village. People are uneasy because they thought Leo—" He broke off in chagrin.

"I can imagine. I overheard stories about Leo possessing magical powers and being in league with the devil when I visited the bakery two days ago." Jocelyn shook her head as she recalled the discussion, broken off abruptly when the ladies discovered her presence. "I don't understand why people would think Leo responsible when he was locked in jail. It's ludicrous."

"The situation has brought back memories of Ursula's passing," Hannah said abruptly. "People are afraid. It's understandable."

Jocelyn felt the pain in her and patted Hannah's arm in silent comfort. Losing a family member was difficult, no matter what the circumstances.

"People like to gossip," Peregrine agreed. "I'm not sure Hannah and I should even visit you. Merrivale is obviously a dangerous place." His grin flashed, indicating a joke, albeit in poor taste.

"Peregrine," Hannah chided her brother.

Jocelyn didn't find him funny, nor did she think the rumors and gossip amusing. Leo hadn't murdered Elizabeth. She couldn't believe it of him, despite what the constable had implied when he'd questioned her. Leo had no reason to murder her mother, yet she couldn't help the way apprehension nipped at her heels and stalked her dreams during the middle of the night. The truth was she didn't know what she thought, her mind going one way and then the other in indecision.

"I think we should take Cassie back to Hartscombe with us,"

Hannah said.

Jocelyn blinked, registering the words a few seconds later. "Why?"

"She's not safe here," Hannah said. "What is to stop the murderer returning and repeating his crime?"

"That's enough, Hannah," Leo said. "Cassie is perfectly safe here at Merrivale. Jocelyn has increased security. No harm will fall on Cassie."

"I'm only trying to help." Hannah wrinkled her nose. "I would feel happier if you were here to oversee the security, but you're not."

"It's obvious to anyone with a brain that I am not guilty of the crimes," Leo snapped.

An uncomfortable silence fell, and Jocelyn could see the others were divided on the subject.

"Hannah, I want to thank you again for visiting today," Jocelyn said, in an attempt to soothe ruffled feathers. "I appreciate you and Peregrine attending my mother's funeral in this atrocious weather."

"It's nothing," Hannah said, her sullenness falling away. "Peregrine, the rain has eased. Perhaps we should depart for home before our visitors arrive."

"Of course you should be there to greet your guests." Jocelyn forced a smile. "We're running through the final details for the festival next week. Would you like to join us? We can always do with an extra pair of hands."

"You're not cancelling the event?" Peregrine asked.

"No, I felt that everyone has worked hard with the preparations. Mother was looking forward to the celebration, and I decided to continue with our plans."

Hannah nodded slowly, pleasure suffusing her face. "Thank you. I'd like to help."

Jocelyn gave both Hannah and Peregrine a swift hug. They

said their goodbyes and departed in their carriage. It was the start of the exodus, and soon Leo and Jocelyn were alone with Cartwright.

"We need to leave too," Cartwright said.

"Give us a few minutes?" Leo asked. "I'd like to escort Jocelyn to her chamber."

"Five minutes," Cartwright said after surveying his pocket watch. He slipped it in his pocket before walking over to the tray of refreshments. "I'll wait here and sip on another glass of this fine brandy."

Leo offered her his arm. "You need your rest. You look tired."

"I am a little fatigued," she confessed.

They walked up the stairs together. Leo halted at the door of her chamber. "I'm hopeful Cartwright will release me soon. Perhaps we'll visit Melburn for a few days once this is over. Take some time away from Merrivale."

"I'd like that." If Leo wasn't responsible for the murders, then someone else was. She chewed her lip, biting down hard to prevent the escalation of fear, for there was a murderer stalking the inhabitants of Merrivale. The only doubt in everyone's minds was the murderer's identity.

CHAPTER 15

JOCELYN KEPT BUSY WITH festival preparations during the days following the funeral, trying to outrun thoughts of her mother and murder.

From her chamber window, she scanned the sky for unacceptable changes in the weather. This morning the sky appeared a brilliant blue with not a cloud to mar the pristine hue. She let the curtain drop back into place. "It's not raining."

Susan smoothed the covers of the bed and straightened the pillows. "My mother thinks we'll have a fine spell. None of the frogs are croaking in the village pond."

"Are frogs reliable indicators of weather?"

"According to my mother." Susan moved on to the dressing table, tidying away ribbons and earrings with brisk efficiency. "How are you feeling this morning?"

"Good." Amazingly, she didn't feel a hint of nausea, not after eating several pieces of dry bread.

"Keep some bread handy, Mrs. Sherbourne. My sister said the nausea can strike at any time of the day." She pulled back the rest of the curtains, letting in a burst of sunshine. "It looks like today will be a fine one. I'm sure tomorrow will be perfect for the festival."

"That's reassuring. The weather is the one thing Mrs. Allenby can't order to jump to attention."

Susan giggled as she assisted Jocelyn to dress in a black gown. Jocelyn smiled until she recalled her mother. Despite the footmen and Woodley plus several of the gardening staff watching the house at night, she didn't feel easy.

"Your...um...visitor left his gloves. Where should I put them?"

"My visitor? Oh!" Suddenly Jocelyn understood. Susan thought Jocelyn was conducting an affair. Bother, she could hardly tell her maid the truth. "Leave them on the dresser. I'll make sure he gets them back."

"Of course." A prim note entered Susan's voice—a touch of disapproval.

"How is Ella? Do you think she'd like to come back to work?"

Susan's frown deepened. "She wakes screaming in the middle of the night. Small noises make her jump."

"That's understandable. I have no objection to her working shorter hours if she'd like to get out of the cottage."

"I suggested she return to work, but it's the manor." Susan hesitated, swallowing audibly.

"Speak freely, Susan."

"She doesn't want to be reminded of Mr. Sherbourne," Susan said grimly.

Jocelyn bit back her instinctive protest, but there was nothing she could say in Leo's defense—not when everyone remained convinced he was responsible for Ella's abduction.

"I WANT TO ATTEND the Harvest festival," Leo said when Cartwright made his nightly appearance to release him from captivity. He raised his hand when Cartwright started to speak. "No, hear me out. I'm willing to help as much as you require, but I was thinking if the real murderer thought I was out of jail, they might attempt to frame me again."

"That's all very well, but I need to keep watch on the abbey."

"But you're attending the celebrations?"

"Yes. Most people in the village are excited about the festival."

"Why don't I stay at Merrivale tonight after we finish at the abbey and attend with Jocelyn. If you're there too we can watch the locals' reactions as they arrive. See if we can shake any apples off the tree."

Cartwright's bushy brows drew together. "And what excuse am I going to give everyone who asks why I've released a murderer from jail?"

"The clever ones will already have realized I couldn't have killed Elizabeth." Leo's lips twisted. "The ones who don't believe I'm in league with the devil, that is."

A snort erupted from Cartwright. "You weren't in your cell."

"We've had this discussion before. I want to clear my name, damn it. I want to spend time with my wife and get back to my farm work."

Cartwright issued a heavy sigh. "You're right of course. All the evidence against you is circumstantial. The maid isn't a reliable witness—not when she's so traumatized."

"I didn't abduct her," Leo snapped.

Cartwright pursed his lips then nodded agreement. "Keep a low profile until most of the locals have arrived. I'll make sure

I'm early so I can witness individual reactions to your presence."

"Thank you." In a buoyant mood after persuading Cartwright to let him out of the musty cell, he whistled a tune as he followed the constable outside.

They rode by horseback to a shepherd's cottage and left their horses in a pen at the rear until their return. In silence, they walked along the narrow sheep track, which led to their favored vantage point above the abbey. They settled in to wait.

"Have you checked the abbey during the day?"

"There's nothing." Cartwright heaved a sigh. "They're careful. I'll give them that."

"But you believe me," Leo persisted.

"I wouldn't be out in the middle of the night at all hours if I didn't believe you," Cartwright said gruffly. "Both Peregrine and Sir James have visitors. If there's ever a time for them to use the abbey again it's now."

"I hope you're right. Nothing happened last time." Not only was he tired of staring at barred doors, but he wanted the women of Merrivale to feel safe. They wouldn't feel secure until the real murderer was captured. And he wanted his name cleared, damn it.

"Horses coming," Cartwright said, gesturing toward their right.

They both peered through the darkness.

"Damn, I can't see a thing. We need to move closer."

Leo stayed him with an outthrust hand. "By the time we get down there, they'll be gone again. Wait. The moon might come out again."

"What are they doing?"

"Is that a package of some sort?"

The clouds shifted, allowing them better vision. A feminine laugh rang out, followed by a masculine chuckle.

"Ah," Cartwright said. "Maybe this isn't what we hoped."

"Not all the women I saw were unwilling."

Cartwright glanced at him. "You're saying that she's there for something more than a tup?"

"Could be."

Half an hour later, the men exited the abbey, but the woman was nowhere to be seen. They mounted their horses and trotted off.

"What do you think? Recognize the horses?" Cartwright asked.

"Difficult to tell in this light, but I think we should check the abbey and discover what happened to the woman."

Five minutes passed before they made their way down the hill. The entrance to the ruins yawned in front of them, a huge black hole.

"How are we going to search the abbey in this light?" Leo asked.

"I found a cache of candles the other day," Cartwright said, sounding a trifle smug.

"Lead the way."

Cartwright groped for a candle and lit it before handing it to Leo. "Can you hear something?"

"It sounds like crying."

Holding his candle aloft, Cartwright hurried in the direction of the noise, Leo following swiftly behind. They came across a woman locked in a makeshift room, her hands tied behind her back.

"Isn't that the blacksmith's wife?" Leo murmured.

Her eyes widened on seeing them, and she opened her mouth as if to scream.

"It's Captain Cartwright, the parish constable," Cartwright said hurriedly. "We've come to help. Turn around. Let Leo unfasten your bonds."

"He's not a murderer?"

Leo's mouth twisted in irritation as he made short work of untying her. "No, madam. I am not a murderer."

"Who left you here?" Cartwright asked.

"That Sir James and his friend, Boynton. They promised they'd give me coin if I let them tup me. Bastards went back on their word. They dragged me here and left me alone in the dark."

"Do you know why?" Cartwright asked.

"They didn't tell me." The woman sniffed, rubbing the back of her hand across her nose. "Heard 'em mention tomorrow."

Leo nodded, his excitement growing. A witness. At last they had a witness.

"Would you be willing to testify against Sir James and his friend?"

The woman tossed her head, flipping a tendril of black hair away from her cheek. "Ye'd take my word?" She paused. "Wot will ye pay me?"

Cartwright ignored her request for payment. "Do you know if any other local men are involved?"

"I only seen those two gents. They told me to pretend I be running off. Outside of town, they came for me. Stashed me in a right nice room." Her eyes flashed anger in the candlelight. "Until tonight. If I be knowing they intended to leave me in the dark I wouldn't 'ave gone for their schemes."

"What schemes?" Leo demanded.

Cartwright sent him a chiding look, and Leo gave a clipped nod to indicate his silence.

"What schemes?" Cartwright asked, his tone far more gentle and coaxing than Leo's.

"They're having a big party. Invited me, they did."

Leo bit back a curse and stepped away to stop himself throttling the woman. It was easy to imagine squeezing the answers from her. The damn woman had found her equilibrium quickly after her scare. The blacksmith was well rid of her.

"When is the party and where?" Cartwright asked, never losing his patient manner.

"They be 'avin' it here at the abbey. A masked ball tomorrow night. Accordin' to them. They told me I'd be sure to find a gentleman to look after me." Her bottom lip shot out in a pout. "I think they be tellin' me lies."

"Tomorrow." Cartwright scratched his chin, the abrasive sound amplified in the enclosed space.

"They might come back," Leo said. "We should go."

"'ere! What about me?"

"Would you like to help us catch these men?" Cartwright asked.

"Catch 'em? No laws against a party, is there?"

"We believe these men are responsible for murder."

She jerked her chin in Leo's direction. "Everyone thinks he did it."

Leo couldn't prevent his frustrated growl. He took half a step toward the woman. She let out a squeak of alarm and darted behind Cartwright.

"Sherbourne," Cartwright snapped and turned to the woman. "He didn't do it."

"Then why he be in jail?"

"We need you to help us catch the true murderer."

She twirled a lock of her hair between finger and thumb, shifty intelligence flitting through her eyes. "What's in it for me?"

IT WAS EARLY MORNING when Leo skulked through the shadows and entered the manor in his usual clandestine method.

"Who's there?" a crisp voice demanded.

"Fuck!" Leo muttered, almost leaping out of his boots.

"Stay right there or I'll put a bullet through you."

A light flared, and Leo squinted against the sudden brightness.

"Mr. Sherbourne," Woodley said, lowering his pistol. "You'll be wanting to see your wife. Best take the servants' stairs. There's a footman lurking at the bottom of the main staircase."

"Right. Thank you." Leo walked past and turned, curiosity getting the better of him. "Aren't you concerned about my presence?"

"I reckon if you had murder on your mind, you'd have done it on one of the nights you visited Mrs. Sherbourne," Woodley said. "I've been keeping an eye on your chamber, tidying away evidence so none of the maids suspected anything."

Leo offered a chagrined smile. "Thank you, Woodley. I'm attending the festival tomorrow."

"Mrs. Sherbourne will like that. Good night, sir."

"Good night, Woodley."

Leo made his way to Jocelyn's chamber, eager to see her again. He slipped inside and inhaled deeply, pausing to enjoy the floral scent on the air.

Seconds later, he disrobed rapidly, pulled back the covers and slipped into the bed. Jocelyn didn't wake, but it didn't matter. This was home.

He woke hours later, only to realize Jocelyn was no longer in the bed.

"Jocelyn?"

"You're awake."

"What are you doing?" It was warm under the covers and the sheets smelled of Jocelyn. Flowers again.

"Checking the weather. I want to see if it's raining."

242

"Come back to bed." Leo stretched, his senses alive, relaxed—yet not.

Her husband's husky voice told Jocelyn exactly what he had on his mind. "What sort of incentive are you offering?"

His dark tousled head poked above the covers. A crooked grin lit his handsome face, and her heart jogged against her ribs. "Is that a challenge? Come closer."

"Said the fox to the rabbit?"

"Jocelyn." His lazy smile lured her, tempted her.

She hurried back to her bed and slipped between the sheets.

"Ow, woman. Your feet are cold."

Jocelyn laughed and cuddled closer, unperturbed by his complaints. His arms wrapped around her, and she burrowed against him, soaking in his heat. She brushed a kiss against his throat and lifted her head to grin when he grumbled another complaint.

"I need to warm you." His hand stroked over her head, smoothing down the wayward locks. She'd given up braiding her hair while preparing for bed. The first thing Leo did whenever he came to her was unfasten her braid.

"I'm warming up already."

"I have a better way."

Jocelyn drew back to study his face. "Oh?"

He rolled without warning, caging her within his arms and laughing down at her. "I think we can dispense with your chemise."

"That won't keep me warm."

"Trust me." He licked along her jawline, wringing a shiver from her. Her breasts prickled, the sensation echoing low between her thighs.

She didn't reply but wrapped her hands around his neck,

drawing him closer until his weight rested on her. He allowed it for an instant before moving. He whisked off her chemise and settled against her again. Their mouths joined, and she greedily met his kiss. His taste and masculine scent washed over her while his warm hand cupped the slight mound of her stomach. She gasped at the touch, somehow intimate and loving, and a wave of emotion almost choked her. In that moment, she wanted to tell Leo she loved him, but doubts—her uncertainty—overruled her.

He caressed the upper curves of her breasts and followed his fingers with his tongue. His touch made her breath catch, her pulse race. His proximity seduced her. She jerked when he nibbled at the juncture of her neck and shoulder and sighed when he soothed the sting with a lick of his tongue. A hungry noise escaped as his hands skimmed her body, his mouth moving downward to tongue her sensitive nipple.

"Leo," she whispered, the tension stretching to breaking point inside her. "I want you now." She wriggled a fraction, parting her legs and silently encouraging him to hurry. Thankfully, he did. He slipped between her legs and pushed into her with an easy glide.

His mouth fused with hers, his first sweet kiss changing swiftly to insistent. His hands glided across her body, loving and tender. He made her feel precious. She wondered at his silence, then the thought drifted away, shoved from her mind as his muscles flexed and rippled against her. A fine sheen of sweat grew on their bodies.

"Jocelyn, you make me happy." He forged into her again, filling her as he spoke. "I'm glad I followed my instincts and offered you marriage. I appreciate your support through all this. Your trust."

The glow in his eyes warmed her all the way through. Words of love flickered through her mind again, but caution kept them contained. It was enough that the emotions had grown in her.

She clasped his shoulders, luxuriating in the sensations coursing through her. One hand crept down to caress his rump, the shift of firm muscles giving her an intense thrill. He changed the angle of his stroke, and a flash of pleasure shocked a cry from her. She bit her lip, holding back a whimper. Her gaze went to his face—the stark muscles and flashing eyes, all determination with a contrasting gentleness when he noticed her close attention.

Another thrust pushed her over the edge. Waves of heat and pressure tossed her into a maelstrom. Leo hammered into her with fast, almost brutal strokes. She clung to him, glorying in his need. He gave one final thrust, his breath a heated rush past her ear. His heart thudded against her chest, and for an instant his weight fell on her again. She ran her tongue over his biceps, the tang of sweat salty. She realized she felt happy, despite the loss of her mother. She'd done her best for her parent, and surely that was all anyone could ask. Now was the time to focus on the present and her own family.

Leo separated their bodies and drew her into his embrace.

"What happens if I have a girl?"

"As long as you both come through the birth safely, I'll be happy."

Surprised, she stared at him. "Most men want an heir."

"Of course I'd like a son, but you're important to me."

It was almost a declaration of love, and Jocelyn beamed at him. "I'll do my best to have a son."

A tap on her bedchamber door told of the passing time.

"Leo," she whispered in consternation. She bounded out of bed and thrust her arms into her robe. She belted it with jerky moves. "You shouldn't have stayed so long."

"It's all right. Cartwright knows I'm here. I'll be attending the festival later and greeting the guests at your side."

"Has Cartwright found the murderer?"

"Not yet."

"Oh." Jocelyn worried her bottom lip and considered the reasoning for freeing Leo.

Another knock sounded on the door. "Mrs. Sherbourne."

Sighing, Leo rolled out of bed. He picked up his breeches and pulled them on. "Don't overdo things today. If you start to get tired, make sure you take a rest. Everyone will understand. I'd better not let Susan see me." He picked up his shirt.

The door burst open. "Mrs. Sherbourne— You!" Susan came to a halt, an appalled expression on her face. "Murderer!" She whirled away, signaling an intention to leave, but Leo grabbed her and shut the door.

"Leo," Jocelyn protested.

Susan screeched, and Leo clapped a hand over her mouth to mute the sound.

"What are you doing? Let Susan go."

"I can't have her telling people I'm out of jail," Leo said. "Hand me my shirt." He indicated the shirt he'd dropped when he'd grabbed Susan.

All of Jocelyn's fears rushed back to swamp her newfound equilibrium. Was he telling the truth? Had Cartwright really released him?

Another knock sounded on the door, and Jocelyn hurried to answer. Her room felt like the front room of a coaching inn this morning.

"Mrs. Sherbourne," Woodley said. "Captain Cartwright has arrived. He wishes to go over the plans with Mr. Sherbourne. I have put him in the study."

"Let Woodley in," Leo instructed.

Wordlessly, Jocelyn opened the door and gestured for the butler to enter.

"Susan, I'm going to take my hand away," Leo said. "Don't

246

scream." He slowly removed his hand.

A panicked cry rippled through the room.

Leo slapped his hand over Susan's mouth again, cutting off the noise. Jocelyn risked a glance at Woodley as her maid kicked in an attempt to gain freedom.

"Stop that racket this instant," Woodley snapped, acting the stern butler from his rigid expression to his upright carriage.

Susan stilled, but Jocelyn could see her panicked eyes, could imagine the frantic race of her heart.

"Mr. Sherbourne didn't commit those murders," Woodley said in a crisp voice. "Captain Cartwright is here to speak with him. Mr. Sherbourne isn't brandishing a weapon, nor is he threatening Mrs. Sherbourne, which tells me the master didn't escape jail in order to murder us in our beds. Now remain silent, and Mr. Sherbourne will release you."

Leo carefully let her go, and Susan darted over to Jocelyn, standing protectively in front of her. "You will not hurt Mrs. Sherbourne."

Leo gaped at her. "Why would I hurt Jocelyn?"

"Because she's been—" Susan stopped abruptly and clapped her hand over her mouth. "Never mind."

"What are you going to do?" Leo asked, giving the maid a hard stare.

Leo didn't cow Susan. She squared her shoulders and glared right back. "I will speak with Captain Cartwright and come to a decision," she said in a haughty voice.

"This way." Woodley marched off without a backward glance, clearly expecting Susan to follow him.

Leo waited until they'd disappeared. "What is she talking about?"

"I have a feeling Susan thought I was having an affair while you were locked up. Hannah thinks the same, by the way." Her hand smoothed over her belly. "Susan assumes that man is the father of my baby."

Leo barked out a laugh. "I'll have to challenge him to a duel."

They chuckled together and Jocelyn acknowledged her earlier fears were silly. Leo would never hurt her. She was displaying the same mad tendencies as her mother for thinking that of her husband.

"I'd better go and see Cartwright," Leo said, bending to kiss her cheek. "I believe he wants me to stay out of sight until later. I'll see you then."

Jocelyn started to dress herself, and Susan arrived ten minutes later.

"This isn't right," she burst out on seeing Jocelyn.

"What are you going to do?"

"I intend to watch him," Susan said, shooting a militant glance at Jocelyn. "I'd persuaded Ella to attend today. I don't know what she'll do when she sees him."

Instead of reprimanding her maid, Jocelyn merely nodded. She understood her loyalty, admired it even. And in truth, she could hardly blame Susan for her behavior.

"Watch the other gentlemen too," Jocelyn said.

"You haven't heard Ella," Susan said grimly. "In her mind she's convinced Mr. Sherbourne kidnapped and violated her. You should take care. Beneath his charm and pretty face, your husband is a ruthless man. I'll go and get you breakfast." Susan marched off, leaving Jocelyn staring after her. Her maid sounded so positive.

Could her faith in Leo be misplaced? Was she stubbornly seeing what she wanted to see?

The morning hours passed rapidly. Jocelyn kept busy with questions and tasks, although her mind flitted from one worry to the next.

A loud noise sounded behind her, and Jocelyn jerked. She whirled around, her heart attempting to leap out of her chest.

"Careful with the tables," Woodley admonished one of the footmen.

Jocelyn gave a shaky laugh and returned to her list. Her mother would have enjoyed the bustle, and the last minute panic to finish everything in preparation for their guests. Later this afternoon, they'd organized a cricket match with the male Merrivale staff playing against the men from the village. She was positive the children would enjoy their games, and after the cricket, the maze would open for everyone to explore. A group of traveling players was stopping by to perform a play, and the vicar had organized a puppet show, which both young and old would enjoy. A feast would follow the entertainment along with a bonfire and dancing.

Finally the guests started to arrive.

A figure appeared from the direction of the rear garden, drawing her attention. *Leo.* Her breath caught as she stared at him. Tall and handsome, he wore black breeches and a matching jacket. The silver embroidery on his waistcoat sparkled in the sun. Casually, he strolled to her location, his head held high. On reaching her, he flashed a charming smile, unperturbed by the stunned bystanders.

She was vaguely aware of the shocked whispers from the newly arrived guests. Leo paid them scant attention, focusing fully on her. "You look radiant." Despite their audience, he kissed her on the lips. "You're beautiful, and I'm proud to call you wife." He pulled back and placed her hand on the crook of his arm.

More villagers arrived on foot and via other various modes of transport. Soon a collection of carts, gigs and carriages filled the entrance near the stables. Excited greetings carried on the air. The gaiety faltered once the new arrivals noticed Leo.

Leo remained smiling at her side and unfailingly polite. He introduced her to every new arrival, never hesitating with his greetings. Captain Cartwright appeared and some of her uneasiness dispersed when he didn't haul Leo away in chains.

"Who is ready for arm wrestling?" Leo asked.

Enthusiastic shouts of agreement sounded, and the men left for a bout in the area under the oak trees. Some of the younger women and wives went to watch while Jocelyn, with the aid of Mrs. Allenby, organized the children for footraces.

Jocelyn tried to enjoy herself, but her gaze kept diverting to Leo. A hard knot of worry stirred, churning her belly relentlessly. This was one ill a piece of dry bread wouldn't fix.

The women from the village were cautious but soon thawed once she drew them out with questions about their offspring.

"I thought your husband was in jail for murder," the baker's wife said in a challenging voice. "Why is he here?"

"Because the parish constable said he isn't guilty." Jocelyn prayed her words were true. The locals seemed positive of his guilt. How could it not play on her mind?

"How is everything going?" Leo slipped his arm around her shoulders.

Jocelyn jumped. "Leo, you gave me a fright." Aware her tone held shades of a London fishwife, she took a deep breath and let it ease out slowly. Yet still her heart pounded in an unnatural manner.

"You're not used to strange men wrapping their arms around you."

"I should think not," she said tartly. "How did you go in the arm wrestling?"

"I came up against the blacksmith," Leo said. "It was simple to predict the winner."

"It's probably best you didn't win." Jocelyn was uncomfortable with the stares and whispers, but Leo never faltered.

"I had no intention of winning." A twinkle in his eyes made

her smile. "This was a good idea."

"You know it was Mrs. Allenby's idea. The vicar's wife is a determined woman. She's organizing games for the children."

"I haven't seen Hannah or Peregrine yet. I thought they'd attend. I heard their parents have returned from their trip to London. I've seen several of their staff."

"Maybe they'll come later this evening. Hannah is bringing someone with her. She was a little secretive. A new beau, I think."

"Nothing would please me more," Leo said. "There's Peregrine now. Who is that with—" He cursed suddenly, earning a loud *tsk* from the baker's wife. "My apologies," Leo said in a steely voice. "I need to take care of something."

"Leo, what is it?" The tension thrumming through him set her on edge.

"That is Jaego, my former best friend."

"Not the one who—"

"Excuse me." Leo strode off without another word.

Jocelyn hurried after him. Several of the locals ceased their activities to stare, but Leo ignored them, and Jocelyn saw he remained wholly focused on Peregrine and Jaego.

"Leo, wait," Jocelyn called.

Cartwright stepped from behind a bush and spoke to Leo. Leo slowed, allowing Jocelyn to catch up with him.

"Madam, I suggest you return to your duties," Leo said, both face and voice harsh and uncompromising.

She halted, struck by his lack of emotion. It was as if they meant nothing to each other. Too bad. Leo wasn't going to make a scene and spoil the fair if she could help it. She grasped his forearm and dug in her heels. "Will you listen to me?"

"This is nothing to do with you."

"It has everything to do with me," she retorted. "Please. If you don't agree with me after I've spoken my piece, I'll let you be."

Cartwright's solid shoulders were stiff with tension, his gaze watchful.

Leo gave a clipped nod, but his gaze fastened on the two men and didn't leave them.

Jocelyn tugged on his sleeve, demanding his attention. "Ursula wasn't a good wife. I don't condone what your friend did, but from what I understand, it wasn't the first time Ursula cuckolded you. She's dead now and it's all in the past. We're happy together." When he didn't reply, she gave his sleeve another sharp tug. "Aren't we happy?"

His breath hissed out. "Yes."

Relief made her knees weak. "Then Jaego's appearance means nothing to us. We should greet him together and ignore past history."

"He could even be the man we seek," Cartwright said in an undertone. "We did see him the other night."

Leo's glare didn't waver. "Despite my dislike of the man, I don't see him as a murderer. Why don't we offer our greetings before we return to the rest of our guests?"

"Thank you." Jocelyn placed her hand on the crook of his arm and stepped forward confidently at his side. A façade. Inside she trembled with the strain of maintaining a calm demeanor. She recalled Hannah's tearful request to invite friends. The woman wasn't to be trusted. It made Jocelyn dread to learn the identity of Hannah's guest.

"Peregrine. Jaego," Leo said in a smooth voice. "Welcome to Merrivale Manor."

"What are you doing here?" Peregrine asked. "I thought you were arrested for murder."

Jaego stepped forward, his attention on Leo. He stretched out his right hand. "Thank you for inviting me. Most men wouldn't be as generous, given the circumstances."

Jocelyn waited anxiously, praying Leo wouldn't make a scene.

"Jaego." Leo ignored the outstretched hand, giving a stiff nod instead. Jaego finally dropped his hand back to his side. "This is my wife, Jocelyn."

Jocelyn inclined her head, not offering her hand either. She wanted to make it plain where her loyalties lay. *Where they should lie.* There were moments of discomfort as the silence stretched, but Jocelyn didn't intervene to smooth the awkwardness. She would follow Leo's lead now that she knew he wouldn't cause a disturbance. His ex-friend simply seemed relieved Leo hadn't pulled a pistol on him.

Peregrine spied Cartwright standing in the background. "What's going on?" he demanded.

"I'm an innocent man," Leo said softly.

The shout went up to summon the men to play cricket.

"I must go," Leo said. "I am the host after all."

"Wait, I wanted to speak with you," Jaego said.

"I don't think so," Leo said, turning away.

"I say," Peregrine said. "Jaego has come all the way from London to see you. Don't you think you could make the time to entertain him?"

"You could have visited me in jail," Leo said. "From what I understand you've been in the area for a while now."

Jaego's throat worked, his blond hair almost the exact shade of Cassie's. Jocelyn bit back her shock. There were other similarities between this man and her stepdaughter. Had Leo noticed? It was a motive for murder.

"Not now," Jocelyn said, frowning at them both. "Leo is busy."

Leo led her away, tension evident in the tight lines of his body.

"Are you good at cricket?" Conversation would lighten the rigidity in Leo's shoulders.

"Yes."

"No false modesty," she teased.

"Thank you, Jocelyn. Your presence has helped. I'm not sure I could've kept my hands to myself if I'd been on my own."

"How long have you known him?"

"We were children together. He used to live at Duxton before Sir James. I believe he rented Duxton to Sir James after Ursula..." Leo trailed off, his muscles tensing again.

"Some things cross the bounds of friendship," Jocelyn said.

"Yes."

Together, they walked to the area the gardeners had mown in preparation for the match. Jocelyn parted from him and went to join the other women seated in a shady area to watch the game. Several of the women were whispering excitedly, their heads close together. When she arrived, the frantic whispers cut off abruptly. Jocelyn smiled and pretended she hadn't interrupted a gossip session. She sat on one of the seats they'd provided, fluffing out her black skirts to avoid crinkling the fabric.

"Susan said you're with child," one of the women said after another nudged her with an elbow.

"Yes," Jocelyn said calmly.

The fraught silence made her want to scream, but she kept her eyes raised, her carriage straight and erect. Pride and her mother's training kept her focused. The village women could count and suspected she'd broken her wedding vows.

Sighing, she concentrated on the cricket game. She clapped and cheered with each run the Merrivale male staff managed, and gradually the village women shifted their focus to the game too.

Much shouting ensued during the next two hours. Jocelyn had imagined she'd joke and laugh with the other women while watching the match, but this didn't happen. When Leo walked up to the stumps, the encouragement halted. Everyone fell silent, but she appreciated Leo's quick bow of acknowledgment in her direction. Ironic, really. The one person who paid her attention was the one who caused doubts to rise to the surface.

She glanced over at the other groups watching the match from different vantage points. Spotting Hannah, she raised her right hand to wave. She froze when she saw the face of the man standing next to her.

Jack Boynton.

As she stared with horror at the man who had caused her so much pain and terror, Hannah turned her head. Their gazes met. Jocelyn couldn't read Hannah's expression from this distance, but Boynton's presence shrieked of mischief.

CHAPTER 16

LEO HADN'T SEEN JOCELYN since the end of the cricket match. She wasn't with the women serving food or those helping to entertain the children.

"Have you seen Jocelyn?" he asked Mrs. Allenby.

"She went to organize more refreshments," the vicar's wife said. "It's been a lovely day, just perfect. I want to thank you for hosting the festival. I know you were reluctant, but everyone has enjoyed it so much."

"You're welcome." Ursula had always disappeared during social engagements, usually to meet a lover. But Jocelyn wasn't missing. She was seeing to a domestic matter. "It's good to see everyone looking happy."

Could he move on without causing offense? He wanted to find Jocelyn, merely to reassure himself of her good health. He nodded at Mrs. Allenby, relieved when she didn't attempt to delay him or ask questions about his release from jail. So far the villagers had given him a wide berth unless forced into an exchange of words.

"Are you all right?" Cartwright asked in a gruff voice from

behind him.

"I didn't expect a welcome, but the whispers and averted gazes are disconcerting. No one is brave enough to say anything to my face. They're worried about their livelihoods."

"It's difficult to blame them," Cartwright said easily.

Leo let out a snort. The flames of the bonfire highlighted the faces of the people sitting around the fire. He couldn't see Jocelyn and moved on, past the couples dancing. The music of the fiddle rang out, a joyous sound and one he hadn't heard at Merrivale for too long. It reminded him of his childhood. A happy time spent playing with his cousins and running wild. The idea of his own children playing with Melburn's offspring brought a spark of happiness. The picture grew to include Jocelyn with a bright smile on her face, her delightful laughter filling the air, the sun striking her hair and turning it into a fiery blaze and her flowery scent. God, he loved her flowers.

He loved her.

The thought sprang into his mind and felt natural, going some way to lighten the tension gripping in his chest. Jocelyn had won him over with her generous nature and determination to make the best of the obstacles life threw her way. He promised himself he'd make love to her at the next opportunity.

The landlord from the village pub stopped him. "Everyone has enjoyed today."

"Your lady did a good job," the landlord's wife piped up.

"Aye," the landlord agreed. "You've a good one there, not like—" He broke off when his wife elbowed him in the ribs. "The constable let you out of jail then."

His wife dug him in the ribs again, and he glared at her.

Not like Ursula. "I thank my cousin for introducing us," Leo said, pretending he'd missed the interest regarding his release. "I'm very lucky."

"Rumor says you're expecting a child," the landlord's wife

said.

He grinned. "Rumor is true." They'd known him since he was a child himself and felt free to ask nosy questions. "We're pleased. Have you seen my wife? I want to make sure she isn't overdoing things."

"Aye," the landlord said. "She was talking to Hannah." His brow furrowed. "I noticed because your lady appeared angry when she always has a smile for everyone."

"Where?" Jocelyn had mentioned Hannah was becoming a friend. Certainly Cassie's behavior had changed for the better without the sulkiness Hannah's visits normally triggered.

"She was on the other side of the bonfire," the landlord said with a wave of his hand.

With a farewell, Leo strode in the direction the landlord had indicated. Cartwright trotted behind him, and Leo paid him no mind. If Jocelyn was arguing with Hannah, something was wrong.

HANNAH HAD ARRANGED BOYNTON'S visit. In hindsight Jocelyn should have told Leo more about her problems with Boynton, especially after she'd seen the man in Tavistock. Made Leo understand how dangerous and unpredictable the other man was with his nasty moods.

How long had they planned this? Had the face she'd seen in the window belonged to Boynton and not her imagination as she'd convinced herself?

The more she considered Hannah's traitorous actions, the harder her head ached.

The woman sauntered from the direction of the maze, and her languid gait reminded Jocelyn of a stable cat stalking an

258

unwary mouse. When Hannah glided to a stop in front of her, it wasn't difficult to discern her malice. The woman had planned this scenario to cause Jocelyn grief.

"I understand you know Boynton," Hannah purred.

Jocelyn's mouth compressed while she battled her temper. "Who?"

"Boynton knows you well." Hannah's smile turned gloating. "He has fond memories of your...beauty mark." Hannah's gaze drifted to Jocelyn's arse before returning to her face. "Does Leo know you're a whore?"

Jocelyn's heart beat so loud it was all she could hear—the roar of thunderous fears crashing through her head. This wasn't fair. She'd been happy with Leo and now gossip would spread. More gossip. Both she and Leo were offering rare delicacies for the locals to devour and dissect.

Hannah's gaze drifted to Jocelyn's belly, her sneer contorting her face into an ugly mask. "That's not even Leo's child."

"The wind might change," Jocelyn said, pretending a calm she didn't feel. Maybe it wasn't a good idea to prod Hannah, but she didn't intend to let the woman walk over her either. "It would be a tragedy for your face to remain in that grotesque grimace."

"I wonder what Leo would say if he knew you'd been meeting Boynton and entertaining him in your bedroom while Leo was tucked away in jail?"

Jocelyn gasped. "That's a lie."

"I saw you meet by the river," Hannah said. "I should have told Leo about your treachery. I'm shocked you'd entertain a man in your chamber, in your husband's house. Criminal." Her eyes gleamed with spiteful enjoyment. The friendship she'd offered during the past weeks a façade while she schemed to remove Jocelyn from Merrivale.

"Leo won't believe you." Jocelyn turned away. She didn't

have to listen to Hannah's fabrications.

Hannah grasped her shoulder, jerking her painfully to halt her departure. Despite Hannah's slight frame and Jocelyn's greater height, the woman possessed a strength Jocelyn wouldn't have suspected. "I mentioned the matter to Peregrine, and I believe he told his friends."

"How do you know Boynton? He doesn't have estates down this way." Jocelyn had to learn how she'd given away her location. She'd felt safe at Merrivale Manor—for a time. Perhaps Boynton—no, as much as she disliked the man and knew him for a bully, the only one he'd wanted to hurt was her. A man's pride was a fragile thing, and she'd stomped all over Boynton's when she'd left him. "How did he know where I lived?"

Hannah's sly chortle raised the hairs at the back of Jocelyn's neck. "A mere coincidence."

"How?" Jocelyn had to know.

"I met him at Duxton. One of Sir James's private parties. He was in his cups, whining about a woman called Jocelyn who managed to escape him. I waited until he was sober, and the next day we conducted an interesting discussion. He knew a Jocelyn. I knew a Jocelyn, and both had red hair." She cast a disparaging look at Jocelyn's nose and her glee jumped to new heights. "And a host of freckles. I did Boynton a favor pointing out your location. He was most grateful."

Hannah tightened her grip until a pained moan escaped Jocelyn.

"Let me go." She wrenched free only to come face-to-face with Boynton.

"We meet again, my dear." His husky tone bore none of the brutality she knew lurked beneath his suave surface.

Jocelyn backed up and bumped into Hannah.

"Peregrine wondered if madness ran in your family," Hannah whispered in her ear.

"I am *not* mad. Leo will see through your lies." *By St. Bridget!* She glanced left and right, dismay striking her. Without her realizing, they'd managed to maneuver her to a quiet part of the garden.

The strong scent of roses combined with Hannah's violet perfume to produce a bout of queasiness, and Jocelyn clapped a hand over her mouth. The delicate scent did not suit Hannah's treacherous personality.

"Ah, my dear. That's where you're wrong." Boynton grasped her arm and forcibly propelled her deeper into the shadows. "You won't have an opportunity to tell your husband anything because you're running off with me. We're going to create gossip that will do the rounds for years."

"No!"

He chuckled, the rich sound contrasting with the roughness of his grip. His blunt nails dug into her flesh. She struggled, called out, but he was quick. He covered her mouth, muffling her cries.

"Can you deal with her?" Hannah asked.

"With pleasure," Boynton replied.

Jocelyn swallowed her fear and wrapped herself in unconcern. A façade when terror danced a jig through her mind. She knew the atrocities Boynton was capable of, had experienced his attentions before.

LEO FAILED TO LOCATE Jocelyn, and worry hastened his pace. Maybe she'd felt ill and had retired indoors for a brief respite. He retraced his steps to ask Woodley and Tilly.

"Is something wrong?" Cartwright asked.

"I can't find Jocelyn. She knows not to wander off with a

murderer on the loose."

Cartwright's bushy brows drew together. "Do you think someone has grabbed her?"

"No, I—maybe," he said, addressing his concerns. "I'd feel better if I could locate her."

"Leo." Jaego forced Leo to come to an abrupt halt.

"I thought I made it clear our friendship was over when I found you fucking my wife," Leo snapped.

"But Hannah said you'd softened, that you'd be amenable to reconciliation."

"Hannah." Leo snorted. "You put stock in anything she says?"

Jaego paused in clear confusion. "She lied?"

"Of course she did. You were my best friend. I didn't expect betrayal, and nothing will make me forgive you. Is that clear enough?"

"Please, Leo, you must forgive me. Ursula...she...she bewitched me."

Leo bit off a laugh. "One thing we have in common. She drew me in like a siren, snaring me before I knew better. The woman was poison, and I'm well rid of her. I'd like to thank the person who freed me of the viperous bitch."

Jaego's expression froze in a comical mask. "You...you didn't strangle her?"

Leo barked out a humorless laugh. "I didn't have that pleasure. Jaego, Hannah lied to you. I have no interest in renewing our friendship. If you're wise you'll leave now before I decide my daughter bears a distressing likeness to you." Leo turned away, but Jaego stilled him with a hand on the shoulder. At the end of his patience, Leo lashed out with his fist, putting every bit of his grief and fury into the punch.

One second Jaego was standing. The next, he lay sprawled at Leo's feet. Leo shook his hand, ignoring the throb and stalked away from his past without looking back.

"I bet that felt good," Cartwright said.

"Instead of trailing me, why don't you help me search for Jocelyn?" Leo demanded. A tight band of worry constricted his chest, making each breath difficult. Where the devil was she?

"Of course," Cartwright said. "I'll search the bonfire and refreshment area."

"I'll start with the gardens and meet you there." Leo found Woodley and Tilly enjoying the music and watching the dancers. "Have you seen Jocelyn?"

"Not since the feast." Tilly's brow wrinkled. "Is something amiss?"

"I don't think so." He thought of Hannah's machinations. "Maybe. I'd rest easier if I could check she isn't overdoing things."

"Good grief," Woodley said, looking past Leo. "What is wrong with Miss Hannah?"

Leo swung around. Locks of Hannah's hair hung around her face in disarray. A green leaf clung to one side of her head while the hem of her black gown bore splotches of dirt. Her chest heaved as she gasped for air. "Leo, thank goodness I've found you."

"What is it? What's wrong?"

"Oh, dear. I don't know if I should tell you this." Indecision rode her expression, and the silence grew until Leo wanted to shake words from her.

"Have you seen Jocelyn?"

"Yes. I don't like to be the bearer of bad news..."

"Spit it out." He didn't have time for this. "Where is she?"

Woodley and Tilly stood, flanking him, united in their concern for Jocelyn.

"Is something wrong with her?" Woodley asked.

"Where is she?" Tilly demanded. "Tell me so I can go to her."

"This is rather embarrassing," Hannah said.

"Hannah." Leo's hands bunched. "If you know where my wife is, tell me now."

A tear slipped down Hannah's cheek, taking him aback. She never succumbed to tears, not even as a child. She was the one who made other boys and girls cry.

"She went with Jack Boynton. I-I thought Boynton was interested in me, but h-he used me to arrange a clandestine meeting with Jocelyn. They-they're lovers."

Leo stood stock still. Jocelyn wouldn't do this to him, not after everything they'd faced together. "No." The denial whispered past his lips. "No."

"Rubbish," Tilly snapped. "Jocelyn hates Boynton. She's terrified of him."

"Tilly." Woodley shushed his wife.

"Don't listen to her," Tilly said to Leo. "No matter what she says, Jocelyn wouldn't go willingly with that brute."

"Where is she?" Leo demanded.

"They were walking in the direction of the river," Hannah said. "There's no need to take your anger out on me. I was only trying to help." She turned away, but Leo grasped her elbow and dragged her to a halt.

"Tell me what you're playing at."

A single tear tracked down Hannah's cheek. "You'd believe them over me?"

"I'm withholding judgment until I speak to Jocelyn," Leo gritted out.

"We'll come with you," Woodley said.

"No, please wait here in case Jocelyn comes this way. Captain Cartwright is searching for her too. Please send a footman to tell Cartwright what's happening. Tell him what Hannah said and that I intend to search the riverbank."

"Of course, Mr. Sherbourne," Woodley said.

"I'm going home," Hannah said.

"You're coming with me." Leo hustled Hannah away from the house, determined strides taking him in the direction of the river.

"Stop dragging me around like a parcel," Hannah snapped.

Leo didn't release his grip. "I notice you're not shouting for help. Is that because you don't want our friends and neighbors to witness your shame?"

"Don't be silly. I don't wish to cause gossip. Surely you want the same thing? Don't you realize the locals are convinced you're a murderer? Why, I've even heard renewed rumors about you killing Ursula."

"I didn't kill your sister."

"I heard the two of you arguing. I heard you tell Ursula you'd kill her rather than let her take Cassie away."

"How do you know that? The only way you could know is if Ursula told you."

Hannah shrugged. "We were close. We told each other everything."

"You couldn't stand your sister. You were jealous of her. This isn't helping me find my wife."

Away from the merriment of the bonfire, Leo paused to listen. He couldn't hear any sounds to indicate a cooing couple.

"Leo, please." Without warning, Hannah threw herself at him. She mashed their mouths together, kissing him without finesse. Shock froze him for an instant before he thrust her away.

"What the hell do you think you're doing?" he snapped. "I'm a married man."

JOCELYN FOUGHT, ATTEMPTING TO dislodge Boynton's iron

grip. Her feet struck at his shins, unladylike grunts emerging with each blow. "You can't do this," she cried. "People will search for me." *Please let someone come soon.*

"I can and I will," Boynton said. "You're going to pay for making me a laughingstock. Damn it, stop kicking. You're soiling my clothes."

"You brought it on yourself," she said rashly, taking great pleasure in landing a strike and smearing dirt down his pale breeches. "You're a bully."

"You liked me well enough when you had me in your bed."

She caught the building fury in him, instinct screaming for her to back away, to cease her taunts. "I put up with your advances. You have the bedroom skills of a green boy." No, she shouldn't needle him, yet experience and bravado lent her steel. She didn't have to put up with his brutish treatment.

Boynton released her abruptly, his hand swinging in a precision arc. The sharp crack of fist meeting flesh shocked her. The ripple of pain sent her staggering, the ringing in her ears, the wavering black spots in her vision upsetting her balance. She fell against a scratchy, green bush, the thorns on the branches clutching her in a macabre embrace while she struggled for equilibrium.

With a snarl, he jerked her free, the rent of fabric another sharp slap of reality. She sucked in a breath and screamed. A small ineffectual sound emerged, pitiful and of little use to attract aid.

"Stop it!" He shook her vigorously, her head snapping back with the force.

"Please s-stop."

The shaking ended abruptly. A foreign sound intruded. A voice.

"Don't you dare," he ground out, dragging her into the dark shadows of the garden. He drew her against his chest, tension radiating from him. The voices receded, and her hope wilted.

Her hand crept up to finger her chin and her fingers came away damp. With rough hands, he directed her to the maze. Her mind worked frantically, searching for a way to escape. She was familiar with the garden and its secluded places, and she doubted he knew his way as well as her—except he'd managed to spy on her without discovery. The knowledge froze her mind like a chunk of fresh ice. She wouldn't have the advantage of familiarity after all.

He hauled her into the maze. Two hours ago the hedge puzzle had been full of laughter and excited shouts from disorientated men, women and children. Now it stood silent, everyone partaking of food and drink, enjoying the music and the dancing in the flickering light of the bonfire.

"Did you think to avoid me? I've known of your location ever since you escaped. I've spent several weeks with Sir James and hugely enjoyed the entertainment in the region. Even helped with the organization."

Jocelyn stared at him, her heart battering her breastbone. The smugness on his heavy-jowled face told her it was the truth. How had she not known? Surely she would have sensed his presence? When Melburn had whisked her off to London, she'd jumped at every sound, but gradually she'd relaxed, feeling safe under Melburn's care.

"Your mother saw me." Satisfaction throbbed in him, and she caught the gloating flash of his smirk. "A delightful game it proved, learning how quickly I could push her into madness."

"You?" All this time she'd thought her mother was seeing things, conjuring ghosts where there were none. Guilt surfaced almost driving out her fear.

"I hired actors to haunt her when I needed to conduct business elsewhere."

Jocelyn spat out a curse and fought him with renewed

determination. He subdued her with little effort, laughing when she repeated the slur against his manhood.

"My dear, I'll happily prove you wrong." His hand slipped down to squeeze one breast, the sharp pain making her cry out. "We'll have a good time at the abbey. Such a fortuitous discovery."

She slithered away as far as his punishing grasp allowed, shooting him a glare of dislike. "Did you kill my mother?"

"I heard she died. I also heard your husband did it." His lips twisted, and she saw his spite. He cared nothing for her pain, reveling in her grief. "Not that I blame him. Who wants a madwoman living in their nest?" He shoved her deeper into the maze, helping her along with a rough hand in the middle of her back. "No one wants to worry about someone attacking them in their bed. I'd say your husband is a clever man."

No, she'd settled this matter in her mind. "Leo's not like that. He's decent."

"He'll reject you too, my dear, especially after I've fucked you and passed you to my friends. It won't take much to circulate rumors around Merrivale and Tavistock. People will laugh because Sherbourne married a courtesan. I told Hannah. She'll make sure everyone learns of your scandalous reputation."

Leo knew. He wouldn't reject her because of renewed gossip. But despite the thought, panic was a stealthy beast, stalking her mind, making her want to curl up and cry at the injustice. People would think the worst of her.

"You can't do this. I'm a married woman." A clear tremor wove through her words. A living nightmare, and there was no way out.

Boynton chuckled, the spiteful humor telling her he was enjoying her plight. "From what I hear your husband is a jealous man. By the time I've finished with you he'll refuse to have you back. You'll be soiled goods. No decent man will want you."

The worst part was she feared Boynton might be right. After Leo's experience with his first wife, he'd believe the worst. A sob caught in her throat, the ache of regret like a cage around her chest. Her hand crept down to caress her unborn child. "Leo will search for me." She knew this with certainty, but what would he do with her once he found her?

"Of course he will, which is why I'm going to make it appear as if we've enjoyed a tryst." He dragged her to a painful stop. "Look at me."

She drew her shoulders back. Her instinct to disobey disregarded because he was bigger, stronger. Instead, she took her time, lifting her chin with hauteur.

Boynton cursed. "Damn this gloom in here."

Jocelyn backed up, gathering herself to run. Unfortunately, he noticed. His hand snapped out to grip the neckline of her gown. The silky fabric was no match for his strength. The tear of fabric made her cry out and she wrenched the mangled bodice back into place.

"Stop! Leave me alone. Help. Help!"

He grabbed her roughly, the hand covering her mouth and nose almost suffocating her. "Cease your shouts, or I'll hurt your stepdaughter. Lots of men will pay for a morsel like her. Fucking a virgin child cures the pox, I've heard." He grunted when she twisted and landed a kick on his shin. His hot breath wafted across her cheek. "And don't pretend you don't care for her. I've had that bitch Hannah whining in my ear for weeks that you've stolen her man and the child likes you better."

Fight. Her breaths exited in a harsh pant. He'd hurt her, no matter what she did. She bit down on his fingers, and when he released her with a howl, she fled, running deeper into the maze.

He thundered after her. Glancing over her shoulder, she could see him gaining. She lifted her skirts and ran, panic giving her speed. Faster. *Faster.* Each successive breath burned, panic a savage beast nipping at her heels.

Where the devil was she? She hadn't kept count of the turnings after they entered the maze. *Fool.* She raced around another corner and came to an abrupt stop, fighting for breath. If she wasn't careful he'd trap her in a dead end, and he wouldn't be stupid enough to let her escape again.

"You can't escape me, Jocelyn."

Bastard. She had to warn Leo. Tell him about Boynton and his threats. *But Leo isn't the only one involved. What if the scandal embroils Melburn too?* She'd never forgive herself if she harmed both men with her soiled reputation.

"Come out, come out wherever you are."

His singsong voice paralyzed her, weakened her knees. She stood in indecision, a hand clamped to her mouth, trapping her dread inside. Footsteps came closer and she fought a whimper. The brush of a limb against hedge indicated he was near.

"You can't escape. My men are guarding the exit."

Yes, but if she could work out where she was and lose him, she'd be able to call for help. If she screamed loud enough someone would hear.

Another footstep. A harsh breath.

"Stop this nonsense, Jocelyn."

Never.

She waited until he drew level with the wall of hedge she cowered behind, waited until the very last minute before striking. She lashed out, chopping him across the throat with the side of her hand. Then, while he was fighting for breath, the air seesawing in and out of him, she kicked him in the balls.

CHAPTER 17

SHE'S RUN OFF WITH Boynton. I told you that. Hannah's triumphant voice echoed through Leo's mind. She'd sounded positive of Jocelyn's betrayal. Pain lashed him, his steps faltering until commonsense reasserted itself. Jocelyn was happy at Merrivale. She was excited about the baby.

A foreign sound pierced his unhappy musing. Leo paused mid-stride, his head cocking to the left. He'd heard a noise. It repeated—this time a pained scream rippled on the air. "Jocelyn!" He was off running before the echoes of the cry died.

"I'm in the maze."

She hadn't run off. "Keep talking. I'll find you." Leo exploded through the maze entrance, past a lingering man. "Jocelyn?"

"Leo, take care. Boynton is here somewhere."

Leo tripped and cursed softly. "Why is he with you?" *Who is he to you?*

"He's not with me, you stupid man," she snapped.

Relief roared through him at her indignation. "Why did you scream?"

"It wasn't me." Her voice sounded closer this time.

"Who—" He rounded the corner, and she was in front of him. "Are you all right?" He embraced her, frantic for reassurance.

"I'm fine. Please, let's leave this maze."

He swiftly guided her through the shadows, down the gravel path to the exit. The man who'd lingered at the entrance had disappeared.

"What happened?" He wanted to scoop her up and hug her to his chest, yet there were so many unanswered questions. "Is Boynton still in the maze?"

"I think so. I kicked him." Her chin lifted in defiance. "Melburn suggested it."

"My cousin?" Now he was intrigued.

"He said if a man accosted me without permission, I should look for an opportunity to kick him in the balls."

Leo winced. "Did his advice work?"

"Yes." She sounded smugly satisfied.

"Let's get you back to the manor."

"I want to rejoin our guests," Jocelyn said.

"I'll escort you back to the manor." He intended to have a word with Boynton. He eyed her, relief at finding her releasing the tightness in his chest. "Everyone will leave soon. You've worked hard today. Go to your room and rest."

Her eyes narrowed. "Is that an order?"

"Yes."

"Because you don't trust me or because you think I might be tired?"

Something twisted inside him, and he had to swallow to dislodge the clog in his throat. He caressed her cheek. "I don't want you to get fatigued. The servants or Mrs. Allenby will supervise the rest of the night. All you need to do is ask."

She winced when his fingers brushed her jaw. "Did I hurt you?" he asked.

"Boynton struck me."

Anger flared again as he turned her face to the light. He trailed his fingers gently down her face until he reached the nasty scratch that marred her silky skin. A trail of smeared blood had dried on her chin, and he rubbed it gently with a damp finger. "He'll pay for this."

"Punch him in the nose."

"You sound bloodthirsty." Her manner calmed his earlier doubts, shame filling him now for even considering Hannah's accusations.

"I hate Boynton, and I hope you put a kink in his beak. He said he intends to spread rumors about my past, if he hasn't already."

Leo grinned, despite his anger at Boynton. "For you, my dear, it will be my pleasure."

JOCELYN CLIMBED THE STAIRS feeling every ache and pain. In her bedchamber, she surveyed her face, probing the sore spot on her jaw. She winced and turned away. Bastard. She should have kicked him harder.

After cleansing the wound and applying one of her mother's salves, she managed to remove her gown and slide into bed. Now that she'd slowed exhaustion struck, but sleep evaded her. Too many thoughts danced in her mind.

Boynton would waste no time spreading the facts of her past. The delicious gossip of a man duped by a courtesan and tricked into marriage would do the rounds in Tavistock and gradually the rumors would wend their way to London. Once the locals learned the sordid truth, they'd turn their backs on her. Leo and Cassie would reap the same treatment by association. Every prediction her sisters had uttered about dire consequences was finally coming to pass. And their baby—what sort of life would he or she have when everyone assaulted them with vicious whispers?

Merrivale was Leo's home. He was a good man and didn't deserve any of this.

Unable to sleep, she tossed and turned, wincing with each twist of her body. Damn, Boynton, and a pox on Hannah.

The hours marched past, and someone knocked on her door. Susan probably. At Jocelyn's muted summons, her maid entered. After setting down a tray, she drew back the curtains. On seeing Jocelyn, her mouth dropped open and her perkiness fled.

"Mrs. Sherbourne. Your face!" She snapped her mouth shut, her lips flattening to a thin line of disapproval. She stole a quick glance at the connecting door.

"Leo didn't do this." Jocelyn rushed to his defense.

"Yes, Mrs. Sherbourne."

Susan didn't believe her. Jocelyn glanced at the pillow beside her, noting the lack of indentation. She frowned, not sure what Leo's failure to join her meant. At the very least she'd expected him to check on her.

"Should I help you out of bed, Mrs. Sherbourne?"

"Yes, please." She noted Susan's anxious glance and sighed. "My babe is fine. I'm merely a little sore."

A sharp hiss escaped Susan when she witnessed the extent of Jocelyn's bruising. "Take a seat and drink your tea while I get some warm water."

Jocelyn obediently limped over to sit in one of the chairs by the window. She caught a glimpse of her face in the looking glass. No wonder Susan was suspicious. She looked as if she'd taken part in a pugilist match. She moved gingerly, biting back an unladylike curse. The idea was to reassure her maid, not alarm her further.

Susan returned with water and, after helping Jocelyn to wash and dress, finally bustled from the room. She must speak with Leo to learn what had happened with Boynton. She and Leo needed to form a plan, present a united front, and they couldn't do that if Leo was avoiding her.

Susan returned with ointment for her bruises.

"I've already applied salve," Jocelyn said. "Is Leo here?"

Susan sniffed. "No one has seen him since last night."

"Please make sure Woodley knows I wish to see Leo as soon as he returns."

"Yes, Mrs. Sherbourne."

Jocelyn spent most of the day pacing the parlor. She read a story to Cassie and told her she'd walked into a tree branch in the dark when her stepdaughter expressed curiosity about her face. It was the same story she told everyone except Tilly and Woodley.

"What are you going to do?" Tilly asked after Jocelyn admitted the truth of her injuries.

"The man has not a shred of honor," Woodley added.

"I'll speak to Leo. If the wretched man ever decides to return to Merrivale. My husband, I mean."

As the day progressed, and Leo didn't arrive, her frustration grew. When the man finally made an appearance she might just flay him with her tongue.

"Is the woman all right?" Leo asked. While he was loathe to leave Jocelyn after Boynton's attempted abduction, she'd be safe at the manor. It was time to clear his name and finish the investigation he'd started on his own, before the constable had tossed him in a cell. Besides, Cartwright had stuck by him, and Leo could do no less now when the constable required his help.

This time they surveyed the abbey from another vantage point. It was closer with better views, and they'd manage to ferret out identities if the men didn't wear masks.,

"The woman is fine. She said a servant took her food and ale. If you ask me they'd drugged it because she said she slept. Her eyes didn't look right."

"What the devil do you think they're up to?" Leo asked, his hands wrapped around a brandy flask as if to ward off the chill. Each exhalation created a puff of steam. "I was sure they'd appear at the abbey last night."

"They'll come tonight," Cartwright said with an air of confidence. "The men I've hired are in place and will move when I give the signal."

Leo wished he held the same certainty. To his mind, the men were playing with them, like a child teasing a kitten. "We know they kidnapped Ella and probably the maid found in the maze. They enticed the blacksmith's wife." Leo's brow crinkled as he stared down at the abbey. "Ursula and Elizabeth were clearly strangled. It's still puzzling me. Why?"

A rumble of laughter came from Cartwright. "Not just a pretty face. I'll make a parish constable out of you yet. I wondered if you'd twig to the differences in the deaths."

"What does it mean?"

"Maybe nothing," Cartwright said. "It might mean they take turns getting rid of loose ends and have different methods of disposing of the women."

"Or there are two separate murderers at work."

"There is that theory," Cartwright agreed.

Leo tossed over the information they had. "I've been thinking about this for days. I don't understand why someone would strangle Elizabeth. She was a harmless elderly woman." He shifted to a more comfortable position. "Unless she saw something. It's possible she witnessed a crime, but her behavior was erratic. Half her words didn't make sense."

"But an odd moment of lucidity might have meant disaster for the person concerned," Cartwright mused.

"Or Elizabeth might have been murdered because of me," Leo said, voicing the idea that had plagued him for some time. "As an act of revenge."

"You haven't considered Jocelyn or the woman who looked after Elizabeth?"

"No, Jocelyn didn't murder her mother," Leo said. "She gave up everything to keep her mother safe, and Tilly is devoted to Jocelyn. I doubt she did it either."

"You didn't even pause to think about it," Cartwright observed.

"I know my wife. She's generous and loving. She—"

"We have a group of horsemen approaching," Cartwright said.

Leo watched the men canter up to the abbey and dismount. The raucous screech of feminine laughter floated to him, and an open carriage came into view. Torches and lanterns soon lit the entrance.

"The men are masked," Cartwright said.

"Gives them a sense of anonymity, makes them feel safe. Don't worry," Leo said in a grim voice. "I recognize the horses. The bay with the white socks belongs to Peregrine Richards. The horses all come from the Richards' stable, which means his guests are with him."

"But Sir James isn't here."

"Give him time."

A man helped the women from the carriage, sweeping them off their feet into his arms. Shrieks of laughter rang out, bolstered by masculine banter.

"It's early," Leo said. "They'll want to have their fun first."

Another carriage arrived, horsemen riding either side. The carriage pulled to a halt and four men climbed out. One reached back into the carriage and lifted out something.

"Another woman?"

"I'd lay money on it. I don't like the escort." Cartwright watched the men enter the abbey. Two remained at the entrance. "They're armed. That will present difficulties."

"Yes, we need to get inside the abbey."

Cartwright shifted his weight, stretching his limbs. "We'll have to get rid of the guards." He scratched his chin then smirked. "Let's dispose of the guards and replace them with two of my men."

"I'll take the one nearest the big oak," Leo said. "We'll have to disable the carriage drivers too."

"We won't have to," Cartwright said with a jerk of his chin. "They're leaving."

Leo squinted through the growing darkness. "That's a good plan on their part. They won't want to attract attention."

Once they no longer heard the rattle of the carriages, Leo and Cartwright crept from their vantage point, stalking their chosen quarry. Leo stole toward the oak, his gaze on his target. He was almost on the man when the crack of the wood beneath his boot sounded like gunfire. The man whirled, gun cocked. Desperate, Leo lunged, his fists swinging. The gun fired and pain screamed through his biceps.

Leo grunted and swung a heavy fist, despite the fiery burn in his arm. The man crumpled, and Leo dragged him behind the oak. He grabbed the man's cloak and swung it over his shoulders.

"You," a voice called from the ruins. "Who fired the gun?"

"'Twas me," Leo said, dropping into local dialect. "'Twere only a bird. Frightened the wits out o' me."

"You're sure it was a bird?"

Leo recognized Sir James's voice. "Aye, sir." He dipped his head, feigning respect. *Bah!* He'd like to wring the man's neck. "'Twas an owl."

The mournful hoot of an owl came on the heels of his words, Cartwright's signal to his men. Leo saw Sir James nod and watched his retreat.

Leo backed into the shadows to inspect his arm. A scratch. He'd been lucky this time, but it burned like the fires of Hell. He dabbed the wound with the tail of his cloak.

"You all right?" a gruff voice asked.

"Bullet scratched me. I'm bleeding but I'll live."

"Let me see." Cartwright angled Leo's arm to the light and nodded. He pulled a kerchief from within his cloak and bound Leo's arm in the competent moves of one experienced with gunshots. "Have you bound and gagged your man?"

"Not yet. He's out cold behind the oak."

Cartwright took care of the chore, pausing to hoot another signal. By the time he'd finished a dozen men stood with them in the shadows.

"We'll wait half an hour to give them time to settle. Once we move, Jed and Harry, you guard the entrance. Stop anyone who tries to depart. I don't want any shooting unless you're being fired upon. Clear?"

"Aye," the men said in a low chorus.

"The rest of you are with me. I want every man and woman inside the abbey ruins detained for questioning. I don't care who the hell they are or what title they possess. No exceptions."

"We'll find them in the main body of the abbey where the roof is still intact," Leo said. "Some of the men might be in the old cells where the monks used to sleep."

"We'll get them, sir," one of the men said, his voice rough from smoking tobacco.

279

Once the half hour elapsed, Leo trailed into the abbey with the other men, the glowing torches making their furtive task easier. The scent of smoke and tobacco hung on the air, along with the sweet scent of something else. Leo recognized the smell as the same one he'd noticed during his previous visit.

Although they hadn't lingered outside, the orgy was in full progress. Leo grimaced as they passed a cell. Pale limbs reflected the light, grunts of physical exertion loud and animalistic. A woman groaned but didn't seem to participate much. One of Cartwright's men slid into the cell, his weapon cocked.

Leo noticed a blond man standing in the shadows. Jaego. His smile turned feral as he stalked forward, ignoring the discomfort in his arm. Time for payback.

Jocelyn retired late that night, exhausted but furious, only to wake several hours later, aware of someone entering her chamber.

"Leo?"

"Who else are you expecting to join you in bed?"

"That isn't funny," she muttered, turning to glare at him in the candlelight. "Where have you been? Why didn't you join me last night? I haven't done anything wrong, and I don't deserve this treatment. I'm your wife!" Her voice rose with each successive word, and the slight quirk of his lips only made her angrier.

"Tell me about Boynton."

"Did you find him?"

"We got him." Satisfaction laced his voice as he stripped off his clothing.

Her gaze came to rest on his upper arm. "You're hurt." Her

anger fled, replaced by concern. She slithered off the bed and rounded it to stand in front of him, her fingers unfastening the makeshift bandage.

He winced, the air hissing from him when she tugged the cloth free. Blood started to flow anew.

"What happened?"

"I stood on a stick and frightened a man. He shot before asking questions."

"This isn't a joke," she snapped.

"It's a scratch. I won't die."

"You will if it becomes infected. Let me cleanse it for you." She retrieved water and a cloth, her actions revealing the extent of the injury. It was as he said—a mere scratch. She held a pad to the wound until the bleeding ceased and applied another pad smeared with her mother's salve. "Are you going to tell me what happened?"

"Sir James Harvey, aided by Jack Boynton, started a club at the abbey—their version of the Hell Fire Club."

Jocelyn's mind raced ahead. "They're responsible for the murders."

"Cartwright thinks so, although they haven't confessed their crimes."

"Boynton never liked Mother," Jocelyn said. "He told me he's been lurking around the manor for weeks."

Leo nodded. "Tell me everything he said."

Jocelyn repeated Boynton's words from the night of the Harvest festival.

"Hannah said you asked her to invite Boynton."

"Ha! She would say that. My past mightn't be pristine, but I'm not a liar." Jocelyn glowered at him, incensed he'd spoken to Hannah before bothering to hear her side of the tale. "She thought you'd marry her. The truth is she asked me if she could bring two guests. Stupidly, I assumed both she and Peregrine would bring one guest each of the opposite sex."

"She brought Jaego and Boynton, men who were guaranteed to upset us."

"Yes." Jocelyn's brows drew together. "Which tells us what?"

"That she planned this entire debacle to cause dissension between us."

Some of Jocelyn's apprehension dispersed. "Hannah has never liked me. Her goal was to wed you, and she hasn't given up, not even after our marriage."

"I'll talk to her and make sure she ceases her troublemaking. What about Boynton?"

"I told you. He threatened to tell everyone of my past."

The flicker of the candle he'd set on the dresser highlighted his scowl of displeasure. "I wish I could have stayed to reassure you. Cartwright needed my help. Most constables would have locked me away and refused to listen to reason. I doubt Boynton will bother you any longer. He'll be too busy trying to save his own skin."

Jocelyn frowned. "But what if he's already spread rumors?"

Leo laced their fingers together. "If he has we'll face the trouble together."

"But we're not the only ones involved. What about Cassie and our baby? The gossip will stain their reputations too. Maybe even Melburn."

"We'll learn who our real friends are." Leo sighed. "But I don't think we'll need to worry. The gossip from tonight will overshadow everything else. Along with Sir James and Boynton, Peregrine and Jaego were arrested plus several of their visitors."

"Was anyone hurt?"

"They'd drugged some of the women to keep them calm, but Cartwright thinks they'll recover."

"So it's really over? They're responsible for terrorizing Ella?"

"I think so. Cartwright will question them about the murders and the other missing women." Leo drew her into his arms, freezing when he heard her faint cry. "I didn't ask you how you were. Hades, I'm sorry, Jocelyn." He carefully turned her face to the light, swearing when he saw the slight swelling and the bruises. "I'm going to kill him."

"Susan thinks you did it."

"The devil she does."

"Believe me. She thinks much worse. She still thinks you're guilty of murder and that I've been having an affair behind your back. It might be a good idea for her to find us both in here tomorrow morning," Jocelyn said with a teasing smile. She sobered when her thoughts returned to Boynton. "I'm happy here at Merrivale with you, Leo. I'm happier than I ever thought I would be, given my past. Tell me you don't regret our marriage."

"Of course not." Leo lifted her carefully into his arms and placed her on the bed. He rapidly stripped the rest of his clothes and joined her, pulling the covers over them.

She settled against him, savoring his warmth and the weight of his arms around her. His breathing slowed as he drifted to sleep, and she smiled in satisfaction until she replayed the last minutes of their conversation. Leo hadn't returned her sentiments.

Leo stalked from Merrivale, a swagger in his step. His limbs were loose and limber, a sense of wellbeing pervading him. There was something to be said for an ex-courtesan as a wife. Jocelyn never hesitated in her loving, and the memories of her mouth stretched around his cock would bring a smile for the rest of the day. Susan's dismay at his presence made his good humor fade. It would take time for everyone to trust him, but soon word would circulate about Cartwright's latest arrests. His name would be cleared.

Now it was time to deal with Hannah, and he wasn't looking

forward to the task.

He strode to the stables. Once in the saddle, he turned his horse for Hartscombe. It was time to confront Hannah and let her know his loyalties lay with Jocelyn.

After a gallop across the moors, he trotted up to the castle, handing his mount off to one of the stable lads. Fractious kicking and neighing from one of the stalls told him Hannah hadn't visited the stables this morning. She was one of the few who could control the bay stallion. The butler showed him into the breakfast room where he found Hannah's parents breaking their fast.

"Leo, what brings you for a visit?" Viscount Hartscombe waved at an empty chair, his weathered face wreathed in a smile. "Have a seat. Join us."

Leo grimaced inwardly. They didn't know, and he didn't want to be the one to tell them. "I came to see Hannah."

"Ah," the viscountess said, her blue eyes bright in an unfashionably tan face. "I believe Alfred said she'd gone for a ride, perhaps to join Peregrine and our other guests."

"Her horse was still in the stables."

"She probably went out the side door and you missed her," Viscount Hartscombe said. "Can we help with anything?"

"Not unless you're involved with her scheming to upset my wife," Leo said, watching Hannah's parents closely for their reaction.

"Oh, dear," the viscountess said. "I thought she was past her infatuation with you. What has she done now?"

"It doesn't signify," Leo said in a curt voice. "She won't repeat the action after I've spoken with her."

"Jaego's appearance, I presume," the viscountess said. "After all that has happened, I admit I was surprised to hear he'd received an invitation to visit the manor."

"Have the charges against you been dropped?" Viscount

Hartscombe asked.

"Yes. I believe Cartwright captured the real culprits last night."

"Oh? We hadn't heard, but what a relief," the viscountess said. "The maids have been quite silly about the situation."

Leo gave a curt nod. Silly? Several women had died. "If Hannah returns please let her know I wish to speak with her." After another strained smile, he strode from the breakfast room. He'd talk to the stable lads. Hopefully they'd give him an indication of where to find Hannah.

Hannah's horse was gone when he arrived, even though she must've seen his mount and known he was looking for her. Avoiding him. Too bad. He intended to settle this matter between them today. Hannah's behavior wasn't fair to Jocelyn. It was no wonder he'd caught Jocelyn studying him with uncertainty. She might think he hadn't observed her fear and her struggle to contain it, but he noticed everything about Jocelyn. His wife delighted him, and he'd do anything to make her happy.

As he'd hoped, the stable lads pointed him in the direction Hannah had ridden. He headed onto the moor, past craggy rocks. Normally, he loved riding in the moors, but today he wanted to settle things with Hannah and make sure she knew not to upset Jocelyn again. If that meant barring her from the manor and refusing to let her see Cassie then he'd do it. Jocelyn meant that much to him, and he wouldn't see her distressed.

After half an hour he finally spotted Hannah galloping alongside the river. He guided his horse in the same direction, intending to intercept her. To his frustration, Hannah didn't slacken pace.

Unwilling to risk his black, he slowed to a trot. "She'll break her bloody neck before I get a chance to do it for her," he muttered. By Hades, the woman was a menace. He didn't intend to chase her all over Dartmoor. Leo swung his horse back toward Merrivale, only slowing when he heard the thunder of hooves behind him.

"Leo, you didn't take up my challenge." Hannah pouted, her fair hair tousled from her mad gallop, her cheeks rosy and eyes bright with excitement. She was a beautiful woman, but not for him.

"I'm not willing to break my neck in a stupid race."

"Pooh, you never used to be so strait-laced."

"I have responsibilities."

Some of her gaiety faded, her mouth crimping into a firm line. "You shouldn't have married her. She's a whore."

His mouth tightened. "She's my wife."

"I bet you didn't know she earned her living lying on her back."

"If you insist on spreading vicious rumors about Jocelyn, you won't be welcome at Merrivale Manor."

"Bah! Shouldn't you be worried about her past soiling your good name? Cassie's good name? Even Peregrine and I will be sullied by the gossip."

Leo glared at his sister-in-law. "It's your prerogative to feel that way, but Jocelyn is my wife, and I intend to stand by her. I won't tolerate your mischief. I know you invited Boynton and Jaego to the festivities with the sole purpose of causing trouble." He spurred his horse into a canter and rode off without another word.

JOCELYN WANDERED THE GARDEN with Tilly, a basket dangling over her arm. "I'd like to make some of the healing ointment. It helps with the pain of my bruises. Do you know the salve I mean?"

"I watched Elizabeth make it many times. We'll need at least three handfuls of willow bark. Mrs. Green told Elizabeth there are several willows growing on the riverbank. Do you feel up to a walk?"

A pang went through Jocelyn at the mention of her mother. Guilt settled uneasily on her shoulders. Boynton had killed her mother because of Jocelyn's actions. "Of course I can walk. It's when I stop that the aches become worse."

"I'd feel better if you rested and ate something before we went. I promised Mr. Leo I'd look after you. You must consider your babe."

Warmth rippled through Jocelyn. She hadn't realized Leo had made a special point to ensure her care and the considerate nature of his request made her wish for his presence now. Her husband had given her much. Subconsciously, she caressed her belly, her lips twitching when she realized what she was doing. It had become a habit to soothe her when she was troubled or vexed.

"Very well, Tilly. I'll humor you and rest. We'll go for a walk this afternoon."

Several hours later she and Tilly left the garden via a small gate near the fruit orchard. Tiny brown birds flitted through the trees, and she caught a flash of movement to her right.

"Ooh, look. It's a rabbit," she said, pausing to watch the creature hop into the hedgerow. "How adorable."

"They're better in a pie," Tilly said. "The gardeners are always trying to trap them. You should hear them complain about the beasties eating their vegetables."

Jocelyn started walking again, wondering if she should summon a footman to accompany them. No, Leo had said they'd captured those responsible for the murders. "Did everyone enjoy the Harvest Festival?"

"Oh, yes. They'll be talking about it for weeks to come. In the past, the staff wasn't allowed to attend. They were expected to organize food for the guests, so they were very excited when you made sure they could participate."

"Everyone worked hard with the preparations. It was only right they enjoy the festivities with everyone else."

Tilly slipped her a sideward glance. "From what I understand the staff was worried Mr. Leo would marry Hannah."

"They were slow to warm to me," Jocelyn remarked. "I thought they preferred Hannah. She's very beautiful."

"That one trades on her beauty and expects everyone to jump at her demands." Tilly wrinkled her nose. "She isn't beautiful inside. They say she has a temper."

Jocelyn had seen Hannah in a sulky mood and sometimes a little snappish, but she'd never seen her lose control. "Maybe she's learned to rein in her rage."

"Maybe." Tilly didn't sound certain.

"We shouldn't gossip," Jocelyn said. "Are we taking this fork in the path?"

"No, the next one leads directly to the riverbank."

"I thought they said it rained a lot in Dartmoor." The path narrowed, and Tilly slowed to walk behind her.

"I expect the winter will be cold."

"Oh, curse it." Jocelyn slowed to untangle her skirts from a protruding branch. "The path is very overgrown. I didn't think it would be such an obstacle course."

"I don't think anyone comes here much. Mrs. Green mentioned the locals think this particular spot is haunted after the first Mrs. Sherbourne died in the vicinity."

"I don't believe in ghosts," Jocelyn said. "All the ghosts I've heard of recently have turned out to be human."

"You keep thinking that," Tilly said. "And if a ghost attacks you can beat them away with a stout stick."

"Tilly," Jocelyn remonstrated. "You sound as if you believe in ghosts."

"I don't disbelieve," Tilly said.

Jocelyn laughed. "Next you'll be telling me the tales of fairies and evil pixies, black dogs and evil witches roaming Dartmoor are true."

"The locals believe the tales."

"Yes, they do." A shiver drew a rash of goose bumps to her arms and legs. "We should talk about something more cheerful."

"How are your aches and pains?"

"That is not a cheerful memory," Jocelyn said.

They walked single file, climbed over the trunk of a fallen tree and stopped to untangle brambles from their skirts.

Jocelyn picked a blackberry and popped it into her mouth. "The berries are delicious."

"I wonder if Cook would make us a pie," Tilly said.

Jocelyn plucked several more berries from the bush and dropped them into her basket. "I would love a pie."

They lingered, picking berries until purple juices stained their fingertips.

"We'd better collect the willow bark," Jocelyn said. "Leo said he wouldn't be late tonight. He had to ride over to Hartscombe, and I believe he intended to visit Cartwright."

Tilly increased her pace, leading the way down the path.

"How far is it?" Jocelyn was suddenly weary.

"Not much farther. I can hear the water."

The path ended abruptly, the abundance of brambles and undergrowth giving way to a rocky beach on the bank of the river. An elegant wading bird probed the mud at the water's edge, searching for food. Their arrival spooked it, and the bird took off with a raucous cry of alarm.

"Where...oh, look," Jocelyn said. "We've taken the wrong path. There's another one just over there and it looks as if it goes straight past the willows."

"Never mind. We'll know for next time," Tilly said. "You're looking a mite tired. Why don't you take a seat and let me cut the bark? It won't take me long, and we'll be on our way."

Jocelyn nodded and followed Tilly along the riverbank. She handed Tilly the knife from her basket and sat to wait on a large stone.

Tilly disappeared beneath the nearest willow. A cluck of disapproval emanated from under the tree. "It looks as if someone has already cut the bark on this trunk. I don't want to take more and kill it." She backed from beneath the branches. "Stay there, Jocelyn. I'll check the other trees and will be back in a trice."

After Tilly disappeared, Jocelyn tipped back her head to study the clouds and pick out shapes. "A dog, I think." She tilted her head to the right. Yes, that looked like a playful puppy.

Half an hour passed, and she started to wonder what had happened to Tilly. The other trees were nearby. It shouldn't take her this long.

The *clip-clop* of a horse's hooves brought a rush of excitement. Leo. She shot to her feet, a smile curling her lips until she identified the rider. Hannah.

"Oh, I thought it was Leo. Have you come to visit Cassie?" Jocelyn moved behind the stone she'd been sitting on, not wanting to get too close to the restive horse. It snorted and danced, but Hannah held it effortlessly in check.

"No." Hannah's face twisted in anger, her ire settling on Jocelyn. "I don't understand why he married you. You're plain and ugly and your hair...it's horrid. Brazen, really."

No matter how many times Jocelyn heard the insult, it still held the power to hurt. The words made her feel less, but as always, she lifted her chin to meet Hannah's scorn. The other woman might be a renowned beauty, but today an icy chill glittered in her blue eyes.

In truth, Jocelyn could hardly refute Hannah. She'd never be a beauty, but despite that, she and Leo were happy. He mightn't have told her he loved her, but he treated her with care and respect and sought her company.

Hannah's horse sidestepped, dancing with impatience as she reined him in, smoothly exerting control. Something in Hannah's mocking expression raised Jocelyn's hackles. A stab of anxiety stirred in her stomach. She looked past Hannah and her mount, praying Tilly would hurry her chore and return.

When Hannah remained and Tilly didn't reappear, Jocelyn edged off the path out of the way. "Don't let me hold you up."

"You have something that belongs to me. I want it back." Hannah dismounted and led her horse to a tree. She looped the reins over a sturdy branch before sauntering back to Jocelyn.

"Whatever do you mean?" Jocelyn's unease deepened and she backed up a fraction more. Her boot struck a rock and her foot rolled. A sharp pain streaked up her leg and her cry rang out. "By St. Bridget, that hurt." She hobbled to the large stone and perched on it to prod delicately at her ankle through her boots. A dull throb emanated from the wrenched area. "Did you see Tilly?"

"Oh, yes." Hannah tapped her boot with her riding crop.

"Do you think she'll be long? I'd like to return to the manor."

"She won't be coming." Hannah struck her boot again without taking her gaze from Jocelyn.

Whack. Whack. Whack.

"I don't understand." With each beat of Hannah's crop Jocelyn's uneasiness increased. "She said she'd be right back."

The swat of the whip ceased. "I struck her over the head, and she fell down."

"I beg your pardon?" When Hannah merely regarded her with a mocking smile, Jocelyn frowned in confusion. "She's hurt? Where is she?"

She started in the direction Tilly had gone, limping heavily. She paused, sucking in a deep breath, praying the dull ache would subside. Tilly needed her.

A hand shot out to grasp her upper arm. "You're not going anywhere."

Jocelyn wrenched away and glared at Hannah. "If Tilly is hurt, she needs my help."

"It's too late for you to aid her."

The maniac light in Hannah's eyes set Jocelyn's heart racing. "Whatever do you mean?"

"You're the stupid one." Hannah's voice held condescension. Clear amusement. "Leo belongs with me, and I intend to have him."

"How?" Jocelyn gaped at Hannah. "Leo is my husband. He loves me." Leo mightn't have spoken the words aloud, but he showed signs of caring for her.

Hannah burst into laughter, a sweet tinkling sound that contrasted sharply with the furious glitter in her expression. "You poor deluded thing. Leo and I laugh about you when we're together. Why would a woman like you interest Leo?"

Pain battered Jocelyn, propelled with a true aim by Hannah's viperous tongue. "I-I don't believe you. Leo married me."

"In a fit of pique," Hannah said. "We argued and Leo went off to London. Of course we'd argued before, but this time the stupid man wanted to teach me a lesson. He regrets his actions now."

"No," Jocelyn whispered.

"Leo realized he made a mistake," Hannah continued. "He doesn't want you."

"Why are you telling me? Doesn't Leo have the guts?" She couldn't quite pull off the hauteur she'd aimed for.

Hannah shrugged, unconcerned by Jocelyn's devastation.

"You know what men are like. They think they're in charge, but they rely on their women. I promised him I'd tell you to spare him the trouble. Come back to the castle. I can provide a carriage to take you away. You needn't face him again."

"But my things." Jocelyn's mind screamed this was wrong. Hannah wasn't telling the truth. Leo wasn't the sort of man who relied on others to fix his problems. He resembled his cousin in his honesty. No, she wouldn't—couldn't—believe Hannah. Jocelyn's chin lifted. "Leo isn't like that. We're having a child."

"It was a mistake. I told you we had a disagreement."

"You must argue a lot because Leo spends every night in my bed." It was the wrong thing to say. Jocelyn knew it the instant the words left her mouth.

Hannah's features contorted with ugliness. Her nostrils flared. "You don't understand. I've done everything for you. I freed you from your mother." Her hands fisted as she stalked closer. "She was a burden, threatening to drag you down. Now that she's gone you have freedom to start a new life."

"My mother?"

"I helped you," Hannah spat. "She belonged in an institution."

Jocelyn listened with growing disbelief. "What did you do?"

"I put her to sleep."

"You murdered my mother?" Jocelyn's breath caught in her throat as she gawked at Hannah. "I thought Boynton—"

"You should be grateful."

Another thought occurred, one that tore at her guts. Had Leo known? The thought didn't bear thinking about, yet she couldn't let it go. "Did Leo know?"

"Of course Leo knew," Hannah said. "It'll be easier for you to return to London and find another protector without your mother in tow."

"No." She recoiled, horror filling her eyes with tears. No, she couldn't believe it. "How..." she trailed off, unable to complete her sentence.

"Pooh, it was simple to climb up the creepers. The catch on the window is easy to open from the outside. It's how Ursula used to sneak from the manor."

"Oh." Jocelyn gave Hannah a sidelong glance. Did she know who murdered her sister? Her eyebrows shot up and she blinked with incredulity as an idea formed.

Hannah had murdered her sister.

No, that didn't make sense because she wouldn't have wanted to implicate Leo. She opened her mouth to ask and thought better of it. She didn't want to know.

"You shouldn't have upset Boynton. The man would have secured your future."

Going anywhere with Boynton would have guaranteed her a life of misery. He'd constantly mocked her plainness and always fucked her in the dark because her face offended him.

"Answer me," Hannah snapped.

"You didn't ask a question."

"Do you want to leave with Boynton? I might be able to talk him around."

"No, thank you. I'll return to the manor and wait for Leo to arrive home. He can tell me to leave, if that's what he wants. I'll go as soon as I find Tilly."

"No." Hannah's hand shot out to grip her arm with bruising force. "Come with me now."

"I want to speak with Leo."

Hannah's hand whipped out. She struck, snapping Jocelyn's head back with the force of the blow. "Why doesn't anyone listen to me?" Her screech rang out, startling her horse. The bay yanked at its reins, snorting, eyes rolling in terror. "No one listens to me. I do the neighborly thing and give you a warning.

You should have listened." With fury glittering in her eyes, she advanced on Jocelyn.

Jocelyn's jaw throbbed. Tears welled in her eyes, and she backed away without taking her gaze off Hannah. The woman was unhinged.

A murderer.

Not looking where she was going, she stumbled. Before she recovered Hannah was on her, hands circling her neck, squeezing.

CHAPTER 18

"MR. SHERBOURNE!"

Tilly burst into his study, looking as demented as Elizabeth on a bad day. "You have to come." Tendrils of gray hair had escaped her normally impeccable style, and she'd lost her cap. A trail of blood ran down one cheek and dirt clung to her gown. Her chest heaved as she struggled to breathe, to speak.

Woodley followed his wife, alarm etched into his face. "Tilly, what is it?"

"Jo-Jocelyn."

Leo surged to his feet. "Where is Jocelyn?"

Tilly wheezed. "River. Hannah."

"Where?" he demanded.

"Near pussy willows," she gasped out. "Careful. Hannah is dangerous."

Leo dallied only long enough to seize his pistol. "Fetch as many men as you can and send them after me."

"Yes, Mr. Sherbourne," Woodley said.

Leo left the manor at a run, his mind rife with horrid possibilities. If something happened to Jocelyn, he'd never forgive himself. He sprinted through the garden, jumping the gate without breaking stride. Years of familiarity had him at the riverbank in less than ten minutes. The anxious snort of a horse drew his attention.

Voices.

Instinct slowed his steps. A scream propelled him to speed again. He burst around a bend in the path to see Hannah attempting to choke the life out of Jocelyn.

"Hannah!" He reached them in seconds, grabbing Hannah by her shoulders and tearing her from Jocelyn. Instead of struggling as he thought she would, Hannah turned to him with a radiant smile.

"Darling, you came." She curled her arms around his neck and leaned against his chest.

He could hear Jocelyn, gulping for air. Alarmed, he thrust Hannah away and hurried to his wife's side. "Are you all right, Jocelyn, love?"

Ignoring the shocked screech behind him, he slid his arms under Jocelyn's legs and cradled her against his chest. The beginnings of another bruise marred her jaw and dirt covered her black gown. Her ripped bodice revealed the curve of one breast, and her breaths came in raw gasps. Bright red finger imprints spanned her throat.

An icy chill swept him as he cataloged the sight. The marks on Jocelyn's neck—they were familiar.

"H-Hannah." Jocelyn swallowed, speech taking great effort.

"Leo, she isn't worth the trouble." Hannah's tone was cool. "She's so plain."

Leo was watching Jocelyn as he listened to Hannah. He caught the pain in her eyes and his heart ached. It wasn't true. Jocelyn was beautiful, especially inside where it counted. "Can you stand?" he asked her.

Jocelyn nodded, and he helped her to her feet, angling slightly to keep an eye on Hannah.

"Leo, tell her," Hannah insisted.

"Tell her what?" His grip tightened on Jocelyn, only loosening it when she winced.

"That we're going to be together at last. Tell her I'm carrying your child."

Jocelyn's gasp cut through his stunned shock. "That's a lie," he snapped. "I have never shared your bed. Jocelyn, she's lying."

"Leo," Hannah said. "I've made sacrifices. It was for us, so we could be together."

The passion, the conviction on her face sickened him. At one time, he'd considered marrying her. Instinct had held him back. Her performance after his marriage to Ursula had brought a sense of relief at his escape. Marriage to Hannah would've been as hellish as his marriage to Ursula. Hannah's exquisite shell hid a black heart.

Several footmen arrived, and he surreptitiously signaled them to stay back.

The truth. He had to learn what had happened.

Swallowing, he forced out the question that needed asking. "What happened between you and Ursula?"

Hannah sneered. "We argued."

"About what?"

"She stood in the way of my marriage to you."

"So you murdered her."

The truth blazed on her face—a hint of triumph and smugness because she thought she'd been clever.

"Ursula didn't love you," she said. "All she wanted was the prestige of a good marriage."

"Maybe so, but that didn't mean she needed to die." They'd been happy at first, but Ursula had changed after Cassie's birth, chafing at their union. She'd wanted to attend balls and parties, and the seclusion of Merrivale had hampered the social butterfly.

Hannah studied him earnestly, hands outstretched in a pleading manner. "Don't you see, Leo? It was the only way for us to be together."

"But it was murder." The casual ease with which she spoke of taking a life sickened him. She spoke of her sister's death as if it meant nothing more than squashing a bug. Her actions had almost destroyed him and cost Cassie a father as well as a mother. He signaled with a jerk of his head, indicating the footmen should come from hiding.

Hannah frowned. "What are they here for?"

"The constable will want to speak with you."

Her brows winged upward, her forehead furrowing. "You'd turn on me? Betray me?"

"Restrain her," Leo ordered.

"No!" Hannah darted out of reach and ran to her horse.

The sudden influx of people, the shouts and the rush of movement spooked the creature. He reared, jerking the reins from Hannah's grasp. His front hoof struck her shoulder, and she fell with a pained screech.

Leo thrust Jocelyn behind a tree and lunged for the horse before it hurt someone else. Two footmen subdued Hannah. She kicked and struggled like a wild creature. An animal-like shriek rippled from her throat, echoing through the riverside clearing.

The footmen dragged Hannah to her feet and hustled her toward the manor. Another footman took charge of her horse and led it off.

"Jocelyn, you can come out now," Leo said.

Jocelyn limped from behind the sturdy tree trunk. "Have you seen Tilly? Did...did Hannah kill her too?"

"Tilly is at the manor. She raised the alarm."

She clapped a hand to her chest, tears sparkling in her eyes when she looked at him. "Hannah killed my mother."

Leo went to hug her, but she jerked away.

"Hannah said you and she laughed about me. Do you love her?"

"No! I almost married her before Ursula returned to Hartscombe, but instinct stopped me. I was right to hesitate." He stroked her cheek with the fingers of one hand. "The only woman I want as my wife is you. Come, let me take you back to the manor."

"Do you hate looking at my plain face?" Her voice trembled, and his heart turned over at the anguish in her expression. "I'm sick of people lying to me."

"We'll discuss this later after we return to the manor." This time he didn't allow her to balk. Taking her arm, he set off for the house. When she limped painfully, he swept her into his arms and carried her.

When they arrived, Woodley and Mrs. Green appeared instantly.

"We've secured Hannah, and I've sent for the constable," Woodley said.

Leo gave a grateful nod.

"How is Tilly?" Jocelyn wriggled and tugged from his grip once he set her down, putting several feet between them.

"She has a bad bump on her head," Mrs. Green said. "I've put her to bed, but she'll recover without serious harm."

"I'll go to her."

"A quick visit," Leo said. "You need to rest. I'll see you in your bedchamber as soon as I've spoken with Hannah."

Jocelyn's quick frown told him she wanted to argue, but he didn't intend to let her retreat. They would talk about Hannah, and by the time he'd finished, Jocelyn would have no doubt as to his feelings for her.

·❤· ·❤· ·❤· ·❤· ·❤·

"Thank goodness you're all right, Tilly. I thought Hannah had killed you." Tears welled in Jocelyn's eyes. "I'm so sorry."

"Why? You didn't hit me." Tilly struggled to sit, and Jocelyn rushed to help. "Look at your face! You should be abed, not fussing over me."

"I'll heal. She didn't hurt me." But that wasn't quite the truth. Hannah had inflicted invisible wounds, ones that quietly festered and held the power to wreak havoc.

"You should still be in bed, resting."

"Soon." Jocelyn dismissed Tilly's concerns. "Tell me what happened."

"Hannah crept up behind me and struck me over the head. I heard a noise and moved at the last minute, or it could have been worse. I fell, and I think she thought she'd done me in because she left."

"Oh, Tilly."

"The woman has a black heart."

"She has no heart," Jocelyn retorted, her mind on the painful revelations. Of course she was plain. Her sisters' taunts flooded her thoughts, still holding the ability to hurt like stabs of a sharp knife. Unable to change the truth or her looks, she did what she always did. She drew herself up and contained her pain, inside, where no one else could see it.

A dull ache throbbed at her temple.

"Go to your chamber and rest for a few hours. You need to look after yourself, for the babe's sake."

"Do you need anything?"

"Mrs. Green has everything in hand," Tilly said. "Please, I'll feel better if I know you're resting."

Jocelyn forced an encouraging response, her lips flexing upward. "I'll check in on you later." She left the room, exhaustion striking her. When she reached her chamber, Susan was waiting for her, an apologetic expression fixed on her face.

"Oh, Mrs. Sherbourne." She wrung her hands. "You look pale. Let me tend your face."

Jocelyn stoically sat through Susan's ministrations. Five minutes later she was tucked between the sheets. Alone, the nagging ache engulfed her, tears streaming from her eyes, dampening her pillow. She'd thought Leo liked her and was as excited about their child as she. Her instincts had failed her.

Leo stalked into her chamber, shutting the door with a decisive click.

He didn't give her a chance to speak. "Why would you believe Hannah rather than me? Ever since you arrived at Merrivale, she's treated you with disdain. I made a mistake. I should have made it clear to her you were my choice. My only choice."

"I thought our marriage delivered that message," Jocelyn said.

"We married quickly and quietly. Hannah thought it meant I didn't care about you."

Jocelyn shrugged. "I have no illusions. You were quite clear at the start that ours would be a marriage of convenience."

"Jocelyn." Leo dragged a hand through his hair, his agitation finally propelling him to motion. "I thought I wanted a practical marriage. I'd done passion and it didn't work. My marriage with Ursula was a disaster. She was headstrong and rebellious, and we wanted different things." He paced in front of her bed before rounding it to stand at her side. "Please don't let Hannah's words and actions poison what we have together."

The ache in her chest grew bigger, more painful. It was like a weight pressing down, threatening to suffocate her. "I can't help the way I look. People laugh behind my back."

"Jocelyn, stop." He plonked on the edge of the bed, the scent of the outdoors wafting to her.

Her eyes welled with renewed tears. "I'm merely speaking the truth. I'm not beautiful."

"Not my truth." He reached for her hand. "I might have started our marriage with the intent of a convenient arrangement, but I soon changed my mind. I'm proud to call you my wife. When I look at you I see your glorious blue eyes and the goodness shining from inside you. I feel your silky skin and the way your quim clings to my cock. I hear the sound of your laughter, the passionate cries you produce when we make love. I see the joy you've brought with you to Merrivale. I love you, Jocelyn. Please let me show you."

She stared at him, trying to gauge his sincerity. "I don't know what to believe."

"Believe this." He leaned close and kissed one cheek. "I. Love. You." Between each word, he kissed her again, moving nearer to her mouth. Finally his lips settled over hers in a gentle, lingering kiss. His flavor and outdoors scent flowed over her, and she sighed. She'd always enjoyed his kisses, the way he took his time and teased, driving her mad with desire. He used his hands to stroke and caress.

He was always touching her, she realized. A pat on the shoulder, an arm slipped around her waist, the subtle guiding of his hand at the small of her back.

Groaning, he continued kissing her, tangling their tongues. He stretched out alongside her and wrapped his arms around her. He licked her mouth, trailed kisses down her neck and nibbled at a sensitive part of her neck until she focused entirely on him and the feelings his touch engendered. He wasn't acting as if he couldn't bear to look at her.

Pulling away, she turned her face to the window, knowing the light would strike her with merciless attention, highlighting her red hair and freckles.

Leo smiled and cupped her cheek, not even hesitating in his attentions. "Let me love you."

"Now?"

"Of course, if you feel up to it. I can't think of anything I'd like better."

"Yes." She melted under his determined charm, letting him remove the clean chemise Susan had helped her don. A few aches and pains from her bruises confirmed she was alive. Others weren't so lucky. He surged off the bed and hurriedly yanked off his boots. His jacket and waistcoat flew in different directions, his haste bringing a warm sensation to Jocelyn's chest.

Leo joined her again, rolling them together and kissing her hungrily. His hands wandered her back, her bare bottom. He kissed her as if he craved her more than anything or one else, and it was a potent sensation. Gaining her confidence again, Jocelyn touched Leo in return. She ran her hands over his shoulders down to bulging biceps, gulping in air when he rearranged her body and settled in to feast on one breast. His mouth closed around her nipple, and he drew hard. A strangled note of pleasure emerged from her.

She clasped his head to her. "Leo." When he looked at her the passion and yearning she saw left her breathless.

"I love you, Jocelyn. If I have to spend every day for the rest of my life showing you how much I adore you, then so be it."

He moved down her body and pressed a kiss to the swell of her abdomen. Her heart thumped extra hard on seeing his tender smile.

"I can't wait to hold our child in my arms," he said.

A rich rush of desire filled her, and she made a soft, yielding sound. Leo watched her while he swirled his warm tongue over her belly. The atmosphere thickened between them, and pure need raged through her body.

"Leo." His name signified surrender. If it weren't for Hannah, she wouldn't have doubted him, and he deserved a chance because he was an innocent man. Wasn't she behaving just as badly as the people who were rude enough to comment on her looks?

"Do you trust me?"

Surprise shot through her at the question. "Of course."

"Then believe me when I tell you I'm not interested in another woman. I don't require the services of a mistress. All I want is my wife. You."

"But, Leo. I know the perfect candidate for your mistress."

He stilled, his lips and tongue ceasing the caress that sent sensations flaring through her quim, and lifted his head to glare. "I don't want her."

Jocelyn battled the urge to smile. "But she has experience."

"I have you. My wife," he said with satisfaction. "Cease your prattling about mistresses." He shifted his weight, guiding his cock into her warmth. With a slow push, he sank to the hilt and halted, groaning at her heat surrounding him.

"Am I not mistress of Merrivale?" Jocelyn asked in a deceptively innocent voice.

His expression told her he understood. "You are indeed, my love. I'm a lucky man." He plundered her mouth with a kiss designed to inflame her, consume her. With whimpers she couldn't contain, he drove deep, pleasuring both of them. He claimed her with each touch until all she could do was clutch his shoulders and ride out the storm. Pleasure exploded deep within her, and it felt as if she were flying.

Leo let out a cry, snapping his hips, stroking into her, then stilling to grip her tightly.

"Jocelyn, you are everything to me."

She smoothed a lock of hair off his brow and smiled. "I believe you. I've loved you for a long time."

"Why didn't you tell me?" He rearranged their bodies and drew up the covers.

She bit her lip, before deciding to tell him the truth. "I feared rejection, and with all that was going on, there was a time when I wondered if I was married to a murderer."

"Me? A murderer?" He laughed a little, searched her gaze and finally nodded. "Hell, there were times when I wondered, given the conviction of everyone accusing me. One thing you need to remember, Jocelyn. I picked you. When Melburn told me he had the perfect woman for me, I trusted his judgment. Once I met you, my decision was easy."

"You wanted a wife so Hannah wouldn't bother you."

Leo sighed. "That's true, and unfortunately, my decision forced Hannah to react."

"What will happen to her?"

"She'll probably hang for her crimes."

"I feel sorry for her family."

"They must have suspected she was unbalanced," Leo said.

"If they did, they ignored her behavior. I can't believe she murdered her sister. Jealousy is a terrible thing."

"You have nothing to worry about. I'm happy with you. Very happy."

"When you look at me that way, I feel loved and treasured." Jocelyn smiled, happiness filling her despite the tinge of sadness at her mother's unexpected death. Despite all her sisters' words of doom, she was happy and fulfilled. She had a husband and stepdaughter and soon she'd have a baby. Three people to shower with love.

"You are loved." His eyes glowed. "My wife. My lover. My mistress."

"Mistress of Merrivale," she whispered.

"Indeed," Leo said, and he kissed her again, proving his love beyond doubt.

THANK YOU FOR READING Mistress of Merrivale.

Would you do me a favor? Word-of-mouth is crucial for an author to succeed. If you enjoyed *Mistress of Merrivale*, please consider leaving a review. Even if it's only a few lines, it would be a tremendous help.

Please turn the page for a glimpse of my other historical romances. *The Unwilling Viscount and the Vixen* is another marriage of convenience romance with a hint of Gothic danger while *Evening Tryst* takes place in a small English village during World War II and is a second-chance romance.

Enjoy!

Shelley

The Unwilling Viscount and the Vixen

EXCERPT

THE CARRIAGE SWAYED AND bounced over the rutted road. With each successive pothole, the driver cursed more colorfully. Rosalind gripped a carriage strap, the excessive jolting doing nothing for her agitated nerves. At the completion of this journey, she would meet her betrothed for the first time. Questions pounded inside her head. Would he like her? And would he accept her, despite her...faults?

Her childhood friend and maidservant, Mary, pressed her nose to the carriage window. "Oh, miss! I think we're almost there."

Rosalind tensed. She forced a smile and bit back a cry of alarm when the carriage lurched. Grabbing the seat to avoid a tumble to the floor, she righted herself and slid along the seat to Mary. "Can you see Castle St. Clare?" She peered out the dusty window, attempting to see her future home.

A snarling gargoyle appeared inches from their faces. Rosalind's breath escaped with a gasp.

Beside her, Mary screamed and jerked away from the window. "Miss Rosalind, do you think we should turn around and return to Stow-on-the-Wold?" She clutched Rosalind's forearm, her voice rising to a squeak. Mary's dread, her frenetic thoughts of monsters, bombarded Rosalind and she shrugged from her maid's grip to break the emotional connection.

"The earl is expecting us, Mary. We can't go back."

They sped past a rundown gatehouse, the carriage jolting from one pothole to the next. As they clattered through a stone gateway, Rosalind glimpsed the gargoyle's twin. It leered from atop a stone wall and seemed alive, as if it could step from its granite prison on a whim.

The carriage made a sharp swing to the right, the coachman cursing his team of straining horses as the gradient increased sharply. The whip cracked. Without warning, the interior of the carriage turned pitch black. Mary yelped, the shrill cry hurting her ears.

Rosalind swallowed her gasp, rearranged the skirts of her best blue riding habit trimmed in gold, and patted Mary on the arm. "It's all right," she soothed, yet the hand hidden in her skirts trembled. For a moment, the temptation to turn back teased at her, then she recalled the situation she'd return to—relations who resented her presence. The reality pushed aside her fears. Ugly gargoyles or not, she silently vowed to continue her journey.

An object scraped along the carriage sides, sending a shiver down her spine. Mary's piercing shriek resounded within the confines of the enclosed space. Goose bumps rose on Rosalind's arms. Her gaze whipped about the carriage. The noise repeated with an eerie echo.

"Hush, Mary." Rosalind's heart was pounding so loudly

she could barely hear herself think. Mustering every shred of courage, she pressed her nose to the cold glass of the carriage window.

This was meant to be a grand adventure, her last opportunity to seize a secure future. Rosalind, the afflicted one, the one the people of Stow-on-the-Wold whispered would never catch a husband. The cousin destined to stay on the shelf. This was her chance to prove them all wrong, despite her accursed gift.

Leaves swept against the windows, followed by the same scraping sound. The cold knot of fear in her stomach twisted. A flash of ghostly fingers waved before her startled eyes. A branch. That was surely a branch. The fear clogging her throat lessened a fraction, and she relaxed against the plush cushions of the St. Clare coach with a tremulous sigh of relief.

"It's a branch," she said to Mary. "We're driving along an avenue of trees. I fear they need trimming to let in the sunlight."

"Are you sure, Miss Rosalind?"

"Of course I'm sure." Rosalind made her voice firm and decisive. "Look out the window. You can make out the branches if you look hard enough." As she spoke, the darkness in the carriage lifted. Then they were in daylight again. "There, what did I tell you?"

Mary grabbed her arm and tugged. Frantically. "Miss. Miss. Look!"

Rosalind swallowed. This was where she was to live? She studied the fortress perched atop the cliff like a menacing monolith. Built of stone, the castle appeared solid and strong enough to withstand the winds that howled across the English Channel. Arrow slits glared at her like malignant eyes. Hardly the welcoming home she had envisioned.

"We're almost there. I can see the gate and the courtyard beyond." Mary turned, her eyes huge brown rounds in her freckled face. "There are people waiting to meet us."

Rosalind's hands crept up to check that her lacy cap sat straight. Uncertainties assailed her, threatening her fragile composure. Repeated swallowing did little to clear the lump in her throat. They said Hastings was mad. Perhaps she should have refused to marry him, but she'd promised her uncle, Sir John Chandler. He'd signed the papers when she and her cousin Miranda were babes. One of them had to marry Hastings.

Miranda had flatly refused so it was up to Rosalind to fulfill family obligations. At least she'd have a home of her own. That was what she wanted, wasn't it? A home of her own, a husband and, if she was fortunate, lots of chubby, laughing babies.

Security.

"Whoa, there!" the coachman bellowed. A horse snorted. A harness jangled, and a piercing screech rent the air as the coachman hauled on the brake to halt the ponderous carriage.

The door flew open, and a footman dressed in green livery placed a step down for them to alight. Rosalind pushed aside her apprehension, swept up her skirts and placed her hand into the footman's to descend. She relinquished his aid almost instantly and stepped aside. Seconds later, Mary exited and stood beside her, blinking in the early afternoon sun.

The earl, much older than she recalled, bowed before her. Tall and thin with stooped shoulders, his clothing hung loosely while his powdered wig drew attention to his extreme pallor. "Rosalind, my dear, it is good to see you again."

Rosalind sank into a deep curtsey, her eyes modestly lowered to hide her sudden nervousness. Her betrothed was here, standing right behind his father, but she was too frightened to look. Her cousin's hysterical words rang through her mind. Viscount Hastings was an ogre. A beast.

The earl interrupted her panic. "Child, let me look at you." Rosalind straightened and met the frank gaze of the elderly earl. "You have the look of your grandmother."

She smiled. "Thank you, my lord. I count that a compliment indeed."

Certainly, her grandmother had been the one person who understood how she felt, since she suffered from the same family affliction. Rosalind had found the past three years since her grandmother's death both difficult and lonely.

The earl urged her forward. "Let me introduce you to my son and nephew. You will meet my sister, Lady Augusta, later."

A chill swept through Rosalind and her lashes lowered to screen her fears. The moment she had both anticipated and dreaded—the first meeting with her betrothed.

"Rosalind Chandler, may I present my son, Viscount Hastings, and my nephew, Charles Soulden?"

Viscount Hastings thrust out a hand, and Rosalind placed her trembling one in his, wishing she had remembered to pull on her gloves. It was too late to worry now. She sank into another curtsey, too nervous to meet his gaze. She registered his size first and then a number of erratic pictures flickered through her mind. She shoved them away, concentrating on the tangible man. He towered above her by a good ten inches, making her acutely aware of her own lack in that area.

The callused hand holding hers tightened, and Rosalind looked up, startled. Her breath caught when she saw her betrothed clearly. Clad in a somber black jacket and breeches, and as dark as she imagined the devil to be, he disdained the fashionable wigs and powder the other men wore. Instead, his hair tumbled in loose, disheveled curls about his head. His face was tanned, as if he spent many hours outside under the sun. But what really caught her attention was the angry scar that slashed his face, running from just below his left eye to his jaw. Puckered and red, it drew the eye.

Rosalind swallowed and looked away, but her gaze clashed with that of her betrothed before she could politely withdraw.

His eyes were a mahogany brown, so dark they were almost black, and they openly mocked her nervous reaction.

Confusion and embarrassment fought within her. She tensed under his sardonic look. She'd known the viscount had suffered an injury while on a Grand Tour in Italy. The gossip about his miraculous return from the dead had spread rapidly through the ballrooms of London. Her stomach churned uneasily, and she averted her eyes to the weathered gray wall surrounding the courtyard.

"Rosalind, enchanted I'm sure." Hastings's low, gravelly voice sent a surge of alarm through her veins.

She inclined her head and valiantly tried to hide her agitation, but she suspected few fooled Hastings. "Thank you, my lord."

Sensations bombarded her mind, fragments of pictures, pieces of a larger puzzle. They were faint at the moment, but she knew from experience more details would come with time. A frustrated scream lodged in her throat. She tugged to free her hand, but he held fast. Why now? Why her betrothed? She'd thought—hoped—he would be one of the people for whom her accursed gift didn't work. She'd felt nothing when she touched the Earl of St. Clare.

The picture of a woman formed in her mind. Dressed in a flowing white gown with a tumble of dark curls about her shoulders, she walked arm in arm with a man. The man was her betrothed, and the woman with him was heavy with child. Rosalind gasped. Her left hand clutched her skirt, and she yanked her right from his grasp. She fanned her face vigorously, fighting for control. "It is hot today."

"Come inside," the earl said. "You must be tired after your long journey."

"Yes," she said, still aware of the viscount's mocking countenance. Her chin rose. "I am a little weary."

"Allow me." Hastings offered his arm. Rosalind caught the

beaming smile on the earl's face as he and Charles Soulden turned toward a flight of stairs leading inside the castle.

"It's not too late to call off the wedding," the viscount murmured.

Rosalind went cold inside at the rejection on his face. The gravel in the courtyard crunched underfoot—the only sound breaking the sudden hush between them.

If she backed out of this wedding, she'd be a laughingstock. A failure, and she'd have no home or chubby, laughing babies. She would end up on the shelf, a charity case depending on her uncle's largesse. A shudder swept her at the thought of being prey to her waspish aunt again. No, she didn't want that, which meant the wedding must go ahead.

Despite the fact that the man walking at her side was in love with another woman.

Evening Tryst

Excerpt

"Are you sure Owen will be there?"

"His squadron always hits the pub on a Friday night after a sortie."

Pamela nodded before she remembered Christine would have trouble seeing in the dark. "Oh." The chances of a pilot living through the war ... they weren't good. Did Christine worry about her man? Of course she did. Everyone worried about the men and women who fought on the front line. Everyone, no matter their identity, had family or friends fighting in the war.

"They tend to stick together. They're more like family than friends because they rely on each other whenever they go on a sortie."

They maintained their silence for a while, neither willing to voice the truth—so many good men had lost their lives already.

Christine opened the front door to the pub, and they darted inside, quickly closing it behind them. The light in the foyer was brighter, good enough to distinguish posters on the walls entreating the public to grow their own vegetables, save coal, and invest in war bonds. The click of Christine's heels signaled her progress across the flagstone floor to the double doors that opened into one of the large rooms inside. When she opened the doors subdued light spilled out along with laughter and chatter and the clink of glasses and bottles. A cloud of cigarette smoke hung in the air. A radio was playing on the bar, the haunting strains of *Somewhere over the Rainbow* combining with the animated chatter.

"There he is," Christine said, bounding through the doorway and into the gaiety, embracing it with a wide smile on her face.

Pamela followed more slowly, her blue and white floral dress and navy summer coat out of place when most of the occupants wore their uniforms, a mixture of Air Force blue with a smattering of Army green and uniforms from the home guard and fire wardens. Even Christine wore her WAAF uniform.

A burst of extra loud laughter came from a group of men in slate blue uniforms who clustered around a table in the corner of the room.

"There's Owen," Christine said over her shoulder, and she put on a burst of extra speed, weaving in and out of the people to get to him.

Pamela trailed after her cousin, another spike of nerves assailing her. She was here for a drink and nothing more. She didn't have to do anything but act friendly and listen. Smiling always helped too. The night would pass quickly, and she'd return to her cozy existence as a respectable widow who worked in the village store.

"Hello, pretty lady. Can I buy you a drink?"

Startled from her anxiety, she glanced upward. The looming shape in front of her was dark. Large. She flinched; a sharp pang of fear hit. "Thomas?" she croaked, the intimidating figure throwing her directly into the past.

The man shifted his weight and came into focus when he turned to the light. Her rapid heartbeat returned to normal when she realized her mistake. Weakly, she offered a smile while she clandestinely wiped her damp palms on her coat.

"Who me? No, I'm not Thomas, but I can be, if that's what you want." One green eye closed in a cheeky wink, and he dragged on his cigarette. He blew the smoke out and waited for her reaction.

Green eyes. Of course this man wasn't Thomas. He'd had brown eyes. Pamela stared for an instant longer, mesmerized and drowning in those green eyes before she realized how odd her reaction must seem. She swallowed and tore her gaze away. Unbidden, her gaze returned to him and wandered to his mouth–quirking lips that laughed at her. No, he didn't really look like Thomas, not when she studied him more closely. Of similar height, they both had dark hair and handsome faces, but this man smiled with his eyes and his mouth. He wore charm like a cloak.

Surreptitiously, she rubbed her forearm. The bone always ached when she thought of Thomas, a reminder of his temper and cruelty. It was the mental viciousness that lingered and made her cautious with other men.

Her mouth opened and closed before she blurted, "I'm here with my cousin."

"I'll escort you to his side," he said firmly. "Too many wolves wandering around this pub. A little lamb like you won't live long to tell the tale."

"Her." Pamela chuckled out loud. She wasn't exactly an innocent. "And it would take a wolf to recognize another." She'd always had a quick tongue, but Thomas's temper taught her to curb clever quips or face his wrath. Amazing. It seemed she was slowly healing, and the thought brought a quick burst of pleasure. Take that, Thomas.

The man slapped his hand across his heart in a dramatic fashion. "She wounds me with her sharp words."

Shaking her head at his silliness, she attempted to force her way over to the corner of the pub where she'd seen Christine disappear. To halt her escape the man seized her hand, his calloused fingers stroking gently across her thumb before he slid them upward to cup her elbow. His contact sent a frisson of sensation running down her arm. She gasped at the surge of pleasure, stunned by his caress and the sexual awareness running through her body. She met a lot of men at the shop but not one of them pulled this sort of reaction from her. With a cautious glance at his handsome face, she studied his expression. Maybe her aunt and cousin were right, and she should stop hiding away. There was no reason she couldn't have a little fun from life, as her cousin said.

"Michael Stedman."

"Pamela Allison."

"Pleased to meet you, Pamela." He rolled her name around his mouth, pursing the sensual curves of his lips in a manner that made her want to touch.

She shivered again, finally admitting the man fascinated her. It was his sparkling green eyes and the daredevil expression lurking in them, his muscular shoulders and his hands. A man's hands shouldn't attract attention, but she didn't have any trouble imagining them running over her bare breasts. Aghast at her thoughts, she ripped her gaze from his fingers to concentrate on his face.

"Why haven't I met you before?"

"I don't go out much."

"We'll need to remedy that, I think."

Good grief. His husky tones brought a distinct prickle to her skin. At the first sexy drawl he'd woken her sleeping libido. Did that mean she was easy? Maybe she should worry about her reputation, but his charismatic smile drew her. If she were a keen fisherman like her uncle, she'd say he was the perfect lure to use for fishing. Maybe too good. Two women at the other end of the bar kept eyeing him like a special prewartime treat. His freshly ironed RAF blue uniform, bearing the distinctive pilot's wings and stripes, garnered everyone's interest. A big man with short black hair, he stood about six inches taller than her. Dark lashes fringed his green eyes, and at the moment, those eyes bore a distinctly predatory look. It should have made her run but instead, the man sent waves of exhilaration skipping through her.

"Do you think so?" A flirtatious smile curved her lips. It brought an answering grin to his, and she wondered what his mouth would feel like brushing against hers. Good, instinct told her, but would she find the courage to let her attraction run its natural course? Only time would tell.

Other Books by Shelley

Historical
Mistress of Merrivale
The Unwilling Viscount and the Vixen
Evening Tryst
Unforgettable

Contemporary

Fancy Free
Protection
Romp
Buzz
Festive

Friendship Chronicles
Secret Lovers
Reunited Lovers
Clandestine Lovers

Part-Time Lovers
Enemy Lovers
Maverick Lovers
Sports Lovers

Military Men
Innocent Next Door
Soldiers with Benefits
Safeguarding Sorrel
Stranded with Ella
Josh's Fake Fiancée
Operation Flower Petal
Protecting the Bride

About Author

USA Today bestselling author Shelley Munro lives in Auckland, the City of Sails, with her husband and a cheeky Jack Russell/mystery breed dog.

Typical New Zealanders, Shelley and her husband left home for their big OE soon after they married (translation of New Zealand speak - big overseas experience). A twelve-month-long adventure lengthened to six years of roaming the world. Enduring memories include being almost sat on by a mountain gorilla in Rwanda, lazing on white sandy beaches in India, whale watching in Alaska, searching for leprechauns in Ireland, and dealing with ghosts in an English pub.

While travel is still a big attraction, these days Shelley is most likely found in front of her computer following another love - that of writing stories of contemporary and paranormal romance and adventure. Other interests include watching rugby (strictly for research purposes), cycling, playing croquet and the ukelele, and curling up with an enjoyable book.

Visit Shelley at her Website
www.shelleymunro.com

Join Shelley's Newsletter www.shelleymunro.com/newsletter